LAZARVS

TAXON

Nick,
I hope you enjoy this reimagining
of the origin of vampires. Best
wishes and have a great holiday!

[signature]

Taylor W Hughes

Charming Scoundrel Publishing
Tacoma, WA

The events contained within these pages are purely works of fiction meant only to entertain. In no way is the author advocating or suggesting the factual existence of the biblical characters fictionally depicted here as being immortal.

I would like to thank my stunning and supportive wife Lindsay, Sandra & William Rades, Claire Blancett, Rev. Luke Timm, Mike Seelan, William Marris, Alan Johns, Dave & Stephanie Farnia, Juliet Gorsuch, Caitlin Hanbury, Dani Brown, Sarah Kutchman, Jennie Ingram, Dan (Thunder) Pace and Brad Alles.

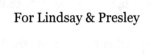

For Lindsay & Presley

Laz·a·rus tax·on (laz-er-uhs ˈtæksɒn)

An organism that disappears from the fossil record,

only to appear again later

1

"And as it is appointed unto men once to die,
but after this the judgment."
-Hebrews 9:27

ISTANBUL, TURKEY
PRESENT

*My name is Ela, and I am dead. This is the story of my life
and of my death.*

Cradling a translucent plastic case inside of his right hand, an
aged man of his early sixties sits aside a venerable and thick
wooden dining table. It is late into the hours of night and
housed inside of this sheer rectangular jacket is a faded and worn
piece of tattered woven fabric. Surrounded by walls draped with
lusterless washed-out mint green wallpaper saturated with vintage
floral patterns, the white haired gentleman is seated at the edge of the
cluttered table. With his left elbow resting on the weathered armrest
of his aged armchair, he buries his forefinger into his upper lip in
reflective contemplation.

At the edge of the rustic table sits an overflowing heap of an
ashtray, which holds the ashy tube of a still burning, but neglected,
cigarette. His dimly lit room is littered with a wide variety of vintage
books, antique statues and an assorted array of religious objects.
Strewn about the large slab-like table is a grouping of four open

notebooks and sketches of a variety of mostly religious objects. Just adjacent to the drawings is an additional collection of black and white photographs of an ancient cross and three stone carvings. With a furled brow, he takes tiny intermittent sips of cheap vodka out of a cordial glass. Except for the rhythmic crackling of the adjacent fireplace, the atmosphere is eerily reticent.

This man is my exceptionally devoted father, Danylo Vlcek. He is a humble man of both profound brilliance and uncompromising integrity. With a multifaceted and remarkable background, he is now a renowned religious archeologist/historian and even more particularly an especially gifted authority on the miracles of the Bible. Presently lodged in Istanbul, Turkey; the demands of his occupation as *the* leading expert of scriptural miracles, often take him away from his permanent residence in Prague. Being a greatly sought after authority on scriptural phenomena, he is abroad for most of the year. Given his highly regarded station in both the theological and historical world community; my father finds himself visiting an abundant variety of locales all over the world. Traversing overseas to far-off destinations as well as simply roving to neighboring countries, he is unequivocally the definitive expert on the miracles of Jesus Christ.

Born and raised in a uniquely privileged household in Prague, my father had an atypical childhood. My grandfather, Alexander, was a distinguished architect who was remarkably successful in spite of the unrest of his time. When I was just a young naïve little girl, both my father and my grandfather would regale me with countless anecdotes of their incredible lives. Just like it was yesterday, I can recall my grandfather fondly recollecting the romantic tale of his first encounter with my grandmother. I lucidly recollect the twinkle in his eye and the tender tenor of his voice when he recounted the circumstances of their fortuitous convergence. In his craggy voice, he described to us with amorous zest, the dawn of their providential history.

A frequent of the international art scene, my grandfather spent most of his time outside of work in museums, theaters and concert halls. He regularly attended a wide variety of art exhibits and classical concerts. One particularly fateful night at the ballet, he saw what he continually described as "a vision of unparalleled grace and elegance." This exquisitely striking sight was that of his future wife and my grandmother, Tanya. A ballerina in the distinguished Czech Ballet Company, Tanya was a young, enchanting and youthful beauty. Immediately following the performance, my grandfather used one of his personal connections at the venue to gain access to the theater's backstage. Adorably humble, whenever he recited the ardent account, he always insisted, that the precious moments after he first introduced himself to her, he could never recall the particular words he nervously uttered, but whatever they were, the two were unusually quickly engaged in evocative conversation. Nevertheless, they were both instantly and irrevocably enthralled with one another. Together, in unqualified love, they shared their passionately mutual admiration of the arts; particularity fine art.

During their courtship, as my grandmother, Tanya, continued to tour with her ballet company, regrettably the two would have to spend weeks and months apart from each other. During those long circuits, she habitually visited the local art museum. Before embarking on the lengthy legs of her tours, my grandfather always told her the same exact thing right before she left. With tender sincerity he would say, "When you find inspiration from a canvas or when you experience an emotional connection with a particular piece think of me. For when the intricate and detailed brush strokes on those oil soaked canvases cause you to stop and only stare at that individual creation, take notice. Even more than that, my darling Tanya, that is how fervently and severe that I have always loved you."

Though truly dreading the time away from her beloved that was an unfortunate necessity of her career, she still anxiously anticipated the opportunities to visit both the old familiar favorites as well as entirely new museums. My devoted grandmother sincerely treasured her time at home but simultaneously embraced the capability to visit the provincial exhibition halls and galleries. Routinely, from country to country; city to city, she frequented as many exhibits as feasibly achievable.

Though her frequently inherent travels often kept them apart for weeks and sometimes months at a time, they managed to seize and cherish every moment they did have together. They were the textbook embodiment of the old adage; "absence truly makes the heart grow fonder."

Upon her atypical eighth and final season, four long and considerably demanding years from the time they first met, my grandmother contentedly said goodbye to her fantastically fulfilling dance career. Taking her final bow at the age of twenty-nine, she gracefully exited out of the prestigious ballet limelight forever. Though bittersweet, she was unreservedly eager to retire from her very gratifying but utterly arduous profession. The loving couple now had the opportunity to share a dramatically more consistent life together. My grandparents joyfully celebrated their long-awaited uninterrupted new life, together, with a grandiose voyage around the world. They traveled to a diverse array of exotic locales.

Upon their return, they immediately intended to take advantage of their newfound stability and start a family. However, just as they were settling into their new life together the unfortunate events leading up to the Second World War were disconcertingly taking shape. During this tumultuous time they had the astute insight to flee the country. Fortuitously, they found solace in a small rustic village in the heart of Spain. There they remained; surprisingly enjoying a most uneventful life despite the turbulent climate caused by the War. Upon the critical conclusion of World War II, my grandfather resumed his former occupation and helped in the restoration and rebuilding of

Europe. Once they reestablished themselves, they immediately began the expansion of their blossoming family. In 1946 they celebrated the birth of their first child, my Aunt Irena. Soon after, in 1948, they welcomed their second child, a healthy baby boy. That infant was my father, Danylo.

As they grew up, my grandmother dotingly imparted her steadfast love and passion of the arts with both of her beloved children. From my father's earliest recollections, she routinely took them to art galleries, museums and exhibition halls at every available opportunity. Her brother, my great uncle Petr, was a virtuous priest in Italy. Because of his position inside of The Vatican, they would frequently journey there to visit him. Vatican City in and of itself, was an incomparable source of precious priceless works of art. The inhabiting museums and galleries teemed with sophisticated sculptures and expressively arresting paintings. Undeniably, my grandfather shared Tonya's deep admiration and respect for her brother, the priest. Likewise, my father and Aunt Irena delighted in a close enriching relationship with their Uncle Petr. Over their formative years, they always spent a fair share of their summers traveling to Italy to visit Petr and enjoyed splendid times as a cheerful and rather fortunate family.

After all of the tours and frequent outings to view vast collections of priceless art in galleries spanning the entire globe; out of all of these innumerable museums, my father and my grandmother shared a unique affinity for one particular painting. This favorite piece was an oil painting by Italian artist Michelangelo Merisida da Caravaggio. It was an eye-catching depiction of the miracle of Jesus raising Lazarus from the dead. Housed at the Museo Regionale in Messina Italy, this lifelike oil painting unexplainably provoked intensely genuine emotions from both my grandmother and her son. One of Caravaggio's final works, the attention-grabbing piece was heavy in contrast and saturated in deeply dark beauty.

As the years carried on, and my father got older, it was

5

said that he excelled in any and everything scholastic. Displaying a spectacularly exclusive intellect, he blazed through school with accelerated ease. From primary to secondary schooling, he finished at the top of every single one of his classes. Though he possessed the unique capacity to literally accomplish anything regarding continuing education, he had always maintained a peculiarly specific focus. Above all else, his heart and mind were staunchly fixed on a predominantly spiritual path. Most likely the result of the amorous relationship with his virtuous uncle Petr, my father felt, deep within the very fiber of his being, that he was preordained to go along a devout avenue. Wholeheartedly believing that this was indeed the proper direction of his future, he fully realized the proper direction for his future. After years of careful consideration, for him, the decision was crystal clear; his steadfast faith was strictly directing him down one particular path; the priesthood.

Immediately following his graduation from his traditional studies, he dutifully attended the local monastery in Prague; beginning his formal and pious instruction. My grandparents were perceptibly surprised by his unconventional choice, but warmly maintained their ardent support for their extraordinarily gifted son. This current course of a spiritual pursuit meant that his current studies were mostly void of the mathematical and scientific stimulation he had become accustomed to. Despite the deeply disciplined and exceptionally intensive nature of his new virtuous vocation, he still retained an unquenchable partiality for conventional high academia. So even though he had seemingly abandoned the anticipated path of his expected traditional education, any spare time he managed to compile at the monastery, he devoted solely to his own personal scientific curiosities. His days were filled with scriptural studies; concentrating explicitly on the sacred rights and holy practices of the church. Though his days belonged almost exclusively to ceremony and theology, his nights were engrossed and consumed by a newfangled veracious pastime, examining the miracles of Christ. Barreling through multiple archeological and anthropological books as he concurrently continued his daily religious disciplines, he had self-cultivated himself into a remarkable religious historical savant.

In hopes of further providing the scientific evidence necessary to support the actuality of miracles, he devoted night after night to his new preoccupation. He spent hours at a time, collecting historical data regarding a multitude of miraculous events surrounding the narrative of Jesus.

Within the first few months of his residence at the abbey, the content of the monastery's library proved to be rather limiting, given his expeditious knack for knowledge. This persuaded him to fortuitously relocate his extracurricular inquiries to the towns more extensive library.

Sofia, one of the young librarians, often eagerly aided him in his research. The accommodating and especially attractive attendant often acquired and transferred in additional finds for him. These supplementary rare and exotic archival books provided additional support for my father's ongoing self-instruction. She found his passion, drive and resilient commitment utterly fascinating. His vast vocabulary and distinctive style of speaking almost immediately set him apart from the other men. Over the next fortuitous cluster of months, they shared an abundant amount of time together. Her consideration and beauty had captured his attention and entirely enraptured her to both his heart and his mind. He was falling for her, and she for him.

As far back as I can recall, my father always had a rather peculiar way of speaking; expressively articulate and semi-formal without being too highbrow. This is only one of his many traits that, for better or worse, I seemed to have inherited. Mother always added that father was not only classically handsome, but most importantly she fancied his exceptional charm. By the same token, my father proudly declared that he was powerless to ignore or deny the overwhelming actuality that he too found her uncontrollably alluring.

Just months before the completion of his studies at the monastery, my father felt he could no longer continue on his chosen path of the priesthood. He no longer felt compelled or proper in his pursuit to be a man of the cloth. He felt fraudulent; given his exceeding captivation with Sofia. To the amazement and mild disappointment of his parents, he abruptly withdrew himself from the monastery; immediately abandoning his aspiration of priesthood.

With uncharacteristic spontaneity, after discarding his plans of the priesthood, my father wasted no time and asked Sofia for her hand in marriage. With great joy and enthusiasm, my mother accepted his impulsive request. They were wonderfully wed only a short couple of months later. Soon after their precipitous union, she gave birth to me, their first and only child. Giving me the name Anzela, which means angel, my parents doted on my every breath. As far back as I can remember, they frequently told me that I was their endless source of happiness. My mother referred to me as her cherished treasure of darling delight.

Though an extraordinary intellectual and ridiculously overqualified academic, my father spent the next year and seven months doing irregular unskilled labor. However, his efforts weren't for just any variety of physical industry, they revolved around several archeological excavations. He had devised a precise plan for his future. Burdening himself with an intensely physically demanding workload was only the temporary means to quickly accumulate the necessary funds for his formal archeology instruction. After earning enough money to pay for his training, he sent out his college applications and transcripts to a variety of esteemed institutions. He was rapidly accepted to Cambridge University. Relocating our family to the United Kingdom, he achieved his ultimate goals in an impressively and uncommonly short period of time. He received both his Doctorate of Philosophy in Religious Archeology and also a Master's degree in Anthropology.

At the beginning of his prestigious career, he concentrated on the journey of Jesus Christ. My father tracked and traced the details and locations that Jesus lived. As he traveled through the Middle East; tracing the very footsteps of Christ, he amassed one of the most impressive collections of trailblazing religious artifacts of all time. After years of examining this broader scope of interest, he developed the uniquely uncontestable urge to explicitly study the miracles that Jesus had performed. By focusing all of his efforts solely on a particular portion of Christ's life, he felt he could have a much broader and more profound impact on individuals and their faith; even greater than what the priesthood could have ever offered. Shedding innovative light on and lending scientific perspective to these religious accounts was his new imperative vocation. This was the perfect culmination of his vastly versatile background and his remarkable wealth of knowledge; this was his proper calling.

Over the years, he ardently researched every last detail of the multiple accounts of Jesus' miracles. Completely captivated by miracles, he was always particularly riveted by the immediate impact these miracles would have had on the surrounding populations of the time. He sought out to uncover their true purpose and give insight into the political implications of the time. While researching the miracle of raising Lazarus from the dead, father fortuitously came across Caravaggio's painting. Remembering the connection he shared with his mother, he instantly reawakened the affinity and kinship toward the dramatic scene. Immediately, he became expressly drawn to the miracle of the Jesus raising Lazarus from the dead. This would become his ultimate objective.

While attempting to describe the fervency the painting provoked from within him, my father would often say: "To properly explicate my purest passion, I need only repeat those words. 'Lazarus, come forth.' And with that modest but authoritative utterance, the Son of God brought a dead man back to life. That act of Jesus retrieving Lazarus from the clutches of death is arguably the preeminent public miracle of His earthly ministry." My father would often elaborate with unbridled enthusiasm; "With stark simplicity, the book of John describes the astounding supernatural spectacle best. The miracle of Jesus Christ raising Lazarus from the dead was done in front of witnesses; the Jews that arrived to mourn the death of Lazarus saw, with their own eyes, Jesus raising Lazarus from the dead. Some of them then went on and reported what they had seen to the Pharisees. They described how Jesus cried out with a loud voice, 'Lazarus, come forth!' And he that was dead came forth! Then many of the Jews who had seen what Jesus did, believed in him."

This, the quintessential miracle of Jesus' ministry, was now the lone concentration of my father's fervent research. Just years into an already burgeoning career, he was considered to be the undisputed authority on the miracle of Lazarus. His distinctively dynamic passion for Lazarus, which originated from the painting he communally admired with his mother, had now fully developed into a flourishing career. As I grew older he traveled the world, gathering new archaeological evidence pertaining to the resurrection of Lazarus. Universities, churches and antiquities dealers across the globe requested his expertise to authenticate old artifacts and positively verify new possible relics.

During his prestigious career, every new discovery only seemed to shed an entirely altered light on the subject. The more fresh evidence he uncovered, the more it only seemed to add to the obscurity of the minutiae behind the initial story. As he probed further and accumulated more information and articles related to the miraculous occasion; the already mystifying story became markedly more incomplete. Because of this confusion, he found himself with an inordinate abundance of unanswered questions regarding the life and times of Lazarus after his shocking resurrection. These discrepancies continuously seemed to be a weird reoccurring theme that surrounded almost every relic related to the Lazarus narrative.

After years of carefully accruing and obsessively reviewing his own unique collection of questions, he had formed an incredibly radical supposition. Judiciously not yet disclosing this fresh thesis to anyone, including me, my father simply described his undefined hypothesis as "an irrational notion driven by consistent inconsistencies."

The most peculiar phenomenon he had noted was that a number of the artifacts he had studied over the years shared one common trait, inscriptions on multiple objects and relics damaged in the same exact location. Certain inscriptions had been, for lack of a better term, "crossed out" by distinctly analogous scoring marks. Another one of the individual objects that had stumped him over the years was a small and extremely rare piece of ragged cloth. This unique fabric fragment was a segment of a handcrafted bishop's pallium. This was believed to have actually been a gift given to Lazarus from Mary, the mother of Jesus herself. My father had always taken great delight in sharing with me the great story behind Mary's gift.

Once Lazarus was raised from the dead, he was dynamic, and the preeminent witness for Jesus and his professed divinity. Because of the power of his resurrection story, many Jews had now believed Jesus was the Messiah. This incident outraged the High Priests. Lazarus became public enemy number one. The Chief Priests agreed that they must get rid of this abomination. A sentence of death had now been dismally bestowed upon Lazarus. These perilous predicaments caused Lazarus to immediately flee his home in Bethany. Forced from his land, he sought out refuge on the island of Cyprus.

Not only was Lazarus distressed from being forced to abandon his home, but he was additionally grieved that he would no longer see Mary, the mother of Jesus. Having been a considerably esteemed friend of Jesus, Lazarus had naturally developed a relationship with Jesus' mother, even embracing her as a mother of sorts. According to tradition, their disconnection directed him to dispatch a ship that would bring Mary to Cyprus for a visit. However, while the ship was in route to Kition, a massive storm carried them off their intended course. Their blown and battered ship ended up near the shores of Mt. Athos, Greece.

Tradition states that Mary turned this adverse adventure into a rare opportunity. She took full advantage of the situation and quickly converted as many Greeks to Christianity as possible. Once her impromptu mission was complete, Mary, once again set sail for Cyprus. Favorably, this second attempt was a success. Once she arrived in Cyprus her son's good friend, Lazarus, warmly received her. That is when she presented Lazarus with the bishop's pallium, which she purportedly crafted herself. Into that fabric, she had meticulously woven the phrase "Lazarus the Friend of Christ." This same exact phrase had been chiseled into the tomb of Lazarus's second burial sight inside of the Church of Saint Lazarus in Larnaca.

Scrupulously reviewing his liberal collection of elaborate notes and numerous photographs pertaining to the miracle of Lazarus, he believes that he has finally found *the* obscure association among his particular pieces. My father firmly believes that the deteriorated fragile textile now gently cradled inside of his hand, is an authentic section of Mary's pallium. This exceptional section could possibly be the enigmatic key to unlocking the mysterious link behind all of these baffling items. Quite curiously, the partial scrap has been marred in the same distinct area as a number of other artifacts. It was as if these similar objects that contained the name of Lazarus, had been purposely defaced or damaged. For years, these uncanny correspondences had goaded him to seek out further clarification of these perplexing parallels. And now, after all of his years pondering the pretext behind the various relics and their comparable markings, this additional piece has taken him closer to a conclusion than ever before. This textile, along with the myriad of assorted "marked" artifacts, may have finally aided in the completion of his radically new and scandalously controversial narrative behind the extraordinary story of Lazarus.

However, since the antiquities market is infamously chocked full of forgeries and reproductions, he is compelled to revisit and scrupulously reinvestigate some of his earlier findings.

Now he sits, in front of his tediously amassed array of Lazarus artifacts. As he peruses sections of the vast heap of his life's work, an overwhelming feeling in the depths of his gut, tells him where to start his final quest for confirmation. Undeniably close to feasibly substantiating the clandestine revelation that has confounded him for years, his instinct implores him to reexamine an alleged burial site of the body of Lazarus.

Centuries ago, Lazarus's remains were transferred from Cyprus to Constantinople until they were then finally relocated to Autun, France. There, set within the bosom of the Cathédrale Saint-Lazare d'Autun lies what are believed to be the remains of Lazarus. Because of its obvious association, my father has traveled there innumerable times before. He is determined to return to this familiar destination in the hopes of further corroborating the necessary evidence to reinforce his progressive notion.

He begins to sort through a few days worth of clothing and arrange some of his basic toiletries. Packing the minimal amount of belongings and the appropriate documents containing his analysis of his previous finds, along with his always present leather bound notebook, he wastes no time in commencing his departure to Autun, France.

Eager to set forth, as he gathers his necessities, he picks up his phone and frantically places a call. Upon dialing the number, he hurriedly sends a scan of some of the recently reviewed engraved images, and anxiously waits for his acquaintance, Santé, to answer his semi impending urgent call.

Santé, a Brazilian priest who lives in Marseilles, France is one my father's oldest friends. Not only one of his old classmates but he is additionally an accomplished linguistics expert. Santé answers the phone; "*Bon soir.*"

Overly excited, my father zealously replies, "*Bonjour!*" earnestly asking; "Old friend, I hate to rush, but I am in an awful hurry to visit our dear friend Phillip in Autun. I have expedited some, how shall I say, 'avant-garde discoveries' and was hoping you could be an old chum and authenticate some of my feeble translations?"

Santé exclaims, "Nothing would please me more then to lend a helping hand to my old comrade, '*Maninho.*'"

He thanks Santé and solemnly adds; "Sorry to be so brief and cryptic, but neither my sensitive data nor my rapidly deteriorating timeframe permit me to divulge too much at this time. However, if Autun progresses as projected, I will be seeing you soon. *À votre bon cœur* for your participation in my crazed quest."

Immediately following that enthusiastic exchange; my father then placed a call to me.

Situated at my kitchen table, midway through my cup of tea and crossword puzzle, I answered my echoing phone; "*Bonjour.*"

"*Bonjour mon Ange*" he replies.

Instantly, I recognize the distinct voice of my father. However, before I can respond he suddenly begins rambling; "So sorry to be in such a rush Angel, but my lofty inquests have sent me on yet another inevitable journey."

"*Oui*"

"Regrettably, due to hypothetical but potentially new insights related to my clumsy and ever changing theory, I must reschedule our customary rendezvous."

Once more, before I can respond, the familiar "clacks" that

accompany another impending call interrupts us. Just as he begins to ask for my permission to answer the incoming phone call, I meekly respond "*Oui*, answer it."

Patiently sitting in the transitory moments of silence, I can discern the subtle sounds of the old blues music faintly emitting from my radio I had just adjusted to a lower volume moments ago as I answered his call. After a rapid, two or three clicking sounds, he reemerged from the reticence: "*Mon Ange?*" he asked.

"*Oui, je suis ici*" I replied.

"That was Phillip in Autun, in response to an earlier correspondence. Phillip has kindly agreed to assist me in the completion of my outrageous theory. Just minutes before calling you, Santé in Marseille has also agreed to help me. I will quickly meet with him immediately following my time in Autun."

After pausing and clearing his throat, he proceeded; "Anzela, might I propose an alternative to our accustomed face to face? In place of Bordeaux; we could possibly meet in enchanting Autun instead? Relocation would be entirely more favorable than cancellation; as brief as it may be?"

The hovering moment of static silence awaiting my response was mildly palpable and unmistakably awkward.

My father continues on the phone, "Phillip has also graciously agreed to house me in the rectory for a few days. The duration, I might add, in addition to the normal, routine access to relics, I will be granted unfettered freedoms to the Tomb and the surrounding newly excavated sites."

With a willing titter and grin, I reply "Of course. I will leave early Sunday morning and drive to meet you in Autun. I will give you a call from the road when I am nearing the outside of the city."

"*Oh, je t'adore, Ange!*" He concludes with enchanted zeal.

"*Je vous adorez trop mon papa.*"

Once I agreed to connect at the Cathedral, I begin packing a day bag for Autun. It was still early Friday night and I wouldn't have to leave until Sunday morning. As fleeting as the visit may be, I know for certain it would break my father's heart if we missed our regular visit. After all, he has only had to cancel on two occasions over the years and he has always gladly made the effort coming all the way to Bordeaux. I continue to arrange my petite bag and glance over the directions for the six-hour drive to Cathédrale Saint-Lazare d'Autun.

Unreservedly anxious to arrive in Autun, my father franticly finishes packing up his own belongings. In addition to his passport and a variety of personal effects, he collects his all-important research materials and data stuffed notebooks. All of his necessities are contained inside of two medium sized duffel bags and one brown leather satchel.

Expeditiously leaving his lodgings and clumsily swinging the door shut behind him. In order to gain another free hand, he tightly bites down on the soft leather strap of his tumbling shoulder bag. With a firm grasp and with his now freed hand, he retrieves the keys from the inside of his pants pocket. After securing the lock at the room's entrance, he continues to his car. Parked on the street in front of him, he continues with notably more ease to his car. His sizable ring of keys rowdily rattles and jingles while he struggles to locate the cars particular key. After a few gawky movements he manages to produce the correct key. Swinging the door open, he is finally able to unburden his straining mouth of the cumbersome kitbag it had been supporting. Tossing his gear into the worn wrinkled leather of the passenger side seat, he quickly settles into his cold seat behind the steering wheel. With a deep inhalation and a substantially mitigating sigh, he slips the key into the ignition. Tightly griping the steering wheel as the auto's engine fires up, he proceeds onto the Serbian Rail station: commencing his lengthy jaunt to Autun.

2

AUTUN, FRANCE
PRESENT

As the daylight rapidly recedes, the city of Autun is ephemerally blanketed by darkness. In the early hours of Saturday evening, Danylo arrives outside of the strikingly gothic architecture of the remarkably impressive Cathedral of St. Lazarus. The taxi approaches the massive sanctuary, and peacefully coasts to an unhurried halt directly adjacent to the curb outside the cathedral's main entrance. Gathering his belongings, Danylo contentedly exits the vehicle. Never taking his eyes away from the impressive Romanesque structure, he smoothly produces money out from the inside of his jacket's chest pocket and compensates the driver. Once financially satisfied and fairly tipped, the taxi driver pulls off. Dwarfed by the imposing, awe-inspiring and magnificent entryway, Danylo is left standing curbside and spellbound.

Though a frequent visitor to the infamous cathedral, given his affinity to the miracle of Lazarus, Danylo is still overwhelmed at the sight of the resplendent structure. Engraved over the west door of the cathedral is an intricate semi-circular decorative depiction of the Last Judgment. Above an elegant set of gigantic, heavy wooden ors lies this meticulously crafted epic carving overflowing with lavish detail. Danylo gazes upon the sophisticated tympanum in roused tranquility.

Suddenly and rather silently a figure emerges from out of the shadows to Danylo's left. Weakly drizzled in the whitish-blue glow of the full moon, as the approaching indistinct character is further doused in the glint of the moon, the figure speaks: "Welcome, my brother."

Recognizing his old familiar friend Phillip, he extends his arms out to the advancing colleague and the two warmly embrace. Phillip cordially receives his friend with a beaming grin and says; "Please, come and retreat from this cold evening."

"*Salutations de mon frère.*" Danylo replies. "Yes, let us withdraw from the cold and warm up in the company of old friends." His right hand slowly creeps out of his duffel, and Danylo proudly unveils a crown-shaped glass bottle of Regalia Vodka. The two give one another a playful nod and continue into the cozy confines of the cathedral. They slowly make their way toward Phillip's residence.

Passing through the ornately festooned doors, making their way through the expansive narthex, they arrive at Phillips modestly regal residence. The spacious one-bedroom rectory is an elegantly fashioned quaint chamber rooted in the inner workings of the sacred structure. Concealed by long, flowing curtains attached to a high vaulted ceiling, stands the comparatively undersized entryway to his quarters. Phillip, fluidly easing the fabric aside, benevolently invites Danylo to be the first to enter. The two move into the charming and intricately decorated dwelling. Blanketed by various sized statues of the Virgin Mary, other honored Saints and a multitude of crucifixes; the room is dully lit by dozens of diminutive white candles. The only artificial light illuminating the area is a table lamp with a brass stand and green glass lampshade resting on a stubby secretary desk beside a massive gold-framed oil painting of the Holy Mother.

Toward the middle of the room sits a medium-sized circular

table with a crimson red tablecloth draped over the top. Stretching out his slightly shaking arms across the table, Phillip collects a number of books and assorted papers that lay strewn across the table and hurriedly places them onto the adjacent, wooden end table smothered with decorative doilies. With his left palm facing up he sweeps his arm across the table, motioning to his old friend to sit down. Sharply turning around, Phillip shuffles himself toward a tall mahogany cabinet wedged into the crook of the room. As Danylo situates himself at the table, Phillip spins around, auspiciously revealing two double tall shot glasses. He returns to the table and with both hands he heartily plunks the glasses down in the middle of the table. Once more he gestures kindly to his comrade with the swipe of his open arm.

"*S'il vous plaît, asseyez-vous*" Phillip cheerfully blurts.

"*Dekuji*" Danylo gratefully replies as he sets his effects on a nearby bench and approaches the table with the vodka still in hand. Both approach the table and exhaustively sink further into their chairs.

"Welcome back Danylo, it is good to see you and have a drink with you once again, old friend."

"*Bonsoir*, Phillip" Danylo reaches for the unique bottle of vodka. With the twist of the sealed cap, he gently tilts and pours the clear elixir.

"As always I am indebted to you for receiving me, particularly upon so little understanding of my exact purpose and such short notification. For that, I thank you."

Harmoniously raising each of their tall slender glasses, they give each other a welcoming bow of their heads and punctually toss back the shot. Phillips eye's slam shut and begin to water the tiniest bit. Briskly exhaling through his nose, he briefly shakes his head while giving a hearty grunt of relief. Danylo haughtily chuckles and pours the two of them another.

Regaling themselves with reminiscent stories of their past, they persevere both well into the night and well into the substantial bottle.

Stumbling slightly and mildly inebriated, Phillip snappishly stands up from the table and conclusively declares; "Tomorrow then!" Ebbing away from the table he sets off to retire to his bedroom for the evening. "May you find what you are looking for, or what *He* has intended you to uncover, my friend."

Once outside of the door to his bedroom, he bids Danylo one more, "goodnight" and then disappears into his neighboring room. With a clamorous thump, he inelegantly shuts the thick wooden door, leaving only a sliver of light creeping out from underneath it. Seconds later, the light recedes and the area surrounding his room is draped in darkness.

Rising up from his stiff seat at the table, Danylo takes one last draft directly from the nearly terminated bottle. He promptly directs himself toward his awaiting bed. Tucked into a small rectangular extension of the main room is a guest bed. This prepared bedstead is furnished with a variety of multiple sized blankets, pillows and throws. Gently crouching down, he leisurely takes a seat at the foot of the bed. Turning to the opposing side of the bed he glances out the cloudy window that is just beside his bed. In an excited trance, he gazes out of the opaque pane. Outside of the murky window is the spectacular moonlit landscape of Autun, propelling bursts of excitement and childlike enthusiasm throughout his previously tired and weary disposition.

Unable to silence the conjectural notions swirling about his brain, he stands up, and silently slinks over to his leather sack. Opening the well-worn flap, he salvages his notebook. He begins riffling through the pages until he settles on one particular page, placing his index finger between the pages for placement, and quickly clamps the book shut. Retrieving his coat, he tersely looks over his left shoulder, peering back at Phillips fastened doorway. Quietly and carefully, he tiptoes toward the room's front entryway. Tenderly twisting the knob and partially propping open the dense door, he slinks out and delicately secures the door behind him.

Gingerly traveling down the expansive darkened corridors of the cathedral, he tactically saunters through the hallowed halls and onto his ultimate destination. Cautiously proceeding down a familiar but awkwardly dark staircase, he tentatively treads toward the tomb of Lazarus. The pitch-black chamber is merely being illuminated by the singular beam of light emanating from a flashlight fastened to Danylo's key ring. His senses are swiftly saturated by the customary stale odor and chalky taste of grit of the ancient enclosure. Amid the stone constructed compartment sits a rectangular sarcophagus fashioned in grayish-tan marble. At eye level, just above the ancient crypt, hangs an elaborate array of unlit white votive candles tucked inside translucent red holders. Draped over the tomb's veneer is an elegant and intricate white woven cloth made of the finest linen and elegant silk.

His heart spiritedly thumping faster and faster, Danylo meticulously draws back the covering, revealing the archaic engraving scribed into the crypt. The uncovered inscription sends a wave of exhilarating delight throughout his otherwise tired body. Procuring his notebook from out of the untidy depths of his satchel, he additionally retrieves his favored fountain pen. Without delay, he hectically scribbles down his spiraling upsurge of ideas. He turns back through the book, comparing multiple pages to his newly jotted markings.

Brimming with wild intrigue, he discreetly opens the decorative facade of the sarcophagus. With a gentle stroke of the back of his hand, Danylo wipes away the obscuring dusty debris lying atop of the stone cap. Bending over, he drops his head toward the stone and blows away some of the finer obfuscating dust. Staring intently at the exposed markings, and, overwhelmed with emotion, he takes a brief moment to brood over his newly substantiated supposition. Noticeably overwhelmingly awestruck by what he has uncovered, he remains in obstinate reticence. Ripping out an empty page from out of his notebook, he proceeds to rifle through his multiple jacket pockets, and, after poking around several pockets, swiftly withdraws his fist; firmly clutching a partially worn red crayon. Gripping the waxy implement on its side, he places the paper directly on top of the engraving. Pressing the horizontal crayon to the page, he rubs it back and forth across the paper, creating a negative of the chiseled markings. Stiffly clinching the sheet, he holds the embossed image up to his eyes for further inspection. Suddenly a brief distant cracking sound startles him. Suspending himself in utter stillness, he listens for the sound again.

"Clank!" Once more he is spooked by the clattery thud of what would seem to be approaching footsteps.

Waiting in absolute stillness, Danylo holds his breath and intently listens for another set of the jolting noises. In his maintained hush there is only silence once again. Though temporarily stunned, he gleefully reverts back to his state of satisfaction regarding his new dazzling discovery. After all, it was probably just Phillip checking in on his old impatient comrade. Retracing his steps, Danylo begins the journey back to the cozy confines of his guest quarters.

"Crink!" Again he hears the unexpected snapping sound echoing in the darkness. Taken aback once again, he stays still for another few seconds. Gathering his wits he shrugs the noises off once more and continues back.

"Clang!" The curious clamorous blasts resonate yet again; seemingly louder and closer than before.

Inquisitively shouting out, "Phillip?" Danylo thought to himself: Phillip would have announced himself in order to not to unnecessarily startle him. Not only was their no response, but there also seemed to be two distinctly separate sets of foots

Increasingly alarmed by the inexplicable mysterious sounds, he presses on. With every cautious step, he is progressively even more suspicious around every corner. Overtly overcome by the eerie feeling of being covertly followed and anonymously observed, he navigates through the darkness; finally returning back to his residence. The shocking commotions have entirely subsided. His heart beats with excessive vigor. Thoroughly relieved, Danylo attempts to relax by descending down into the comfortable depths of the dark brown leather recliner in the middle of the quiet quarters. Taking a few deep breaths, he begins to unwind. The sounds had now subsided and a feeling of ease washed over his intellect. It must have been his imagination. Now entirely calm, unconcerned and exhaustively content, he tightly clutches his notebook and breathes an extended sigh of reprieve. Serenely sinking further into the chair, he tranquilly closes his eyes; cascading into a deep peaceful slumber.

He is crudely awoken from his peaceful respite. Slowly opening his eyes, to his astonishment and horror he has been bound and gagged. His feet, arms and chest have been tightly secured to the leather chair. The ivory white sheet that previously covered his bed had vindictively been wrapped around him. With blurry vision, unable to fully acclimate himself, Danylo peers upward. Amid his incoherent intellect, he is hazily able to make out the shadowy indistinct figure of a man standing above him. Squinting, he makes every effort to get a better look at his captor. However, with the disorienting bright beam of light burning behind the silhouette, any attempt at distinguishing details is futile. Suddenly, the dark figures' arms come violently crashing down upon his chest, leaving Danylo absolutely motionless.

The fateful blow surprisingly leaves no bruises or contusions. Without any sign of a struggle or indication of violent occurrences, the cause of death would undoubtedly appear as an unassuming heart attack. Judiciously leaving not a trace of his presence, the shadowy visitor surreptitiously retreats. The unassuming but deadly restraints have been removed and meticulously placed back onto the bed. The anonymous murderer slips away, vanishing back into the darkness. Although taken by surprise and sadistically slain, Danylo's face maintains a very peaceful expression and remarkably his body shows no sign of being restrained. In the out-and-out reticence of the night, his body is left lifeless in the dusky brown cracked leather chair giving the impression he had simply passed away peacefully in his sleep.

3

"What hath night to do with sleep?"
-John Milton, *Paradise Lost*

NEW YORK CITY, UNITED STATES
PRESENT

Mirrored atop the cracked and puddled moist asphalt surface of the city street, reflects the twinkling of flashing streetlights and the hapless glow of foreboding neon signs. Tucked into this corner of the grease coated, dirt stained district of downtown New York stands a partially dilapidated bar. This area is less of a district and more of a sin sodden cesspool of dregs; a waste tank for corrupted slime and sleazy perverts. The derelict dive before me is known as the Candy Club. However, it isn't just a bar; the Club is purely a charming façade. The degenerate saloon is merely a veneer concealing access to an even more nefariously repugnant retreat. Concealed within the club's walls is the secret entrance into an illicit, unlicensed and definitely illegal underground society of the truly wicked: The Devil's Den. Not only is it a hangout for putrid creeps, but also a safe haven for both Bleeders and Feeders.

My name is Simon and I am charged with the pursuit and eradication of all the Bleeders and Feeders around the world. More commonly known as vampires and werewolves, these unholy atrocities proudly feast upon the innocent blood and flesh of mortals.

Eclipsed by the ceaselessly customary cover of night, I stand in front of what appears to be just another typical grimy New York bar. However, swimming amidst the lingering sweet-vinegar stench of trash, I detect the faintest whiff of an all too familiar iron-tinged odor. Bleeders are most certainly nearby. But, I have been pursuing something even more savage than Bleeders. Accompanying their foul fragrance is the distinctly wretched stink of sulfur, rotting flowers and burning excrement. That pungent aroma always gives his position away. Of course *he* would keep company with Bleeders. His vile trail has led me straight to the Candy Club. The chase ends here.

Beyond this seedy façade of the dingy bar is something much more dangerous than Bleeders. Somewhere among this lawless gathering of creeps and monsters is Legion, an unprincipled horde of uncontrollable demons. The rebellious group of tormenting demons violently seizes a human body and then possesses that individual with the sole purpose of inciting as much chaos as they can possibly create. Lucky for me, his old habits die hard. Though this habitual hunt up until now has been for the most part straightforward; he never goes easy.

As the "U" in the tacky red neon sign above the entrance sporadically blinks off and on, I slowly gait toward the club's doorway. Lodged between towering walls of worn black brick, topped with rows of shattered windows painted rich pitchy violet from the inside, the front entrance is only fortified with one bouncer. The sounds of ear-splitting screams and the pounding of deafening bass that somehow passes for music these days intensifies with every step closer to the entrance. As I arrive at the door, "Should I Stay or Should I Go" by The Clash appreciatively interrupts the former grating noise. The obnoxious odors swell with gushing intensity. He is close.

Casually crossing the threshold from the empty streets into the realm of undesirables, I am greeted by the slapping stink of at least 100 cigarettes and the overwhelming perfume of stale beer and cheap hooch. Upon my intrusion, all but a few of the patrons turn and fling uninviting snarls in my direction. The crowd of street toughs and wannabe heavies attempt to hurl intimidating and ghoulish stares at me, the unfamiliar and therefore unwelcome intruder. Ignoring my objectionable sordid hosts, I slowly drift through the paltry crowd of tattooed freaks and woolly whiskered weirdoes. I make my way through leather clad biker impersonators mixed with obnoxious would-be goon punks with multicolored hair. This skuzzy collection of misguided recluses and pointless misanthropes consisted mostly of only aspiring criminal wannabes, but there is much more impending business. Bleeders are far more malicious than these make believing mortals. Even more malicious then most Bleeders, is Legion. By the loathsome and expanding foulness in the air, that flesh pirate is somewhere in this room.

Driving through the sea of shoving shoulders and squints of oozing umbrage, I plant myself on a stool at the far end of the bar. I observe a group of alabaster tinted gothic girls scantily clad in constricting black and red shiny vinyl. The mass of amatory misfits is huddled around a vintage jukebox directly over my left shoulder. To my right is squatted a grossly plump young man, dewy with sweat and biting down on a nauseating cheap cigar with brownish-yellow tarnished teeth. Attired in black denim from head to toe; cut-off at both the sleeves and the knees and complete with a ridiculous partially bleached blonde Mohawk, the lumpy boy turns his moist beefy head to me. Peering at me through the corners of his yellow eyes, he grumbles and shrugs his shoulders while promptly turning his considerably large back to me.

The bartender, a greasy slick and sickly thin fellow ornamented with multiple body piercings as well as clear clusters of telling track marks, makes his way toward me. Looking me dead in the eyes, "Skinny" leisurely approaches me and then deliberately speeds his pace and continues on; not just refusing me service, he was sending the clear message that I was categorically unwanted. Sternly perched atop my bar stool, I steadily continue my undeterred fixed gaze forward.

Directly above my head and behind the bar, hangs a television quietly buzzing with a news program. A news anchor articulates the feature story of latest outbreaks of the deadly Ebola virus and a revolutionary new vaccine. "...Given the recent number of Ebola outbreaks in both the United States and the U.K., the President is also pressing congress for hundreds of millions of dollars to set up healthcare facilities in West Africa and to additionally airlift much needed supplies to Liberia. He is also demanding additional millions in order to assist in dramatically bumping forward the Human Vaccine's timetable."

It seems the latest innovative immunization is scheduled to conclude its test trials in the near future. The radical injection will soon be ready for worldwide distribution. Loudly interrupting the news cast, one of the surly patrons squawks at the bartender from somewhere amongst the crowd:

"Hey ass-breath, change the damn channel!"

Like a clamorous zoo, the bar immediately erupts with ill-tempered cheers and raspy yelps. The bartender shouts back, "Screw you!" and promptly changes to a channel airing the already in progress, *A Nightmare on Elm Street*.

Amidst the bellowing jeers and riotous hecklers, I endure in silence; inflexibly focused on my scanning senses. He is close. Indifferent from "Skinny" and his band of imbeciles, I stay put and patiently wait.

All at once the bouquet of decay gets patently stronger. With an insignificant tilt of my head I peripherally glance to my right: nothing. Sweeping back over my left shoulder, I spot him. The tall, well-built and truculent black man across the room is the current flesh casing for the collective of body bandits. His profoundly inked and branded dark muscular physique, united with a razor shaved glossy head is all too familiar indicators. However, under the heavy silver eyebrow ring that garnishes his fuming tightly furled brow, sits the unmistakable irritated red and emerald colored eyes, the definitive confirmation that Legion has taken the bulky form over. Rising up from out of a corner booth the strapping flesh finger-puppet slowly parades to the back of the room.

Although brilliantly disguised inside of a human form, Legion always has a tell. Not only do the inhabitant's eyes appear excessively bloodshot and the iris's turn an unnatural shade of intense green, but additionally, the hijacked human's skin turns slightly translucent. This rapid skin transformation unveils unusual groupings of blue and red tinted veins around the eyes, mouth and brow. Not to mention, Legion never fails to indulge in his peculiar penchant for predominantly possessing two varieties of hosts. Habitually, these usual specimens are either generously tattooed, athletically developed black-skinned gents or antithetically, white, heavy-set bearded men, who happen to have a weakness for donning women's apparel. It's him alright. His current host is exceptionally bigger and substantially stronger than previous bodies. This could get interesting.

Deathly still, I remain convincingly unseen; at least I don't think he saw me. Just as I hoped, he had only just arrived to the Club. Dropping by the booth to give his regards to some scruffy scumbag acquaintance, he was now headed to the real party.

At the back of this lousy sullen hole-in-the-wall is an unassuming rust-stained door. This door marked "Employees Only," is the gateway to a dramatically more sickening and outrageously evil underworld. Just beyond the door is the confidential entrance to the Devil's Den. Infested with heaps of illegal drugs, prostitution and gambling there is only one prerequisite for entry into the Devil's Den you are one of three things: a demon, a Bleeder or a Feeder. The patrons of this secretive sin-filled establishment are an obscenely unpleasant and rather beastly congregation of murderous immortals; creatures radically worse than the laughably costumed humans of the Candy Club

As luck would have it, my objective, Legion, has led me directly to another stop on my long list of immortal establishments to obliterate. I am going to deliver all of them directly into the bleak beyond. Tonight, they are all going to Hell.

As Legion approaches the exclusive back door, he reaches out his clamped paw, and pounds his fist against the fist of the colossal sentinel resolutely parked at the perimeter of the private passageway. This looming guardian of the entrance is a literal giant. Towering over the length of Legion's massive figure, the willowy beast stands at least seven-feet tall. With stringy muddy brown hair and chunky black sunglasses, the willowy goon stands guard in front of the restricted entrance. His pale, emaciated face and crimson stained cracked dry lips, not to mention the hazy but undeniable smell of sweaty nickel, instantly gives him away. This oak of a man is unquestionably a Bleeder.

Just as Legion is permitted access to the private quadrant, he slows his gate. I try to watch casually from my undetected position. Mid stride, he glances back over his shoulder. Did the iniquitous meat thief spot me? Almost through the door, he catches me out of the corner of his characteristically gleaming jade and blushing eyes. Hesitating for a moment, he flashes a mischievous smirk and rapidly hurls the door shut behind him. Given that particular grin; yeah, he definitely saw me.

Slowly crossing his trunk-like arms, the hefty tattooed ox takes his wide-legged stance in front of the secret doorway and stands guard once again.

No time like the present. Taking my cue from the song's chorus, I engage them... all of them. No need for real hardware. Faithless, foul, and unmistakably corrupt as this sordid crowd is, they are still only human. It is the wretched undead that lie beyond that door that I am after.

Without hesitation, Simon produces two retractable batons out from the inside of his long draping raven-black trench coat. Simon swiftly swats both of his arms down by his side, simultaneously extending his less than lethal weapons.

While the hooded Simon battles the club's seedy patrons, Legion has continued past the doorway and down the lengthy dim lit passage way that leads into the heart of the Devil's Den. Emerging out of the other end of the narrow hall, Legion is greeted by the sinful social club's second set of security. The mob of five pale skinned overweight and oversized gorillas stand shoulder to shoulder: Round and bulbous shoulder to round and bulbous shoulder. Keeping guard over this second entrance to the even more fallacious club, the husky apes are all outfitted in bulging black tuxedos with black shirts with red bowties and additionally armed with a variety of firearms. AR-15s, M-11s and M-16s, these silenced and shoulder strapped semi-automatic machine guns dangle like jumbo jewelry from around the men's stout necks. All five of the firm force of massive egg-shaped men, stand tough and steadfast.

Recognized by the bulky men, Legion effortlessly saunters past them and growls; "There's a hard ass starting some shit out there." The prodigious primates with their shaved heads and sleek black sunglasses focus on the Den's entrance. The beefy bunch firmly plants itself; facing forward, down the narrow hallway. Holding soundly, their inflexible faces of rigid stone anticipate the arrival of the forthcoming intruder. .

Casually cruising past the immovable cluster of hired muscle, Legion seizes one of the guard's hidden halfway consumed bottles of cheap rum. Reaching into his pants pocket and producing a book of matches, Legion riotously hurls the glass container against the floor. Scattering the bottle into pieces, the booze now completely covers and saturates a section of the wall and the floor around a nearby trash receptacle. Striking one of the matches, he slightly tilts the single flame, which in turn ignites the entire book in a flash of flame. Tossing the fireball into the liquor-soaked trashcan, he then steadily makes his way to the main chamber of the Den. With a steady stroll, Legion collides with a rapidly approaching Den member in a grey suit. Legion clashes with the silvery sharkskin suited thin man, purposely slamming his sturdy shoulder forcibly into the man's softly padded shoulder. In an instant, locking his eyes with the unaware bystander, an emerald green puff of smoke-like vapor rapidly erupts from Legions eyes, directly shooting into the eyes of the man with the slender suit.

Legion momentarily possesses the boney body of the slender passerby. Like a callous, pitiless puppeteer, Legion guides the man to grab his own fountain pen from the inside of his jacket pocket. Gripping it firmly he controls the man to disturbingly thrust the pen rigorously into his host's own face, neck and chest. At once a profuse amount of blood sprays from out of the multiple wounds. The gushing torrents splash against the hallway wall and stream down the shimmery suit of the thin man. This juicy mutilation propels the overwhelming scent of fresh blood in the air, a number of nearby members impulsively swarm around the self-mutilating man. Unable to resist the bloody offering, the group of Bleeders heedlessly hoard over his gushing body in a tumultuous feeding frenzy.

Temporarily obscured by the flame and smoke of the slightly escalating trash fire, in a smoldering surge of gleaming green smoke, Legion dashes back into his original muscular form and then further into the depths of the Den. Both the insignificant inferno and the scraggy blood-spewing Bleeder were merely diversions. He simply needed a few extra seconds to formulate his evasion of the advancing Simon. Just as the hulking Bleeders huddle around the bloodied body, the small fire bursts out of the receptacle, spilling onto the floor, igniting the spattered alcohol. Once introduced, they create a roaring, broader blaze. The swelling flames instantly trigger both the building's strident fire alarm and its ample sprinkler system. The hallway is filled with the steady throbbing of screeching sirens as well as thoroughly doused in a dusting of cold water from above. These small distractions should be just enough to facilitate Legion's getaway. The startled, water soaked crowd in the Den stand up, and promptly scurry about, a bit disoriented by the unidentified confusion. While most of the crowd scampers closer to the main entrance, Legion moves against the tumultuous current of the tangle of bodies; spiritedly proceeding to the back of the Den.

Meanwhile, during the burgeoning bustle in the back room, the shrouded Simon begins his arduous jaunt through the Den's furtive entrance. From the moment he first lunged from his barstool, he has already incapacitated six of the bar's characters with only two fluidly precise movements of his adept hand held instruments. As most of the decadent crowd scatters, frantically fleeing out the front door to escape, a group of mortal curiosities approach Simon. Five grizzly men and two robust and quite masculine females surround their unfamiliar guest. With absolute stillness and a calm face vacant of expression, Simon, the cloaked agitator, is positioned directly in the center of the now encircling gaggle of freaks. As the first of his combatants springs toward him, he swiftly makes short work of all seven. In merely four lightning fast strategic strokes, they are deftly defeated. Clearly out of commission, the seven will live, though severely stunned and provisionally immobilized.

Victorious and still absent of a facial expression or any appearance of effort, he makes his way toward the only figure left in the Candy Club. The towering shaggy bouncer still resolutely tending to the disguised doorway is now the only thing that stands between him and the Den. The beastly tree of a man reaching out his lumbering

33

arms clinches his teeth together and lets out an animalistic roar as he confidently stomps toward his modest opponent. Standing his ground, Simon grips the bottom of one of his batons and instantly draws out a thin metallic wire that is wound and tethered to the inside base of the baton. As the seven-foot ogre charges toward his undersized and seemingly inconsequential challenger, Simon punctually extends the fine wire. In a faintly fast imperceptible motion he wraps the wire around the advancing colossal creature's neck. Nearly capturing his would be victim, the giant just barely misses Simon; forcing him to come to a sudden halt. Momentarily taking a brief pause, the oaf composes himself and as he stands up straight, his bitter expression morphs into a dazed look of dismay. Gradually, the lanky brood's head slips down his neck and topples down to the dingy, beer-soaked bar floor.

As the rest of his titanic figure tumbles to the ground, the wire retracts back into Simon's baton. Triumphant, Simon returns his batons back into his jacket and kneels down beside the huge headless corpse. Outwardly extending his right arm above the body, he smoothly gestures the sign of the cross over the beheaded form. In Latin, he recites;

"*Ecce crucem, fugite partes adversæ.*"

"Behold the Cross of the Lord, flee bands of enemies."

In an instant, the massive mangled body turns into a shriveled pile of decaying debris. Reaching into the slimy waste of where the mammoth man's hand used to be, he retrieves a small key chain. This tiny pendant is the remote that controls the automated opening of the Den's mechanized entryways. Rising back to his feet, Simon now treads toward the rusted doorway. Dynamically kicking down the heavy iron door, he reveals what looks to be simply an unassuming supply closet. Lined with numerous shelves and stocked heavily with various cleaning chemicals, the room is littered with several buckets accompanying a disgusting collection of grimy mops and brooms. Stepping into the modest space he pushes the button on the recovered remote. Instantly the entire wall in front of him begins to rotate. During the room's revolution, he seizes an intricately decorated flask out from the inside of his coat. This decorative metal wrapped glass flask is filled with richly red essential fluid. He takes a hearty draught. Completing its rotation, the moved room reveals the dark narrow passage that leads to the infamous Devil's Den.

Amidst the clanging fire alarm and the raining sprinkler system, the five ape-like armed guards eagerly await to greet their audacious intruder. Simon steadily heads toward the herd of guards. Reaching once again inside his flowing jacket, he produces two more weapons. Unlike the relatively benign batons, the short bladed swords are both exceptionally sharp and exceedingly lethal. With his new weapons drawn, Simon continues intently through the downpour; staunchly toward his anticipatory challengers. The hulky group furiously fires multiple rounds toward their rapidly approaching hooded assailant. Entirely ineffective, the squad's timid warning shots do not sway Simon in the least. Continuing on his unswerving path, they continue to open fire. Countless muzzle flashes and gun smoke mix with the flashing floodlights and gusts of smoke from the now extinguished trash fire. This blustery blend makes a dense fog-like atmosphere that momentarily obscures their ominous forthcoming foe.

Amidst the haze of their seemingly confusing cloud, Simon craftily weaves around the husky shooters in a blur of brisk movements. One by one the heads of the gunmen are swiftly severed from their upright bodies. Sequentially, the headless bodies collapse to the ground. In the twinkling of an eye, all five carcasses lie motionless amid the swirling pools of water and blood. Just as the final body inelegantly slumps to the ground, the water raining down from the ceiling suddenly ceases.

Formulaically crouching to the ground once again, Simon

motions the sign of the cross over the group of truncated corpses. Again he recites; "*Ecce crucem, fugite partes adversæ.*" Upon conclusion of his recitation, the hill of bodies mutates into another heap of muddy sludge and blackened decay. As the air clears, the intensely violent scene suddenly comes to a tranquil halt.

Beholding the upsetting spectacle, a group of startled Bleeders stands momentarily paused at the edge of where the hallway connects to the Den's main room. The agitated and bloodthirsty cluster is comprised of both men and woman outfitted in a variety of gothic get-ups. Routine red velvet jackets, black leather trench coats and skin-tight vinyl purple corsets are just some of the regular regalia. Tightly bunched together, they stand craving to collide with Simon, their curious infiltrator. Directly in the middle of the mass stands a beefy muscular man with tattooed arms bursting from his sleeveless black tuxedo jacket. With a heavy black tribal tattoo wrapping around his aged eye socket, he peers out from behind his sleek dark sunglasses. Out from underneath his charcoal grey and pointed beard, his lips pull apart and curl as he begins to growl. The bearded brute slowly crouches down, maintaining his aimed glare with Simon. Flexing his enormous inked arms, he lets out a primal cry and leads his riled associates in a charge toward Simon.

The brigade of Bleeders hurls themselves clumsily toward their shrouded opponent. Though vastly outnumbering Simon roughly thirty-to-one, the assailants are patently unorganized and rather sloppy. As the barreling horde closes in, Simon reacts with brief but systematic strokes of his deadly accurate blades. The animals don't stand a chance against the methodical force that composedly stands prepared before them. In a matter of seconds, his brisk strikes and keen lashes result in another mound of headless bodies. Ritualistically kneeling and gesturing over the defeated bunch of bodies, Simon once again ceremonially recites the Latin utterance and once more the hefty piles melt into murky slush.

Rapidly arising to his feet, Simon rushes into the main chamber of the Devil's Den. Surveying the sizable room, he is able to spot his target across the wide expanse of the now evacuated nightclub. In his attempt to escape, Legion had unsuccessfully tried to liberate himself from the Den using a back door that had been unknowingly barricaded. Simon now had him uncompromisingly cornered. With no chance of escape, Legion cocks his head from side to side, brashly cracking his vertebrae. Clinching his beefy fists, he prepares for the inevitable battle with his determined pursuer. With a great big smirk emerging on his face, Legion slyly spouts; "Good to see you again... 'Simon' is it?"

Upon displaying this smug and toothy grin, Legion ferociously leaps toward Simon. Rushing directly into his considerably smaller adversary, he thrusts his massive shoulders heartily into Simon's core. Bowling him over, Legion violently sends both of them crashing directly to the ground. Relatively motionless, Simon slides off and rolls to the side of Legions brawny form. Flat on his back, Legion frantically glances down to his shoulders and is stunned to see that he has been not only wounded but also perplexingly incapacitated. Inexplicably during his abrupt assault, Simon somehow pierced and subdued him. Penetrated by two cross-shaped daggers now protruding from his shoulders, Legion is now helplessly pinned to the floor.

Gradually rising victoriously back to his feet, Simon hovers above his constrained and defeated foe. Slowly, Simon slips the hood from off the top of his head. With outstretched arms he fervidly gestures the sign of the cross atop his furiously writhing captive. Reaching down, he sturdily places his right hand on the forehead of the hysterically squirming Legion. With a deep inhale he firmly presses his hands over the subdued Legion's eyes and shoves his sweaty baldhead into the water and blood coated concrete floor, Simon begins to chant. This time is a bit more in depth and intensely than the previously rudimentary ritualistic words of expulsion. As his monotonic words of exorcism are about to reach their conclusion, he is interrupted by a resounding clang. These rustling reverberations were curiously coming from somewhere above the two combatants. A startled Simon briefly looks upward toward the commotion overhead.

Suspended from the ceiling in the center of the room hangs a large round glass enclosure. This glass compartment served as a dangling stripper booth. Encased inside of the elaborate cage were three scantily clad, curvaceous and painfully frightened young women. Enslaved against their will, the women remain helplessly captive and completely petrified by the perplexing and ultra violent incidents. Managing to crawl to the edge of her booth, one of the fazed girls peers down from her floating cage.

Her rowdy rattle from the overhanging pen is just the distraction Legion needed. The disruption of Simon's incantation allows him the fleeting opportunity to lock his eyes with those of the on looking girl. In an instant, the greenish smoky substance gushes from his eyes and shoots upward. Hurling through the air, the misty green vapor is torpedoed directly into the eyes of the terrified onlooker. Penetrating her bright blue panic stricken eyes, the smoke instantly transforms her previously youthful eyes to that of the characteristic bloodshot and bright glowing green gaze of the occupant Legion. At that same moment her skin instantly turns a transparent shade of alabaster; revealing vascular patterns of red and blue. Still pinned to the floor, but released from his demonic inhabitor, the menacing muscular form is entirely motionless. Legion has now possessed and is in complete control of his new female victim. Like a morbid marionette, he abruptly whips the girl's head unnaturally to the side, forcing her to fix her burning green gaze on the other two fear frozen half-dressed female captives. Spontaneously, Legion desperately scatters his company of demons; distributing them between the three helpless young prisoners. Three sets of glowing green eyes instantly indicate that Legion has clearly taken whole possession of each woman.

Now hanging directly above Simon, who only moments ago, nearly had him pinned, Legion looks down at him through the three's green eyes. Cruelly taking control and dynamically operating their bodies, Legion manipulates the young girls to compulsorily hurl themselves from their cage. Simultaneously, the three wildly break through the imprisoning glass enclosure and leap from the high swaying platform and onto the surrounding catwalks. Completely covered from head to toe in shards of broken glass now trickling with blood; they disperse and madly run in three different directions. Sprinting across the suspended catwalks just above Simon, the women vault toward the blacked-out windows that embellish the Den's high reaching walls. Simon patiently observes; standing at the ready as all three ladies slam their bodies through the windowpanes. The scantily clad young women promptly propel themselves through the room's small rectangular windows.

With a massive burst of jagged debris, they securely land on the building's fire escape. Now liberated from the Den, Legion influences his female forms to assure his escape by flinging themselves as far away from Simon as possible. He directs the first girl to jump from the balcony, her limbs flailing hysterically as she sails through the night air   Plunging down into the dark alley below, she violently slams into the windshield of a vacant car, smashing her head through the window. Subsequently, he maneuvers his second victim to clumsily hurdle the fire escape's railing. Awkwardly falling through the air, she splashes into an adjacent second story storefront glass window. Inelegantly rolling backwards from off of the window's edge, she haphazardly flops her mangled body onto the pointed post of a wrought iron fence below. The sharp iron dowel gruesomely juts out from her temple.

The third and final possessed girl lands on the far end of the fire escape after bursting out of the Den. She promptly dashes down the grated landing. Illogically sprinting toward the railing, she recklessly leaps from the far end of the platform. Soaring through the elevated space between the two buildings, she propelled herself into a knotty collection of rusty chains that are dangling from the side of the adjacent building. As she collides with the chains, she gets instantly tangled inside of the muddled metal cables. The dingy chain links wrap around her neck like a noose. The force of her falling body horrifically snaps the poor girl's snagged neck leaving her lifeless body swinging back and forth above the dimly lit alleyway. In a "poof" the green cloud of mist that is Legion disperses. Because of the alarming commotion, a small crowd has now gathered at the edge of the alley. The emerald vapor disperses into multiple individuals in the assembled group of astonished bystanders. Because of the commotion, Legion is unfortunately able to flee by disbanding into several of the surrounding spellbound spectators.

Upon scaling the Den's walls and impulsively in pursuit of the three young female victims Simon darts down the suspended catwalk. Rushing toward the shattered windows he promptly peers out of the breach and out past the escape. Hurriedly skimming over the shadowy surroundings he scarcely observes Legion's devastating discharge into the crowd.

Outwardly serene, thwarted Simon is utterly unable to pursue the expansive breadth of dispersing individuals. Composedly disenchanted, he quietly retreats. Perfectly undetected by the onlookers, Simon repositions his veiling hood upon his head and recedes; slowly vanishing into the obscuring shadows of the city.

4

"For God doth know that in the day ye eat thereof, then your eyes shall be opened, and ye shall be as gods, knowing good and evil."
-Genesis 3:4-5

LONDON, ENGLAND
PRESENT

Poised behind an ornate hand-carved and throne-like gothic chair is the dusky silhouette of a slender man. From his stance tucked behind an opulent antique mahogany desk he looks out at an elevated and stately view of London. Peering through the towering two-story high narrow column of windows, the slim man of Middle Eastern descent smugly beholds the grand view. With his mildly olive complexion and long jet-black hair that is tightly slicked back into a ponytail, the debonair man intensely gazes out upon the bustling cityscape. Not only offering an imposingly splendid glimpse of the River Thames, the lavish study is also bursting with an elaborate selection of antique furniture, priceless works of art and a notably vast library. Filled from wall to wall and from floor to ceiling, the extensive and impressive collection is almost exclusively comprised of extremely rare and first edition books. Everything rests above a gathering of colorfully refined Persian rugs blanketing a meticulously extravagant marble floor.

Attired in a perfectly tailored custom-crafted black suit draped over a pearly crisp white shirt adorned with a crimson red tie, the man continues his unbroken stare out of the picturesque window. With a flawlessly fashioned full Windsor knot, the svelte figure has his back turned to the computer monitor sitting atop the lush desk. Engaged in an intense video communication with one of his subordinates, the man intently listens to his underling's update. Predominantly almost inanimate, the sleek man has been receiving unsatisfactory status reports from his principal associate, Monkey. The previously tranquil advisor is now noticeably becoming increasingly disconcerted with his assistant.

Aboard a freighter boat, the faithful subservient Monkey is vigilantly scouring a section of the Mediterranean Sea. He is tasked with the recovery of a very particular set of sunken artifact. These imperative objects previously belonged to the lean man in the office. Donning an avocado green-dyed mohawk and large gauge plugs stretching the lobes of his ear, Monkey is noticeably reluctant and fearful to convey his frustrating update to his intolerant director.

In his dense cockney accent, thick as the infamous fog of London, Monkey stammers: "We have been out here for twenty-three blinking days, sir...as of now; the boys have been having Barney Rubble fetching the last two of your silver coins. My apologies sir, but I regret to report that we still have found sod all regarding signs of..."

Cut off by his dismayed master, the distempered supervisor injects; "Monkey, before you utter another foolish word; I don't care. I refuse excuses and I will not tolerate failure."

Blatantly sarcastic, he continues: "Of course they are going to be difficult to find, that was my intention, was it not?" With a chagrined breath out he commandingly concludes, "I have provided you with everything you need to find them all. You have exactly twenty-six hours to retrieve the rest of my silver. Until then, I see no reason for you to contact me again. Bring me what is mine!"

As the final words of his sentence draw to a close, the irked boss smoothly reaches behind himself. With an extended index finger, he blindly presses down on the keyboard, abruptly bringing the heated transmission to an end. Ostensibly calm once again, the silhouetted man grows increasingly displeased; stewing in his own stoic stillness. Maintaining his intense gaze upon the bustling city below, he stands stationary. Following his concentrated survey of the city beneath him, he lazily spins around to the desk and fixes his keen eyes on an extensive stack of large-scale blueprints. With an acutely attentive eye, he ponderously shifts his focus to the abundant research in front of him. The detailed plans and schematics appear to be the layout of a thoroughly fortified compound. Attached to the obviously confiscated architectural designs and satellite photographs are detailed illustrations of a complex and state of the art security system. Now fixed above the gathered materials, the man continues to brood over them in a steady state of assessment. Clearly this is a considerably precarious situation of rather exceptional importance.

Lethargically hovering over his mammoth desk, the dark stranger leans over an exquisitely decorative silver platter containing an immense pile of fine white powder. Stiffly bending downward at the waist, with one hefty and energetic inhalation, he sprightly snorts a sizable amount of the cocaine. Adjacent to the copious heap of coke is an array of miscellaneous multicolored pills. While reverting back to his original upright stance, he promptly pops an abundant handful of the colorful capsules. Reaching out for his posh crystal highball glass that is teeming with amber alcohol, he swiftly washes his indulgences down with one strapping belt of amply aged Scotch.

Monkey, the man's "errand boy," is a young Japanese man in his mid twenties. Gawkily slim and extensively wrapped in colorful tattoos from head to toe, Monkey is an exceptionally capable genius. Intellectually liberally endowed in physics, mathematics and molecular biology, he is an unparalleled bonafide virtuoso in nearly every aspect of academia. This brilliant brainiac, born "Akira," was discovered and hand selected by his authoritative overseer only seven short years ago.

Although growing up in an exceedingly westernized Japanese household, at an early age, Akira was still traditionally pressured to primarily and achieve academically. His father, a wealthy businessman who regularly commuted between Japan, The United States and the United Kingdom, proudly promoted the values and languages of both traditional Eastern and modern Western cultures. Immediately displaying signs of advanced and distinctively uncommon intelligence, Akira's path in life seemed obvious.

During these impressionable years, Akira and his family tediously traveled the globe. His father's business demands left him and his family frequently vaulting from East to West. This incessant jarring back and forth was certainly affecting him. Unfortunately, Akira was being negatively impacted in intensely terrible ways.

Breezing through his conventional educational systems in multiple institutions in both Japan and the UK, he progressed through his studies at an astonishingly accelerated rate. By the young age of nine, his future had been precisely mapped out by his tremendously controlling father. By the pliable age of fourteen, Akira was shipped off to MIT. After effortlessly exceeding the already lofty expectations placed upon him, he rapidly received some of the highest honors available. Upon earning simultaneous mathematical degrees after only two and a half years, he stringently abided to the next phase of his father's plan. Without delay, Akira was consequently transported to England to attend Cambridge University.

At the age of only seventeen, while working on some of the highest profile theoretical projects in the world, Akira became grossly disillusioned and because of this he began to critically question his entire childhood. Over the years he had gradually become more of an introvert. A conventional childhood had been substituted by a life gorged with scholastic competitions and any semblance of a normal adolescence was disrupted by his father's exacting aspirations and grueling collegiate preparation. Though he was routinely surrounded by a massive ensemble of some of the brightest minds in the world and virtually hundreds of academic acquaintances, there wasn't a single person Akira actually called a "friend." As the pressures from everyone exponentially increased, he was suddenly struck with an unbearable fear of failure; second guessing the entire scope of his proficiencies.

In order to remedy both his rapidly deteriorating self-confidence and his lacking social experience, Akira took an interest in using drugs. Increasingly self-scrutinizing his academic abilities, he convinced himself that self-medication was the only answer. After researching a variety of illicit pharmaceuticals, he decided to try methamphetamines.

Obtaining the speed from the black markets of London, he instantly felt the benefits of his potent psychostimulant. He basked in his newfound ability to stay more alert and reveled in the immediate surge of energy. Things came easier now. Not only was he dramatically more alert, but he was also thriving with unwavering self-certainty. Rejoicing in his brand-new, substance regulated stimulation, Akira hurriedly progressed to harder and even more dangerous illegal substances. Cocaine, mescaline and heroin were now part of his unremitting routine. Transforming from privileged genius and distinguished introvert to every day substance regulated junkie, he was now absolutely addicted and controlled by a compulsory multitude of uppers and downers. At first, his colleagues and administrators attempted to ignore his declining condition. Despite his wilting performance, they were willing to look the other way because of how extraordinary invaluable his raw intellect was. However, as he progressively gave into his new addictions, he became utterly uncontrollable. His behavior became so hazardously bizarre that his supervisors could no longer excuse or cover up his sporadic actions. Unequivocally immersed into the unhealthy preoccupations of a severe addict, Akira was subsequently dismissed from the University. Unwilling to notify his father or solicit assistance from anyone of his family, he was directly relinquished to the streets.

Desperately destitute, he continued on his path of chemical compulsion and self-destruction, fully submerging himself into the warped realm of the decadent London underground. In addition to his now innumerable drug habits, he swiftly became similarly addicted to gambling. Frequenting every black market casino inside of London's arcane underworld, Akira now replaced his life of academia with a seedy existence with ruthless bookies and degenerate two-timing gamesters. Consistently building up extensive debts with far too many bookmakers to keep track of, he found himself regularly dodging ugly and unyielding collectors and their hired muscle. Solely driven by his severe addictions and inundated with an infinite amount of debt, Akira was running out of dope and places to hide. He had not only hit rock bottom regarding his drug dependence, but with such tremendous debt to all the wrong people; his days were numbered.

Mortally fraught, he increasingly deserted any hope of survival. After narrowly evading the threat of yet another hired thug appointed to collect money from him, he resigned to surrender to his dire situation. During the early hours of a frigid English morning, he hopelessly drudged out to the middle of a soaring bridge. Shaking from the chilled air but mostly from his obstinate withdrawal, he managed to crawl to the stony edge of the steep bridge. Bleakly primed, ready to hurl himself from the lofty structure, he was abruptly interrupted by the authoritative declarations of a mysterious character.

"It is entirely beyond me why you would purposely want to extinguish such an abundantly intellectual inferno as yourself? The loss of such a scintillating and complex erudite as you would be a monumental tragedy."

Calling out from the darkened midst of the desolate overhang, the assertive voice baffled the would-be jumper. Teeming with petrifying trepidation, he found himself momentarily impeded by the petulantly poised but strangely calming voice of this unseen spectator. Already hopelessly distressed and juddering uncontrollably from withdrawal, Akira stood petrified in wonderment. Squinting his tear-filled eyes as he scans his darkened surroundings, he nervously waits for another sound to emanate from the murky shadows. Again the anonymous voice bellowed out:

"I know what you are, Akira. Your true nature and the breadth of your amazing capabilities are far beyond what you have ever imagined. I, and I alone, can actually grasp the greatness of which you are destined to achieve."

Considerably spooked, Akira stood firmly frozen in consummate shock. Keeping a steady gaze on the thickset darkness that interred the origination of the curious orator, he timidly awaited for yet another proclamation. Then suddenly, from out of the pitch, strutted the slender figure of a suavely suited man. Creeping out from the ominous darkness with his hands behind his long sleek overcoat, the distinctively sophisticated but perceptibly sinister fellow ethereally glided toward the debilitated recluse. The enigmatic stranger drew closer. Overcome with frightening confusion, a speechless Akira blankly paused in baffling awe as the anonymous supporter continued his approach.

Towering above the squatting reject, the pompous stranger stretched out his sturdy right arm and firmly took hold of Akira's arm. Staring down at the sickly limb, riddled with track marks and scars, the unidentified visitor said:

"Failed attempts and broken dreams, my young squire. Always trying to fill that vast void that inhabits the vacant hollow where a soul should be. Young man, I know that sensation and your circumstances all too well. I too, am a misfit of sorts."

Flinging his left arm from out behind his body, the stranger lobs a round shaped object toward Akira's tensely fixed feet.

"All your debt has been consummately eliminated," oozes charitably from the lips of the unexpected visitor. "You can call me Mr. Shepherd."

Deeply puzzled, Akira looks down to discern the tossed article. He shockingly recognizes the unsettling projectile. To his astonishing disbelief it is the severed, blood-spattered head of his prominent relentless bookkeeper.

"That bothersome void you have in your heart and the assiduous ache in the pit of your rotting belly is a stubbornly voracious craving. Akira, I am the key to satisfying that remarkably rare and relentless appetite. I can offer you the life that you desire and more importantly I can make all of your pain... 'Poof!' disappear. I can be the nurturing, understanding and faithful father that you never had. Come with me and indulge your hunger: gratify that agonizing stomach."

After a generous pause, Akira still quite stunned, closed his eyes and slowly lowered his head. With a nod of his head; he accepted Mr. Shepherd's altruistic proposition.

"Magnificent!" the insidious stranger exuberantly roared, sharply breaking the tense atmosphere.

"Your defeated attempts at a fulfilling life will be a distant memory." Throwing his arms around the nervous young man, he asserts; "I will bestow unto you all that you covet. You will bathe in endless perversion and revel in lavish lasciviousness."

Intensely looking Akira straight in the eyes Mr. Shepherd goes on to additionally promise; "I am your committed benefactor and you will be my uncompromised facilitator. Wealth, dominion, women, and most importantly, understanding, are yours. All I ask in return is simply unlimited access to that remarkable intellect of yours. I am your benevolent master and you; you will be my honored little monkey."

From that moment on, Akira was referred to as "Monkey."

His treacherous sponsor, Mr. Shepherd fulfilled his commitment and Monkey was in fact compensated far beyond his wildest expectations. For his assorted tasks, he received prolific riches and wielded previously unimaginable authority. Hands down, his favored reparations were the unrestricted access to endless supplies of both high-end ladies and high-priced drugs. Living the ritzy rock 'n' roll lifestyle as the errand boy for a menacingly influential superior, Monkey now had a rewarding reason to perform his intellectual stunts. Unlike the demanding expectations placed upon him by his apathetic father, there was no hidden agenda. Simply put, this was an even exchange. Though a mysterious man of many secrets, Mr. Shepherd had been entirely forthright and open with his proposition. As Monkey's benefactor, Mr. Shepherd had not only accepted and even appreciated the unorthodox inclinations of the ingenious prodigy; he perfectly endorsed and encouraged his new life of errant excess.

5

"The object of persecution is persecution.
The object of torture is torture.
The object of power is power."
-George Orwell, *1984*

BORDEAUX, FRANCE
PRESENT

Comfortably asleep in my cozy bed inside of my Bordeaux apartment, I am abruptly awakened by the incessant vibrating of my mobile phone. The persistent incoming call is an unknown number. Before picking up the tenacious request, with the use of only one partially opened eye, I glance to see who it is that is calling me. Directly below the "unknown caller" alert, is a digital display of the time; it is barely past five o'clock in the morning. Before I can ponder the possibilities of the pending party, I habitually answer: "*Bonjour, qui etes-vous?*" Flopping back my warm comforter, I sluggishly stand up from my bed and walk toward the washroom for a glass of water. "*Bonjour?*"

Following an awkwardly lingering hesitation, the caller speaks in an overtly somber tone: "Anzela *allô*, It is Abbe Phillip, in Autun. Ela... I have some rather upsetting news. Your father, I am sorry to say this over the phone, my dear, but your father has unexpectedly passed on."

Immediately my legs become wobbly and weak. Receiving this earth shattering report of my father's ghastly death, I begin to shiver uncontrollably. Like a flakey dry tree branch snapped by a hearty gust of wind, I collapse to my knees and begin to weep. Waiting in simple sympathetic silence, Phillip graciously allows me the time to gain some semblance of composure. My sudden weeping turned into unyielding and uncontrollable sobbing. Overcome with rich misery, my hefty sunken gulps for air were followed only by sputtering bursts of spit. Why? How can this be? What happened? A countless collection of clamorous queries surged throughout my brain. Staggering distress satiated my marrow. My sporadic sharp drawn pants now slowed to a stammering wheeze of balmy steam. After a few steady breaths, I was composed enough to reply.

"How did he? What happened?" I confoundedly asked.

Abbe Phillip went on to delicately describe his macabre morning. To his great horror, he had only discovered my father's motionless body just under an hour ago. He said that the two of them were up late the night before and when he left my father, everything seemed perfectly normal. When Phillip woke up, he proceeded directly into the kitchen; finding his my father peacefully settled into a chair, he softly snickered to himself. Assuming my father had never made it to his bed from both too much excitement and too much vodka, he went to prepare them both some tea. Once the water was boiled, he went back to wake up my father; presenting him with his morning tea. However, as soon as he approached him, an eerie sensation washed over Phillip. He instantly knew something was wrong. As he drew in closer, it was woefully obvious that my father was not merely asleep: his body was entirely void of any sign of vitality. Cold to the touch and not an ounce of breath; seemingly he had probably departed quietly in his sleep sometime in the early hours of the morning.

My knotted gut twisted more and more with the details of the troubling account. Settling down, as much as presently possible,

I simply respond. "I can be there by early afternoon, Abbe. *Au revoir. Je vous remercie et je vais vous voir bientôt.*"

Concluding the woeful exchange, with the heaviest of hearts, I hastily prepared for my compulsory gloomy spree to Autun. Quite perplexed and jarringly dazed, I managed to scramble together some essentials and promptly set forth for Autun.

While barreling down the highway, my grieving mind was obligated to reflect on my relationship with my father and the events that had altered our relationship forever.

Nearly six years ago, my mother passed away. After her laborious life-long battle with diabetes, later in her life she was dealt yet another crushing blow. Only a few years ago, after complaining of shortness of breath, she cautiously visited her doctor. Shockingly, my benevolent mother received the awful and grim news; one of her test results showed that she had developed lung cancer. Upon further examination and multiple tests, they determined the merciless cancer unknowingly had rapidly spread throughout her entire body. Bravely, my mother fiercely fought back with multiple rounds of exhausting chemotherapy. She had already been forced to fight diabetes her entire life, so now when faced with cancer, she knew no other way than to fight back some more.

Upon initiating her strenuous treatments, my father took a temporary leave of absence from his research. I took as much time as possible to be home with my mother during her horrendous sessions. My father was determined and insistent to taking care of my ailing mother himself. However, as the weeks and months went by, he felt pressure from his administration to return to work, if only at a part time capacity. He continually rejected their proposals and declined their offers. However, eventually, under the administrations tremendous pressure, he accepted a part time role. Whether it was financially driven or purely a matter of his feeling of responsibility and satisfying expectations, he only agreed to this temporary and brief duty because of its diminutive nature. As my mother was at the end of her lengthy treatment and since her prognosis looked remarkably positive, he felt confident that his fleeting absences would prove to be auspiciously insignificant. This new and part-time position only took him out of town on extremely short-term occasions.

Inopportunely, to our gruesome surprise, just as he had resumed his third week of work, my mother suddenly died. We were absolutely shocked. It was later discovered she had developed an unrelenting bacterial infection that had gone undiagnosed and therefore untreated. Beyond devastated, my father was surpassingly ashamed and, to the best of my knowledge, has never forgiven himself for his absence during her passing.

In a fraught attempt to validate the time he had expended on his research and disagreeably detached him from my mother's side, he entirely engrossed himself into his work. Stemming not only from his need to prove the efforts were not in vain but also a developing fixation on the substantial subject of life and death, my father intensely immersed himself into his work. His research had always revolved around the re-animating of Lazarus and more intriguingly, the vague and scarcely mentioned circumstances surrounding the particulars of his life post his being resurrected from the dead.

I always understood that my father was enveloped in a dreadfully difficult position, but our relationship has never been the same since my mother's passing. The complicated and lousy circumstances clearly drove a wedge between us. Admittedly, I suppose I never really overcame his poorly timed absence. Following the upsetting funeral and forlorn burial, I moved away. I simply couldn't escape my persistent resentment. Feeling inexorably compelled to distance myself from my father and avoid the anguish of the entire situation, I morosely moved to Bordeaux.

Since then, my father and I have routinely met the second Sunday of every other month. Normally, we reunite at one of my favorite cafés. Reconnecting over tea and pastries, we catch up with each other and discuss the latest happenings and developments in our lives. He shares his distant travels and odd findings with me and I fill him in on the generally inconsequential details of my life. Though the occasional innocuous argument, our rapport has been generally complacent and altogether quite sterile. Nevertheless, there is a noticeable change from our previous relationship. I am of the opinion that the change we feel; that change is the poignant void of our dearly missed and entirely irreplaceable mother and wife. I was never sure if either one of us could ever really recover.

I arrived at the cathedral just shy of six hours from when I first received Phillip's call. Being so sorrowfully fettered with intense lament; the lengthy commute flew by in a fleeting flash. It seems my heavy heart had influenced a heavy foot as well. As my car came to a rest directly adjacent to my father's, I slowly exit the car. Forlornly looking down at my father's auto, I stood subdued in mournful malaise.

Similarly distraught, Phillip considerately came out to receive me just outside of my parked car. Without hesitation, he extends his arms; fully embracing me with the benevolence of someone all too familiar with consoling the grieving. With soft but firm snugness, he comforts me. Still quite baffled and seeping tears, I clinch him tighter in his enveloping squeeze. Drawing closer, with another sturdy squeeze, we separate from our lock. He escorts me toward the cathedral.

As we walk through the imposingly monumental main entrance, Abbe Phillip reiterates his commiseration; "I am deeply sorry Ela, how are you holding up, my dear?"

"I can only say that I am incredibly devastated. This is so... unexpected. I'm stunned... I just cannot believe..."

Being one of my father's most favored destinations, I had toured the cathedral on many occasions. However, it was now bluntly apparent to me, that this was my first visit to the building without my father. Though I frequented this cathedral countless times as a child, I still marveled at its elaborately ornamental entrance. Slowly treading through the intricate entryway, Phillip leads me toward the core of the massive chancel. With his arm gently draped around my shoulders, he supports my wobbly fragile posture. Through spacious artfully adorned passages we arrive at his residence. A somber crowd has congregated outside of the doorway to Abbe Phillips quarters. Despite the assembly of twenty or so melancholy groups, the hallway stands exceptionally reticent.

"These are some of our employees and a few parishioners were here this morning. Besides the police, I have tried to contain the news, until after you arrived. Please, come this way."

Crossing through the crowd, we entered into Phillips lodging and gradually saunter to the center of his room. Almost directly in the middle of the room rests the back of a single chair. This is where my father passed. With every strenuous step closer to the back side of the leather armchair, my heart slows its beating and my throat goes uncomfortably dry. The morbid scene saturates my soul in difficult lament. Reticently advancing toward the looming sight of my father's abrupt demise, my heart is once again ambushed with gushes of abundant sorrow.

Continuing further into the room, with a deep breath, I attempt to prime myself as we approach the troubling site of my father's death. Progressively, I am introduced to the awful scene. In front of me sits the empty chair where my father silently left this world forever. Irrepressibly shutting my eyes, I am instantly confronted with the vivid imagery of his lifeless body settled inside of this seat. My heart momentarily stops as a shiver swells throughout my body. My swollen eyes immediately send tears streaming down my cheeks and with this distraught temperament; I turn to Phillip for support. Treading to my side, the doleful friend of my father reaches out and kindly consoles me with a tender wrap of his arms.

Finding momentary relief within Phillip's embrace, once

again I let loose a steady tide of tears. Overwhelmed by my flowing grief, my posture becomes slightly feeble. I can feel the weight of my body dependently held up by my devoted sympathizer. Generously patient and compassionate, Abbe Phillip tends to my frail demeanor. I find myself unable to concentrate with my wet gasps of sobbing short breaths. Unmoved in superlative empathy, I stand nuzzled gently into his warm seizing arms, unburdening my doleful emotions.

This liberating release of my despondency calms my restless mind; slowly I begin to process the reality of the situation. Thankfully, Phillip's warmth has somewhat acclimated me to the bitter acceptance of my father's mortality.

"Merci pour tout, Phillip. Mon père vous remercie de votre gentillesse." I graciously thank Abbe Phillip for both his console and his very vital soothing presence.

He solemnly responds; *"C'est moi qui est reconnaisSanté de vous voir. Cependant, je suis désolé c'est à cause de cela."*

Gradually loosening our grasp on each other, we slowly withdraw from one another. As we let loose of our compassionate lock, we are approached by a man wearing both a grey suit and a rather serious expression. Additionally donning a stiff-lipped expression underneath a faint mustache of stubble, the average sized man draws nearer to us, the bereaved. As he closes in, he raises his right hand up; offering an invitation to a shake his end. Accepting his customary gesture, I naturally take grip of his rugged hand.

"Bonjour Mademoiselle, mon nom est l'agent de Sandro Moretti avec ICPO. Je suis très désolé pour votre perte."

I nod and airily respond, *"Merci. Je suis Ela, sa fille."*

"Yes, I know, Abbe Phillip speaks very highly of you."

"Interpol?" I asked, thrown off by the unexpected involvement by an international policeman.

"Yes. Please, forgive me; I happen to have an unusual connection with the unfortunate circumstances. My sincerest condolences Mademoiselle; I do not mean to intrude. However, once you have settled in, I must ask you a few routine questions."

"The long drive, though tranquil, was fairly exhausting. Though I could desperately use a glass of water and the use a washroom, I would be satisfied to just get them over with. The meditative stretch and my time with Abbe Phillip, I have been able largely progress past the initial shock of this all."

Phillip gestures to the washroom and politely insists to get the water while I freshen up as the edges of the agents lip curls up into a slight grin of agreement. Abbe Phillip attentively ambles into his kitchen for water and the considerate agent patiently waits in the middle of the room. With water in hand, Abbe Phillip rejoins Agent Moretti; the two quietly make conversation.

Upon my return, both men mindfully turn toward me, immediately discontinuing their exchange. Gathered around the dining room table, I am welcomed back with their considerate but visibly forced half-smiles. Before taking his own seat, Agent Moretti politely waits for me to be seated. Taking a place next to Abbe Phillip at the table, I rest my elbows atop the surface. In preparation of the forthcoming line of questioning from the mysterious agent, I tightly clench my hands together.

Abbe Phillip presents me with my glass of water; I take hold of the refreshment with both hands and take a modest gulp. Peering up, I watch as both men stare back at me. It seems that all three of us are hesitant to begin the awkward Q&A about to take place. A rough and worn man in his mid to late forties, Agent Moretti has an amicable ruggedness about him. His pleasantly unpretentious character looks somewhat out of place tucked inside of the marginally wrinkled and mildly out of date suit. With his stubble-coated chin, canyons of wrinkles around his eyes and his loose, shoddily knotted tie, he looks more like an overdressed utilities worker than the stylish Interpol agents of cinema. Though demonstrably surly, there is a sense of soft sincerity that accompanies his coarse exterior. Directly peaking into my weary eyes, Agent Moretti pointedly breaks the quiet pause:

"Again, I am sorry... I am sorry you should be here. Your father was..."

Foregoing the obligatory formalities, I promptly cut him off, "*Merci*, Agent Moretti, please just tell me why an agent from Interpol is here?"

Pursing his lips together Agent Moretti sternly nods his head, conveying his understanding that I wish to simply skip the customary pleasantries.

"There are no signs of a struggle or any indications of foul play; however, I have reason to believe your father's death may have not been one of natural causes" he says.

Allowing me to process that difficult information he continues; "I had been previously assigned to discreetly monitor and observe someone in Marseilles. This individual was going to be testifying in an upcoming court case. This case was of an exceptionally high and public profile. Besides following his every movement, I also had to tap his phone in the off chance that he received a threat."

Taking a momentary pause, he clarifies; "Ela, that man was a renowned linguistics expert Abbe Santé Laurent. Not only had your father had just recently contacted his former colleague, but I regret to inform you that earlier today, Abbe Laurent was found dead."

"My God!" I sighed, bewildered by the disconcerting information being laid out before me.

"When they discovered Abbe Laurent's body, I was automatically suspicious. Upon our initial inspection, his death surprisingly seemed entirely natural and he passed peacefully in his sleep. The initial word from the coroner is that there is no sign of any struggle or any evidence that would suggest any criminal activity. All of the evidence suggests that. And without any sign of forced entry it seems to be a relatively straightforward case of crazy coincidence.

However, I can't ignore my instincts and swallow that supposition. I had been monitoring all of his communications and following him for weeks; something just did not sit well with me. While walking the perimeter of the building, I heard a police scanner briefly mention your father's passing here in Autun. It is by pure chance, we were listening in on Abbe Laurent; therefore making the unlikely connection between him and your father. Once I referenced the two events I realized the estimated times of death for both men were remarkably similar: almost simultaneous. Both men were intended to have presumably died innocuously in their sleep. I promptly ordered the thorough autopsy of Abbe Laurent and came here. I can only imagine how this all must sound to you, but I must find out if there is any legitimacy to my clumsy hunch."

Smothered by waves of lament that violently crashed into gusts of deep puzzlement, I sat dumbfounded by his surreal theory. "You think they are related; that my father's death was somehow connected with Santé's involvement in that court case?"

"Given the bizarre timing of the conjoint occurrences, I simply wish to be thorough. I don't mean to alarm you Mademoiselle."

He proceeds with a tactfully sarcastic tone. "All that I have to go on are the mysteriously simultaneous passing of two acquaintances, just hours after they had contact with each other. A peculiar set of corresponding incidents, possibly nothing more than plain coincidence."

Humbly confident he has incited enough of my suspicion me to at least partially believe his intuitive theory, he ostensibly continues; "The records show that you were in contact with your father at the same time he had a conversation with Laurent. What did you talking about? Did he mention anything peculiar?"

Continually looking me directly in the eyes, his words, though unsettling, carry a tone of genuine concern and immediacy.

"And what is it that you believe this further inquest of my

father could reveal exactly?" Rashly replying with a somewhat irritated temperament, I felt compelled to hurry his line of questioning along.

"My father had simply contacted Abbe Laurent to review some of his current research. Frequently my father reached out to his old friend in the hopes he could offer an additional outlook on his analysis."

"We do have the transcripts from those communications; I was hoping you could offer additional details or any other information pertaining to their previous correspondences?" Agent Moretti replies while tilting his head slightly upward and fervidly maintaining his steady stare into my eyes. His hearty look of concern along with the immediacy behind his gruff voice was profoundly intense. Though lacking the tact that a soft and subtle tone suggests, his frank, awkward honesty were strangely comforting.

Retracting my previous accent of aggravation, I collectedly replied, "I was on hold with my father during that conversation. The only particulars my father told me of that short conversation were exactly as I stated before. I imagine that it provided the same information afforded by the conversation that you were auspiciously listening in on."

"Fair enough," he said. "Forgive my brashness, but there is no easy way to ask this; do not worry about answering right away, but I will need your permission to run a more extensive autopsy on your father's body?"

Clearly consumed by growing disquiet, I supportively state; "If there really is some violent treachery surrounding these circumstances, I am grateful not only for your involvement but also for your persistence."

Briefly taking a pause and gazing down to the table, Agent Moretti flashes the tinniest expression of an understandingly gracious grin.

"*Encore une fois, je suis tellement désolé pour votre perte.*

Please *Mademoiselle*, call me if you need anything or if you have any questions. If you can think of anything that might be useful, please do not hesitate." With that he nimbly rises up from the table and firmly hands me his business card.

Glancing over his information, I notice he had personally penned onto his card, the number to his personal mobile. Stumblingly, he raises his hands upward to shake mine. This candid attempt at a personal and sympathetic gesture, as uncoordinated as it may be, was truly authentic.

He assures me, "Please Ela, I know this is a difficult time, I only want to find the truth." Letting go of my hand, he takes a step back and lowers his head like a subtle bow-like motion.

"*Oui*, Agent Moretti." I said as he began to walk away. "You have my permission to do the examination."

"*Mademoiselle*" He appreciatively responds and advances out of the room.

As Moretti exits the scene, a somber Abbe Phillip stands staunchly by my side. Tucked within his two clenched hands, are a couple of mysterious objects. Unfolding his wrinkled fingers and lightly trembling hands, he uncovers two precious trinkets my father always had in his possession, and benevolently presents me with them.. His thoughtful gift is coupled with the kindhearted words; "I believe these should now be in your care, Angel."

The first object was his old black and silver beaded rosary from his time at the monastery. The other precious item was a locket that had belonged to my mother. He had dotingly given her the exquisite antique silver locket for their tenth wedding anniversary. Inside of it was my father's favorite picture of me as an infant. After my mother had passed, he kept it as a reminder of both his beloved wife and me, his only child. In his chest pocket; snuggly pressed against his heart, he faithfully retained the memento at all times.

Strikingly overwhelmed with warm but torrent emotions,

I accept the sentimental articles. Carefully clutching both of them, I immediately press them vehemently to my despairingly nostalgic chest. At that moment, for the first time, the situation became painfully palpable. Just as I took possession of the pieces; I immediately sensed the soothing spirit of my father folding me in his arms and lovingly squeezing me back. A chill jolted throughout my weary body. I had no family left and these precious ornaments were my emotional inheritance. Housing the tender memories of my father and my mother, I held them tight.

"*Merci*, Phillip." I flimsily say to my father's understanding confidant.

With yet another conscientious lull, Abbe Phillip bestowed upon me yet another one of my father's venerated particulars. Reaching into his pocket, he materialized my father's most recent notebook. It was a well-worn handcrafted leather bound notebook. I recognized the book immediately. It was part of a set he had special ordered from an antique bookseller outside of my home in Bordeaux. Just like the other trinkets, he never traveled anywhere without at least one of the notebooks.

Within these notebooks, he recorded some of his most sensitive observations of rare or inconclusive findings. In order to guarantee their confidentiality, he only wrote down his notes about them in this unofficial journal. This, his most recent, contained a wide variety of scattered statements, cryptic data and a collection rough doodles and detailed sketches. Flipping through the well-saturated pages, I am inundated with numerous fond memories of my father. A brief smile forces its way onto my face as I remember how he would often use the bookstore where he had these made as an excuse to come and visit me. These notebooks were the secretive collections of my father's most exclusive observations. This was my father's legacy. However honorable the possibility of completing some of my father's final inconclusive discoveries could be, it is entirely too exhaustive to even contemplate. The grand effort it would take to even initiate such a task is grueling at best.

The small but clamorous crowd that has been lingering around the room continues in their hushed discretion. Their conversations, though indiscernible, create a continuous hum and stir of activity that circulates just below the solemn tones of our heavy, sensitive dialogue. Delicately closing the notebook, I turn my sidetracked focus back to Abbe Phillip. We still have to make the necessary arrangements for my father's funeral.

Abbe Phillip says; "I have already taken the liberty and have readied the necessary steps to hold an intimate observance later tonight, with your blessing and approval of course. It would be a small affair, just so some of his local acquaintances can pay their respects."

He kindly adds, "I believe he would have liked to have rested here for a moment before reuniting with his long since passed and reverently awaiting family."

"Of course, Abbe." I said with affectionate candor. "He would have appreciated this, his favorite sanctuary, play a role in his final farewell. He had a profound respect for you and this church. My father cared for you very much and truly treasured his time here."

With that being said, I lofted my arms listlessly over Phillips shoulders; hugging him to show my sincerest gratitude. Securely squeezing me back, we draw away from the embrace. Still tightly clutching my father's trinkets in my hands, we both take pause. Face to face, we bask in the mitigating stillness.

As I gently place the three articles into my canvas satchel draped over my shoulder, Abbe Phillip leads me out of his bustling quarters and out into the expansive halls of the cathedral. Passing through the tiny crowd of mourners still tacitly roving the perimeter of Phillip's dwelling, I receive their continued deferential regard. Once past the crowd, he accompanies me to an adjacent chamber. Coming to a halt inside of the diminutive area, he turns directly to me once more and gently grips me by the shoulders. With a robust squeeze he looks me earnestly in the eyes and intently says, "Now Anzela... Angel, you have always been like a daughter to me and your father like a brother. Please, anything you need, trust I am here for you... anytime."

As a single tear trickled out of the corner of my eye, I reply; "*Merci*, Phillip. I just need to unwind a bit. Maybe I will get some fresh air and just stroll about the grounds a while. Perhaps a bit of a stretch might help in clearing my mind."

"Agreed." He pleasingly replies. Following our private moment of tranquility among the surrounding whirl of activity, we leisurely exit the modest side chamber. Stepping back into the narrow but vast hallways of the colossal cathedral, we continue onward.

"He was here to examine the tomb again, correct?"

"*Oui*." Phillip responds with absolute certainty. "I believe he was going to investigate something to do with the sarcophagus. There was something about its markings or inscriptions."

"Would it be too much to ask, Abbe; is it possible to see the tomb now? It could be freeing and fitting to pause and reflect on the subject of my father's life's work."

"It would be my pleasure. Please, this way." With a delicate voice he fluidly guides me down the extensive hallway. Descending down the narrow and unfinished ridged steps we slowly proceed into the cold stale stone structure. This faintly damp and scarcely lit room houses the very tomb of St. Lazarus. Illuminated solely by clusters of decorative votive holders dangling from the ceiling with burning candles inside, the rocky room had a distinct aroma of earthy-ore combined with a tiny bouquet of lavender and other fresh flowers. Now poised immediately in front of the marble crypt, we stand in unnatural silence. Void of any extraneous noise, the ghostly room is substantially spine chilling.

Sentimentally recollecting the many occasions my father had eagerly brought me here; it suddenly strikes me that it has been at least seven years since I was last here. Nostalgic before the Saint's grave, I thoroughly survey the familiar room. Recalling several moments from our countless visits, I came to the ominous conclusion that realistically, I might never set foot in this hallowed area ever again. Pleasantly scanning memorable objects and appreciating certain forgotten features of the space, I attempt to mentally capture the scene. Knowing my father, he would have been strangely placated to have spent his last moments here. Likewise, he would be overjoyed that after all of these passing years, I would be paying my respects while surrounded by his revered St. Lazarus.

Gathered together inside of the cold but strangely cozy compartment, Abbe Phillip and I stand reticent, silently reflecting on the influential life of our dear friend and father. Minutes pass as we reminisce in bittersweet contemplation. Suddenly our wordless tribute is interrupted by the rhythmic repetition of Abbe Phillips vibrating mobile. With an expression of embarrassment, he hastily reaches into his pocket and sharply silences the intrusive alarm. Pulling the phone out, he peers down and squints at the screen. As he reads the impending message a look of disappointment washes over his face. He turns to me and apologetically states, "Regretfully, my duties call me to yet another matter. Please excuse me, Anzela. Please make yourself at home and I will reconnect with you in a while."

With a sincere tone I acknowledge my understanding of his attentions; "*Merci*, Abbe, I can let myself out."

With a brief but gracious hug he departs to attend to his ensuing situation. Now alone, I take one more sweeping glimpse of the evocative crypt. The collection of vivid memories still wildly resonated throughout my mind. With a tiny wistful simper creeping to my lips, I whispered, "Pleasant journey father."

Daintily placing my right hand upon the white cloth elegantly draped atop the tomb, I tenderly glide my fingertips across a small section as I unhurriedly began to exit the room. Readily rising back up the stone staircase I begin my casual wandering drift through the historic cathedral.

Traipsing down the expansive corridors, my recollections of my childhood visits become increasingly vivid. The buildings ornate architectural and fancy marble features progressively evoke the memories of the many days we frequented these hallowed halls. I explicitly remember how as a child, I felt the elaborate surroundings seemed entirely infinite. They were so surreal that they absolutely overwhelmed me then, just as they still do now. Walking back to the Abbe's quarters I paused, mid-stride, in one of the many enormous hallways. Looking up to the majestic arched ceiling, I thanked God to have shared so many wonderful occasions with my father in this resplendent house of worship. Just as I terribly miss my dearest mother; I now miss my father too. Overrun with the extensive range of exhausting emotions, I feel the eminent approach of fatigue. This has been an exceptionally long day, to say the least. Growing weaker and wearier by the moment, I quickly continue back to Abbe Phillip's lodging. With my swirling mind struggling to stay afloat and eyes beginning to burn just attempting to stay alert, my body is obviously begging for relief. It is time I tried to get some rest.

Back to the busy room, I walk through the assorted crowd of police and parishioners. Casually retrieving my bag and jacket, I browse the dwelling for Abbe Phillip to inform him of my temporary departure. Thoughtlessly reaching down form my bag, I inadvertently notice a miniscule red fleck clinging to the bottom of my father's notebook. Somehow, my tired mind recalls recently seeing something very similar. Yes, there was a small collection of the same crimson, wax-like shards atop the tomb of Lazarus. Just at the edge of the where the decorative white cloth adorning the sarcophagus ended, there lay distinctly similar shavings. At the time, I merely though they were candle drippings and thought nothing of it. But now, what seemed to be the same substance was oddly compressed against my father's notebook.

Without hesitation I flip through the book, scanning page after page in hopes of any additional clue or clarification. Almost midway through the notebook, I discover an empty page that contains yet another matching miniscule red bit. Puzzled by these presumably connected scraps, my mind is a tumultuous cyclone of probable explanations and ridiculous interpretations. Where did the red clumps come from? What are they, exactly? And most importantly, why are these scrapings found both on Lazarus's tomb and my father's journal?

Apparently my father's abstract reasoning and sporadic paranoia was undeniably passed along to me. I took a deep breath and realized I was entirely too neurotic. Not only is there an abundance of red candles about the cathedral, but also my father had sometimes used crayons for certain sketches in his journal.

Clearing my ridiculous queries I once more set my sights on finding Abbe Phillip in order to say goodbye. At that moment he returned to his dwelling. Collecting both my jacket and my shoulder bag, I started toward him. Just inside of the entryway to his residence, we once again stood face to face in a brief moment of sedate silence.

"I am exhausted, Abbe. Once I check into my hotel, I am going to try and get some rest. I will see you at the service tonight. *Merci encore pour tout.*"

He pensively gives me his favorable and compassionate nod and courteously accompanies me to my car. The short journey to my auto was serenely placid.

"*Que Dieu bénisse, mon Ange.*" He says as he delicately swings my car door shut. With a heavy disposition and the gentle wave of his hand, I was off to get some much-needed sleep.

Proceeding directly to my temporary lodging, I eagerly reported to the front desk and hurriedly check in. With the swipe of my key, I swing open the door and stare directly at the welcoming bed in front of me. Haphazardly releasing my belongings from my grasp, I watch them collapse to the carpeted floor. Mentally bankrupt and physically overexerted, I toddled to the foot of the bed. Closing my frazzled eyes, I let my wilting body succumb to the fatigue. Crumbling onto the bed, I instantly fell into a deep, peaceful and quintessential sleep.

Wobbly, I wake up from my obligatorily slumber; groggy from the potent combination of both ponderous travel and exasperating emotions. I slowly regain consciousness from the depths of my lethargic state. Still yawning uncontrollably, I firmly press my palms into my face; rubbing my stiff cheeks and adjusting eyes. As my eyes begin to gradually focus I turn to the clock atop the bedside table. The impending ceremony for my father begins in four hours. Prudently arranged by Abbe Phillip, the service was to be a momentary tribute, not only act as a ceremonial last rights but simultaneously as a public acknowledgment of his honorable research on the history of the miracle of Lazarus. As one of the premier sights related to the Lazarus, the cathedral and its parishioners clearly held both the raised Saint and my father in the highest regard. Though physically awake, I remained in a confounding daze.

After a brisk shower, I returned back to the sorrow stocked church. Staggering through a massive sea of mourners solidly stuffed inside the monumental sanctuary, I became smothered by utmost vacantness. I took my place at the front-most pew. There I sat; completely alone and at the end of an otherwise empty row. My mind began to dull its operations and I became sluggishly unaware and effectively disengaged from my surroundings.

Ritually going through the motions, I inexplicably have no recollection of the specifics of the affectionate tribute. Customary chanting along with Abbe Phillip's compassionate accolades and anecdotes of his dear friend, sounded throughout the vast building. My own perpetual retrospection of my loving father is the only memory I have of the solemn service. Concurrently preoccupied and yet barren of any functional attention, my mind can only retain my distant tenuous memories of the past. Though I cannot recall the particulars of the service, I know in my heart that it was a thoughtful tribute that was attended by a courteous collection of residents of Autun.

Immediately following the kind commemoration, Abbe Phillip attentively navigates me through the gathered masses. Past the crowds, we sit in his office and he graciously assists me in arranging the transportation of my father's body to Prague. There, in his family's plot, he will once more be enduringly reunited with my beloved mother. However, this would have to wait until the conclusion of Agent Moretti's forthcoming autopsy.

Agent Moretti had predicted the evaluation would hopefully be concluded by tomorrow afternoon. After reviewing and approving the new and necessary sensitive arrangements, Abbe Phillip familiarly escorts me once more to my car. After another tongue-tied farewell, I leave drive away from the cathedral and joylessly return to my hotel.

As soon as I parked, I mechanically proceeded to back to my room. Passing the hotel's bar, I slow my stride. Taking pause, I fixed my tired gape on a stranger's enticingly generous pour of red wine, but then reluctantly soldier on to my room. Though my exceptionally long day has been emotionally taxing, I needed to get some genuine sleep. The looming early morning will undoubtedly emerge all too soon. With my mind drifting in a turbulent sea of infernal malaise, my surplus of drowsiness directly advances me to my provisional bed. Amid my distracting despair, I lay dormant once again.

In what felt like only a few minutes, the incessant screeching of my mobile abruptly awakened me. Not quite alert yet, I reach out and instinctively answer; "*Bonjour.*"

"*Bonjour manquer. C'est l'agent Moretti.*"

"*Oui.*"

"Sorry about the hour, *Mademoiselle*," Twisting to glance at the tiny clock atop the nightstand; it curtly apprises me of the time. It is just after five o'clock in the morning.

"Abbe Phillip told me to inform you when your father's autops..." Hesitating for a bit, he considerately rephrases his wording. "...when my office has completed its investigation." Considerably dulling his tone he continues; "We have everything we need and I can proceed with his transportation earlier than anticipated."

"*Merci*. I am curious; did your inquiry produce any additional information?"

"There is nothing of concern in the preliminary search. However I am still waiting for some of the other results."

With a notable pause and slight mutter of reluctance he continues; "I can't say conclusively, but so far there is nothing out of the ordinary, but you will be the first person I contact when I receive the official results."

Appreciative of his candor as well as his well-intentioned conduct, I reply; "*Merci*, Agent Moretti. I will be returning to Bordeaux later today. You can reach me on my mobile."

In his scruffy but cordial voice he concludes; "Again, I am sorry for your loss, *Mademoiselle*. Drive safe and I will be in touch."

Ending the conversation, I place my phone back onto the bedside table. Realizing the alarm I had set the night before was going to wake me up within the hour, I decide to get an earlier start to my day. Springing up from the bed, I proceed to the shower. Promptly freshened up, dressed and having repacked my belongings, I after checking out, I quickly return to the all too familiar seat of my car. Placing the key into the ignition, I look at my weary reflection in the rear view mirror. With a turn of the key, I begin my tour back home. Undertaking the six-hour commute to Bordeaux my mind is bubbling over with scattered thoughts of my beloved father. In my recently customary daze, I carry on with my mind set on an autopilot of sorts. Absorbed with unforeseeable grief, my mind wanders and I zone-out.

Meanwhile the operator side of my consciousness routinely forges home. Emotionally depleted and physically drained, confusingly minutes feel like hours and the hours feel like minutes. With all that had happened, during my drive home, I found myself fixated on one thing. I barely remember the drive and disconcertingly, I scarcely remember arriving at my home later that day. I was solely preoccupied with the nagging notion that there was something indescribably unusual about those red shavings.

6

"The meaning of life is that it stops."
-Franz Kafka

ROME, ITALY
PRESENT

Concealed deep beneath the heart of historical Rome, is the undisclosed headquarters of a secret society. This ancient and international order of men is known as The Obedience. Embedded below the picturesque metropolis, The Sanctum acts as the nerve center for this excessively esoteric group. Though religious in nature and arguably operating on behalf of the church, it is declared as purely fictitious; even emphatically denied to exist by The Vatican. Rightfully so, The Obedience is essentially so obscure, that truthfully no one presently inside of the Catholic church actually does know of its existence. The ultra-covert society tracks down and destroys the unthinkable: the immortal beasts and creatures of legends. Hunting down so-called Bleeders and Feeders, these individuals are simultaneously devout men of the cloth as well as lethal world-class soldiers. Obedience members travel the globe, ruthlessly seeking out wretched immortals. Consisting of no more than sixty individuals at one time, these religious soldiers are singularly dedicated to ridding the world of every fallaciously foul monster on the planet.

Originally named the Order of St. Lazarus, The initial group was a virtuous order of religious warriors led by the infamous man

Jesus had raised from the dead. Soon after his return to the land of the living, Lazarus felt overwhelmingly obligated to bring the word of Jesus to other nations. He felt it was his sacred duty and that evangelization was the exclusive reason for his resurrection. In addition to spreading the account of Jesus, his army would also charitably protect the communities that had nobly risked their very lives distributing the gospel. Because of the severely unstable religious climate of the time, many early Christians were persecuted. Brutal and often fatal violence was the all too common reaction to the religious concept of early Christianity. These savage acts compelled Lazarus to coordinate a righteous group of spiritual men who also possessed a militaristic background. It was of great importance to Lazarus that his men maintain the difficult balance of both compassionate restraint and the necessary potent physical force required to protect the persecuted.

Just over thirty men strong, his disciplined force ventured throughout the ancient world. The Order progressed from town to town, honorably guarding, and at times defending the religiously oppressed. Many tyrants fell and some of the tortured and afflicted were rescued. However, not everyone could be recovered. Not everyone could be delivered from evil. An all too lengthy list of who we consider now to be the earliest pioneers of Christianity, they became the first wave of martyrs.

Eventually, the oppressors resorted to even more ruthless tactics. Increasingly aggravated by the Order, the antagonists began to punish the members by capturing their families and friends. A staggering forty-three innocent women and children were senselessly slain as a penalty for the acts of the religious militia. This retaliation led to the fictional disbanding of The Order of St. Lazarus. Pretending to concede and seemingly abandoning their cause, the remaining men dispersed to various surrounding countries. This course of action preserved the lives of the diminutive collection of their remaining families and acquaintances.

Though voluntarily resigned to never return to their loved ones or set foot upon their native soil again, the scattered compatriots vowed to establish a version of The Order wherever they settled. Lazarus himself was detached and isolated to protect those who knew him best. Self-exiled to the outlying expanse around his homeland, Lazarus soon initiated his new rendition of the secret religious army. The Obedience was that result. For years he quietly but effectively spread the Gospel while protecting those who accepted it. Upon Lazarus' death, The Obedience still continued its' crusade. Over the years, generations trained in secret; passing down the tradition to their successors.

At present, the operational center of The Obedience is rooted inside of the spacious catacombs beneath a prominent hotel. This historic building unknowingly acts as The Sanctum's façade. A distinctive combination of classic stone and marble Roman architecture and crisp, clean contemporary renovations, The Sanctum's space consists of offices, meeting rooms and well-stocked armories. Integrated with modern conveniences and advanced technologies, this voluminous operational post is strikingly silent due to its scrupulous soundproof embellishments. Cold stark metal and luminous glass partitions section off the venerable library that stands at the central corridor and focal point of the headquarters.

Encased in a circular structure of thick impervious glass, delicate age-old documents are distinctively displayed as a reminder of the group's essential legacy. Inset into the marble floor at the foot of the expansive book filled foyer is the giant seal of The Obedience. The substantial circular image of a slim snake consuming its own tail that encompasses a symmetrical Maltese cross made up of four arrow shaped pieces that adjoin at their points.

Just off to the left of the esteemed repository resides the main conference room. Roughly twenty members are gathered behind its closed doors. Surrounding a long shiny black conference table, the seated men are attentively being briefed by their leader. Heading the assembly stands the esteemed and intimidating Prior James. At six foot three with an impressively athletic build, The Prior is the current commander of the organization. Prior James has every member's complete attention as he routinely distributes informational updates and delegates their next missions. Dutifully listening to their highly regarded director, the men compliantly concentrate on the directives imparted to them by their pious Prior.

"Two Brothers are already positioned in France. They will provide you with a detailed report on both locations. We are still awaiting further intel regarding the cause of the death of the two parties. No immediate actions will be taken at this time. The Obedience has been charged only with the observation and evaluation of these questionable fatalities. Aggressive tactics have been officially deemed unnecessary. Quietly observe, document and only if absolutely unavoidable, protect the involved. If you encounter any outside interference or hostiles, as always; go with God and stay out of sight." The room is totally silent as the amenable members heed their commander.

"Now we move onto the deteriorating mission outside of Alexandria. Because of the current situation, we must dispatch two more men to Egypt. The escalating unrest in the region, Brother Thomas and Brother Christopher will require additional manpower. Upon arrival, Brother Mark and Brother David you will advance to the 'Z- Quadrant' and rendezvous with them there."

Gradually standing and casually turning his attention toward the door, a young man retreats from the table; passively withdrawing from the ongoing deliberations. Meekly stepping toward the door, he stealthily exits the room. Judiciously closing the door behind him, he directly advances across the wide-open corridor and into the washroom. Though he attempts to still be cautious, his steady steps still echo throughout the soaring arched catacombs; percussively reverberating with every stride. He enters the dimly lit lavatory.

Sturdily standing in front of the sink he slowly twists the knob for cold water. Leisurely rinsing his hands, he glares directly into the eyes of his reflection in the mirror.

The commonly average looking young man with tightly combed chestnut tinted hair intensely scowls back at his own reflection. This clean-shaven man is John, a twenty-seven year old member of The Obedience. Outfitted in the Obedience's customary drab coffee-brown suit, stiff, white point collar shirt and scarlet shaded tie, he turns the water off and unhurriedly shakes his hands dry. Continuing his unbroken peer into the mirror he gazes beyond his reflection into the shadowy indistinct corner of the already scarcely lit room.

"Who authorized it?" An expressively curt and pithy tone crisply utters from inside the murky depths of the shadows.

John upsettingly responds directly into the mirror in a moderate whisper. "Despite what you might think, it wasn't us." "You know as well as I do that we've known for years that he was onto something. But, however close Danylo was, he was close enough for our intervention!" John anxiously awaits a response from the darkened corner. "Simon, I assure you, this was not The Obedience."

"Who was there?" Simon asked.

"How can I convince you, we were not involved?" John recklessly blurts out.

"Truth be told, the brothers are just as surprised and upset as you are." With a distressingly uneasy pause, John divulges; "His daughter Anzela; we think she could be in danger. She is his only surviving relative. *If* in fact, there was an outside aggressor, they would probably want to 'tie up loose ends.' We want answers too. Brother David has been assigned to follow her from a distance and observe her activity."

"Where?"

"She *was* in Autun. We believe she has returned to her home in Bordeaux. Did you find Legion?"

"Simon?"

"Simon?"

Just as quickly as his voice seemed to virtually materialize from out of nowhere, so the dark depths were vacant of sound once again. Routinely Simon had suddenly turned up to collect pertinent information from John. Thereon commonly he would also abruptly vanish. Though a faithful member of The Obedience; John was also simultaneously an invaluable informant for Simon.

With veritable unparalleled skills, Simon, was the ultimate weapon against the undead. However, over the years, The Obedience and their technology were similarly invaluable. Because of his long and turbulent history with The Obedience, Simon was eventually compelled to secretly extract intelligence assets from someone within the organization. The role of spy had been passed down to John from generations before him. The delicate guise of both devoted brother of The Obedience and staunch messenger to Simon was a complicated but necessary role in eradicating immortals.

Once more turning the water on, John bends over the sink; flippantly splashing chilled water against his face. Turns the water off again, he pulls a thin white paper towel from a wall mounted dispenser. Gently messaging his face, he continues to dry off his marginally troubled face. Carelessly tossing the crumbled cloth into the trash, he abandons the washroom and returns back to the informational proceedings.

7

"I saw the woman, drunk with the blood of the saints and with the blood of the martyrs of Jesus. And when I saw her, I marveled with great amazement."
-Revelation 17:6

BORDEAUX, FRANCE
PRESENT

Upon my arrival home I trudge through the door of my apartment, set down my purse and bag and traipse directly to the comforts of my own bed. En route to my bedroom, I collect my father's notebook and a much deserved bottle of Sancerre rouge. Elatedly opening the bottle, I immediately pour myself a liberal sum into my robust glass and turn on the radio. As I slowly sift through the journal, the piercing harmonica and slow blues gallop of Jimmy Reed's "Little Rain" echoes about my room.

I had nothing but time during my returning drive home to think. For six hours, the suspicions of Agent Moretti persistently reverberated inside of my head. I additionally brooded over the red wax adhered to the book. I found myself unable to shake the unusual, increasing sensation inside of my gut that his death was not only untimely but in all probability, also unnatural. Although I am incredibly exhausted, these unfounded but growing suspicions lead me to sort through his to belongings. Immediately, in an attempt to uncover anything out of the ordinary, I scour through some of his most recent notebook. Maybe, just maybe there is some sort of tiny indication to his untimely death. After all, I had not received any further information from Agent Moretti, and if there were in fact villainous activities involved, it would most likely be attributed to my father's research.

Shamefully not allowing the accustomed time to breathe, I impatiently take an excessive swig of wine. As the music slowly dissipates, the radio personality remarks:

"The UN Secretary General just announcing an emergency session on Ebola, before the UN Security Council this Thursday. The President of the United States is headed to Atlanta for a briefing at the center for disease control. Both the US and Great Britain have had unusually massive outbreaks of Ebola and now measles. The release date of the highly anticipated Human Vaccine is expected to be announced in the next couple of weeks, stay tuned for the release of any further details."

After the brief interruption of breaking news, the music carries on with "The Big Change" by Big Mama Thornton.

Before long, I am ¾ of the way through both my father's notebook and my bottle of wine. My afternoon of examining page after page of my father's notes has left me frustrated and even more exhausted than before. In my silly attempt to discover some sort of clue, my eyes have grown surpassingly fatigued. They feel as if they may actually burst out of my sockets. Just on the threshold of giving up, I think I may in fact have stumbled upon something. Though barely visible, I notice a diminutive mark of blue ink on the outer edge of a page. What is rather peculiar is that the surrounding pages contain only black ink. Upon further inspection, my intuition screams that a page or pages must have been removed. Could this be the significant lead my gut was pressing me to find? If there was a missing page, who ripped it out? My father used these notebooks to organize his thoughts. Reviewing *every* entry and *every* scribble was their entire purpose. To the best of my knowledge he would have never removed a page.

The notion suddenly hits me to have someone take a closer look at it. Better yet; why not the actual person who made it? This was originally part of a set he that he had purchased years ago from the bookstore just outside of Bordeaux. My still stunned intellect was now overflowing with spurious suspicion. Snatching the journal along with my jacket; I anxiously spring my car and proceed directly to the bookseller. Through the now pouring rain, I arrive at the store within the hour. Completely brimming with fervent curiosity, my previously drained spirit has received a surprising second wind.

Squeezed between a bustling fragrant bistro and a vacant commercial space, sits the narrow brick storefront of the bookstore. Slipping my father's book underneath my mostly dry jacket, I flee my car and leap toward the storefront. Above the unusually narrow doorway hangs the hand-crated, paint chipped sign "*Le Livre Ouvert*." The boisterous clang of a door chime rings out robustly as I dash out of the rain and through the front door.

Along with the elegant resonance of classical melody flowing from a record player I am met with a powerfully stuffy sensation. The stale, musty smell of old books is simultaneously realized along with the absence of any customers. Furnished with wall-to-wall shelves bursting with books, the congested room is swelling with a vast variety of aged texts. Tucked away in the back corner of the narrow room is a tiny and disorganized counter. The owner of the store, an old and slightly rotund black woman with long grey dense and curly hair appears from out behind the cluttered counter. A warm and courteous woman in her early seventies, she stands up with the assistance of her handcrafted wooden cane. With her welcoming smile she greets me with; "*Accueil*."

"*Merci*" I reply.

Retrieving the book from out of my jacket I ask: "This belonged to my father."

As I present the book to the woman, she kindly takes notice of the delicate way in which I hold my father's book and diplomatically handles it with extreme consideration. While she draws it closer to her pondering face, I say; "I was hoping you could tell me if any of these pages have been tampered with."

Taking a moment, suddenly her expression changes. Readily lifting her head from the book and redirecting her focus on me, a pleasant look of recognition drifts over her face.

"Your father was Danylo, the Lazarus man. Yes, and you, you had bought him the 'Moravus Incunabula, De Civitate Dei' I believe?"

"*Oui, c'est vrai*"

Genuinely surprised by her exceptional memory, I ask; "I would be indebted to you if you could tell me if there is anything out of the ordinary; particularly in this set of pages. I have a lingering suspicion that at the very least; a page has been removed."

Elevating the set of dangling bifocals up to her squinting eyes, she leans even closer to the book.

She recalls "I remember hand crafting this set for him several years ago."

Grabbing a magnifying glass, she draws even closer to the pages and their binding. She grabs a tweezers and extracts a tiny fragment of a page that was left behind. She determines; "My dear, there are in fact a couple of pages missing from this binding. One sheet has been ripped out quite hastily, however there was yet another."

Straining her ripened eyes even more intently, she adds, "That absent folio was altered using remarkable precision. If I had not made these, I wouldn't have even noticed."

My suspicions are indeed authenticated. It seems Agent Moretti and his unsubstantiated gut, may actually have some solid foundation after all.

8

"Where justice is denied,... and where any one class is made to feel that society is an organized conspiracy to oppress, rob and degrade them, neither persons nor property will be safe."
-Frederick Douglas

MARSEILLES, FRANCE
PRESENT

Returning to his original post outside of Abbe Laurent's parish, Agent Moretti continues to actively audit his previous transcripts of Laurent's communications. In his tenacious attempt to uncover any further indications of foul play, he painstakingly revisits his original notes. As well as his own records he likewise thoroughly thumbs through the memos of his colleagues. After reanalyzing his original interviews of Laurent, he makes arrangements to question some of the local persons at the parish for a second time.

While he eagerly awaited the official autopsy results, the coroner had given him an off the record report that they, "had observed nothing indicative of either assault or murder." Regrettably, Moretti doubts the optimism of his associate's premature assumption. Even though he strenuously believes in his own hunch, he does truly hope to exhaustively conclude that the deaths, though ostensibly suspiciously as they may seem, are in fact a case of far-fetched coincidence. He is determined to either unearth a mysterious ruse behind the two deaths or totally confirm that his suspicions are downright unwarranted. Although it would be the first time that his instincts were wrong, he welcomed the opportunity to not be inundated by villainy once more.

Squished behind his makeshift desk positioned inside of the observational van outside the Marseilles Cathedral, Moretti broods over his mound of notes. While he discouragingly mulling through the case's documentation, he cannot help but contemplate the series of actions that placed him inside of the surveillance vehicle in the first place.

Several months earlier, Moretti was informally reprimanded by his director. His duties were restricted due to his chronic unpredictable behavior. A seasoned law enforcement officer, he had previously been warned on multiple occasions regarding his use of questionable tactics. His unadvisable conduct with both presumed perpetrators and established criminals was infamous among his colleagues at Interpol. Regularly cautioned, he was often sternly advised to cease his precarious methods and to proceed with extreme prudence. Unfortunately, this recent suggestive warning was given in concert with his last case that concerned the abuse of a child. This revolting incident involved the appalling sexual assault of a nine-year old girl. Granting Moretti was veritably hardened to the grisliest of crime scenes, he was never able to stomach the spectacle of an abused child.

While in the custody of the police, the lead suspect who distinctly fit the detailed description of multiple witnesses was confoundedly released. To Agent Moretti's absolute disgust, just over 36 hours following his hasty release, police apprehended the rapist at gunpoint.

It started with a highway patrolman on a somewhat routine stop. The officer had pulled over to assist a car flashing its hazard lights. With the car innocently stalled on the side of the road, the officer naively approached the man's car with the intent to see if the motorist required any assistance. As the officer approached the driver's side window, the man took out his knife and concealed it between him and the door. Placing his left hand on the edge of the vehicle's rolled-down window, the officer leaned over and addressed the stranded motorist. Just as the man in uniform was about to speak, the man impulsively jerked out his arm and rashly slashed the unsuspecting patrolman's neck. Tumbling to the ground, the bloody officer managed to bravely draw his firearm and shoot the pedophile in the shoulder before collapsing.

Wounded and desperately frantic he hastily entered the police car and directly fled the gruesome scene. Hopelessly hustling down the highway, he was completely unable to decide his destination. Rapidly losing blood, the depraved man lost consciousness; uncontrollably crashing the car into an embankment on the side of the road. Extensively broadcasting the horrifying news of the terrible incident, the police were able to quickly locate, capture and detain the sick assailant.

Unconscious but relatively stable, the man was once again placed into custody and taken directly to the nearest hospital. While searching through the criminal's vehicle, the crime scene investigators were utterly shocked by their disturbing discovery: the repulsively contorted remains of a young girl had been stashed inside of the assailant's trunk. The mutilated body was that of a ten-year old girl that had gone missing only in the last 24 hours. Later, the autopsy would conclude her time of death to be only several hours after his recent release.

Moretti cursed the broken system. This unhesitant predator was able to rape and kill another innocent young girl simply because of malfunctioning legalities and flawed municipal technicalities. Righteously aggravated, Moretti raised absolute hell with his superiors. Grotesquely infuriated, he stormed into his director's office. Wildly slamming the door behind him, he passionately articulated his unadulterated disdain for the fractured system that governed Interpol and all of its agents. He ferociously ranted on the faults and defects of the Interpol director himself and his coinciding organizations. Additionally he expressed his deep disparagement of the obvious defects affixed to the agencies legal components. He zealously declared his strenuous request for an immediate call to action. Given the recent incidence, Agent Moretti demanded that his director take a stand and immediately insist on an adjustment to their damaged policies. Notably insulted and publicly challenged, the director summarily suspended Moretti. Immediately following his two-week suspension for insubordination, he was assigned the task of monitoring the communications of Abbe Laurent in Marseilles. At his point in his career, observation detail was an unequivocal demotion; a direct punishment for his brash actions and insolent behavior toward his slighted superiors.

Now ridiculed and snubbed by most of his jeering colleagues, the unrefined but unquestionably honorable agent remained dedicated to his compulsory commitment to law enforcement. No matter what the appointment, upholding the law is all that he knew how to do. Right is right and wrong is wrong; these principles had always governed his every action.

Currently charged with the edict to ensure the unfeigned assessment of two analogous deaths, Agent Moretti tirelessly sorts through his gathered evidence. Accustomed to much more sinister scenarios, he is still compelled to apply the same extensive scrutiny to this substantially less dubious case. Amidst a complete lack of supporting evidence, his experience still maintains the lingering impression that the two deaths are connected. Keeping a skeptical watch over the seemingly passive conclusions, he diligently continues his investigation.

Currently reflecting on the unexceptional and innocent

responses from both autopsies, Agent Moretti sits entirely frustrated by the prospect that his inclinations could be so mistaken. The lingering disconnection of forthcoming conclusions and his continual hunch were exhaustingly contradictory.

Tensely uneasy, he cautiously places another concerned call to Ela. As his outgoing call is promptly directed to her voicemail, he leaves an uncharacteristically subtle cautionary communiqué. The Agents uncertainty has made his stomach queasy from the thought of both unfounded paranoia and the misleading sense of security he ultimately could be dispensing to her. However, this was the right thing to do.

"*Bonjour mademoiselle, cela est agent de Sandro Moretti avec ICPO,* my sympathies once again to you and your family. Regarding the suspicion of foul play, our official conclusion is that this was mere coincidence. I am sorry for any additional concern or stress this investigation may have caused, but I assure you it was done only with the best of intentions. Please feel free to call me with any further questions you may have. *Encore une fois mes plus sincères condoléances. Au revoir.*"

Upon ending the call, he is immediately flooded with uneasiness from the potential false security he has just given her. Even with the complete lack of tangible evidence, he genuinely remained convinced there is an underlying treacherous plot behind the insipid events. Confident in his baseless notion of conspiracy, he concedes to give her some closure. Compelled to keep an eye on Ela, even though his formal investigation will soon be officially concluded, his cautious intent will remain fixed on her. It would be a delicate balance, but it is exactly what must be done for the sake of both parties.

9

"Woe to the inhabitants of the earth and of the sea!
For the devil is come down to you, having great wrath,
because he knoweth that he hath but a short time."
-Revelation 12:12

BORDEAUX, FRANCE
PRESENT

Wholly disturbed from the book dealer's affirmation of meticulous meddling, I forgo returning directly to my home. With my mind preoccupied with incongruities, I am inclined to take refuge at a quiet local of contemplation. In an attempt to unclutter my mind, I elect to pay a visit to my nearly daily-frequented café. Walking through the front door; I give an admittedly half-hearted wave to staff before progressing back outside. Promptly proceeding to my customary table, I collapse into the heavy metallic and familiar chair. Taking a much-needed deep breath, I relax into a seat that is elatedly *not* the driver's seat of my car. Etienne, my tall, dark and *married* attendant approaches: "*Bonsoir, Ela. Votre habitude?*"

"*Bonsoir Jean, merci.*"

In my earnest attempt to wind down and settle my mind, I immediately give in to the urge to delve into the notebook once again. Optimistically, I revisit the cryptic contents in the hopes of discovering any additional evidence of tampering. As I flipped through the ink-laden pages, my mobile in my purse begins to vibrate. I ignore the incoming call as Etienne has returned with my customary sparkling water with a single lime slice and most essentially, my sweltering hot cappuccino.

"*Merci.*"

While accepting the demitasse cup with both hands, I have a sudden realization. As Etienne withdraws from the table, I begin to tumultuously turn through the pages; looking for specific content I had docilely skimmed past earlier. If I remember correctly, the pages in question were only a few pages before the tampered section. After quickly locating the cited entries, I thoroughly examine my father's notes. Just as I thought; the multiple translations are all slight variations of the same phrase:

"*Lazarus, the foundry dead and friend of Christ.*"

For some reason, these particular translations impulsively struck a chord of suspicion within my intellect. Briefly pausing for clarity, I take the lime wedge and squeeze its juice into the bubbling water. Taking a cautious sip of my cappuccino, I hope for a revelation. Looking up to the voluminous starry night sky, I closed my eyes and momentarily held my breath. Biting down on the inside of my lower lip, I tightly squeeze the lids of my eyes even closer together. Magically, my ephemeral anticipation of clarity was not in vain.

Within seconds I received a jarring realization. I begin to rapidly whirl through the pages once again. This time, there was a particular sketch I was looking for. Once I located the proper page, I concentrated one specific drawing. My father had scrawled a rudimentary doodle of the Tomb of Lazarus in Autun, specifically the inner sarcophagus. Underneath this image was another illustration of the inscription. This depiction had the word, "*Filiou*" scratched out. "*Filiou*" was friend. Another caption below that contained the word, "pallium." My father had just recently obtained what he believed to be a segment of a pallium that actually belonged to Lazarus.

At that exact moment, I vividly called to mind the engraving atop Lazarus's tomb. Precisely where I had noticed the red wax shavings; this is a depiction of that inscription. Immediately, my intellect is inundated with a furious squall of postulations! Had my father used a red crayon to make a relief of that inscription? Was this the particular subject that had brought him back to Autun? Was his journal meddled with because it contained an imprint of the tomb? Or was this somehow connected to his recent acquisition of the cloth fragment?

Overwhelmed by my escalating paranoia, I decelerate and slowly sip my cappuccino and reflect on the multifaceted suppositions. Dramatically even more baffled than before, I irritably slam the journal shut. Rubbing my brow with my palms, I run my fingers back through my hair. Sitting back I recognize that my attempt to clear my mind has left me only more anxious than before. Leaving the last of my coffee, I drop my payment on the table and wearily begin to drudge home. I cannot prove anything tonight. What I *can* do is get some decent sleep.

Leaving the café, I traipse down the sparsely lit boulevard toward my car. With ponderous thoughts still swirling around in my brain, I trudge down the vacant road. Not far from my car I detect the sound of multiple footsteps. Heeding the puzzling stomps, I turn around. Oddly, no one is there. With a heavy exhale of relief I turn back around. To my alarming astonishment there stand three figures less than a meter directly in front of me. Severely startled, I instantly panic; aggressively advancing even faster toward my car. To my terrifying fright, the unnerving men quicken toward me. One of the men gruffly pins me up against the wall. Intensely petrified and ultimately cornered by the three strangers, I stood there completely scared stiff.

Lit only from behind, the brutish group of men stood entirely enveloped in shadowed obscurity. Chillingly identically outfitted in long black trench coats and concealing fedoras, the looming men drew uncomfortably closer to me. The only other distinguishing detail I could note was the glimmer of a pin fixed to each one of their lapels. Each of the creepy assailants had this distinctive circular badge with a Maltese cross-shaped icon inlay fastened to their overcoats. Stricken with absolute terror and recoiling even more against the cold brick wall, I hysterically cry out for help. Reacting to my shriek, one of the men slams his leather glove covered hand against my jaw; violently clasping my mouth shut. Utterly fearful, my legs instantly gave way as I partially collapse to the ground. Now bent at the waist and awkwardly twisted, I am degraded down to one knee. Looking upward I helplessly watch as one of the men extracts a syringe from the interior of his chest pocket. Mortified beyond words, I simply froze, unprepared for the chilling unknown.

Unexpectedly, another indistinguishable figure abruptly soars over my head. His flowing black jacket streams through the damp night air above me; flying over my petrified position. Plummeting to the ground, landing just behind the others, the hooded stranger descends upon my three assailants. With swiftly intricate movements, that of a delicate, all be it violent dance, he slyly subdues my unfamiliar foreign foes. In a blur of practically imperceptible movements, the man sweeps across all three men; laying waste to them with elegant ease. With the thrashed attackers now writhing on the ground, the hooded man twists around and sternly faces me. Pounding his black boot to the ground, he shatters the one man's exposed hypodermic needle. Suddenly, the shadowy stranger lunges directly toward me.

Firmly planted only centimeters from my cowering self, he sharply fixes his eyes on mine. The stranger, still shrouded in darkness earnestly says; "Follow me."

With an outstretched hand, he gestures for me to come with him. Still paralyzed with fear, I remain totally motionless.

Whipping his head over his shoulder, he reviews the status of the three thwarted combatants. Looking back, he again turns his focus on my stationary stare.

Oddly serene, he adds; "They will not stop."

Ridiculously rattled, I accept his hand and he helps me to my feet. Faithfully, I follow my anonymous defender away from the chaotic scene. Just as he turns around, our escape is obstructed by one of the original three men armed with a gun. My shrouded guardian positions himself firmly by my side; unyielding to the threatening aggressor. Rapidly raising his arm, he aims the pistol at my chest and "BANG!"

Somehow, with impossible speed, my protector shifts in front of me; directly into the bullet's path. At almost point blank range, the stranger took a direct round to the chest! Shocked to the core, I watch in absolute horrific astonishment as the shielding stranger isn't the least bit fazed!

Without hesitation, he quickly reaches out to the shooter and agilely seizes his gun. Dynamically, he hammers the butt of the gun against the culprit's temple. Keeling over headfirst into the ground, the man is rendered motionless.

Terrified, I remain incapacitated by the recent startling events. Spinning around, the hooded hero wraps his arm over me. Wrenching me close, he engulfs me into his jacket; shielding me with his stiff and sturdy lock. Maintaining the locking grip around me, he pilots us to a nearby car. Opening the back driver-side door, he gently guides me inside. However, my weakening faculties recklessly send me sailing headfirst into the backseat; sliding like a rag doll across the brown leather interior. Closing the door shut behind me, he jolts to the front; rapidly taking his position behind the wheel. Turning the ignition, he shoves the car into gear, sharply thrusting us away from the jarring chain of events. Accelerating into the night; we are propelled into the void.

Discerning what I can of the crazy events that have just taken place I sit upright and collect what I can of my jumbled intellect. Throbbing from being tossed about, my head is flooded with a blustery excess of emotions. Speeding down the city streets toward the countryside, I sat in an incessant trance. Streetlights intermittently flash bursts of light as we hurriedly continue down the route of our escape. With his eyes firmly fixed on the road, my arcane deliverer is settled calmly into the silence.

Unable to tolerate the creepy quiet, I finally manage to blurt out; "What the hell is going on?"

"They are part of a secret society; those men who were trying to kill you." He says while glancing at me coolly in the rear view mirror.

"A secret society? Why is a secret society trying to kill me? Why are they trying to kill you?"

The absurd activities had spun me into a disorienting daze when suddenly it occurs to me; "You were shot!"

In a faint and rather nonchalant tone, he replies; "I'm fine."

"That's rather gallant of you, but I saw him shoot you in the chest; you can't just be *fine*."

"I am as right as rain." He casually insists.

He must receive treatment. He says he's fine, but I was right there; even the slightest flesh wound can get dangerously infected or worse, he could be bleeding uncontrollably. Scrambling over the seat, I stubbornly make an attempt to inspect his injury. Pawing at his jacket in an attempt to survey the damage, he sharply captures my hand. Loosening his hold he, deliberately guides my hand away from him.

Increasingly frantic and concerned, I inflexibly insist; "You need to go to a hospital, you need medical attention!"

Remarkably composed he again responds in his bizarrely tranquil tone: "I was shot, yes... but it's complicated." He slowly utters back with a simplistic manner. "I am quite splendid, I assure you."

"Whoever you are, thank you for saving me, but this is insane; what the hell is going on?"

With brief earnestness he relies; "This is just the beginning. They will not stop, but stay with me and you will be safe."

Overcome with dithering disorientation I bewilderingly blurt out: "How could this possibly get any worse?"

Attempting to grasp the outrageousness of the situation I add; "This 'secret society', who are they? Who are *you*?"

Following a momentary lull, he bluntly specifies with genuine authority; "I am obligated to keeping you alive."

His peculiar stoic demeanor was simultaneously unnerving and yet somehow strangely comforting. His soothing collected composure was certainly a calming crutch to lean on; putting me slightly more at ease than expected. Though I found myself extraordinarily frightened like never before; his serenity was indisputably reassuring.

"I really do *not* understand..."

His calm countenance in the rear view window gestures down to my still shaking hands. Securely clasped to my chest with my interlocking and white-knuckled fingers, is my father's notebook. Discerning his obvious sharp glance directly fixed upon the worn document, I impulsively clutched it closer to my enveloping hold. Easing his scrutinizing eye upon my father's journal, he casually turns his concentration back to the ever-darkening stretch of road.

"Simon, my name is Simon."

The adrenaline still wildly coursing through my veins I stumblingly replied; "My name is Anz..."

"I know who you are, Ela." He coolly intrudes before I can even articulate my entire name.

"I knew your father. I'm deeply sorry for your loss. Danylo was a good man. I am uniquely familiar with his particular area of expertise." He warily glances yet again toward the weathered notebook.

Unnerved by the grand spectacle of violence that has just

93

occurred, I acutely react; "*That* is what all of this absurdity is about; my father's research?"

Punctually but guardedly he responds; "Those men and the organization they represent are convinced that your father and his research may eventually expose some exceptionally enigmatic actualities. Their organization is called The Obedience and they have worked diligently over countless centuries to suppress these truths. Your father was in the rare position to potentially expose them."

Increasing his air of solemnity, he continues in serious candor; "Ela, *that* impending possibility of their exposure is why I believe they murdered your father. Unfortunately, that is why they are now after you."

With a crisp tenor, he additionally enquires, "When was the last time you were in contact with Agent Moretti?"

"Just this past hour, he had left me a message." Wait, how does he know about Agent Moretti?

"Did you reply?"

"No, I haven't even listened to it yet."

He petitions; "Listen to it, but do not reply."

Moreover stressing with persuasive paranoia; "By now, The Obedience as well as Interpol will be monitoring your mobile."

"This is lunacy." I strain with a bitter tone of impassioned agitation while promptly begin playing back the cautionary message left by Agent Moretti. Impossibly, I become even more filled with increasing anxiety.

"My father studied miracles performed over two thousand years ago. What could possibly be so sensitive to compel this *Obedience* to take such malicious actions?"

Abruptly taking the phone out from my hand, Simon inadvertently tosses it over his shoulder and out of the car window and subsequently responds; "Your father was a visionary who had an incredibly unorthodox way of examining circumstances. Scientifically thorough yet creatively fantastic, his observations were so original, that they often led to even more imaginative questions. Some of the answers, as whimsical though they may seem, where in actually, legitimate conclusions."

Recognizably taking a transitory pause, Simon's already critical tone gets even more severe.

"His unprecedented perspective of the raising of Lazarus could prove more veracious than even he could believe. His wild interpretation could in fact shake the very foundation of Christianity. Your father was about to uncover one of the largest cover-ups of all time."

"I'm not aware of any controversial or 'earth shattering' theories. In reverence to the church, he had the utmost discretion with anything that was in any way provocative."

"Over the years he had unknowingly collected the pieces of a puzzle that were never supposed to be rejoined. Some methodically buried and some simply lying dormant; these pieces were intentionally disconnected and therefore became conveniently indiscernible. That is until a few years ago, when he randomly 'resurrected' one of these key elements. With a wild but incredibly accurate hunch, he began putting the pieces together of an ageless and volatile mystery. Ela, you are familiar with 'The Order of Saint Lazarus', yes?"

In response to Simon I fervently say; "Yes."

"How much do you know about The Order?" He asks.

"According to legend, they were an elite military order comprised of advocates for Jesus. My father could go on for hours talking about them. Inspired by Lazarus, their sole objective was to protect the early followers of Christ from persecution and death. If I recall, there has never been any substantial evidence to support claims that a militant segment of The Order actually existed. The militant 'Order of Saint Lazarus' is just an idealistic myth."

"That 'myth' just tried to kill you." He mockingly states.

With a mordant look, Simon continues; "Led by Lazarus himself, The Order was not only factual, but it was a revolutionary force that tactilely safeguarded early Christians from dire brutality. Traversing from town to town they challenged the corrupted attackers. These devout men righteously struggled to defend as many early Christians as possible.

However, after years of shielding countless populations of Christ followers; The Order was publicly disbanded. Outwardly dissolved, in actuality the force simply scattered to various locations. Covertly, the obedient members kept their same vocation; saving Christians. This latest group of soldiers renamed themselves The Obedience."

Once again peering humorlessly into the rearview mirror, Simon glares directly into my eyes and continues.

"However, much of the post-resurrected life of Lazarus was of the story was omitted from the gospels. The actual account is uniquely complicated. In order to protect the lives of his men and their families, Lazarus faked his own second death while he still secretly commanded his holy warriors.

The Obedience has quietly endured throughout the ages, defending the faith. Membership into this brotherhood is passed down from generation to generation. Possessors of this birthright are predominantly responsible for the preservation of the Christian faith. They still exist and to this day, they remain as uncompromising as ever. Existing in absolute obscurity, these high protectors of faith were who attacked you tonight. I am sorry to tell you this Ela, those men are members of The Obedience and I believe they are the same men responsible for the death of your father."

Already plagued with an overwhelming rush of emotions from the recent ridiculous goings-on; I am now suddenly struck with this outrageous and awful new insight.

"I still don't understand; why would they kill him? Even if

he *had* successfully connected the ambiguous evidence, he would have had to still publicly form a hypothesis of his revolutionary theory. Besides having some unfinished observations that appear quite innocently in his journals, how could they possibly be threatened by him?"

With a restraint but forewarning tone Simon says; "Sadly, they have silenced men in the past for far less."

Coupled with the slightest touch of remorseful reticence, Simon continues; "Their mission is to effectively erase any and all breaches of their otherwise secure station. Unfortunately in this case, that includes eradicating you as well."

"But that still does not explain why they maintain such excessive sensitivity? Why take such extreme measures to suppress their already vastly unidentified existence?"

Proceeding with a sober temperament, he replies; "That is precisely wherein the true complexity of the situation lies. As an exceptional investigator of fraudulent claims; I know you are inflexibly skeptical, but the truth of the matter is..."

Taking a pause and a breath; Simon genuinely continues; "When Jesus raised Lazarus from the dead, he was reborn as *the* undying witness to the true omnipotence of the son of God. That man Lazarus, the leader of The Order, he never actually died a second death. Lazarus was an immortal."

"That's grossly absurd." I blurt out in tremendous disbelief.

"In light of recent circumstances and your noble heroics and not to mention the fact that I am absolutely terrified, you did have my undivided attention. I was already struggling to swallow the bit about the actuality of The Obedience, but now you have increased the level of irrationality from the highly improbable to the categorically impossible! Thank you for rescuing me, but you can't actually expect me to swallow this ludicrous fairytale of immortality?"

Except for the whooshing of wind against us, the car is

totally silent.

Solemnly grave and with a ponderous pause, Simon lifts up the collar of his jacket. Adamantly peering directly downward, he staunchly fixes his stare upon the recently made bullet hole blown through his lapel.

"That bullet was meant for you Ela." Shifting the coat slightly to the side he adjusts his gaze to yet another hole through the shirt below. With two fingers, he stretches the fabric downward, revealing the all-together baffling site: there is absolutely no sign of any injury... not a scratch! Upon further inspection, it is obvious his entire shoulder and chest are inexplicably unaffected: unbelievably free of any and all trauma.

Slightly squinting his lids, with an eagle-eyed cast he profoundly articulates. "You were right there; you saw him shoot me, Ela."

Steadily tilting his head forward, he once again turns his sedate watch to the rear view mirror. Directing his intense leer straight back to me, I see an even more explicit and severe sincerity behind his weighty observance. He was telling the truth.

As if it wasn't bizarre enough, nothing could have prepared me for what came next. With unsmiling eeriness he delivers another unimaginable bombshell:

"My real name is not Simon. The name I was given at birth was Lazarus. *I* am Lazarus of Bethany, Ela. Many centuries ago, my friend Jesus raised me from the dead and now I cannot die."

There I sat, stupefied in sheer silence; muzzled by his oddly outrageously claim.

"I understand this is difficult, but you must try to relax. I will tell you more, but first it is imperative we get to a secure location. Give your mind and body the time to regroup. You are safe now and I assure you, everything will be explained."

Bombarded with mind-boggling claims of immortality from

a complete stranger, who just moments ago took a bullet meant for me, I struggle with the tenuous mélange of upsetting circumstances swirling recklessly inside of my head. The abundant boosts of adrenaline are now showing clear signs of wearing off; my body quickly begins to crash. The transient streetlights and the occasional headlight illuminate the glowing droplets of rain on the window of the vehicle. These sporadic waves of light slowly put me into a glittery trance. In a moment I swiftly transition from entirely alert and exceedingly roused, to being exceptionally exhausted. Suddenly stricken with commanding fatigue, my heavy eyes are bulldozed shut and my shifting thoughts dissolve into an unconscious void.

Involuntarily weakened; everything goes dark.

10

"I am in so far in blood that sin will pluck sin."
-William Shakespeare, *Richard III*

BASEL, SWITZERLAND
PRESENT

Slowly bringing my blurry eyes into focus, I am woken up from my temporary crossing into acute unconsciousness by the voice of a familiar stranger. Gradually recollecting the outrageous chain of events that led to my black out some hours ago, I am instantly struck with a mighty rush of anxiety. Once again, Simon tries waking me up while informing me that we have reached our destination. Parked outside of what looks to be an abandoned electrical station, Simon apprises me that we are somewhere in the Swiss countryside and that this building, partially consumed by the surrounding foliage, is our new lodging. Apparently this is only one of many safe houses he has around the world. After firmly engaging the car's parking brake, Simon exits the car with only a brown paper bag in hand.

With his authentic gaze of attentive consideration, he patiently waits for me to willingly withdraw from the car. Finally regaining the majority of my cognizance, steadily exit the vehicle. I'm not exactly sure what to think of it all, but my concerned apprehensions are currently undermined by my need of his protection. Lit only by the patchy bluish bursts of the moon peering through the dense woods, he strides to the front of the car. His eyes remain fixed upon me as he glides around to my side. Even when I look away, I can still feel his steadfast watch. Characteristically emotionless, he pauses for a moment, as he stands face-to-face with me. Surprisingly breaking his continuous stare he drops his head down. With his descending gaze in sync with his falling head, he utters; "I'm sorry."

Stumbling to reply, I say; "This is..."

He interrupts, "Ela. I am truly sorry. For *all* of this... I am..."

Returning the favor I directly interrupt him; "Thank you. Thank you for rescuing me. Undoubtedly, you saved my life. Though *inconceivable* doesn't even begin to describe everything; thank you."

For a second, there is a fleeting instant of indescribably irregular calm.

"This is all so ridiculous; I am overwhelmed and disoriented to say the least. I don't know what the hell is happening?" I additionally assert.

Our flashing exchange is suddenly halted by a "clang" from far inside the thicket. Startled, the noise quickly reminds me of the rather perilous situation I was in. As I flinched in fear, an unaffected Simon instantly scans our surroundings. Obviously assured the noise was harmless, Simon turns around and treads toward the small, concrete square of a building tucked inside the thick brush.

"Follow me." He says.

Shaking off the startling moment I continue. Like a trusting child faithfully shadowing their parent, I carefully follow in his footsteps. Stepping toward the boxy bunker, I do not know what to expect. Flipping open the small cover that conceals a hidden keypad, he enters in a numeric code. Directly adjacent to the perceived door, a separate camouflaged door rapidly jerks open. He enters into the structure and with a nod, motions me to follow. With anxious uncertainty and a peculiar sense of credible trust, I progress through the entryway.

Surprisingly, the inside of the unkempt shelter is refreshingly charming. The unassumingly quaint space is equipped with minimal but modern conveniences. Guiding us to a modest wooden table and chairs at the opposite corner of the room, Simon evenly suggests; "Please, have a seat."

Still reacting with judiciously timid trust; not to mention my still recovering disposition, I immediately sit down. As I take a seat, Simon opens the paper bag. After digging through the bag, he curiously produces my specific brand of sparkling water along with two limes and a cup. After opening the effervescent bottle, he pours some into the cup and places it down on the table. In a flash, he produces a pocketknife and delicately slices a thin sliver of lime. He pinches the wedge and places it into the water. Softly sliding the container toward me I sit befuddled at the personal details of his offering. I remain frozen; glancing at the glass with obvious skepticism.

In reaction to my hesitant reception, he directly sits down across from me. Drawing closer, he reaches for the drink he had just presented me and summarily pours some of the water into a glass already on the table and takes a hefty sip.

With acrimonious jolt I blurt out; "But aren't you immortal?"

With a sarcastic grin and an air of light hearted humor I continue; "Really?"

"Fair enough." He replies in a lightheartedly bland tone.

With that slight but playful exchange, I accept his offer; taking a tiny taste. With a tentative pause I take a larger gulp of the refreshing drink. After a few more substantial gulps, my weakened body begins to feel partially refreshed. Simon simply looks on in stiff silence. Gradually revitalized, I peer around at the simple but mysterious surroundings. Studying the sparsely furnished room, I take notice of a set of long narrow banners hanging on the wall; particularly because they are the only embellishments on the walls.

"That is Japanese, yes?"

Simon nods.

Maybe trivial small talk could bring some levity to the situation.

"When I was fifteen, I studied abroad in Japan. Embarrassingly enough, I have forgotten most of what I had learned. What do they say?"

Pointing sequentially to each grouping he judiciously responds; "Do not sleep under a roof. Carry no money or food. Go alone to places that are frightening to the common brand of man. Become a criminal on purpose. Be put in jail and extricate yourself by your own wisdom."

"Are they a reminder?" I ask.

Willingly, he responds; "Centuries ago I had a number of skirmishes with Samurai; these encounters never ended without profound effort. Because they served something much greater than the individual; Samurai had unparalleled power. Because of their impressive successes, I turned to their methods for guidance; finding invaluable direction in the virtues of bushido."

With a candid and faintly tender tone of gratitude, he gestures to the symbols on the foremost edge of the room.

"Justice, courage, mercy, politeness, sincerity, honor, loyalty, character and the most important element, self-restraint; these were their fundamental directives. Bushido taught his pupils to behave according to this absolute moral standard."

My face conclusively washed over with solid skepticism, I sit in utter silence; intently waiting in considerable confusion over the irrationality of his proposed past. Acknowledging the rapidly increasing inquisitive expression on my face, with a concentrated breath in, Simon begins to recount the narrative of his alleged immortality.

"I realize how preposterous that sounds; I really should start at the beginning. I really am Lazarus, the man who Jesus brought back from the dead."

BETHANY, ISRAEL
31A.D.

"The man known as Jesus, the Son of God and the Savior of the entire World, I knew as Yeshua, and he was my close and dearest friend. We were like brothers; we ate together and we laughed together. We would also travel together and cast nets together. It was like he was part of my family. He truly was the purest combination of two separate individuals; both divinely complex and subserviently simple. I would have done anything for him and he would have done the same for me. While passing through Bethany, he would frequently stay with my sisters, Mary and Martha and me. Jesus was not only a virtuous man and spiritual teacher, but he was the finest of friends.

In the days leading up to what is now Palm Sunday I quickly became consumed by a mysterious illness. At first, I only developed a persistent cough and experienced a minor loss of appetite due to unimaginable nausea. Bizarrely losing a dangerous amount of even more weight, I became increasingly feeble; forcing me to sleep through most of the day. Swiftly ravaging my body, this strange malady engulfed me with severe discomfort. Absurdly weak, I found myself within close proximity to death. Suffering from extreme pain and overwhelming malnourishment, mortality was staring me in directly in the face.

Faithfully, I cried out to God for mercy, but he did not answer. I had unmistakably felt His presence before, but now...I felt nothing; nothing but perpetual pain. Helplessly watching me wasting away in anguish, in a desperate attempt for a miracle, my friends dispatched word of my condition Jesus. Many of us had seen Him perform miracles; most of which were for complete strangers. They were all certain he would come to the aid of a dying friend. I was particularly confident that he would release me from this awful illness. But just as God gave me no reply, I similarly received a surprising lack of response from Jesus as well.

After two insufferable days of forcing the smallest amount of sustenance into my now shell of a body, I could actually feel my organs slowly failing as I withered away. Overtaken by violent spasms, I endured well over sixty-four hours of the most intensely excruciating pain beyond anything I had ever imagined. After this agonizing eternity of infinite pain, I was finally dispatched from my earthly body. At last I was relieved of this frail flesh prison; I was dead.

At the exact moment of my passing, I experienced what I can only refer to as being absolutely saturated by pure light. Like being gently submerged into comforting warm water, the soothing sensation seeped over my skin. Beyond that particular feeling of perfect calm, I had no other specific sensations to speak of except for the resounding knowledge that I was in God's presence.

What a stark contrast from my dying days of severe suffering. The atrocious pain was gone. Being in that presence and that light... was everything. Suddenly, I was experiencing unqualified peace beyond any words. 'Perfect serenity' and 'exquisitely unscathed'; using these words to describe heaven would be like saying a sunrise is 'neat'.

Unfortunately, my experience was fleeting.

Upon receiving word of my condition, Jesus arrived at my home, only to find He was too late. Martha sorrowfully told Him that I had died and my body had already been placed in a tomb. Jesus wept. Composing himself, he calmly proposed I was merely asleep.

Four days had passed since I had perished. My lifeless, soulless body was prepared and wrapped in linen and shrouds. I was laid to rest in a stone vessel and sealed inside a tomb.

'Lazarus, come forth!' Jesus cried out as he eagerly approached my tomb. By way of the miraculous authority of His powerful command, I was instantaneously extracted from heaven and returned to earth. Just as quickly as I was delivered into the benevolent hands of God, I was likewise abruptly plucked from His presence.

Given that time simply does not exist in that flawless realm, in a flash, my four days in paradise were suddenly terminated. My experience simultaneously felt like a beautiful eternity and a disheartening split second. The warming light of relief became depressingly dark as the distinct feeling of separation scattered throughout my insides. As the light vanished, I began to feel human sensations once again. God was forcing me back into my previously failed faculties; I was being reunited with my frail earthly form.

Overwrought with confusion, my body compulsively began to walk out of the dismal tomb. Impulsively obeying Jesus' directive, I was stunned to suddenly be standing in front of a small crowd stricken with similar uncertainty.

'He was dead!' and 'How can this be?' They horrifically gasped.

Though awkwardly disillusioned to be transported to utter bliss, only to be brought back to earth, I was elated to see my two sisters. I embraced the fact that I had additional time with Martha and Mary. It would have been selfish of me to disobey the will of my God. My jarring journey back into the drab landscape of this world seemed validated by both the joyous reunion with my precious sisters and to be in the service of the Lord

By bringing me back to life, Jesus displayed the actuality of His divine omnipotence. Such a massive showing of what it meant to be true God and true man; I was now the living, breathing proof of Jesus' sovereignty. This was the evidence that He had the ultimate authority; authority over mortality itself.

As I began my new life as the amazing affirmation of Christ's divinity; I was celebrated as a blessed, celebrity of sorts. Crowds frequently gathered outside of our home; simply to get a glimpse of me, the walking miracle. Besides the natural progression of this saintly celebrity disfiguring itself into a kind of freak show; my new position of the ultimate miracle came at a steep price. The multitudes that traveled to behold Jesus' greatest miracle to date first hand logically caught the attention of the religious elders. Unfortunately, I swiftly became the main focus of the Chief Priests and other religious officials of the time.

As a result of my numinous resurrection, multitudes of Jews had chosen to follow Jesus as the one true Messiah. However, because of this widely circulated threat to the very foundation of their beliefs, the Chief Priests quickly consorted to change that. I was not only a threat to their religion, but against their very way of life. They plotted to kill me and this time, my death would be a permanent one. Even though I was somewhat secluded, the mere idea of my existence could not be tolerated. It was decided, that I had to be dealt with; all evidence of the man Jesus raised from the dead, had to be suppressed.

At first I only received a handful of verbal threats and petty, foolish taunting. However, that quickly escalated into a full out assault; not just on me, but of my entire family. But, no matter how hard the Chief Priests tried, they could not dissuade me from my new vocation. At the height of their desperation they put a rather hefty price on my head. Finally feeling the intense effects of their pressure, I began to fear for my sisters' safety. I decided that we should go into hiding. We took refuge at a home in the countryside. Sympathetic neighbors helped establish a perimeter around the village. For months we lived in tense paranoia; constantly looking over our shoulders.

For thirteen months we lived as prisoners in our own home until one day my courageously sister Martha decided that she had had enough. Unable to tolerate the uncertainty of our safety, she devised a plan to allow for both my continuing existence as the premier illustration of Jesus' divinity and also grant their uncompromised security. Her suggestion was that the two of them leave me and proceed to an undisclosed location; a location even undisclosed to me. Only then, could they ever hope to be truly out of harm's way. Selfishly, I did not wish them to leave, but I could not deny the legitimacy of Martha's conclusions. Our current turbulent reality was impossible to disregard. Reluctantly, I agreed to her proposition and began preparations for their departure.

Though I knew it was a necessary measure to ensure their lasting well-being; I lamented the disheartening consequence of my loyalty. Before the sun had set the following day, we had said our final goodbyes. Before carrying on to their new destination, I passionately embraced my treasured Mary and my beloved Martha for one final time. Upon a final kiss, I watched in merciless melancholy as my devoted sisters walked out of my life, forever.

The next day, I began my own relocation. The particulars of my journey were contaminated by the dispiriting sorrow and heartache left by the sad departure of my sisters. To this day, I don't recall most of my passage. In all honesty, the traumatically vivid memory of our separation actually surpassed the pain I experienced while dying. First I was separated from God and now I was separated from my benevolent sisters.

Wasting no time, I stowed away on a boat that delivered me to the Greek island of Cyprus. This seemed to be the safest location to resume my necessary vocation while distancing myself from my original home and even further from my now estranged sisters. Although my displacement was abrupt and quite jolting, within days I happened to encounter a fellow follower of Jesus. Nikolas, an ardently hospitable local man quickly welcomed me into his home just outside of Kition, on the islands southern coast. His entire family received me as one of their own and I effortlessly settled into their home. To my pleasant surprise, their quaint community rapidly became my affable homestead. The sympathetic citizens responded to my disparity with open arms.

A generous patriarch, Nikolas and his wife Amara allowed me to live in their home along with their only child, a son, Petros. Over time, the sting of my sister's departure somewhat lessened in intensity and the town remarkably began to feel like home.

Meanwhile, the Chief Priests however, remained remarkably relentless. Following my disappearance, they immediately dispatched their soldiers, spies and even hired mercenaries to acquire my latest position. They even offered rich rewards for any information leading to my capture. Eventually, one of the villagers gave word of my location to the awaiting Priests. Once they had received the coordinates of my whereabouts, they immediately sent out another group of men to kill me. This time they employed a special unit of skilled soldiers to conclusively exterminate me. Hastily, they invaded my new settlement. However, when they arrived at my new home, they were disappointed to find that I was not there. That morning, Nikolas and I had gone into Kition and regrettably the only ones at the residence were Amara and Petros. In the wake of my absence, they brutally took both of them into their custody. Though contracted by the church, the contemptuous men thought it necessary to claim their own personal trophies before carrying out the obligatory arrangements set forward by their pious authorities. Savagely, they abused her and ruthlessly made her watch as they tormented her son. Through these acts of limitless depravity, the soldiers exposed their true selfish nature. Their animalistic hypocrisy was proudly paraded and on full display.

After tormenting both of them for hours, the callous thugs set Amara free. It seemed the brutes' degeneracy knew no boundaries. In the hopes of luring me out of hiding, the men kept her young son to use as bait. Once freed, they expected Amara to go directly to her husband who in turn would lead them to me. Upon her release, she did manage to find Nikolas and apprise him of the horrific situation. However, Nikolas and I had parted ways in the village; leaving me entirely unaware of the gruesome activities. At the same time that anguished Amara had tracked down Nikolas, I was already headed home.

As I naively approached our homestead, I took notice of a

group of unfamiliar men gathered outside of our home. Cautiously advancing toward the group, upon further examination, I could plainly see by their weapons and attire, that they were soldiers. Behind the soldiers, was the battered body of young Petros. They were clearly using the boy as bait in order to get to me. My insides churned with utter disgust. These soldiers, dispatched by the appallingly corrupt elders, would stop at nothing to capture or kill me.

Sadly, as I surrendered to the strange soldiers, they mercilessly killed Petros anyway.

I was consumed by sheer and uproarious anger. It seemed that their sordid plan did work, but not exactly the way they had anticipated. Their ghastly exhibition of wickedness drove me into an uncompromising rage like never before. Madly infuriated, I accepted their grisly invitation; I slaughtered the bastards where they stood.

After slaying the heartless mercenaries, I surveyed the grounds for any sign of his Nickolas or Amara. Finding no sign of them, I swiftly retreated into the surrounding fields. If his parents were actually still alive; I could never face either of them ever again.

Wandering through the countryside, I agonized over the tragic circumstances. Though I had killed the men who had viciously murdered an innocent child, I felt no satisfaction, only profuse sadness. The unsettling sight of lifeless Petros sent me into a profound and bottomless pit of depression. Riddled with remorse, I was unable to shake the feeling of personal responsibility for the death of my kindhearted caretaker's only child.

Drifting further into the countryside, as night fell I took refuge inside of a nearby cave. There was nothing left for me to feel but unparalleled anger. Once more, I felt slighted by God. First I was forced to abandon my loving sisters and now I had an innocent child's blood on my hands. None of this would have happened without my newfound miserable immortality. Never the less, I maintained the belief that this is all according to God's will. My abiding faith in God and my absolute trust in my friend, Jesus, compelled me to redirect my anger toward the true evil; the loathsome leaders who dispatched those soldiers. The High Priests and other murderous authorities had to be stopped. Taking cover inside the depths of the land, I began to plot my thoroughly intemperate revenge.

Emaciated and perpetually unchanged, my days consisted mostly of continuously recollecting the awful images of Petros' death and contemplating the unknown whereabouts of my beloved sisters. Over and over, those memories repeated in my mind. Deciding on my strategy of vengeance, I initiated my righteous reckoning against the Jewish leaders that were responsible for the death of an innocent child. Petitioning to a modest collective of Christ followers outside of Kition, I secretly instituted my own band of religious warriors. This freshly created group would be a militant order that would strike at the very core of our religious oppressors. Our mission was simple; to aid and protect the early followers of Jesus who were erroneously persecuted. We would come to be known as The Order of St. Lazarus.

I could no longer live with the typical temperance of my previous life. No longer did I have the disposition of an average citizen, I was now an aggressive and emotionless military leader. The Order's goal was to spread the story of Jesus and simultaneously offer protection for the newly converted. However, my own quest was for unadulterated vengeance, and we were good at it.

As time went on and stories of our deeds spread, it was evident that I could be an even more effective leader of the growing Order, as a martyr. So, we faked my death. A ceremony was enacted to mourn the second and conclusive death of Lazarus, 'the miracle man.' An elaborate tomb was constructed in my honor. On this stone was inscribed 'Lazarus, The Foundry Dead and Friend of Christ.' God's walking/talking object lesson was now the martyred and even more powerful everlasting inspiration.

Those first couple of years the numbers new followers

dramatically multiplied and volunteers into The Order rapidly increased. As a nameless leader, year after year, century upon century, my religious soldiers and I marched through hundreds of cities and countless countrysides, devotedly converting and defending new followers of Christ. We were righteously rigid and extremely effective. No matter how many lives I took or how many lives I saved, I still remained tormented by my past. Night after night I was haunted by the vivid recollections of Petros and his horribly graphic murder. But, as time passed and I helplessly watched as my loyal soldiers, loving friends and earnest cohorts grew old, withered and finally surrendered to the inevitable passage of time my memories grew distressingly more lurid by the year. Unaffected by time itself, I discouragingly existed just as I was; perpetually recalling the upsetting details of their violent deaths. That is, until one distinctively dissimilar day, they began to miraculously subside.

One uneventful afternoon, the sister of one of my many soldiers offered me some water. In a time of perpetual bloodshed, her modest gesture of compassion somehow made my previously numb heart feel. A sense of calm and humanity crept back into my soul the moment that I saw her. Her name was Sarah. Besides her undeniable beauty, there was something much more. She was genuinely compassionate and had a tender serenity that I had not felt in ages.

My anaesthetized manner once more began to change. I gave thanks to God for His timely gift of companionship. Kindly befriending me, we rapidly became close friends. Sarah became a long over-due, but most pleasant distraction from my violent existence. Comforted, I felt a tranquil period I hadn't remotely felt since I was in the company of my dear sisters.

But like everything else in my long lamentable life, that feeling would be all too brief and fleeting.

One dark and misty morning, my men and I returned back from a mission. As we approached the outskirts of the town, we noticed the gates had been broken down. We hurriedly proceeded into the town, and found that home after home, from top to bottom, were thoroughly demolished. Only the charred remnants of what used to be our lively village remained. Once more my life was frustratingly reduced to wreckage.

As the men surveyed the severity of the situation, I ran toward Sarah's dwelling. Rapidly approaching the ruins of her home, I thrashed around the ashy rubble to recover any hope of her survival. Increasingly unlikely, I grew progressively agitated and frantically searched for any sign of her. Fury surged through my veins.

Among the overwhelming odor of smoke, lingered the unmistakable putrid stench of death. Ominously, toward the middle of the ravaged room there sat a stone case that rested slightly higher than the surrounding debris. I approached the troubling slab, and daring to peer into it to see its undoubtedly dreadful contents, I opened it. As I lifted the lid of the stone compartment, I recoiled back in complete horror. It was Sarah. Curled up into a twisted and mangled fetal position, the contents of the rock case were the gruesome leathery fragments of her partially burnt corpse.

In an attempt to hide from the intruders, she obviously had concealed herself inside of the compartment. It would seem that the aggressors discovered her and placed heavy stones atop of the lid. She was trapped. When they decimated the town, she was burned alive.

My spirit was instantly incensed beyond words. My insides unstably seethed with bitter animosity.

In retaliation for my loyal service to God and my friend Jesus, another innocent person had been brutally murdered by a group of irrational religious zealots.

My mind was flooded with the horrendous memories of a Petros' grievous death, more than ever before. Rage, anger, indignation, furious and hysteria did not remotely begin to describe the state of dejection that coursed through my boiling veins!

Disgustingly detailed images instantly rifled through my infuriated mind's eye, overwhelming my senses; entirely paralyzing my consciousness. Rapid visions and soul crushing imagery surged, penetrating every cell in my partially withered body. With that rush of uncountable, sickly sadistic memories that purged my intellect, I lost the last, and only, remnants of a human being that I had left. Any and all semblance of humanity was swiftly stripped from my soul. To say I was a broken man would be an unparalleled understatement and entirely inaccurate. I was no longer a man, I *was* hatred.

As my loyal men approached the disturbing scene, they earnestly tried to console me. Two of them attempted to pull me away, but silently simmering in anguish I would not be moved. One of the troops extended his hand to me. At that exact moment, I had had enough of God and His means. My service, my sacrifices and my faith had left me with nothing. I had lost both my patience with Him along with any remaining traces of humanity. Consumed with errant anger, just as his outstretched hand was about to touch my shoulder, without thinking, I violently grabbed the young man's wrist.

Twisting his hand back and disabling him, I spun around and grabbed him by the neck, coldly snapping his spine. As the next man advanced; without hesitation I delivered a kick that brought him directly to his knees. Towering above the defenseless boy, grasping his jaw, I snapped his head completely backward. The other men of The Order looked on in bewildering horror as his lifeless body dropped to the ground.

Rapidly, they surrounded me, their out of control leader. Without a second thought, in an infuriated blur, I viciously dispatched my young pupils.

Beyond my own weighted respiration, I was temporarily frozen. There I stood among the bodies, piles of ash and the blood soaked earth. I vaguely remember trying rather unsuccessfully to control the raging impulses. My barbaric actions might somehow be restrained if only I were able to feel any other emotion but anger. But at that moment, my soul was lost and all that remained inside of me was emptiness. There I stood writhing in pure, venomous rage; I was powerless against it. Manipulated and ultimately dominated by hostile resentment, I was totally transformed. Even though blankness took hold of my expression; violence had fully filled my lungs. Hatred had replaced the beats of my now blackened heart. My God had neglectfully deserted me for the last time.

After brief moments of wrathful hesitation, I took the leather pouch from my belt and I delicately filled it with the gritty ash that used to be Sarah. Cinching it shut, I hung the pouch around my neck where it gently rested outside of my tormented heart.

Fleeing the scene in my insufferable state, I immediately hastened to the sight of my fake burial. Now stained and irrevocably transformed by gross devastation, I longed to destroy the shell of a man I used to be. Already abandoning my existence as Lazarus, it was time to forsake the rest. The nameless man that was a prophetic crusader for God was no longer. I had truly believed that he actually had a plan. I had trusted Him, but I was deceived. Selfishly, God had ripped me from paradise and made me immortal only to be His witness. My faith had cost me everything. My undying devotion and uncompromised loyalty had resulted in unjust penalties that ultimately destroyed everything I had ever loved. I was now at odds with God himself. He had used me. My friend Jesus Himself had manipulated me for His own narcissistic purposes. God wanted me as His ultimate undying prophet, but now He had created a relentless adversary.

He wanted an eternal saintly soldier but now he would have to contend with *my* plan. Sealed with blood just as His sacred sacrament, I would devise my own covenant. My blood oath would pledge my everlasting life to a radically different purpose. Instead of scurrying around doing 'God's bidding,' I would now plow through the ages disrupting His so-called plans. My new eternal life would be one of pure vengeance to the God who betrayed me.

As I stood before my own tomb, staring at the forgery of my mortality, I heard two brethren approach. My two top prodigies had caught wind of my heinous actions. They were there to impede any more murderous outbursts.

Samuel, my current second in command called out; 'Halt, Brother Lazarus!'

My other man pleaded with me; 'Please brother, you are out of control! This is not part of His plan; this is appalling!'

'You know you must be stopped!' Samuel vehemently exclaimed with pious conviction.

At that moment, nine other members of my Order appeared. My faithful brethren had come to put a stop to my deplorable actions, but they were too late. I was too far down my dark path. Their attempts would prove to be dramatically futile. I was a heartless beast.

Calling out, I warned the men; 'This is between your heavenly Father and I. Do you not see? He is using you just as He used me. We are but toys to Him. Leave now and I will spare your meaningless lives.'

'If that is your choice...' Samuel replied, 'Then it is our duty to expedite your meeting with Him. He can judge you!'

Saturated by unbridled hostility, as the men advanced, I distributed death with the ease of breathing. Shamelessly tearing through them like gusting winds tearing through a fragile seaside town, in mere moments, my former brethren were extinguished as effortlessly as blowing out a tiny flame.

After mauling over my former brethren, I went straight to Samuel, who I had purposely left alive, but wounded. Standing above his injured body, I looked down and watched his furious gaze turn to me. When our eyes met, I watched as disappointment, anger and confusion combined into one solitary expression. With this glance, he began to pray; he was praying for my forgiveness and praying for the strength to die with grace.

His undying faith; his devotion to the great Messiah, only infuriated me even further. I dragged him across the chamber by his shoulders and propped him against my fictitious tomb. Hoisting him up over the empty grave I took a strong grip of his neck as I lifted him above my head. I thrust him down onto the stone slab. Pinning him down to the top of my fabricated final resting place, I initiated my plot for revenge.

I was already engaged in a vengeful feud with God, the egocentric deity responsible for this new life; a life perpetually filled with turmoil and agony.

With boisterous torment I bellowed; 'No longer will I surrender to Your will. No longer will I be subject to Your rules. No longer tolerating a position as your lowly servant, I not only renounce You as my heavenly father, but I pledge to forever be Your vicious adversary.'

With those roaring words I took my dagger and heedlessly thrust it into Samuel's chest. My sharp-edged dagger forcibly advanced through his body, digging deep into the tablet below. Dragging his body across the surface, I jaggedly scraped into the stone while shouting; 'I renounce You, o Lord. I reject and abhor You. You are no longer my God and I vow to destroy Your creations and feed on Your children who will forever detest me!'

The word *Friend* upon my counterfeit crypt was not only the ultimate insult but also counterfeit in and of itself. My friend had preyed on my undying devotion. Friend; I was God's new nemesis. Teeming with spite, I wielded the blade I had driven through Samuel's chest and vigorously gashed-out the inscription "Friend of Christ." My forged epitaph was now unnecessarily stained with the blood of yet another one of His faithful disciples. Samuels's death and the deaths of the other men were merely the beginning. I would have my revenge.

While reaching for the pouch around my neck containing the partial collection of Sarah's ashes, I lifted Samuel's expiring head up by his sopping wet hair. I poured a handful of ash over his blood soaked face. As I showered him with the charred remnants of my beloved Sarah, I shrieked 'This was her body, shed for *You*; for *Your* sin.'

With those words, I commenced my unholy communion.

Screeching to the heavens, I heatedly continued; 'This blood institutes my pledge, my new and dark covenant to protest and defy You. Once You had only Your one begotten son, but you have given birth to yet another child. I am your bastard son; spawned from your greedy will and narcissistic intentions."

Hoisting the head in my hands up to my mouth I cried out: 'With this blood, I will live a new life in absolute impudence to Your will. Like Your own holy arch angels, I will attack at night; plaguing Your world with death and devastation.'

I slashed Samuel's throat and drank his gushing blood frenziedly. Thrusting my mouth to the cavernous gash inside of his neck, I tried to take a drink. Gagging and gasping as the substantial mouthful heaved down my throat, I eventually managed to swallow it down.

'The blood of Your creations will be the life source for my life anew as your savage antagonist!'

My life, that God himself irrevocably altered, was now permanently transformed by blood. Immediately, I began to feel the intensification of my abilities and my ravenous appetite for blood was instant... I had become a monster. Certain effectiveness now coursed through my being. With every taste, I felt the distinct acquisition of strange and unique capabilities.

My dark covenant had now left me with an insatiable thirst for blood that incessantly controlled my death-defiant existence. Consumed by spiteful contempt, from that moment on, my path was consummate death. My unfading grudge endured and I delivered on my promise of ceaseless destruction. A prolific killer, I soon realized the ability to impart my immortality unto others. With only a simple drop of my corrupted blood, I could bestow upon them my same abilities.

I am shamefully responsible for the existence of hundreds upon thousands of immortals. I call them Bleeders. I am guilty of reprehensible acts of depravity and centuries of immeasurable murders and worse; I am behind some of the most vile and catastrophic tragedies in all of history."

With a single teardrop trickling from his eye, I saw the candid resentment and intolerable remorse behind his stone-faced appearance. This awkwardly epic confession had left me stunned to the core. Though frightened and insufferably befuddled, inexplicably I still managed to feel safe in his presence.

He decreed; "I detest my past, Ela and I am unequivocally ashamed of my contemptuous deeds. I alone am categorically guilty of some of the world's greatest atrocities and darkest events. I do not bother to ask God for His forgiveness, but only humbly request the opportunity to nullify the evil I have unleashed."

11

"When I say unto the wicked, O wicked man,
thou shalt surely die; if thou dost not speak to warn
the wicked from his way, that wicked man shall die
in his iniquity; but his blood will I require at thine hand."
-Ezekiel 33:9

EAST LONDON, ENGLAND
PRESENT

Amidst the shadowy cover of a starry night, a group of heavily armed men stand outside the perimeter of an old rundown warehouse. The rhythmic resounding hum of a train vibrates in the distance as the camouflaged militia stealthily descends upon the dilapidated structure. On the back of their inconspicuous combat fatigues was boldly stamped in white lettering that read, "SOCA"; Serious Organized Crime Agency is a government outfit of highly trained soldiers. Complete with state of the art night vision goggles and a variety of flashing hand signals, the covert group stands at the ready in intense anticipation; well prepared for a synchronized assault.

Wrapped in the delicate muffled chirp of nearby insects, the men wait in careful silence. With one jerky gesture, the leader of the strike team directs his men into action. Breaking down the door of the main entrance, they methodically infringe upon the warehouse.

Additional men burst through the side windows as the sly invaders close in upon the middle of the vast and indistinct interior. Weapons at the ready; the group becomes increasingly weary of their suspiciously vacant surroundings. Gradually, the men begin to regroup. Coming to a standstill, the alert twelve-man unit stands frozen in uncertainty.

After thoroughly surveying the unexpectedly deserted darkness, the confounded men look toward their team leader with uncertainty. With another cautious scan of the tenebrous space, the leader orders his men to hold tight in their current positions. In a blinding flash of light, the blazing lights from the lofty ceiling illuminate the space, instantly disorienting the strike team. In that fleeting moment, they are sharply surrounded by another group of extensively armed commandos. Outmanned as well as outgunned, the SOCA soldiers stand surprised but steadfast.

Out from the depths of the substantial mass of gunmen, bellowed a commandingly articulate voice of Mr. Shepherd; "Gentlemen; unfortunately for you, this is *not* going to be the venerable drug bust of your careers. This is in fact, an ambush."

Stunned, the SOCA operatives stubbornly stand firm and anxiously listen to their unfamiliar rival with heightened uncertainty. Strolling around the band of bewildered soldiers, Mr. Shepherd confidently pronounces; "I have brought you here for a purpose. You have been deliberately chosen for your team's impressive methods of incursion; save this little blunder. I have a particular mission of great importance and for that; I desire nothing less than the very crème de la crème."

Ambling toward the team's leader, the Mr. Shepherd continues; "Allow me to introduce myself. You may call me Mr. Shepherd. How 'bout I forgo all of these pointless formalities and cut right to the chase. I have recruited you to be my subservient little drudgelings. I am now your master and make no mistake; *You. Are. Mine.*" Now increasingly disconcerted, the faction vulnerably listens as Mr. Shepherd carries on.

"To answer the lingering question regarding both my intentions and my capabilities, I assure you gentlemen, I am the most dedicated, resourceful and potently evil fiend you have ever had the misfortune of being introduced."

Directly behind one of the men, Mr. Shepherd vociferously whispers; "I *am* evil incarnate."

Securely stalwart, but increasingly alarmed, the troops prevail in their awestruck silence.

"In order to avoid the inevitable questioning of my sincerity or the actuality of my consummate grasp over you, I need only tell you this: In the blink of an eye, I can locate your supple girlfriends, your haggard wives and your precious children. However, that information is entirely parochial. The extent of my malicious tenacity is far more profound. I will not only slaughter your family, I will additionally kill that crafty accountant, Ross, who annually prepares you taxes. I will gleefully butcher that little slut Becky Ann you took to your prom."

Slowly extending his arm, Mr. Shepherd presses his stretched out index finger into the forehead of the stunned captive.

"Monkey; let's start with this one." Mr. Shepherd says.

Smashing his pointed digit right between the eyes of the still and stationary soldier, he removes his depressing gesture, and turns his attentive gaze to his subordinate, Monkey.

Promptly tapping information into his compact tablet, Monkey turns the screen toward the man while he giggles uncontrollably to himself. Mr. Shepherd proudly reads aloud; "Lt. James Reginald Turner. Your wife Elizabeth Jane is quite the alluring brunette. Daughters Stella age five and Marissa age three are both delectable blondes and as chaste as heavenly angels. A marmalade colored cat named Lulu."

Momentarily pausing, Mr. Shepherd fractures the slightest grin and snickers to himself while continuing his recital of the man's supposed to be confidential information. With a furrowed and sweaty brow, Lt. Turner is still composed but progressively distressed.

"Oh, I'm just getting started. You have a degenerate Uncle Stewart who is an alcoholic and an excessively matronly Aunt Mildred. Oh, and let us not forget your shamelessly sleazy Aunt Laura, yummy. Cousins Kate, Robert, Cecile and Alyssa Mae along with a neighbor named Sara, who incidentally has a delightful young child, Amanda. Amanda has piano lessons at four o'clock every Monday and Thursday with the ever so crotchety Mrs. Eleanor Perry."

With smug sarcasm, Mr. Shepherd asks the terrified company: "Shall I go on?"

Now comprehensively aghast, the SOCA militia stands disjointedly thunderstruck.

"Now then, what I desire of you is quite simple. I need you to go and fetch something for me."

Systematically frozen in despair, the men maintain their inflexible positions. Each man, still stubbornly persevering with their weapons at the ready, surveys their colleague's discriminating stare. With gazes of unbending allegiance, the troops motion to each other with a distinctly affirmative look in their eyes; they agree to endure.

"Please gentlemen, need I move onto Lt. Grayson and his darling twin daughters and their little bitty piggy tails? You *are* finished."

Unanimously they continue their sustained resistance the inexplicable but undeniably overpowering opponents.

"I do applaud your proud reluctance, but allow me dowse your tiny little heads of any glimmering hope of prevailing."

The SOCA agents continue to reject their deplorable adversary though inwardly heaving with trepidation, the men remain still in their quiet stalemate.

"Well then, I suppose I must dispute your foolish defiance of my arrangement. Do not make the mistake of allowing my flare for the dramatic in any way diminish your acceptance of the magnitude of my abilities. Do not confuse my melodramatics with politeness; this was *not* an offer, gentlemen."

Casually taking a confident step toward the now unnerved group, Mr. Shepherd unhurriedly approaches one of the agents. Deliberately positioning himself intimidatingly in front of the motionless soldier, he stares directly into the man's fretful eyes. Mr. Shepherd was imposing, but even more so was the heavily armed enclave surrounding them. Retrieving the handgun from out of the shoulder holster of his own adjacent henchman, Mr. Shepherd, presses the barrel of the gun harshly into the man's temple. Promptly pulling the trigger, he shoots the agent in the head; explosively blowing a hole through the man's head.

Bearing fierce expressions of pure terror and unsettling astonishment, the stunned soldiers watch in horrific dismay as their fellow agent's head is propelled backwards. His lifeless body rashly collapses to the cold concrete floor.

Swiftly replacing the borrowed weapon of execution, back into the sheath of his subordinate, Mr. Smith glances briefly at his retracting right hand. Taking notice of a small collection of blood that had been splattered from his victim's wound; he gradually brings it up to his lips. Peering at it for a moment he morbidly samples the stain with his tongue; lapping it up in relishing gratification.

"Permit my theatrical tendencies to only further the futile question of your fallacious options."

With a look of defeat, despite their determined protest, the SOCA operatives surrender and relinquish their firearms with disparaged apprehension. Placing their weapons on the ground, the trounced men remain entirely disappointed and stationary. Upon discarding their defeated combatants' ammunitions, Mr. Shepherd's men round up their captives, and direct the commandos out of the warehouse and toward an awaiting fleet of six black utility vehicles.

Ushering the detainees into the burnished Cadillac Escalades. Once situated, both armies deploy and caravan to their mysterious location. The humiliated agents await their unsettlingly new undertaking.

As all of the departing vehicles disappear into the veiling pitch of night, two silhouettes stand motionless outside of the shabby warehouse. Only Monkey and Mr. Shepherd remain among the scrap heaps scattered about the abandoned building. Mr. Shepherd leisurely surveys the surrounding black-blanketed landscape.

In subjugate stillness, Monkey looks to his superior for direction. Disrupting their brief moment of tranquility, Mr. Shepherd confidently growls; "Now that we have obtained our silly little pawns; have them devise a plan of attack of the compound."

Slightly apprehensive Monkey replies, "I still don't understand why we have to babysit these pigs. The men and I, we can handle a simple snatch and grab."

With a leering grin and raspy chuckle, Shepherd replies; "My dear boy: Why waste our precious anonymity when we can simply use and frame our very own parade of pork puppets."

Monkey sniggers as Shepherd continues.

"You will lead both our new swine minions and our beastly brethren in the encroachment of Salazar's acropolis. Once you have explicit possession of the Spear, bring it to me. Once you have withdrawn from the compound, our fresh little minions will be sacrificed to guarantee our ambiguity; concealing our true identities for our appropriate circumvention."

As Monkey smirks with unsympathetic indifference; Mr. Shepherd callously imparts; "Monkey, my will be done."

12

"You know that every traitor belongs to me as
my lawful prey...His blood is my property."
-C.S. Lewis, *The Lion, The Witch and The Wardrobe*

BASEL, SWITZERLAND
PRESENT

Speechless and overwhelmed by the staggering suggestion of
Simon's implausible events, we sat in insecure silence, while I
attempted to process his vivid account.

Breaking the muzzled hush, Simon additionally submits;
"Vampires; the ferocious beasts of legends do, in fact, exist. However,
the truth behind them is not as absurdly charming or romantic as the
novels or movies may portray. Blood sucking immortals are not a fairy
tale; I was the first vampire. Once God's faithful servant, I became
devoured by hate and obsessed with revenge. I am the dishonorable
father to multitudes of these fiendish bastards."

With a densely dumbfounded demeanor, I return with hesitant
but trusting disbelief; "Not only do you want me to accept that you
are *the* Lazarus and an immortal, but your expect me to believe that
you became that way after performing your own unholy version of
communion which resulted in your transformation into a vampire?"

"Forgive my bluntness, but if you were so consumed and driven
by revenge against God, how did you find your way back to morality?

I don't mean to seem so cynical, but given those circumstances, a transformation back to righteousness seems rather improbable." I asked with puzzled tonality.

Broadly taking in a large lungful of air, Simon meekly divulges; "My conversion came toward the beginning of the 16th Century: a rather savage period in history. It is only by the sheer grace of God, that I was once more transformed by dreadfully explicit occurrences. After centuries of unforgivable behavior, my disgraceful course was mercifully altered once more. Unfortunately, it took yet another series of tragic events to alter my heart."

Admittedly, I was awkwardly engrossed; itching to hear the continuation of Simon's grand saga.

"For centuries, I killed for vengeance; concentrating on mostly individuals and small groups. After years of deviant contemplation, I sought to exact my revenge on a much grander scale. In order to dispense more death than I alone could deliver, I would turn droves of God's most fervent followers into bloodthirsty mechanisms like me. Turning his loyal advocates into the loathsome creatures He Himself despises, would hopefully turn Christianity upside down and perfectly inside out. I found the perfect stage for my engineered retaliation.

In the years following Columbus, Spanish explorers feverishly swarmed to the New World. Some voyaged in the name of Spain, but in actuality, a large number only sought out the land's endless riches. This New World seemed like the ideal circumstance to manipulate Christians into viciously killing in the name of God. My search for the ideal candidate led me to Francisco Pizarro. In him I found the consummate weapon in exacting my revenge upon God. I had created a monster and he would prove to be extremely effective

Born in 1478, Pizarro was the bastard son of a professional soldier. Severely neglected and abused as a child, he matured early with an abundance of resentment and hate. I had discovered him at just the ideal time. His less than pleasant upbringing along with being distinctly under educated, gave him the unique qualifications required for me to mold him into my perfectly impressionable vessel. By his later teenage years, he was already a seasoned sailor and I had gradually begun to integrate myself into his life. We were first introduced as colleagues on a ship. I rapidly assumed the role of the masculine but attentive mentor; the father figure he never had. Journeying across endless blue seaways of the world, we explored scores of foreign lands. I fed his impressionable mind with stories of unfathomable wealth, riches and power. In no time at all, I secured his complete trust.

Appealing to his greed, misguided faith and obstinate vanity, I delivered my lofty proposition. Surely we could receive the endorsement and full financial backing of the Spanish government by disguising our quest as a righteous crusade. Assuring him that he was ready to command his own vessel, I persuaded him to assemble his own crew and assertively procure a ship. Our sales pitch was straightforward; in the holy name of God and Spain, we would righteously reclaim the lands of the New World and unconditionally convert the 'heathen savages' to Christianity. Of course we would accomplish all of this while stripping away all of the wealth and power from the pagan natives. With minimal resistance, we swiftly received approval for a small exploratory mission, along with ample provisions and a substantial endowment. If our first journey was a success, we could receive full compensation for a colossal crusade.

To additionally finance our quest and appease our governmental financiers, we partnered with another experienced captain Diego de Almagro and an affluent priest, Hernando de Luque. As the news of our continued support spread, by 1526 we began the intensive preparations for our difficult journey into the uncharted New World.

Our expedition would prove to be even more perilous than any of us had ever anticipated. So overtly difficult that it generated divisions among the discouraged crew. This wedge only pushed Pizarro further into his burgeoning obsession. The worse the conditions were, the more fervently obsessed he became with his entitled wealth and rightful power. One night after one of our men complained about his sore stomach and his lack of sleep, Pizarro grabbed the dissenter by the neck and violently strangled him in front of the other men. Looking into the shocked eyes of the surrounding men, he brashly exclaimed: 'Are we not here to do the Lord's work? This is His will and His land. I will not tolerate irreverence on this ship!' I marveled at the magnitude of his brutishness. My plot had worked better that I had ever anticipated; fiercely bestial, he had become a fully self-perpetuating instrument of evil.

Day by day and driven by fear, the exhausted crew pushed onward. But just before we reached land, the men began to slow their progress. Once more, talk of discontent resonated blatantly. Arriving at land, we began to set up camp. Our first night, while sitting fireside in our beach camp, an agitated Pizarro had had enough. Angered with the incessant complaints and apprehension, Pizarro rashly addressed his uneasy crew. Unsheathing the sword from his side and trembling with wild intensity, he gave the men an ultimatum. Provoked by furious exasperation, he and frantically drew a line in the sand and passionately exclaimed:

'There lies Peru and its riches, and here lies poverty. The other side of this line lays danger, hunger, abandonment and the possibility of death. On the other side lies comfort and safety. If you desire wealth beyond comprehension, cross this line and claim what is rightfully yours. Choose, each of you, what best becomes of a brave Castillian.'

He was flawlessly fulfilling the exact tasks I had primed him for.

With spit spluttering from his mouth, he fumingly hollered; 'Those of you who choose to remain on that side of the line; you are relieved of your duties. Go! Go and live out your poor and dishonorable existences. You can watch our prosperous lives play out from Hell!'

Upon his divisive declaration, I, along with twelve other men crossed the line and stood by his side. We would later be referred to as the 'Glorious Thirteen.' Pressing onward, we endured many more hardships and difficulty traveling into the mysterious Inca territory. However the gamble paid off. Scouting the layout of the land under the guise of 'peace negotiations' we painstakingly collected a variety of native treasures. Triumphant, we returned to Spain with hefty samples of precious gold, elegant silver and prized emeralds. Hailed as brave champions of the Church and Spain, we were welcomed home with open arms.

In the absence of the Emperor, we presented the Queen with our loot. These profitable samples would illustrate the opportunity that truly lies in the New World. Gratefully accepting our generous presentation, the Queen declared our exploratory undertaking a victory. This offering guaranteed the immense support needed for our subsequent incursion and eventual conquest of the New World. Not only did our appreciative Queen approve our request, but increased our appropriations tenfold. In addition she made Pizarro an official Captain General. Furthermore, she assigned him as Governor of the South Panama Lands. The Capitulacion de Toledo officially authorized our voyage; giving us the permission to proceed with the conquest of Peru by any means Pizarro deemed necessary.

In January of 1531, The 'Glorious Thirteen' and Pizarro's brothers, Hernando, Juan and Gonzalo, along with 247 soldiers set sail for Peru. Brimming with confidence, we began the familiar but never the less arduous journey into the uncharted world. However, this time, we were ridiculously better financed and vastly more prepared. Along with over 60 horses, we carried a substantial arsenal containing a variety of swords, spears, crossbows and most imposingly early muskets known as arquebuses. Our latest throng of dedicated soldiers was led by a new and mysterious addition,

Teniente General Sebastian Diaz.

General Diaz, having an enigmatic relationship with the Queen, had specifically requested his assignment into our great conquest. The Queen agreed and affably appointed him as the soldiers' General as a term of our contract. The addition of Diaz into the chain of command would give Pizarro separation from the front lines. In the face of the complexity of our mission, this would afford Pizarro more time and not distract him with every little aspect of our conquest.

General Diaz already had a notorious reputation as a brutal military leader among the men. Besides his set of mysterious credentials, the General was infamously known for never removing his distinctly ornate helmet or his elaborate armor. Only once he had retired into the privacy of his tent would he remove his suit of armor. When asked about this peculiar practice, he routinely responded:

'Victory and greatness undeniably coexisted with each other and are generally earned by means regarded as outlandish or extreme. To be a lucrative leader, one must be unequivocally alert and at the ready for attack at every waking moment. I am my armor and my armor is me.'

By early November, expressly rested and reinforced like never before, we left the comforts of the coast and marched into the Andes; directly into the heart of the vast Inca Empire. Further into the Peruvian wilds, we were surprised to discover the native's complex system of roads. Connecting the entire Inca Empire, these impressive roads extended from what is now Ecuador all the way to Chile. It seemed that the inhabitants of the New World were not the primitive savages we had anticipated? Not only was their countryside filled with thousands of miles of well- crafted roads, but it was also bursting with complex structures like suspension bridges and massive, meticulous stone temples. It seemed our original perception of the native people was quite askew.

Continuing further into the jungle and down the extravagant

road we were amazed to come across a giant set of stone steps. The immense staircase led us higher into and unfamiliar and treacherous mountain range. In a few days we arrived at a lofty peak that overlooked what looked to be an Inca city. Staying out of sight, that night we carefully crept closer to survey the city. The vast native camp was lit by so many campfires; it had the eerie resemblance of a starry sky. Upon our further inspection, this was no town; it was an Inca military camp. It was clear the natives were well aware of our arrival and were making ready for an encounter. Our men were stunned to see the 30,000 men strong army.

To our further surprise, King Atahualpa had already dispatched a messenger to our camp. So, just as we had returned; the emissary gave us word that Atahualpa would grant us safe passage into the village, provided our leader agrees to a meeting. Though slightly uncertain, ever-vigilant Pizarro promptly accepted the invitation. In curious anticipation we guardedly shadowed the King's delegate; timidly continuing down another giant descending stone passageway. Our final destination was a large stone platform surrounded by immense natural steam bathes. As we surveyed the misty and mystical surroundings we were shocked to find our native escort had vanished. The designated arcane meeting place was suspiciously vacant.

Palpably skeptical we cautiously awaited the arrival of our mysterious Inca host.

King Atahualpa had only recently become the sovereign Emperor of the Incas. Just two years before we had arrived, his father, King Huayna Capac, had died. While all of his siblings selfishly squabbled over the throne, Atahualpa brutally murdered most of the other possible heirs. After shrewdly disposing of the feuding family members, he not only declared himself to be the new ruler of the people, but their god as well.

Anxiously waiting in uncertainty, we began to hear a confounding sound; from out of the darkness rang the echoes of an ominous song. The bizarre intonations were the chants of the approaching Inca army. The resounding melody was a ceremonial reception officially announcing the King's arrival. Suddenly emerging out of the thickset curtain of steam, a small group of native men appeared. From behind this first wave of men emanated the heavily guarded Inca King, Atahualpa. Sitting upon an elaborate throne that rested on the shoulders of ten of his men, Atahualpa towered above the lot of us. Appearing from amidst the ensconcing vapor, the elaborately decorated King was strikingly stoic. Wearing a glistening robe made from the skins of hundreds of vampire bats, his stately but savage wardrobe was completed by a distinctive red tassel that dangled from his forehead. He was a naturally handsome and intelligent looking young man. As more and more natives emanated from amidst the sheltering steam, all of us stood fast and gripped our weapons tight. Maintaining utmost stillness, we endured in continued amazement of the fascinating ritualistic spectacle; waiting for the ceremonial entrance to conclude.

Once the chants had dissipated and the ceremonial entrance had finally concluded, Atahualpa looked down at us in stiff, preserved silence. With the expressed intent of interrupting the conspicuous quiet, Pizarro, with the aid of his translator, spoke to the foreign sovereign. Addressing the Inca King, Pizarro proudly spoke:

'Your Majesty, high exalted King of the Inca people, thank you for welcoming us into your beautiful land. Lay the foundation of brotherhood and peace that should exist between us, so that you may receive us under your gracious protection. With respect and deeply admiration, we have traveled from afar to be welcomed into your great land. Providing you generously grant us opportunity, I humbly present my services to aid in the fight against any of your enemies. On behalf of his Majesty and all of Spain, we graciously request safe passage.'

Breaking his indomitable demeanor, Atahualpa merely cracked an arrogant smile. He sanctimoniously smirked as if he did not think much of Pizarro, or any of us, for that matter.

Self-assured and inwardly disinterested with the King's actual response, Pizarro confidently approached Atahualpa. Beset directly next to Pizarro stood our priest, Padre Valverde. Striding towards the throne, Pizarro looked upward and brazenly addressed the King, passionately offering our proposition.

'Great King and newfound friend, on behalf of the Spanish government, it is also my privilege and duty to offer you a most invaluable gift. Our generous offering is the gift of salvation. Hear now, the divine law from us and all your people may learn and receive it, for it will be the greatest honor, advantage and salvation to them all.'

At once, Padre Valverde hoisted up his immense bible above his head, exhibiting the peculiar sacred document to the Inca audience.

'This great book; the Holy Bible, contains the story of the one true God and His Holy Son, Jesus Christ. The country of Spain implores you; abandon your heathen indulgences and embrace the only true religion. I pray your hearts will accept the forgiveness of your sins.'

Looking upward directly into Atahualpa's strong stare, he daringly asserted; 'The choice is yours, but I beseech you King Atahualpa, to take great care in sufficiently pondering your decision.'

After a distressingly cumbersome silence, Atahualpa leisurely stepped down from his lofty platform and assuredly presented himself affront Pizarro. With an emotionless expression, he fearlessly took a brazen stance face to face with Pizarro. There they stood in bizarre silence.

Gripping his worn and weathered bible in his hands and with the meticulously crafted metal cross by his side, Padre Valverde stood fearless in front of our nerve-wracking host. The single mission of the priest was to present the godless heathens with the opportunity to share in the sacred religion of Spain.

Face still fixed in calm collection and stoically stern, Atahualpa dauntlessly responded by thunderously stating; 'My people follow our own religion; the undying sun, the fervid moon and the ancient gods of my ancestors. What is your authority for your 'god'?'

Holding up his bulky bible even higher into the air, Valverde presented it to Atahualpa. Looking down at the strange text, Atahualpa took the massive book into his own hands. Slowly raising the hefty manuscript to the side of his steely mannered face, he firmly but tentatively pressed part of the book against his cheek. After a few moments of silent unnerving stillness, he delicately raised it, lifting it just to the side of his left ear. Tepidly shaking it once more, he then lowered the bible and placed it once again against his ear. Once again after a striking amount of quiet, he haughtily exclaimed:

'Your writings, they speak nothing to me. I hear nothing but silence.'

Grappling the book in one hand, Atahualpa tauntingly tossed the lumbering book carelessly back toward Valverde. Forcefully flung through the air, the abraded book landed at the feet of an increasingly provoked Pizarro. Though outwardly offended, this was exactly the outrageous reaction Francisco not only yearned for but also ultimately required. In reality, our gesture was entirely disingenuous. Our religious offering would merely be the much-needed catalyst to validate our desecration of their land. We had merely proposed this artificial option to bring about the consequential annihilation of the strange inhabitants of the new world. This act of insolence was the pretext for the war we craved. This blasphemy was just the affront required to justify our attack. This singular display of disrespect to Spain, endorsed our crusade against the savage Inca Empire.

Upon Atahualpa's provocative actions, Pizarro immediately signaled to the awaiting General Diaz. Along with his bloodthirsty soldiers, Diaz had covertly surrounded the entire city and was zealously at the ready. Upon the signal, Diaz avidly drove his horses and ground troops into the very heart of the unsuspecting native city. Though brimming with admirable resolve, the ill-equipped natives never stood a chance. Even though we were vastly outnumbered, the Inca army was no match for our advanced weaponry. Our crossbows and arquebuses slashed through their defenses with the ease of a blustering wind through a field of brittle slender reeds. I watched with prideful pleasure as Pizarro, my star pupil and vindictive instrument plowed through the battle, proudly plying his sword, killing every opposing soldier in his path. Exercising my superlative plan, he maneuvered toward the conquered Inca king. After swiftly overpowering the King's private guards, Pizarro himself took Atahualpa as his captive. With his dagger rigidly fixed against the King's throat, he ordered that the King be restrained and confined to a makeshift prison.

Thousands of Inca soldiers died that night. As the rains fell in the murky darkness, the square ran crimson red with sooty blood.

Defeated and demoralized, Atahualpa was held helpless inside of the provisional bastille for nine months. Locked inside of a large, dimly lit stone cell in the center of the square and constrained to a commoners chair, sat the once great Inca King

Desperate to be set free, the defeated dignitary knew his only possibility of survival was to appeal to our discernible greed. Sullenly drenched in insulting disgrace, the caged sovereign unhurriedly raised his dishonored head and requested an audience with Francisco. Atahualpa had devised a proposal for his release that would satisfy both our vanity and our proclivity for excess. With genuine curiosity and earnest suspicion, Pizarro went to hear his offer.

Atahualpa solicitously uttered the scenario of his subsequent release.

'My foreign hosts, if you release me, in addition to your continued free passage through my vast land; I offer to you the riches of my people. I can show you riches, far beyond the reasoning of your strange minds. My subjects will assuredly pay the highest ransom for me, their hallowed ruler.'

Instantly seduced by the captivating pitch, Francisco directly responded to his captive; 'Truly you do not actually believe you are in any position to bargain? Your majesty, please regale me with your approximation of such riches. I, along with my men, have quite an extensive supposition as it pertains to wealth.'

Embarrassingly reduced to a common pawn, Atahualpa judiciously detailed the particulars of his payment.

'For my release, I guarantee that my villagers will provide enough gold to fill the two generous rooms beside me from floor to ceiling. They will also fill another room with silver and a variety of gemstones well beyond the reach of a man's arms.'

Inwardly erupting with insatiable exhilaration, Pizarro calmly accepted his subjugated adversary's proposition.

'My esteemed Inca King, I find myself overwhelmed with mercy. I accept the generous terms of your release. I will dispatch my foremost General to collect the lavish payments from your devoted subjects.'

Immediately upon agreeing to the deal, Pizarro staunchly ordered General Diaz to aggressively accumulate the assets from the natives in the surrounding territories. As Diaz and his soldiers took over portions of the Empire, they plundered and enslaved countless natives during which time Pizarro meticulously strategized the next step of his sinister plot. It was now time to maintain control over the savage population through the use of a puppet king.

Even though the Atahualpa held up his end of the bargain, Pizarro was determined to denigrate King Atahualpa, the alleged divine ruler, but also entirely conquer the savage empire and strip it of all of its wealth. Like a pyramid, the Inca Empire was a simple in its nature with the exalted Emperor at the top. The entire infrastructure flowed directly from Atahualpa. Without their all-important King, the empire would be assuredly crippled. The perfect candidate was

Atahualpa's own half-brother, Manco. Pizarro promised Manco that he would be permitted to be the new King as long as he obeyed his instructions. Intimidated, but seduced by power, Manco reluctantly but anxiously agreed. In order to illustrate his preeminent control over him, Pizarro forced Manco to watch as he relentlessly raped his wife. Entirely void of any conscience and displaying an unlimited lack of morality, Pizarro was a monster. This maniacal lesson was repeatedly enacted to unequivocally dash any and all prospects of hope from Manco's intellect.

From that moment on, everything began to turbulently spiral out of control.

While our armies were tyrannically securing the bounteous riches in exchange for the former King's emancipation, Pizarro impudently put Atahualpa on trial. This overaggressive action completely solidified his decisive capacity for outrageous actions.

This absurd public trial heedlessly concluded with a swift 'guilty' verdict. Our biased jury consisted mainly of Pizarro's obviously predispositioned brothers. In front of the remaining Inca community, Pizarro presented the former magistrate to the crowd. Once their exalted and dignified King, Atahualpa now stood before his people, a trite and vitiated prisoner. Consequently found guilty of crimes against the Crown of Spain, along with adultery, idolatry and insurrection, the verdict carried with it a steep penalty: death.

Directly upon the decree of 'guilty,' Atahualpa was given a choice to be either burned alive or death by garrote; slow strangulation by an iron collar. In order to preserve his body for the afterlife, Atahualpa chose to be strangled. Once the collar was attached and just as it was being slowly tightened, Pizarro impulsively ran up to the King and slit his neck. Proudly carving his throat from ear to ear he nearly severed his head from his fettered and still twitching body. As his blood splattered and the life torpidly departed from his mutilated figure, the crowd watched with frightful astonishment as Atahualpa's corpse carelessly flopped to the ground.

The bloodied carcass came to a stop directly at Pizarro's feet. Substantially consumed with considerable power, Pizarro stood above the motionless body. Reveling in his own rampant narcissistic superiority, he positioned himself over the slain king's maimed corpse. With a smug of expression beaming from his face, he repositioned his blade and dragged it across the remains of the marred body. Wiping the blade clean with the King's own ceremonial chest covering, Pizarro rashly dropped the dagger upon the defiled ruler's lifeless chest. In an explicitly mocking tone he uttered; 'A gift to you...*King*.'

Scowling at the on-looking Incas, Pizarro subsequently stepped away from the bloody scene and departed the square.

At that moment, the natives of the land were utterly paralyzed with frightful awe at Pizarro's brutish actions. Sporadically lit by the clusters of surrounding torches, the gathered crowd of Incas and Spanish alike, stood steadfastly silent. For a sustained period, the atmosphere lingered in hauntingly mute reticence. He had unequivocally broken his word and blatantly swindled the villagers. And so the execution of King Atahualpa set in motion the ruthless conquest of the entirety of the Inca lands."

13

"My revenge has just begun! I spread it over centuries and time is on my side."
-Bram Stoker, *Dracula*

PERU

1532

"Thousands of Incas died in the battle of Cajamarca. Over the subsequent months, hundreds of thousands more die as General Sebastian Diaz proudly continued his collection of the steep ransom for King Atahualpa. As Pizarro and Diaz took over portions of the Inca Empire, they plundered and enslaved countless people. Disregarding the fact that that the person who was to be ransomed was now dead. General Diaz viciously devastated every village he came across; annihilating most of the native inhabitants. Sebastian didn't just consider the Inca people to be savages and heathens; he haughtily declared that they were overall 'sub-human.' The death tolls of General Diaz's campaign surpassed well beyond one million Incas. As Diaz aggressively collected the profuse amounts of gold and other vast riches from the native people, explicit stories spread of his cruel and inhumane conduct. Graphic narratives and theatrical lore of Sebastian's total lack of compassion but additionally his callous lust for grotesque self-indulgence had always followed him and his service. Our conquest was no exception. Diaz and his men mercilessly raided village after village; murdering nearly every native they happened upon. Entire families and bloodlines were outright wiped out. Whether acutely exaggerated or actually authentic, gruesome tales of his sadistic nature proliferated throughout the land; adding to his already notorious infamy.

All of these activities were being performed while hiding behind their fraudulent veil of righteous evangelism. My terrible plan of death and devastation was being effectively recognized, well beyond my initial intent. Tales chronicling Sebastian's malicious indulgence of harsh interrogations and his unusually brutal torture techniques continued to grow. Men, women and children alike were ruthlessly slaughtered. Hundreds of women were heinously raped. General Diaz enthusiastically referred to these degenerative exploits as 'entertainment.'

As word spread of Sebastian's ruthless actions, there were also growing reports of soldiers insolently leaving their posts and violating our, all be it liberal code of conduct, to formally participate in the so-called entertainment. Some of the latest accounts were so disgustingly deplorable that they even upset some of my most seasoned and cold-blooded men at arms. Ever since I renounced God, I had only concentrated my vengeful appetite only on men and women. As wildly depraved and villainous as I was, I still maintained a sympathetic regard for children. Irrefutably, they were entirely innocent; they had always been forbidden. Not to mention that if there was a mass lack of discipline among the men, insubordination would not be tolerated. So, without delay, I heedlessly mounted my horse and set out to evaluate both the authenticity and severity of these accusations.

Crossing the countryside, I recall contemplating my twisted assessment of the convoluted situation. Though my evil and deranged pledge was being brought to fruition even more perfectly than anticipated, I remained resolute to maintain uncompromising order among the already difficult to control mercenaries. Though these soldiers had perfectly executed my vengeful plot thus far, if they had abandoned their posts to participate in Diaz's entertainment, they were now guilty of disobeying the chain of command. Determined to regain the proper order to my camp, I had to confront the General himself. He may have been inexplicably acquainted with the Queen, but this sadistic rogue mercenary was not going to undermine me or any of my directives. This stray General had gone too far, and his actions resulted not only in the increasing unruliness of our men, but the monstrous murder of innocent children.

Arriving at the village currently being occupied by the General and his men, I dismounted my horse, and immediately laid witness to the evidence of the dreadful suppositions. Presumably as a celebration in depravity as well as a sturdy warning to rare surviving natives, I was greeted by a rotting inverted corpse, crudely fastened to a freshly fractured tree stump. That first morbid sight was as pleasant as it would get. Stepping further into the newly decimated town of ash, the indistinguishable rancid stench of death in the air was as perennially thickset as viscidly tainted honey.

Previously a lively Inca community, this den of despair now housed the temporary camp of Diaz along with his noxious band of berserk militants. Everything was now burnt and rested in ruins of dust. The only structures left were the transient domiciles of Diaz and the Spanish soldiers. I prudently proceeded further into their camp. Toward the middle of the devastation, I took notice of a banner fixed to the roof of the tallest structure in the area. The recognizable red and black emblem of a warring dog was the distinctive banner of the General himself. Situated just beyond the tents and wreckage before me now, resided the disobedient excuse behind my rash arrival.

Carefully advancing toward his lodging, I heard the energetic shouts and animated cheers of Spanish soldiers. Creeping closer to the rowdy merriment, I peered out from behind a mass of ashen rubble and bared witness to the ghastly validation of the scandalous hearsay.

Amidst the roaring crowds of onlookers stood two adolescent Inca boys, no older than nine years of age. Both boys were blindfolded and tattooed with bruises. Coated from head to toe with dried blood and mud, the lads had crossbows bound to their hands. Restrained to massive wood "x's" fashioned from the scorched remnants of their village, were three similarly petrified young women; positioned only a few meters in front of the frightened children. The frenzy of Spanish soldiers was forcing the terrified boys to shoot at the human targets in front of them. The terrified women cried out for mercy. One of the battered young ladies had already been wounded by an arrow that now protruded from her leg. Quaking with fear, the young women remained helpless as the army of loathsome spectators hollered relentlessly for their demise. As I cautiously drew closer, I watched as the men exchanged money. The sadistic Spaniards, inundated with perverse bliss were placing bets on which of the defenseless captives the terrified boys would involuntarily strike next. As the boys continued to uncontrollably weep and the young girls forsakenly cried out for relief, the men stiffly forced the lads to fire once again. I watched as the projectiles narrowly missed their intended targets. The soldiers simply laughed heartily and continued to exchange wagers. These unconscionable activities were not amusement; they were shameful acts of debauchery and disobedience. After surveying the crowd of soldiers however, the General was nowhere to be found.

As I searched for signs of General Diaz, I inadvertently locked eyes with one of the defenseless women. Even from my covert position, she seemed to inexplicably be staring directly back at me; glaring unnaturally deep into my eyes. Immediately I was inundated with vivid recollections of the events leading up to Petros' death. Unexpectedly the powerfully surreal memory of his callous torture played out in my head. In a flash, I sharply called to mind the haunting circumstance of Petros' heinous murder.

Instantly, I harkened back to the sick particulars of

that awful day. I remembered gasping in horrific outrage at the nauseating and shocking site young Petros in the hands of those sadistic mercenaries. Gruesomely beaten, he had been appallingly fastened to a crudely fashioned wooden cross as well.

Attempting to stealthily cheat closer for a less obstructed glimpse, I accidentally stepped on a brittle branch. Though only the slightest of sounds, the subtle snap was just enough to give away my position. My bungling mistake gave one of the soldiers an indication of my position. The soldier emphatically exclaimed, 'Lazarus, come forth!'

Unmistakably mocking me, the miscreant used the exact and unforgettable words that Christ himself used to bring me back from the grave. The arrogant soldiers wildly snickered and howled with impudence.

Undeniably exposed, I responded; 'I surrender! Let him go and I guarantee my surrender without incident!'

Staggering out from the covering surroundings, I slowly walked toward the soldiers. 'I beg of you, please free the boy; it is me that you want.'

Pleading with them to let him go, I advanced closer. As I yieldingly held out my arms in peaceful submission, the soldiers wildly screamed with amusement as they suddenly lit the cross. Though I had surrendered, they heartlessly set Petros ablaze. I was too far away to stop them and I watched in horrible disillusion as he was burnt alive. His desperate, ear-piercing screams echoed in my infuriated mind. In a spark filled puff, the blaze of brimming flames engulfed him.

Boiling over with hysterical rage, I staunchly proceeded directly toward the three. In the blink of an eye, I took the first by surprise and tackled him into the fire. Somehow managing to seize his spear, I simultaneously thrust it into the second soldier's leg, disabling him for a few moments. Snagging a partially charred log jostled loose from the flame, I wildly swung it in the direction of the advancing third soldier; bludgeoning his face. With one more swing, I violently twisted his neck backward; instantly killing him. Just as the one soldier began removing the spear from his leg, I picked up a rock and forcibly thrust it deep into his forehead; bringing him to his knees. Teeming with crazed madness; the bloodied rock in hand, I continued repeatedly bashing and mashing his face into a puddled pulpy slop. Smeared tissue and blood radiated in every direction. I was saturated in their blood and with pure aggression.

Now standing in that Inca village, to my great surprise, I suddenly felt more than just pure hate. I shockingly, I felt sorrow once again. Even more emotionally potent, I was overwhelmed with profound remorse. Re-living the intense experience of helplessly watching as Petros was burned alive sharply thrust me into a riotous rage once again. But this rage was coupled once again with an inexplicable urge for morality. Erupting with a vicious vengeance unrivaled throughout the ages, I tore through the camp, slaying every self-indulgent soldier within the shattered remains of the ravaged city. My comparatively immature adversaries were easily bested. Though I played a substantial part in training these illiterate cretins, I sincerely expected more opposition. My collective experience of murderous activities through the centuries proved to be a source of profound regret. It seems my rueful indignation solely wanted categorical retribution.

After defeating the Spanish soldiers, I quickly freed the women and children. While I released them, I implicitly recognized that I was ultimately responsible for this and as grateful as they were, I couldn't bear to look any of them in the eyes. I was ashamed. Once they were considerably free from harm, I directed my newfound indignation toward the yet to be seen, the sinister General Sebastian Diaz.

Wasting no time I, along with my heated acrimony, commenced toward his quarters. Loyally standing at the entrance to his grand tent stood two of his personal guards; sturdy, ugly and notably pungent. On top of their offensively strong body odor, I detect the trailing stench of human rot and decay. With marginally more effort than that of my previous aggressors, I still dispatched them within seconds with the edge of my sword.

Brimming with vigilant hostility, I entered into Diaz's quarters. Dimly lit by glowing embers, the dark room was choked-full with confiscated gold and a variety of appropriated riches. The smell of death was oddly abundant. I thought I had seen mankind at its worst, but I was ill prepared for what was actually contained within these walls. I was now standing directly in front of the General. Momentarily stunned, I took in the inhuman display before me.

With a calm disposition there he stood, partially obscured behind the tattered mess of what used to be a native villager. At his feet, lay disfigured body of a young Inca girl. Doused in blood, her entire body was abnormally adorned with hundreds of tiny little slashes. Her wounds were a bizarre combination of bites and crude markings that curiously resembled ancient glyphs. Both Diaz and his latest victims were arranged in front of a large inverted coarsely constructed wooden cross. Sickly secured to the tasteless symbol hung the solidly bound remains of a recently skinned female. Her upside-down corpse was suspended with rope around her midsection and by nails driven through her hands and feet. Substantial chunks of her once chastened flesh had been gnawed of. It seemed the limits to this man's self-indulgent debaucheries had been greatly underestimated.

Monstrous memories of Petros and Sarah violently reverberated in my head as I beheld another body hideously fastened to another cross and the lacerated figure of yet another innocent child.

Beaming with gory gratification, he looked me square in the eyes as he boorishly took one final chomp from the feeble figure before him. Shamefully, I just stood there; frozen at the unexpectedly confusing rapid sequence of events. To my right, there was a mangled heap of countless other bodies on the floor. Obscured beneath a shaggy fur tarp, this additional jumble of bloodied human remains was piled up nearly to the height of a man. In that brief moment of hesitation, I came to the realization that Diaz had been feeding on her and the other villagers for days. He didn't only drink their blood; he had obviously consumed their flesh. Was this part of some blood-oath similar to that of my own unholy communion?

I suddenly felt my previous apathetic existence mutate into conscientious objection and instantly develop into a profoundly newfound utter distain for depravity. The jarring sight of innocent children along with the potent memories of Petros and Sarah and all of the lives I selfishly destroyed were powerful enough to rescue me from the dark depths of my own self-constructed decadence. Even more compelling than the grief and shame and various other senses that had abandoned me centuries ago, I felt crushing remorse. Once again, I actually had a soul.

Looking past his filthy blood-smeared face, I laid my eyes upon the General for the first time without his helmet. I peered deep into his newly exposed scowl. Beyond the splatter and past the dripping gore, was the inexplicably recognizable profile of an alternate identity. Turning his foul face, Diaz looked me firmly in the eyes and smirked at me yet again. As soon as he flashed me that second gloatingly smug smile, I shuttered with grotesque familiarity. Temporarily unable to fully recognize our incredibly unexpected connection, I knew for certain that he was not just his contemporary persona of General Sebastian Diaz. Not only was he not exclusively the twisted General of the present, but he was also bafflingly an indistinct person from my past.

With blood gushing from his grimacing smile, he spit out the chunk of flesh from his young victim's neck and thunderously grunted; 'Greetings, brother Lazarus.'

With those words, the faintest rattle of gargling blood echoed from his sodden throat. The carved up corpse flopped recklessly

147

to the floor. As the lump of mutilated tissue landed at my feet, my now enigmatic foe unswervingly pounced atop my paused figure. Powerfully tackling me to the dirt floor below; my ripe adversary proved to be the ultimate opponent. As I countered his aggression, he was able to match with skillful and quite concrete physicality. We exchanged a barrage of blows and neither one of us seemed to be effected. Both of us gave and both of us received potent punches and commanding wallops. Tirelessly, we stumbled about, tearing the spacious surroundings apart. The tent lay in ruins as our violent quarrel seemed fundamentally ceaseless. Pound for pound, blow for blow, this merciless, fraudulent and unfeeling villain had to be stopped.

Through our turbulent transactions I scanned the dismantled environment, in the hopes of exploiting any items within my reach. However, his riotous retorts made it considerably more difficult to examine. Fortuitously more mindful of my unstable surroundings than my otherwise synonymous opponent, I took found the advantage I was looking for. A slivered piece of timber now precariously protruded in the favorable position just behind Sebastian.

Taking a considerable beating, I patiently waited for the necessary opening to make my perfect move. As that moment fatefully arrived, I promptly pummeled Sebastian directly into the shard; solidly thrusting him into the sharpened tip of the lengthy wooden pillar. Amazingly this seemed to only temporarily weaken Diaz. Picking up his now impaled body, I hoisted him up above my head. With passionate rage I thrust his body against the ground, driving the pillar down into the earth. The wooden stake stood upright like a sturdy post as his still struggling body slid downward. At that moment, just as his body sank deeper, he lay briefly stationary at the midpoint of the wooden stake. Without warning he reclaimed a short dagger from the varied wreckage below and plunged it deep into my chest.

Now totally subdued by the sizable stake bulging through the center of his writhing figure, he flashed yet another one of his shuddersome smirks. Grabbing the blades handle, I attempted to remove the dagger now protruding from my chest. I watched with uncertainty as his body grew skeptically still as it slowly skidded down the steep-set stake. With a quick jerk, I snapped off the dagger's handle, leaving the majority of the blade inside of me. As my skin instantly healed the provisional trauma, the fragment was thusly sealed inside of my chest.

I was overtaken by both profuse guilt and confusion. If Sebastian was in fact an unholy creation like me, I couldn't be sure of how to actually kill him. In order to guarantee his death was permanent, I resigned to just be thorough. With him rendered incapably captive by the wooden stake, I reached for one of the only torches still remaining in the dismantled quarters. Flame in hand, I twisted back, and threw down the torch to set him ablaze. However, somehow in the brief moment I turned my head, Sebastian had vanished without a trace.

As crimson fluid grimly ran down his smirk, and he garishly called me by my given name, I suddenly realized the inconceivable reality behind his true identity. Albeit distorted, the candid tenor of his utterances now clarified my outrageous supposition of his true identity. The impossible revelation shocked me to my very core.

Surveying the devoured surroundings, I distressingly beheld the ruthless consequences of the violent struggle between me and my cryptic antagonist. Among the ruined heaps, lay the charred remnants of what used to be innocent women and children. Leathery scraps and shredded body parts were strewn all around me. Because of my centuries of selfish godlessness, millions of innocent human beings were now reduced to dregs of smoldering ash.

Previously, I had a complete hatred for God; now, I transferred that hatred to my own self and that beastly sewer of a man. That abomination was still out there and I was the only one capable of stopping him. There was no time to waste; I had to attempt to offset the irreparable damage I had done. He had to be permanently eradicated."

14

"Burning for burning, wound for wound,
stripe for stripe."

-Exodus 21:24

PERU

1541

"With the sickening realization of my sadistic and similarly immortal counterpart, I began to strategize a suitable method of eradicating the man currently known as General Sebastian Diaz. While I plotted the necessary subjugation of my uncanny and kindred rival, the admirably resilient Inca people sought out to reclaim both their dignity and their empire. Beyond the devastation of the local populations by warfare, they suffered considerable losses due to our foreign diseases. The Spanish soldiers also took thousands of women from local natives to use as servants and concubines.

Outraged by his treatment and particularly the violation of his wife, Manco, the 'puppet king,' held a secretive meeting. Inviting the remaining soldiers of his dismantled Inca army, under the cover of night, they gathered in a small temple just outside of the city. Surprisingly undiscovered by the Spanish, the unscathed sun temple now housed an assemblage of the provoked Inca rebels. As the consummately riled brigade gathered, the enraged faux-sovereign Manco stood in front of his incited countrymen. Face to face with his slighted subjects, Manco collected himself as best he could and addressed the unstable crowd.

'I summoned you all here, today because it is all too clear now, the true origins and intentions of these awful foreigners. Clearly, these bearded men are not the worthy messengers of their god that they claim to be, but instead, they seem to be the children of Supay, god of death. They assassinated our King and butchered countless numbers of our people. We, the great ones, have obeyed their demand and in return we they have treated us like dogs. We have endured a thousand of their insults and we have suffered enough! At this moment, we must show them the consequence of our great anger and discontent. I implore each of you to summon every last of our people and meet with me here in twenty days' time. On that day, we will take back our land and kill every one of our bearded enemies. Perhaps then, we can awaken from this agonizing nightmare.'

Manco's emotional speech energized the crowd and word quickly and quietly spread of the Inca insurrection. After overhearing rumors the plan, I devoted my particular skill set, to their cause. This was the perfect opportunity to accomplish my immediate task of properly dispose of my abhorrent creation, Francisco Pizarro.

Twenty days later, in June of 1541, we infiltrated Pizarro's palace. Leading the surge was Diego de Almagra II, 'El Mozo,' the son of Pizarro's former partner, Diego de Almagro. A previous member of our 'Thirteen,' Diego had been cruelly betrayed by Pizarro, and been sentenced to death. Once the coup d'etat had been arranged, El Mozo had set his sights on revenge against Pizarro. Myself, El Mozo, and twenty heavily armed men stormed his home while he was hosting a grandiose dinner. The room was choked full of Pizarro's relatives and closest acquaintances. Blazing into his dining hall, I locked eyes with my abominable prodigy. Seated at his flauntingly elegant banquet, he pompously stared back at me with rattled animosity. A true tyrant to the end, he leapt from his seat and nimbly retrieving a decorative sword from the wall, he killed three men before I was able to stop him. There we were, face to face for one final moment.

Looking my regrettably successful student in the eyes, I sharply thrust my sword into his throat. Blood gushed like a fountain from his neck as he grossly guzzled out, 'Jesus!' His butchered body promptly fell to the cold palace floor. A hypocritical bastard to the bitter end, he painted the sign of the cross on the floor with his own blood. Struggling to breath, he piously pressed his expiring lips into the sick symbol and shamelessly kissed it. Feebly crawling along the blood-soaked floor, he sluggishly came to a halt as he finally breathed his last breath. I could not think of a more suitable death for my ruthless invention.

I had begun to fully realize the horrid implications my impish deeds. Whether by battle or disease, our campaign was responsible for millions of native lives. I had shamefully left an irreversible and permanent scar carved deep into humanity. It fell upon my condemned soul to undo the unpardonable actions of my godless life of disobedient opposition. From that day forth, I took an entirely different vow to counteract the damning damage I had done. Delinquent wrongdoers like Pizarro, Diaz and the countless others before them were damnable miscreants of the highest degree. I was responsible for creating the misguided monsters and pestilent evil that now terrorized humanity; Pizarro was only the begging. The man known as General Sebastian Diaz along with all of the other blood-sucking Bleeders I had created over centuries, had to be terminated. Though I wasn't entirely sure of *what* Diaz was, it was evident he was an exceptionally powerful immortal not unlike myself. Because of these formidable capabilities, I needed some additional deadly assets.

Over the ages, I had acquired an abundant repertoire of skills, but this journey required a new and even more effective set of lethal fighting techniques. The first stop in my higher education in the art of death, led me east. There I sought out the assistance of the most virtuous and competent combatant I had ever encountered, The Samurai. The Samurai warrior had long been a formidable adversary. Frugality, loyalty and honor to death; these crucial attributes were entirely absent from my appalling immortal existence. My deranged path had been controlled by pure, fuming hatred toward God. My rebellious violence had to be tempered by wisdom. Death and destruction had to be balanced with serenity. In order to successfully vanquish my remorseless foe, I would have to attain the transcendent skills of the Samurai. This new exotic skill set, coupled with a variety of other deadly defense disciplines, proved to be the ultimate combination to combat my own rapacious creations.

Inevitably, I would receive my own well-deserved punishment from God, but not before I nullified my unhallowed monsters. I could never be saved just as my festering creations could never escape my punitive wrath. In addition to modifying my skill set, I felt it necessary to change my name as well. Lazarus, which means 'God is my help,' felt peculiarly phony, given my new quest for vengeance. Undeserving of grace and my denial of Christ, I abandoned the name Lazarus and replaced it with Simon. 'Lazarus' was the friend of Jesus; I was no longer worthy of that title. Simon was now the deftly proficient instrument to undo all the wrong Lazarus 'the impure immortal' had brought about. It was now my responsability to deliver every Bleeder that I had created, directly into the hollows of Hell."

15

BASEL, SWITZERLAND
PRESENT

Practical disbelief gradually diminishes from my mind as candid curiosity swirls about in my head. Resting my forehead in my palms, I am speechless and fully confused after hearing Simon's outrageous tale. However skeptical I attempted to remain, there was no denying the inexplicably odd things I have seen since meeting Simon. As Simon stands by my side with his steadfast composed demeanor; struggling to comprehend his incredible claims, I demurely inquire; "You're telling me that blood sucking vampires actually exist and you are not just one of them; but the original?"

Sullenly shameful, Simon replies, "vampires, werewolves, witches or any other monster... to some degree, most of them are all too real. At the heart of every legend, there is a pledge. The myth of the vampire is simply an echo of my disgraceful past. Bleeders are the unforgivable result of my rebelliousness. I have turned countless quantities into bloodthirsty beasts and I alone am responsible for their elimination."

I notice myself carefully balancing both cautionary doubt and broadening intrigue.

"The blood, the aversion to daylight, even the wooden stake through the heart; they all stem from *your* past?"

He nods with doleful verification.

Momentarily confounded, I continue my engrossed inquiry.

"So how do you eliminate immortals? How can you kill the undead?"

Without hesitation he reacts; "With Bleeders; I cut off their heads and banish their souls directly to pits of hell."

"How do you actually 'turn' someone?"

"Man's sinful nature is easily corrupted. When someone is bitten, but not totally drained; my blood oath is transferred to them and they become Bleeders. Most everyone instantly gives in; the potent offering of power is simply too great to refuse. The few that actually resist or later regret their transformation eventually kill themselves. Some simply refuse to feed and wither away to nothing: the others find a way to sacrificially condemn themselves. If they have the will; they eventually deliver themselves from the monster they became."

With swelling fascination, I proceed with my exploratory questioning. "There must be thousands, even millions of them out there. How do you find them all?"

"Once I transformed myself into an immortal beast, the remaining members of The Order of St. Lazarus became a covert group of immortal hunters. Changing their name to The Obedience; they dedicated their lives to killing me along with every one of my evil 'creations.'

"After my confrontation with Diaz, and I vowed to undo the irreparable damage I had done, I realized I had underestimated the breadth of my heinous actions. Eliminating thousands upon thousands of immortals proved to be beyond the scope of my own immortal capabilities. Because of this, I turned to a rather unlikely source; the group that was dedicated to killing me. If I could tap into just one man as a resource, I could evade their pursuits while attaining the necessary intelligence to fulfill my new plot of a reckoning.

"Through patience and judicious persuasion, I was fortunately able to successfully appeal to a member of The Obedience. Discreetly convincing him of my reformation and that I was truly deadest on expelling my abominations, the insider became an irreplaceable asset. Secretly keeping me abreast of their intelligence and advancements, this single informant has passed down our confidential relationship from generation to generation.

"For centuries The Obedience has watched and documented immortal activity and they have also managed to keep Bleeders, Feeders and themselves out of the history books as well as the public eye. Over centuries, they have continued this suppression for only one reason: protecting the church."

Infuriated, I passionately interject; "My father was killed to protect the church?"

Simon concernedly responds; "They are only supposed to track and kill immortals; never humans. There have only been a couple of extreme cases when they have actually targeted humans. However, with the death of your father and the attempt on your life, I can't help but suspect their involvement. Even their holy organization is susceptible to corruption.

"I followed you not only to protect you, but I believe you may be something much more than just a 'loose end.' It seems as if they consider you just as much of a threat as your father."

Responding in lurid amazement but festering acceptance I react with, "Vampires... werewolves...this is all unbelievable. I am extremely overwhelmed to say the least."

Resolute and increasingly determined, Simon, my progressively credible guardian unflinchingly replies; "I know it sounds like ridiculous fantasy, but I promise you this; you are only safe with me."

Looking me sternly in the eyes, he continues; "Long ago, I

immersed myself in pure sadistic evil; I am damned. Rehabilitated; I am once again a relentless soldier of God. My only course is to undo my unforgivable transgressions; vanquishing all of my creations from the earth. I'm sorry you are in the middle of all of this."

Responding to Simon in a complicated but progressively sympathetic manner, I say; "My God is a very gracious God, beyond any understanding; surely *He* recognizes your transformation."

With calm abandonment infused with staunch martyrdom, he retorts; "I have an inescapable appointment in Hell and I have no delusions of somehow falling back into His favor and I accept that. But before I go, my immortal plague *will* be eradicated. *All* of the Bleeders and *all* of the Feeders will be wiped out."

Insistent; again I state, "When I was younger, I went through a number of rebellious stages; far too many to count. Preceding my much-deserved discipline, my father would routinely force me read chapter three of Romans. I'm sure you know it; every one of us has sinned and therefore fallen short of His glory. Jesus, your friend, is God's grace. He forgives anyone who asks for His mercy. No better; no worse."

"All *men* do fall short of the glory of God, but you forget that I am no longer a man. I did not merely fall from his favor; I willingly thrust myself away from it. There are so many dreadful, detestable sins in my past; I can neither shed those memories nor can I expect God to forgive them. Trust me; there is no redemption for what I have done."

Amidst the gloomy mood of despondency, I suddenly have a revelation; "That's what General Diaz was; he didn't just drink his victims' blood, he consumed their flesh. Diaz was a werewolf, wasn't he?"

Simon nods.

Awkwardly absorbed by these thrilling insights, I persist; "If Diaz was a werewolf, where did he come from?"

Taking a temporary and remorseful pause, Simon solemnly responds; "The man who called himself General Sebastian Diaz was the first of the Feeders. Though wickedly similar to Bleeders, Feeders have a similarly sinister but slightly different origination.

16

"Betrayal is the only truth that sticks."
-Arthur Miller

MARBELLA, SPAIN
PRESENT

Scarcely lit by the pale light of a crescent sliver of a moon, Mr. Shepherd comfortably occupies the passenger side of voluminous black sport utility vehicle. Under a pitchy, star splattered sky, amidst the laden sweltering temperature rapidly approaching 37 degrees Celsius, the ever-enigmatic Mr. Shepherd takes a sustained pull from his sizzling slender cigarette. Squinting with a forward focused gaze, Shepherd, lingeringly expels the stream of cloudy fume from his snarling nostrils. The murky air, both palpably polluted and faintly anxious, persists in acute silence.

Brashly breaking the stagnant stillness, Shepherd flashes a subtle sideways hand gesture just to the left side of his concentrated expression. The salute sharply signals his recently acquired SOCA recruits waiting in the darkness. One hundred meters before them lays an enormously mountainous mansion. A barrier measuring over three meters in height protects the perimeter of this lavish home. Beyond the fence is the obscenely spacious lair of one of the world's most infamous arms dealers, Alejandro Salazar. With another faint flick of his wrist, he commences the incursion. The coerced commandos tactfully sneak toward the monumental residence.

Salazar is a dangerous munitions trafficker notorious for selling weapons to every-and-all sides. Though widely acknowledged to be arguably *the* preeminent arms dealer, the authorities have been habitually incapable of successfully acquiring even the slightest morsel of physical evidence against him. Pretentiously flamboyant, he has made a remarkable career out of not only dealing profuse quantities of weapons and ammo, but also a brilliant career of skillfully eluding the law. On top of being the world's foremost arms dealer, Salazar is also a passionate collector of occult memorabilia and more specifically exceptionally rare religious artifacts.

Though he has dozens of spacious properties around the world, this extensively well-guarded compound overlooking the breathtakingly scenic Costa del Sol is Salazar's main residence. The grounds feature a meticulously groomed luscious green lawn with an intricately embellished stone patio that surrounds an enormous fifty-meter pool. In the midst of the colossal estate, stands the over four stories high stucco palace. The residence contains over forty stately rooms; including a full size movie theater, a bowling alley, an indoor Olympic sized swimming pool, a restaurant style kitchen, and a tremendously impressive and expansive gallery of fine and priceless works of art. Rumor has it that there are secret cellars hidden below his extensive estate that house the rarest and most elicit items of his collection.

With ever-dutiful Monkey behind the driver's seat, Mr. Shepherd looks on in hushed anticipation as his soldiers begin to invade the villa. Along with the SOCA agents are a small collection of Feeders. The two groups swiftly swarm the immense fortress. In a flash, Shepherd's onslaught of slinking invaders, rapidly suppress the first group of guards at the gate with an absurdly excessive rush of firepower. This over the top outpouring of ammunition takes out at least seven guards and instantly vaporizes the impeding wall in front of them. This first brash wave immediately activates a boisterous alarm.

Collaborating as one unit, both Shepherd's captives and cronies descend upon the inner courtyard of the compound with brute force. The cacophonous alarm blares throughout the compound as emergency lights intensely illuminate the grounds. Through the wafting debris and bellowing bursts of bubbling smoke, the men catch a glimpse of their objective. The militia fixes their eyes upon the extravagantly ostentatious stucco structure that is Casa de Salazar.

Charging through the reduced walls, the soldiers approach the top of the elongated pool. With no shortage of firepower themselves the remaining palace guards desperately fire at their unexpected and overwhelming invaders. With the immortal Feeders leading the charge and taking the bulk of the fire, the SOCA agents and Feeders remain unscathed. Shepherd's soldiers forcibly push them forward, past the posh pool and beyond the accumulation of freshly wasted sentinels. Advancing up the grand marble staircase leading up to the palace's main entrance, the assaulting army secures the perimeter in only a matter of seconds.

Following a transitory pause, the troopers turbulently burst open the humungous double doors; gaining access into the secure fortress. Promptly, the crew systematically trounces the remaining guards. After the boisterous barrage of bullets and the frenzy of screams dissipate; the striking sound of only the clanging alarm remains. One of the Feeders manages to turn off the raucous siren; the men are suddenly surrounded by sheer silence.

Stalwartly stone-faced; Shepherd, still calmly smoking his cigarette inside of his vehicle, turns his head. With Monkey dutifully holding up a two-way radio in front of his boss's mouth, Shepherd priggishly delivers his directions; "Gentlemen, locate the hatch to Senor Alejandro's secret cellar and make it lickety-split. I want my spear."

Scrupulously stashed away beneath Salazar's chateau is the

historically renowned and surpassingly sought after Spear of Destiny.

The Spear of Destiny is the lance that pierced Jesus' side as he clung to the cross and it is believed to contain preserved remnants of the blood of Christ. Due to the alleged traces of Jesus' actual blood on its tip, the Spear is believed to possess prolific supernatural powers. Over centuries, it has become an amalgamation of various materials; some to keep it in one piece, while others have been simply added for decoration. Delicately held together by these additional adornments, the Spear supposedly houses yet another exceptionally rare relic. Carefully concealed inside the center of the jumbled array of artifacts is a nail. This single nail is rumored to be one of the actual nails that held Jesus' body to the cross. Just like the tip of the Spear, this nail is believed to contain traces of Jesus' blood as well. It is said that whoever is in possession of the Spear becomes invincible.

Historical characters ranging from Charlemagne to Barbarossa have been connected to the lore of the Spear. From fanatics to fiends, it has certainly had its fair share of sordid and divergent backgrounds; passing through the hands of emperors, kings, dictators, historians and collectors alike. In 1938, Adolf Hitler took possession of it and had it added to his personal collection of artifacts in Nuremburg. A staunch believer in the occult, Hitler adamantly believed in its profound mystical capabilities.

Years later, in 1945, it was accidentally discovered by an American soldier under the direct command of General Patton. Inside one of Hitler's many bunkers, there it sat inside of an open crate atop a stack of wooden crates. Curiously reaching out to the unique antiquity, the young man grabbed a hold of it, officially transferring possession of the Spear to the United States. As legend would have it, at that very same of exchange, Hitler shot himself in the head.

When the Spear was brought back to their military base, experts immediately recognized the relic as The Spear of Destiny. Shortly after, they respectfully returned the Spear, along with other priceless artifacts and works of art they had rescued back to Vienna, Austria. Carefully housed behind impenetrable glass, the Spear of Destiny has to this day, remained in the secure confines of the Vienna museum.

However, even though this spear is widely believed to be the authentic Spear of Destiny, it may actually be a craftily constructed replica; one of many. At present, there are four separate spears claiming to be *the* authentic Spear. Besides the one in Vienna, there are spears in Krakow, Armenia and also inside of the Vatican. Properly tested and verified, the Vienna spear is indeed the same age as the original, but unfortunately there have been at least seven different "Spears" through the centuries. Whether they are actually counterfeit creations for profit or elaborate decoys to thwart any attempts at world domination, no one yet has been able to absolutely certify which one is the authentic Spear.

Over the years, Mr. Shepherd has laboriously located the other six supposed spears. So far only two have been authenticated to have actually contained genuine components of the original Spear of Longinus. Shepherd believes the Spear entrenched below Alejandro Salazar's once opulent home is the true Spear of Destiny.

As Shepherd's soldiers rigorously rifle through the monumental and largely illegal collection of rare artifacts, one of the men halts their hunt by enthusiastically shouting out; "Bingo! I found it!"

Hoisting the ornate rectangular glass container high above his head, the elated infantry member repeats his declaration, broadcasting it over his radio to the awaiting Mr. Shepherd.

"I've got it!"

Shepherd replies; "Very good! Have one of the agents bring it to me immediately."

With a sooty tongue, he sternly delivers his next set of instructions; "As for the rest of you meffs, search the wreckage for

Salazar's body. I need him to be unequivocally dead."

Continuing his forward fixed stare, the unflinching Shepherd awaits the emergence of the SOCA agent and more importantly, the Spear. Out from underneath the ruins of rubble, the trooper surfaces and hurriedly scuttles toward Shepherd's automobile. Breathing heavily, the nervous commando approaches the Shepherds black SUV. Slowly rolling his window down, Shepherd extends his arm outside of the vehicle and as the agent promptly presents him with the ornamental container. Brimming with restrained rapture, an acutely appeased Shepherd draws the relic back into the vehicle. Once more, Shepherd extends his arm out of the passenger side window. However, this time he is unexpectedly gripping a 9mm pistol. Forcefully jamming the barrel of the gun into the soldier's forehead, he unhesitatingly pulls the trigger. The bullet turbulently torpedoes through the unsuspecting soldier's temple. His inanimate body fluidly flops to the ground.

Smoothly turning back to his subordinate, Shepherd delivers his additional addendum. "Burn it down: all of it."

Monkey stares back at Shepherd with an inquiringly blank expression.

Mr. Shepherd additionally commands with overly dramatic amplified passion; "Blow it to pieces and burn the foundation to cinders and ash."

Monkey questions his superior with perceptible perplexity; "The lot of them? The agents as well as our own; you aren't even going to turn those filthy tossers?"

Peevishly answering his inquiring minion, Shepherd indignantly asserts; "Let not your intellect be troubled, Monkey, with the reasoning of me, your vastly predominant iniquitous superior. Burn it down."

With another hefty exhalation of smoke, he indifferently imparts; "After all, someone should be held accountable for this rather impressive incursion. Leave their remains for the authorities."

Raffishly smirking toward one another, the two begin to giggle incessantly. Grabbing some explosive devices, Monkey promptly exits the vehicle to properly execute his new instructions. As Monkey aptly sets up the more than sufficient amount of explosives, Mr. Shepherd merrily lingers on in his smoldering smog of cigarette smoke.

17

"You have to die a few times
before you can really live"
-Charles Bukowski, *The People Look Like Flowers at Last*

MARSEILLES, FRANCE
PRESENT

Surprisingly restless while awaiting word of any evidence of treachery regarding the peculiarly timed death of Father Santé, Agent Moretti anxiously paces the long hallway of the city's morgue. After performing an unconventionally in-depth autopsy ordered by Moretti, the local law enforcement's most experienced pathologist has almost concluded her expansive inquiry. One of the examiner's assistants exits the lab and continues down the hallway where Moretti impatiently strides. Rolling through a set of swinging steel doors, the young intern briskly approaches Moretti.

"Albeit a long shot, she thinks she has found something. She's running more tests, but she may have found indications of a struggle."

Upon finishing her compulsory update, the reserved assistant retreats back through the fluctuating doors and back into the examining room. Though distinctly stated as being only a possibility; the slightest encouragement of substantiating his instinct was good enough for Moretti. Merely miniscule at best, this possibility only served to validate his unwavering skepticism. At this moment, Agent

Moretti's gut could prove to be rather compelling.

Increasingly frustrated with Ela's continuing absence and lack of any reply to his communications, Moretti grabs his phone from his jacket pocket and tenaciously attempts Ela's mobile once again. Not only perpetually paranoid for the debatable state of her safety, he is still attempting to get any more details she could think of regarding the death of her father. Anything she may have forgotten to disclose or happened recall in the time since their initial encounter, could prove to be valuable, given the confusing circumstances. Sharply elevating the phone up to his ear, he tensely waits for her to answer.

To his expected chagrin, succeeding six lengthy rings, he is disappointedly responded to by her voicemail. Following her all too familiar automated greeting, he resolutely leaves yet another message.

"*Bonjour Mademoiselle,* it is Agent Moretti. Again, not to alarm you, but I would simply like to know that you are alright. I still suggest that there may be an unseen conspiracy behind your father's death, so please take the proper precautions to stay safe. I know this is a difficult time; I am merely concerned for your safety. Please contact me at this number once you have received this."

Discontented once more, Moretti forcefully tucks his tightly gripped mobile back into his jacket. With a grunt-like sigh, he stands frozen in paused deliberation. In this momentary lull, he ponders the scope of his uncompromising convoluted station. Notwithstanding his nearly nil amassment of physical evidence, Moretti has been positively guided by his hunches more often than not. This current predicament was certainly no exception.

With a burdensome conscience and with his unflinching determination, he decides to stay his course and continue to concentrate on Ela's well being. He remains untiringly firm in discovering the uncontaminated truth behind the deaths of Danylo and Father Santé.

BASEL, SWITZERLAND
PRESENT

Prudently keeping us on the move, ever-cautious Simon has procured another vehicle to transport us to our next destination. The indistinct sedan will certainly carry us indistinctly to another one of his safe havens. Gathering a generous variety of weapons, he packs the arsenal alongside a collection of food for me. Completely filling his two sizable black carryalls, he steadily packs the provisions into the vehicle's boot. After arranging the load, he invites me to settle in for the extensive ride.

"It is imperative we stay on the move. I hate shuffling you around like this, Ela but with all of this madness, I can't leave anything to chance."

With the bundles of weaponry and supplies in tow, we embark onto the next precautionary shelter. Progressively trusting but discernibly drained, I sit serenely by Simon's side. Whether it was the tiring commotion of the recent events or my just body's reaction to my circumstantial grief, I slowly begin to succumb to the relaxing rhythmic hum of the motor.

Progressively more lethargic, I curiously concentrate on my reactions to the men attacking me outside of the café. I am a bit embarrassed and disappointed that I simply froze. After a number of deadly terrorist attacks in the US and France, my company offered free self-defense classes to all of the international agents. Surprisingly, I loved it. I immediately added to my routine of fitness and yoga. At the time it was a great workout and a great way to relieve some pent up aggression. But now, I am frustrated that when the critical time did arrive; I just disconcertingly froze.

Looking over to me with woeful concern, Simon interminably turns back to the road and forges us onward to our next refuge. Little by little I gradually slip into an extremely essential slumber.

Hours elapse as we trek across the Swiss countryside. I toggle back and forth between being moderately alert and being totally asleep.

The sunrise slowly begins to illuminate our previously inarticulate scenic surroundings. The indefinite road is suddenly enclosed by sublime shades of emerald green and the blurry sky transforms into a vibrant expanse of gold and blue. I hand over my consciousness in exchange for a sedate trance and Simon continues in muted reverie. Concernedly reflecting upon the calamitous circumstances, our substantial drive has also proved to be a beneficial meditational period. His seasoned faculties are clearly engulfed in heavy contemplation as righteous unrest oozes from his expression. Once more I submit to my drowsiness. Hours seem to pass as mere seconds.

With a bellowing yawn, I stretch my arms above my head while broadly opening my waking eyes. Awaking from my lengthy doze, I swivel around and squint my eyes at the beautiful surroundings. We are driving alongside the edge of a densely lush green forest. Slowly coming into full observant alertness, I yawn once again and childishly curled back into my passenger slot. In oddly sedate silence, the two of us cast our gazes forward and simply savor the arresting surroundings.

Just as the somber quietude settles in and placidity is composedly attained, I interrupt the calm atmosphere. "We need to stop. I'm afraid I must answer nature's impending call."

With the possibility of pestering my already accommodating operator I shyly tack on an additional petition. "I *could* hold out for a toilet situated under the roof of a café?"

"Could you now?" He ripostes in a jesting sarcastic tenor.

With only the slenderest period of passing time, I observe an opportune locale for my brief stop. Faded paint on a rather weathered sign boasted; "Warming your heart with delectable tea and delicious pastries "Café Güte", *Café Kindness*. Auspiciously no more than 20 kilometers ahead of our current position, this could be a welcomed and favorable interim pause. Just as I process the advertisement, I recognize Simon has taken notice of it as well. With a subtle nod and genuine slight tender strain of his eyes, he consents.

"I believe we can manage that." Simon answers with a sly smirk at the corner of his mouth.

In minutes, we stray from the monotonous freeway and proceed toward the roadside café. Simon settles into the parking lot located in the front of the convenient café. We are parked at the end of a narrow strip of seven or eight other cars. Swinging his door open; he motions for me to exit as well. Departing the automobile, he suddenly stands still. Peering back at me through the car's open doors, he coolly states; "Quick to the toilet... and then a brief bite. Then we carry on."

Satisfactorily content and with an amused simper, I replied; "Yes...I got it." Remembering a phrase my father used to frequently utter, I insert; "I will be faster than thought or time."

Completely exiting the car, I dependably walk to Simon's side as we stroll toward the entrance of the café.

The charming café is a quaint, house-like structure stashed along the forest-laden interstate of the Swiss countryside. We are surrounded by high-reaching trees that are swaying in the gentle draft flowing down from the mountains. Completely coated in a soothing tint of sea foam green, the rural eatery has already delivered on its allegation of comfort. The welcoming warm repose of coziness washes over my frazzled senses from head to toe. Run-down and quite weary, the breath of relief afforded from this oasis already proves to be a rather judicious decision.

Holding the café's door open for me, I step into the eatery as Simon breezes in behind me. Taking direction from the sign adhered to the counter in front of us; we proceed to "*Setzen Sie sich*": seat ourselves.

Strolling toward a sufficing table for two, I am instantly reminded of my initial requirement of their lavatory. Twirling around, I embarrassingly blurt out; "*Les toilette.* I won't be a minute."

Simon continues onto the table as I revert back past the entrance and down the tiny corridor leading toward the washroom.

As I head back to the table, Simon slides the empty chair away from the table with his foot; inviting me to sit. Softly snickering to myself, I accept the playful gesture and take a seat. The round rustic tabletop is embellished with a smart handcrafted tablecloth. Between us is a short red ceramic vase with a single but simply radiant white daisy in full bloom.

Facing the door, Simon is customarily reticent and as calmly alert as ever. Though our temporary hiatus seems somewhat hurried, I can already feel my unnerved senses regaining a bit of composure. With a profound breath in, I continued to stare into Simon's unrelenting expression. Somehow his unshakable scowl challenges my fear; rendering most of my angst and uncertainty almost entirely ineffective.

After abiding in our peaceful occasion of wistful reserve, we are pleasantly greeted by our hospitable server. Intently reporting to our cozy table stands the grey haired veteran waitress. With a warm "*Willkommen!*" and gigantic eager smile, she places down an offering of ice water.

"*Hallo und vielen Dank.*" I respond with frank gratitude.

With her cheerful disposition and hospitable manner, she inquires; "What is it that I can get for the two of you?"

Urgently taking a refreshing sip of the icy cold water, I expressly blurt out; "Tea for me, thank you."

Worried about pressing my luck, I expressly blurt out; "Do you have roschti? If you do, I would love a plate, please."

Widening her grin to an approving cast, she turns her

attention toward Simon. Taking heed of her attentiveness he politely asserts; "Nothing for me, thank you."

"Very well, I will be right back with your tea." Cheerfully shuffling away, she retires back into the kitchen.

Out-and-out silence devoured the unassuming atmosphere once again.

Our tranquil quiet is finally disrupted upon the return of our gracious host. Cautiously setting down the steaming pot of hot water, she carefully places a cup and saucer in front of me and skillfully fills my cup to the brim.

"There you are my dear. Careful, it is very hot." She fondly utters and begins to withdraw from the table once again.

Looking compassionately into Simon's steely countenance, she pivots back and concernedly remarks; "Young man, the weight a man carries on his brow, is very telling. If you don't mind me saying so, you should smile more."

Concluding her good-natured observation, I uncontrollably let out a giggle. My clamorous burst of merriment instantly legitimizes her predication. Happily grinning from ear to ear, my escaping snicker was followed with; "I whole heartedly agree. Thank you! You don't know how right you are."

The two of us, now gleefully rejoiced at the amusing moment. The tittering chuckles diminish as our waitress once more returns back to the kitchen. I attempt to attach a sincere statement to my laughter at his expense; "Seriously Simon, do you *ever* actually smile?"

"That's funny. No one has ever said that to me before." He reacts with unmistakable sarcasm.

"Centuries following Sarah's death, I apparently never smiled; not even the slightest. Smiles and glee were entirely absent from my days until one day I realized life's entertaining irony. Sitting in a market, I watched as a man brazenly attempted to steal a clay pot from one of the merchants. Years before, Jesus had frequently referred to humans as clay. The hilarity of a clay vessel stealing another clay vessel suddenly struck me as an intensely amusing endeavor. With that, I laughed for the first time in almost 100 years."

Still chuckling from my previous observation and now the addition of Simon's comical testimony, I seemed to be miraculously unburdened and actually relaxed. Though claiming to be altogether inhuman, Simon had finally manifested his indiscernible side of bona fide humanity. There we sat contently distracted in temporary serenity.

With her impeccable timing, our delightful waitress returned with my delectable roschti. Gently placing the mouthwatering potato dish in front of me, she discreetly slips away as if to not interrupt our playful exchange. A genuine "Thank you" reels from my lips, directed toward the expeditiously regressing server. Unfolding the snowy white napkin before me, I spread it across my lap and take a hefty forkful of the traditional Swiss roschti.

Heavenly bite after heavenly bite, my simple but gratifying dish disappeared in a swift display of unrefined ravenousness. In no time at all, my plate is entirely bare. The high-pitched clink of an empty plate sounded as I recklessly released my fork. Upon curtly satisfying my craving, I looked up to see Simon, still maintaining a solemn stare across from me.

Wiping my gluttonous lips with my napkin, I seized the laid-back moment to address his overall outlook. Maybe the light-hearted atmosphere will mellow the bite of my observation.

"You need a dog or a cat or something... seriously; don't you have any friends?"

Meekly grinning in response to my jesting criticism, he replies; "I have had my fair share of acquaintances over the years: a samurai, a poet, surprisingly a politician; but the closest thing to a friend I have had in centuries was a former enemy turned ally. A total lunatic, 'The Greek' was a unique and invaluable confederate."

And with that sentiment, drab desperation slowly slinks back into his composed expression. Regretting that I soured the mood, I insist; "I know you think your past is far too wicked for God's forgiveness, but it is impossible for anyone to be *too* sinful. The greater the sin the greater the consequence, yes, but no one can run, fall or flee away from God's grace."

Simon gravely counters; "But... I cannot buy or fight my way back in either."

With his persistent glare, he intently prolongs his final stubborn sentiment. "I am only worthy of Hell."

Now stalwartly paused in an unbelievably awkward hush, we sat suspended in unbalanced uneasiness. Our bleak reticence of still disagreement is interrupted by the muddled murmurs of the scant surrounding patrons and the faint clamoring of dishes.

Simon is truly perplexing. Understandably, he is rightfully riddled with guilt because of his previous deeds of horrendous degradation. There he sits, utterly apologetic and resigned to undo his damnable creations but he still remains permanently pessimistic regarding any hope of absolution. He asks for nothing and therefore expects nothing. Capable of horrific, heinous exploits yes, but categorically beyond exoneration he is not; certainly not the venerably ardent God that my father showed me. Heavy-hearted and struck with convoluted grief; I am severely sad for him.

Depressingly wading in this dismal atmosphere of lingering melancholy, we went through the routine motions of concluding our stay at the cozy café. While he pays the waitress, I quickly refresh myself in the washroom once again. Regrouping at the entrance, we have yet to speak a word to one another. There is an indistinct liveliness lacking from my slowing steps. The downward spiraling conversation had taken its toll. Even Simon's invariable barren cast was acutely contaminated with subtle consternation.

Upon leaving the comforts of the quiet café, we progress onto our car. Though slightly disparaged by the discouraging subject of conversation, our stop had still proven to be restfully restoring and a rather beneficial suspension of our current situation.

Just as Simon crouches to get back inside of our latest vehicle, he promptly looks across the car and over my shoulder. Remaining casual, something peculiar seems to have caught his attention. With a distinguishable sharp inhalation and flickering flare of his nostrils, his gaze intensifies.

Following his stringent attentiveness, I swivel around only to find a man nonchalantly smoking a cigarette. Harmlessly leaning against his automobile, the seemingly unassuming stranger is at least five or six cars away from us. I don't see what the danger is. Simon however, has clearly detected something.

Suddenly it hits me; Simon smells the distinct traces of another immortal. It is a Feeder. Directly upon my realization of the situation, the smoking motorist abruptly produces a pistol and instantly fires a shot in our direction. The bullet zips just inches from my head. Before he can fire a second shot, Simon has inexplicably lunged over the row of cars and lands directly to the shooter's side. The unsuspecting Feeder is instantly subdued. Obscured by the extending row of parked cars, I can only surmise Simon is customarily disposing of him as he does all Bleeders and Feeders.

Springing up from behind the cars, Simon composedly but passionately calls out to me, "Ela, let's move!"

All too familiar with the indicative urgency and grave significance of the threatening scenario, I quickly move into the somewhat safer confines of our car. Again with inexplicably impossible speed, Simon expressly dashes directly back into our car. Hurriedly turning the key, he rapidly shoves the car into reverse and we erratically flee the sinister scene.

Agilely accelerating and returning to the spacious motorway, we are soon followed by another errant motorcar. As it makes tremendous headway toward us, Simon continues to accelerate, in the hopes of escaping our devotedly indignant admirers. After giving nimble chase for only a short number of kilometers, Simon unexpectedly hits the brakes. We are jolted forward and the car is brought to a screeching halt.

Now at a standstill in a clearing alongside the highway, Simon briskly bolts out of the driver's side. With his short sword in one hand he assumes an attack position; willingly awaiting our impending enemies.

In no time flat, our pursuers come barreling toward us and slide their car to a grinding halt, squarely in front of Simon. Surging out of the nebulous puff of debris are three enormous and beastly Feeders. All three of the cantankerous creatures have ghostly grayish-white skin and long grease- black hair. With their fanglike yellow teeth, the snarling Feeders barrel toward an eagerly expectant Simon. The savagely aggressive one in the middle boldly pounces toward Simon first as the other two lumber only seconds behind their tussling principal.

The other two hovering hostiles look oddly similar. Both are excessively decorated like a band of colorful rejects from a deranged circus sideshow. They came complete with matching facial tattoos and a variety of ornate designs that adorned their beastlike physiques. In addition to the tattoos, they both had tiny horn like body modifications protruding from their temples. Looking altogether awfully menacing, the two frightening freaks swiftly verged upon the battle. Like undomesticated animals, the miscreants shriek and squeal as they approach the skirmish.

Simon slashes through the first combatant with exacting precision. With the elementary ease he carves into his unholy antagonist. His first slash slices the Feeder's abdomen open just before the second swiftly severs his head. Just as the head haphazardly topples to the ground, Simon is already simultaneously engaged with the other two Feeders. Further enraged by the sight of their suddenly slain cohort, the bizarrely erratic hellions grow rabidly hawkish as they storm Simon with a barrage of frenzied strikes.

Despite their reckless rage and violent gyrations, the acrimonious outbursts prove no match for Simon. Among the flailing motions is the distinguishable stillness of Simon; delivering his deft maneuvers and easily overpowering them. The ridiculous marauders are fluently overpowered. The Feeders are routinely beheaded and expelled.

Performing the ritualistic recitation; Simon kneels down amongst the wolfish wreckage. Gesturing the sign of the cross above the bested corpses, he delivers them into the merciless arms of their esteemed master, Lucifer. The bodies are reduced to the crumbling lump of earthy hued decay. Contentedly rising back to his feet, Simon trudges back toward me.

Reinserting himself into the driver's seat, Simon expressly spouts, "Our unknown adversary has been monitoring us; most likely through a satellite system or even through traffic cameras." Energetically cramming the car into gear and forcibly bearing down on the accelerator we are quickly catapulted back onto the open road.

Simon intently continues, "We will have to use alternative modes of transportation. We have to go off the grid."

Mildly baffled but remarkably semi-accustomed to the increasingly common gruesome bloodshed, I inquire; "Anything you say. I am entirely entrusted to you. What exactly are *alternative modes*?"

With the almost imperceptible peppering of playfulness, Simon responds, "Nothing complicated: hopping a freight train, stowing away in a container ship or hiding inside of a transport truck...the usual."

Affably encouraged by stoic Simon's marginally jesting reply, I attentively await for the next unexpected progression of our improvised itinerary. Once again we agilely venture into the picturesque rural roadway.

18

"But what's puzzling you
Is the nature of my game"
-The Rolling Stones, "Sympathy For The Devil"

VERONA, ITALY
PRESENT

Riveted by the tree line cruising evenly past my eyes, I brood over the latest activities in our amassment of incredibly far-fetched circumstances. As the overshadowed trees and electrical wires whizzes past my introspective watch, intermittent bursts of dim lights flash across my lamenting face. Accompanying the rhythmic dissonant rumbling of the train is the raucous and quite ear-piercing screech of the steel wheels scraping along the rusted tracks. Once again sharing chronically familiar contemplative quietude, Simon and are now precariously entrenched inside of a crudely corroded and relentlessly vibrating galloping freight train. Departing the Swiss countryside and voyaging through Northern Italy, I nervously anticipate our arrival to our newest destination. We are en route to another one of Simon's many safe houses. Somewhere neighboring the Province of Verona, our second secure stop will hopefully prove to be considerably more auspicious than the last. Since all indications point to our successful extrication from the watchful eye of our yet to be specified adversary, the perpetually serene Simon believes we will find our much needed respite there.

As we are submerged in the murky nebulous of a starless night, I muse over the wild events that led to our current locomotive lodging. Only eight short hours ago we began our excursion on the railway. After fleeing the café in Switzerland we directly drove into a brush covered hallow in the dense woods. Hurriedly hiking toward a set of railroad tracks, we briskly made our way toward a tiny clearing near the tracks. Feeling the grumbling quake of a nearing freight train, we had providentially arrived mere seconds before an approaching train.

Evidently well acquainted with the challenging task of actually vaulting onto a moving locomotive, Simon took me securely into his arms and began to run. Amazingly, he somehow sprinted fast enough to match the speed of the locomotive. Strongly enfolding me at his side with one arm, he tirelessly dashed alongside a wide-open compartment door. By some astonishingly impossible means and without any warning, he launched me up and inside of the train. As harshly jarring as his actions should have been, I was remarkably catapulted with considerably delicate fluidity. Landing with only the slightest graceless thump, I gently came to a rolling stop. Now safely shielded inside of our new temporary steel dwelling, I watched as Simon curiously swooped himself into the chamber with ridiculous leisure.

Confident in our prospective refuge provided by his Italian safe house, Simon remained guarded but tentatively settled.

For eight hours I have anxiously waited for our successful passage to his provincial asylum. Only one more hour and we should be there. My hope is that our dangerous departure from the freight train will proceed with as much affluence as our surprisingly easygoing entry. Securely settled next to Simon, I continue to gaze out at the blackened sky.

Suddenly with a squawk and violent jerk, our compartment

is roughly yanked out its rhythmic trot. Unexpectedly thrust forward, it seems that our current mode of crude transportation is coming to a halt. I attempt to regain my balance as we are bucked, jostled and uncontrollably forced frontward. Dynamically rising to his feet, Simon unhesitatingly darts to the compartment's gaping door. Agilely leaning out of the shaking locomotive, his already stern profile takes on an intensely upsetting scowl. He's not just startled or concerned... he is enraged. Snappily swiveling back to me, he declares; "We need to leave now! It's them."

As the braking train rattles while maintaining its hasty deceleration we are both startled by an enormous explosion.

Stumblingly springing to my feet, I join Simon and peer out of the precarious opening. Simon grapples me by my waist, securing me as I inspect the compelling goings on. Just ahead, swelling smoke and blazing flames surge upward into the night sky. In the distance, there looks to be the contorted wreckage of what looks to be a colossal fiery accident. Upon further scrutiny, the calamitous cluster looks to be the mutilated ruins of at least seven or even ten demolished vehicles.

As the cacophonous blasts draw closer, Simon demands that we immediately desert of our bustling habitat. Grabbing me even tighter into his preservative embrace, he springs us out from the train. With impossible dexterity and accuracy, Simon lunges us from the train; indescribably settling us safely on the ground. Standing temporarily stagnant from the spontaneous exit, I look up to Simon for essential direction. Catching a closer glimpse of the massive disturbance, Simon is determined that this was deliberate malicious obstruction.

Simon declares: "They tracked us, I don't know how, but they tracked us. How else could they have found us so fast?"

This was no accident, this was an intentional barricade; a feigned ambush to capture the two of us.

As our recently deserted train continues to decelerate;

easing closer to the entrapping disaster, we tuck ourselves into the surrounding brush. Shrewdly meandering upward to inspect the wreckage and the attempted snare, Simon states; "This is far worse than I suspected."

Suddenly suspending his thoughts, a profoundly motionless Simon takes his discernible sniff of detection. Still but acutely at the ready, he shifts his intense expression to the dark void behind us. Reaching into his coat, he produces his flask, promptly gulps down an ample mouthful; dispensing an instant swell of added ability and immediately vaults over my head. As I lift my head to follow his astonishing upsurge, I am utterly awestruck to see him violently slam into an anonymous assailant! Seemingly appearing from out of nowhere, the unforeseen attacker bashes directly into the suddenly expectant clutches of soaring Simon. It's another Feeder.

Intensely entwined, the two turbulently plummet to the ground; strenuously thwacking down to the rigid turf. Their strained scuffle is filled with vehement jabs and rambunctious punches.

From the edges of the gloomy dark surroundings comes the unmistakable droning of multiple motorbikes. While Simon tussles with his aerial combatant, we are suddenly inundated with three clamorous motorcycles. As Simon forcefully twists his enemy's head off of his body, he notices the converging clan of Feeder cyclists. Casting the severed head aside, he impulsively motions the sign of the cross and voices his Latin recitation. The Feeders remains instantly disappear in a sputtering puff of hazy ash as the rapidly approaching maniacally motorists descend upon me. Frightened and altogether unprepared, I desperately cry out; "Simon!"

Without delay, Simon slings his assortment of throwing knives directly into the advancing immortals. The whetted blades embellished with ornate cross-shaped hilts plunge deep into the Feeders with deadly precision. Continuing his resounding invocations, with effortless transitional movement, he progresses to the gesture of the cross; immediately transmitting their dratted spirits to hell. At the moment their bested bodies collapse into withering debris, another wave of raging Feeders uproariously appears from out of the wooded remote. Our surroundings are increasingly illuminated by the flickering lights coming from the nearby catastrophe.

Ostentatiously leading the reprobate group of snarling beastly degenerates is a grossly rotund and burly critter of a man. This shaggy butterball is the very essence of gruff and grimy. He stands complete with slimy slicked back hair and a thickset bush of a beard. With a heavily fat and fuzzy physique, he stands the ultimate cliché of a surly biker, save one gigantic peculiarity; he is outfitted in women's clothing. Shamelessly garnishing his fat sweaty figure is a sapphire blue and disgustingly tight baby doll t-shirt atop an outrageously short red rubber miniskirt. For a fat man in silver heels, he wildly leads the company of god-awful Feeders directly to us with remarkable speed.

Nearing our position, the scruffy ringleader removes his obscuring sunglasses; revealing the true identity of the plump attacker. Sunk inside of the man's veiny blanched skin is a set of conspicuously jade-stained eyes. This quirky shell of a wooly biker is actually the pestilent swarm of dreaded demons known as Legion.

Notorious for massive disorder along with his blatant hatred for any measure of morality, Legion is the very essence of anarchy. Ushering in the enclosing band of hellish Feeders, Legion extends his hairy arm forward, waving in the roused pack of bloodthirsty brutes to quickly converge upon us. The excited immortal mass riotously passes their demonic director and surge toward us. There Legion stood, watching his mischievous mob from behind the driving drove like an unhinged malevolent master.

Simon immediately produces two short swords from the inside of his flowing jacket. As the frenzied Feeders collide with him, the steadily expectant Simon, slices, slashes and severs the heads off of the group of ravaging raiders. Blood splatters in every direction in a blurry haze of furious kicks, stabs and swats. Bursts of crimson shower the scene.

Through the clamorous cloud of sweeping strokes and swinging extremities, the Feeders are reduced to a shriveling heap of dusty remains. Mounds of rot encircle Simon and become floating puffs of ashy particles that dissipate into the cold night air. Faintly through the fleshy fog I observed Simon's silhouette concluding his motioning of the cross.

Entirely unscathed, Simon stringently concentrates on the only person left standing; Legion. Heartily chuckling with deranged trepidation, Legion rowdily rushes toward Simon; still brandishing his deadly deft blades. Despite being unarmed, Legion launching his weighty figure into the air and begins his feverish assault on Simon. His unrestrained bombardment of blustery jabs actually clobbers Simon's swords to the ground. Shockingly, Simon takes a significant amount of lumbering blows. Legion's substantial superhuman strength releases relentless wallops. For the first time, Simon is actually struggling.

Unarmed but clearly not dismayed; an unyielding Simon begins to battle back. With a potent shift, Simon grindingly regains his supremacy; forcibly hurling Legion to the rigid dirt and commandingly overpowering his zealous adversary.

With both of his chubby, hairy arms sturdily pinned underneath Simon's knees, Legion lies restlessly defenseless and entirely subdued. Thrusting his oppressing open hand directly down against Legion's thrashing throat, Simon madly tightens his immovable grip. Securing his crushing hold, Simon sternly asks Legion with increased aggravation:

"This... *this* is not exactly your style, Legion. Who are you working for?"

Futilely restless, Legion crudely spits; spraying a greasy mix of saliva and blood into Simons face. Further constricting his narrowing clench upon his captive's neck, Simon tensely queries once again:

"This lacks your chaotic flare, demon. This isn't your like your usual pointless savagery. Who is pulling your strings? You forget I know your primitive nature; you're too stupid and impulsive for all of this. Who is it behind the curtain?"

Ineffectively struggling underneath Simon's staunch retention, Legion's burdened body momentarily yields; temporarily conceding. With a strained gasp and suspiciously rotten grin upon his haggard, pallid face, Legion hoarsely grunts;

"You naïve devotee: you have absolutely no idea what *he* is up to, do you."

Mildly bewildered, an outwardly agitated Simon momentarily contemplates on exactly who Legion is referring to. During this brief moment of reflection, Legion, in a faint flash, abruptly departs from his hairy host. Instantly he had remarkably disappeared into a flock of black birds overhead that rapidly vanish into the swarthy night sky. The surly man beneath Simon is no longer a threat; he has returned to being only human.

Sweeping to my side, Simon securely cradles me into his arms. The two of us have successfully survived yet another vicious invasion. Just as his consolatory grip collapses me in comfort, he says;

"This has spiraled extensively out of my control. We need answers and I need help."

Concerned with the increasing uncertainty and worsening magnitude of desperation, Simon feels he is left with no other choice but to reluctantly request aid from a resource of last resorts. Without delay, Simon urgently devises a new course of action. We hustle toward the pile-up of cars surrounding the flaming wreckage. Foregoing his previous intentions of staying off the grid, Simon hastily breaks into one of the abandoned cars. As we sit inside vehicle, I curiously take notice of my strangely reassured demeanor in the company of the vigilant Simon.

For at least twenty minutes, we sit in complete silence.

Continuing our dangerously exposed drive, Simon interrupts the quiet:

"I am left with no other options. We are headed to the only place that can help us; The Obedience Headquarters in Rome."

I am once again awestruck. The Obedience was the primary suspect in my father's death, not to mention the same conglomerate whose sole purpose is to hunt and kill Simon.

With obvious frustration, Simon clarifies; "It is clear now that these attacks are not the work of The Obedience nor were they orchestrated by Legion alone. It's him. *He's* back."

Now exhaustively used to the unique sensation of being outrageously baffled and unbearably confused, I query: "Who's back? Who is *he*?"

Our unanticipated and unlikely excursion into the headquarters of The Obedience is sizably reduced by yet another one of Simon's incredible accounts.

"I have withheld some of the truths behind Feeders, Ela. I have the distinct misfortune of knowing the true origination behind the man known as General Sebastian Diaz."

Perpetually attentive, Simon drives us to Rome with acute urgency. Brimming with cumbrous contrition, he divulges to me the startling story of Sebastian and the outrageous reality behind his sinister heritage.

19

"If one good deed in all my life I did,
I do repent it from my very soul."
-William Shakespeare, *Titus Andronicus*

JERUSALEM, ISRAEL
31 A.D.

Judas, the disciple synonymous with the ultimate betrayal of Jesus, was not actually Judas *Iscariot* but rather Judas *Sicariot*. An early translation of the Gospels was altered to hide his extreme background. The Sicarii from the Greek word "assassins" was a group of Judean fanatical nationalists. Judas might as well have been named "Judas the Terrorist." This secret society was mostly composed of militant radicals who believed strongly that the only good Roman was a dead Roman. The Sicarii, were notorious for brutally assassinating individuals in public by using a small, inconspicuous dagger. As they approached their target in a crowd, they would draw their ritualistic blade and repeatedly stab their target. Before the victim's body even hit the ground, the Sicarii would mysteriously vanish into the surrounding unsuspecting and utterly horrified crowd.

The specific rogue sect of fanatic Sicarii that Judas belonged to secretly followed a bizarrely jumbled combination of Jewish tradition, ancient Egyptian beliefs and a variety of assorted collections of pagan rituals. His twisted sect was an amalgamation, some say abomination, of the original fanatical group. Less Sicarii sect and more of a confused cult, they were a convoluted distortion of the already misguided group of wayward men turned overzealous assassins. A more accurate comparison of this organization would be to the rituals and practices of the modern day Free Masons but with psychotic participants. Fascinated by Egyptian myths and lore, they secretly studied and designed customs derived from both Judean customs and ancient Egyptian mysticism.

Being of Judean descent, Judas had already been a sort of outcast from the other disciples who were all Galilean. Judas always felt that he was never be entirely accepted by the disciples. Through his brothers in the Sicarii, he now had a legitimate network of kindred personalities. Judas had agreeably found a group of peers that unconditionally and wholly welcomed him regardless of his Judean heritage, satisfying his tottering need for acceptance.

Being one of the disciples and a close companion to Jesus, Judas was well aware of the detailed prophecies of Jesus and his sacrificial death. Judas was completely convinced that Jesus had to die in order for His spirit to be ultimately released from His earthly body. Being as perversely narcissistic as he was, Judas believed that he was destined to play the necessary role in the story of salvation. He actually believed that by betraying Jesus, he was bringing about the death of Jesus and therefore aiding in the salvation of all mankind. Profoundly misguided and utterly deranged, Judas actually believed that in time, he would be celebrated as a necessary participant in the redemption narrative.

On that fateful night in the Upper Room, the disciples watched as Jesus instituted the sacred act of Holy Communion. Not only did Judas watch as Jesus drank the wine and ate the bread, but he was actually given a piece of bread, by Jesus to directly single him out as His forthcoming betrayer. When Jesus handed it to Judas, he received it with reticent zeal; proudly accepting the gesture entirely disillusioned of the actual repercussions of his convoluted actions.

In his own polluted 'Gospel of Judas,' he perversely portrays himself as a privileged and favored friend of Jesus. He goes on to assert that afterwards, when they continued on to the Garden of Gethsemane, Jesus actually turned to Judas and said; 'Step away from the others and I will share with you the mysteries of the Kingdom. It is a great and boundless realm, which no eye of an angel has ever seen, no thought of the heart, has ever comprehended.'

After Jesus separated from His disciples to pray, He returned to them. Judas slowly approached Him. He looked directly into Judas' eyes and calmly uttered: 'Friend, do what you are here to do.'

Upon those momentous words, Jesus was immediately taken into the custody and later sentenced to death by the utmost barbarically tormenting form of execution, crucifixion.

Thoroughly delusional, Judas still genuinely believed he was a revered hero, for he had facilitated the liberating of Christ's divine spirit for the redemption of all mankind. When he was utterly ostracized and passionately vilified by his fellow disciples, he was genuinely confused. He pleaded with them that Jesus' body was a horrible prison for His heavenly spirit within. Imploring the other disciples, he argued that he was merely an instrument, an instrument wielded by the very hand of God Himself.

Realistically, he had accepted that he would have to sacrifice a segment of his reputation at first. Eventually, people would recognize that he was righteously fulfilling Jesus' own prophecy. However, he had never imagined the lengths of people's actual unadulterated disdain. Judas was instantly reviled and his actions were considered disgracefully heinous and unforgivably corrupt. With this solitary act, he went from holy apostle to pure incarnate evil! Just look at the Gospels, he grows increasingly more evil in each account. By the book of John, he is described as actually having the Devil inside of him.

From his fanatic devotion to the extremist cult to the

irreversible betrayal of Christ due to his incessant narcissism, Judas was undoubtedly a breeding ground for pure evil. His cultivation of violence, hatred and greed formed an unstoppable notion that he *deserved* something more than eternal enmity and scorn. A fraudulent God had used him and maliciously swindled him. Just like me, Judas was determined to become *the* irrefutable antagonist to God, the self-indulgent deity who fundamentally deserted him. More important than his own vindication, he wanted revenge against the God, the recipient of his misguided loyalty.

Just as my heart seethed with pure hatred; enough hatred to contest God himself, Judas similarly planned to counter God's will. He concocted a corrupt covenant designed solely to spit in the very face of God. Just like me, he sought to achieve an eternal life of heretical evil.

The first step in his gaining immortality was to kill his earthly form; delivering himself into the shadowy netherworld. Once there, he intended to make an arrangement with Osiris, the Egyptian god of death. In order to successfully navigate through the unknown realm of the dead, he would need a guide. This pagan escort would require some spiritual currency. The thirty silver pieces found below Judas' body have been dramatically misinterpreted throughout the ages. As greedy as he was, Judas definitely did not betray Jesus for the money. He was more narcissistic than anything else. Already the trusted treasurer of the disciples; he had access to an extensive repository far beyond a mere thirty pieces of silver. This was not an apologetic act of contrition, but rather this was an offering to a pagan guide to guarantee him a consultation with Osiris.

According to tradition, the wife of his brother Seth deceitfully betrayed Osiris. She had an unwavering hunger for both Osiris and causing controversy. Magically taking the form of Osiris' wife Isis, she seduced him; becoming pregnant with his child, Anubis. Outraged at his deceitful wife and insanely jealous of her attraction to his brother, Seth lured Osiris into a coffin and cast it into the river; attempting to drown him in the boggy depths. But Isis recovered her husband's body. Determined to destroying his brother, Seth once again captured Osiris and madly hacked his corpse into many pieces and then scattered them about the vast Egyptian desert. Isis spent multiple years searching for the pieces of her mutilated husband. Save one missing piece, she was ultimately successful. Ceremonially inscribing a pledge into a wall, Isis used her supernatural powers to bring Osiris back to life. The ancient Egyptians believed that inscribing an occurrence into a wall made that written action a substantive reality.

Like his exalted Egyptian demigods, he desperately coveted the ability to transform himself into various creatures. Comparing his own perceived betrayal to the legend of Osiris, Judas aspired to assume other forms just as Isis once did. Woven into his quasi Egyptian/Satanic dark oath, he crudely added his own distorted fragments of the Sacrament. He used 'the body' to aid in the fulfillment of his pledge. Upon consuming the human flesh, he would be granted the ability of unsanctified immortality.

Under the vivid light of a full moon, Judas arrived at a secluded field that all but guaranteed no one would disturb his evil irreverent enterprise. A particular portion of the field had the fragmented remains of a small stone wall into which Judas planned to diabolically carve his pagan pledge. Located just on the brink of a steep rock face overhanging a valley, this section of the desolate field contained a singular tree. This was the perfect spot to carry out his plan.

Equipped with the significant silver payment and the essential ceremonial Egyptian dagger to crudely engrave his pledge, he stood ready to initiate his vile institution. Commencing his carefully concocted deliverance into evil, he began to scrape and scratch the pledge into the stone structure adjacent to the now infamous hanging tree.

Since his twisted ritual also required the additional sacrifice and subsequent consumption of another individuals flesh, he had abducted the vestal daughter of the Chief Priest who had originally hired him. Bound and barely conscious, she laid powerless at his feet as he concluded his inscriptions. Reaching into the leather pouch at his side, he promptly withdrew five of the thirty silver coins. He strategically positioned the five coins into a small tight circle directly in front of him. Slowly turning he intently repeated the same action; dividing the remaining silver coins into five similar groupings. Placed down in precise equidistant positions, the 30 pieces of silver now entirely encompassed him and his helpless captive.

Rigidly taking hold of both his blade and his young prisoner, he dementedly he frantically began to carve into her feeble skin. Wildly slicing into her skin, she was now spoiled with hundreds of pagan symbols and polytheistic glyphs taken from the Egyptian book of the dead.

Staunchly grabbing her by the back of her hair, he madly hoisted her to her knees and violently jerked back her head. Slamming his open mouth into her exposed neck, his expanded jaws clamped down on the narrow supple extended side of her neck. Savagely tearing into her skin, he gruesomely proceeded until he hit bone. Her desecrated corpse and the surrounding scene were now fully soaked in blood. With his mouth brimming with flesh and blood, he slowly descended to his knees and began to chant his self-contrived immoral incantations.

After removing his blood-saturated cloak, he ripped it lengthwise; fashioning it into a rudimentary noose. Wrapping it around the thickest branch of the tree and placed the loop around his bloody head. Using the mutilated corpse as a step he lifted himself up and euphorically collapsed; propelling his falling figure downward. With a forceful wrench, he successfully hung himself. His lifeless body dangled and swayed from the tree atop the lofty precipice.

His plan worked; the unholy offering expedited his soul

directly into Hades. Though his spirit was delivered into hell, his earthly figure was temporarily suspended on this terrestrial plain. He made his deal and he was granted immortality and the ability to shapeshift. Everything went according to plan with one exception. With his tainted soul eternally exiled to the netherworld, even when he regained control of his earthly form, he would be forever lacking of any and all sensations facilitated by the soul. Upon returning to earth, he was granted immortality, but he was also cursed to an existence of absolute numbness. Devouring flesh not only necessary to his pledge, but it was the only way he could satisfy the voluminous void left by his absent soul.

Veiled by his armor of anonymity provided by his ability to shape-shift, he continued throughout history entirely unknown and unidentified. From simple face changes to entirely different forms; his incredible ability to transform himself into limitless amalgamations of both people and creatures alike is his indomitable assets. Because of this, my evil counterpart; my bastard of a brother has always managed to keep himself cloaked by an impressive cape of uncompromised secrecy. Lucratively shrouding himself in unconditional shadow, he has vilely ventured through the ages, stirring up as much death and devastation as he could wield.

His favored form happens to be that of the hyena. This nocturnal beast is notoriously vicious; exhibiting the deadliest attributes of canines and felines alike.

However impressive as his unique aptitude may be, he does have a weakness. Fortunately, a considerable amount of concentration and energy is necessary to fully transform his appearance. Because of this, he generally only manipulates smaller details of his face for extended periods of time. In order to maintain an extensively different form requires a severe abundance of both intense focus and plentiful strength. He can be a full on beast; but only for a limited amount of time.

Amusingly, even though he has the ability to shape-shift, Judas is unable to see anything but his original likeness when he looks into a mirror. It's remarkably peculiar; as narcissistic as he is, he absolutely detests his own reflection. Being a perpetual reminder of his mortal origins and ill-reputed past as Judas, he unreservedly loathes mirrors.

For over a thousand years, I was completely unaware of his existence. Like me, Judas has been responsible for an incredible amount death and turmoil for centuries. He has sculpted, influenced and hand crafted some of the world's cruelest warlords and criminals. And like me, he was able to maintain his anonymity simply by influencing and sometimes puppeteering corruptible individuals.

For centuries I was entirely unaware of his existence; that is until that fateful day he revealed himself to me in the early sixteenth century.

When I stormed into General Diaz's tent and he removed his helmet; I had a shocking revelation: Sebastian Diaz *was* actually Judas.

For centuries, he had known of my existence and secretly observed my activities. It seems his playful inclinations urged him to see how close he could actually get to me. But he never anticipated my conversion back to morality. From that moment on, we became dedicated adversaries from one century to the next.

My contemptuous immortal counterpart was the inciting mastermind of some of history's most despicable mass murderers. Jack the Ripper, H.H. Holmes and Luis 'The Beast' Garavito, he was their inspiration. Exponentially worse, he is behind such atrocities as Mao's 'Great Leap Forward' and most of the African Slave trade! His most recent pupil carried out one of the most reprehensible genocides of all time. Adolf Hitler is the self-proclaimed feather in his malignant cap. Judas watched with pride as his most accomplished student grotesquely mutilated and murdered millions of Jews during the

Holocaust. His unspeakable acts are overwhelmingly irreparable. At the time, I was useless to stop him. He had anticipated my every move and managed to slyly thwart my every attempt at stopping him. Using Hitler, he was incontestably closer than ever before to achieving mass human extinction through a global takeover.

In spite of the sick scope of the appalling atrocities enacted under Hitler's command, Judas' maniacal mission was fortunately left entirely unaccomplished. Though the unspeakable nature of the Nazi occupation seems supremely devastating; it was intended to be exponentially worse. Judas's unrealized master goal was the complete annihilation of the entire human population of the Earth. Hitler was only the second stage of an elaborate plot of planetary domination.

Directly after his failed attempt, Judas went into hiding. He even taunted me with a letter once that said 'he was finished with his miniscule and frivolous attempts.' Delving deep underground, he wrathfully vowed to focus all of his attention on developing what he referred to as his 'Apocalyptic Masterpiece Solution.'

If Judas is pulling Legion's strings, it seems that time has come. He would only resurface if he had something even more catastrophic up his sleeve. The immediate future could prove to be the most dangerous time in all of history. Only decades ago, he almost fully realized his attempt at earthly extinction; mankind will not survive another one of his dreadful schemes. I failed to kill him the last time; I am going to need all the help I can get.

Locked away deep inside of the catacombs of The Obedience headquarters are the possible means to combat whatever devilish plot he has devised. Along with a variety of rare and enigmatic texts, documents and scrolls is the legendary Gospel of Judas. These primary archives may hold the quintessential key to conclusively combating Judas' transcendent villainous plot.

The only way to bring the monster Judas down is by the hands of another monster. I *will* end this."

20

"And it shall be, if thou do at all forget the Lord thy God, and walk after other gods, and serve them, and worship them, I testify against you this day that ye shall surely perish."
-Deuteronomy 8:19

ROME, ITALY
PRESENT

Amidst the shivery chill of a crisp and cloudy Italian morning, Simon settles our vehicle directly outside of the scenic, façade of The Sanctum. Our already intense journey was teeming with even more urgency. Quickly exiting the car, Simon leads us past the striking exterior of the hotel and through the expansive vestibule. We hurriedly weave through multiple queues and scattered clumps of tourists. Remarkably, we charged past the mass of patrons with unassuming and ease. Once successfully passed through the hotel's resplendent entrance Simon actively navigated us through the building with various left and right turns. With our unremitting rush, we promptly propel down another ornate hallway. Advancing toward the absolute end of the lengthy corridor, it looked as if we were ultimately at an impasse. Though I began to slow my tentative gate as we approached the wall, an intrepid Simon steadfastly continued. Positioned at the end of the prolonged hallway was a petite pedestal topped with a multi-colored bouquet of fresh flowers next to a singular wooden armchair.

From my timidly lagging position, I watched as Simon oddly pawed at the wall next to the isolated seat. Reaching out, he dragged his fingers along the decorative molding and pressed down on a secretive lever beneath the piping. A secretive door is suddenly revealed; hidden amongst the decorative trim. As it slides open, Simon looks me in the eye and gestures for me to immediately step into the awaiting void.

Unnaturally accustomed to his bizarre resources, I faithfully crouch down and enter into the tenebrous tight expanse. Dutifully behind me, Simon quickly inserts himself into the compact area beside me. As he clears the entryway, the hidden entrance abruptly slams shut behind us. Rising to our feet, we stand face to face in a moment of stillness. Simon reaches just over my shoulder and with a forceful tug we are suddenly sent plummeting downward.

Briskly but controllably, we cascade down what appears to be Simon's crude makeshift lift. In an instant, the provisional shaft favorably drops us about ten to twelve meters. The unanticipated descent suddenly comes to a jarring halt, wrenching me compulsorily into Simon's sturdy stance.

Now motionless as the bottom of the rudimentary lift; in an extraordinarily rare tone of mischievous tonality, Simon sedately voices; 'Hold on."

My startled expression swiftly shifted to playful objection. A moving sense of relief washes over me at the sight of Simon's subtle display whimsy. Continuing into the darkened bleakness, Simon leads us from the lift and into a cold, clammy but much larger room. Looking at the raw unfinished walls surrounding us, I assume we are inside of the catacombs far beneath the hotel. Within these subterranean chambers is The Sanctum. This, the ethereal headquarters of The Obedience, is surreptitiously positioned just underneath the city of Rome. With his undisclosed secretive passage and the help of a covert member, he has maintained unrestricted access to The Sanctum and the invaluable archives preserved inside.

Nimbly walking through the coarse corridor, Simon leads us to yet another undisclosed doorway. Just as he reaches out to unlock the furtive portal, he twists his head around and earnestly states; "Just stay calm and follow me."

Pushing through the hidden gateway, he securely grabs my hand and takes a firm hold of me. Stepping through the entryway, I am taken by absolute surprise at the encompassing gathering of about fifteen men at the ready before us. Both the men's stares and semiautomatic guns are firmly fixed upon us. These are the renowned members of The Obedience and they have been anticipating our arrival into their restricted station. Just before we had reached Rome, Simon delivered an urgent and compelling text to Prior James. The communiqué's requested a temporarily truce between them in order to have a necessary consultation regarding the fate of the world. The director had granted his bizarre appointment; temporarily welcoming Simon into the heart of the organization sworn to kill him.

Astonishingly tense beyond words, the strained standoff subsists at an indefinite impasse. Haltingly lifting his arms into the air in submissive deference, Simon subtly interrupts the stiffly silent stalemate. In response, the tautly trembling men take one short step closer to our position. Undoubtedly intimidated by the flagrant face to face with their venerable rival, the members stand fast with heightened anticipation. With his arms held high into the anxiety-filled air, Simon asserts; "Gentlemen, as charming as they may be, we do not have time for these pleasantries."

His audience of Obedience abides in tongue-tied stationary rigidity. Their guns fixed no more than a meter or two away from his head, a steadfastly confident Simon serenely continues; "I'm afraid we have a much larger problem well beyond our incompatible past. *Judas* has returned."

Drastically more startling than ever anticipated, his daunting revelation visibly wallops the men to their core. Flush with guarded uncertainty, every member looks over to their peer in abysmal dismay. I can only assume, from the mum-stricken men, that they recognized the grave gravity of this new intelligence. Clearly affected and concerned with Simon's claim, they keep their guns pointed at the both of us. We remain stagnantly suspended in the stalemate.

With stern conviction, Simon resolutely demands; "This is significantly more important than either of us. You of all men know the obscene magnitude of his sadistic capabilities. I need access to the archives: I have no other play here."

Standing directly in the middle of the group of Obedience members is Prior James. As all of the members look to their general for an order, Prior James firmly clenches his jaw in strained contemplation. The other members persist in their standoff as Simon continues his appeal.

"None of us can afford him the opportunity to finish what he started in Germany. I deserve every unimaginable evil Hell has to offer me, James, but I have vowed to take him and every last one of those bastards with me. Please, we can't dismiss this pressing possibility."

Preceding a broad lingering inhalation, Prior James swiftly lowers his side arm and places it back into his shoulder holster.

While maintaining his deadpan scowl exactly fixed upon Simons similar solid glare, James addresses his anxiously anticipating men with an unenthusiastic order; "Take him to the archives."

With a humble nod of appreciation, Simon sincerely adds; "She stays with me."

Prior James responds with curt strictness; "Remember your place, Lazarus. Do not mistake my charity for weakness. No one outside of The Obedience has ever been permitted into the archives."

Simon obstinately demands with unflinching sincerity; "She does not leave my side."

Retorting with his stiff-necked trepidation; "Tread carefully, Lazarus. These are the same men who have devoted their entire lives to destroying you. Proceed with profound discretion... both of you."

With a meager dip of his head, Simon responds; "Certainly" as we cautiously carry on past the group of desisting men.

Studiously escorted by four members of The Obedience, we hurry down the subterranean corridors of the Sanctum and into the all-important archives. The first two men, Jacob and Marcus, are bizarrely indecipherable. Though certainly not identical, with same height, light complexion and similar facial features, the fellows are distractingly similar in almost every way. The inexpressive clones were even crowned with the same brown hair, the same flat dusty brown like their suits. Their resemblance is truly detracting.

Our two other intent attendants are John, Simon's insider and Matthew, the prominently junior member of the secretive syndicate. Both outfitted with the customary Obedience attire, young Matthew's slightly oversized uniform only served to accentuate his greenness. The ill-fitting suit merely enhanced his already awkwardly youthfully demeanor. The four men promptly lead us further into the dusky cold quarters.

Lodged into the expansive stone arches of the cavernous chamber is The Sanctum's monumental library. Just beyond the thick transparent walls are some of the most rare artifacts and unique historical documents of all time. Standing in front of the sheer secure entryway, we impatiently wait for one of the still hesitant men to let us inside. Under obvious protest, one of the members grudgingly unlocks the sealed gate, granting us access to the exclusive collections.

Rushing past our resentful chaperones, Simon navigates us directly to a particular grouping of seasoned texts and scrolls. Arranged amongst a variety of plinths and rows of voluminous shelves crammed with ancient artifacts, is the object of Simon's increasing concern, the Gospel of Judas.

On an ornate pedestal before us lies the archaic and considerably controversial account of Judas. Advantageously adjacent to the podium resides the accumulation of ancient Egyptian texts affiliated with the infamously secretive Sicarii sect that he had belonged to. Without delay, Simon rapidly but quite delicately sifts through the piles of privileged documents. Page after page, he rifles through the texts in hopes of uncovering any information that could explain Judas' intentions. Intently consumed by the variety of documents in front of him, Simon urges me to bring him the metallic binder from off of the shelf behind me.

Presented with the bulky file, he immediately begins hurling through the pages. He finally settles on a page that is saturated with sketches of assorted symbols and characters. Placing his finger directly atop one of the coarsely rendered illustrations, he blurts out; "This same exact symbol appears multiple times inside of the Egyptian Book of the Dead."

Gesturing to a neighboring vintage photograph, he intensely continues his thought; "This is the inside of an ancient Sicarii dwelling. The walls are completely covered with identical characters. These are the same exact symbols used by Judas in his pledge. These characters were the key to his immortality; they could also be the key to his demise. These symbols are what gave him his power; could they be used to take them away?"

I curiously interject, "What has been bothering me is how Judas was able to make a deal with Osiris? If there is only one true God, who did he make a covenant with?"

Simon turns to me with a concertedly responds; "Any pledge not made to God himself, the devil, my dear, is always happy to indulge."

With a sullen brow he continues; "There are only two things Judas has ever truly been afraid of; the thirty ceremonial silver pieces and the infamous Spear of Longinus. The silver he has displaced long ago due to its crucial role in his ritual. Even if I could recover even one piece; I've never been sure of how I could actually use it to destroy him. The Spear, he has been after the Spear for centuries. I have concluded that its alleged retention of the actual blood of Christ could somehow be an actual liability to his oath of blood. These objects could possibly be the only way of reversing his covenant."

"Judas has always been a complex duality of over-confidence and abundant paranoia. Whenever someone discovers a new religious relic related to the crucifixion, Judas is completely consumed by it. Fortunately, it seems that his scrupulous searches have disappointingly left him with only more questions and curiosities than actual answers."

I interject; "The Spear of Longinus is in Vienna, Austria, no?"

I additionally respond with swelling discouragement; "Wouldn't it be impossible to find the actual silver from over 2,000 years ago!"

"I'm not certain when or where, but the silver is permanently hidden away. We are never going to find it. The Spear however, has proven to be a bit more complicated for him. For at least the last 700 years, he has been actively seeking the Spear with increasing fervor. Over the centuries, there have been a number of relics claiming to be *the* actual Spear of Longinus. With every discovery of yet another alleged Spear, it became increasingly difficult to distinguish the authentic Spear from the insurmountable amount of meticulous forgeries. Currently there are at least four locations claiming to possess the genuine Spear. Vienna, Krakow, Armenia and the Vatican all publicly house a purported version of the Spear. But there is one other. An arms dealer in Spain, Alejandro Salazar, is rumored to have another potentially genuine spear."

Turning to Matthew and John our attending escorts, Simon authoritatively suggests; "I would start there; closely monitor all five of those locations."

Simon proceeds with concerned diligence as the abutting men utilize the archive's impressively progressive digital database.

"Centuries ago, I suspected he had positively identified one of these five spears to be the genuine Spear, but he curiously left it where it was. I think Judas knows which one of them is real and rather ingeniously he purposely left the real Spear in the one of the virtually impregnable strongholds. Until he could find a way to completely destroy it; the real Spear would remain safest where it already was."

As Simon details Judas's uncompromising dedication to preserving his immortality, Matthew and John make use of The Sanctum's state of the art computer network and feverishly scan locations and key words related to Simon's broad suppositions. Surprised by an immediate result, John hastily blurts out; "Authorities in Spain are currently responding to an attack on Alejandro Salazar's compound! It appears it has been entirely incinerated!"

With bright astonishment, his eyes rapidly jolt from side to side while he continues to read on: "It appears to have been entirely incinerated; there doesn't seem to be any survivors."

"He was after The Spear!" Simon powerfully pronounces.

"Undoubtedly he has something up his sleeve, but what? There must be a reason for him to..."

Just at that very moment Matthew, the seemingly unseasoned member of The Obedience awkwardly interrupts Simon and astutely articulates; "He may have found a way to permanently destroy it."

The abashed member soberly looks Simon in the eyes while he persistently continues to vigorously tap at his computer keyboard.

Struck with obvious intrigue Simon reacts; "What did you have in mind, kid?"

Spiritedly plunking away at his computer, Matthew continues: "Theoretically, he could use current developments in advanced molecular technologies in order to obliterate them. You it said yourself, 'wipe them out from existence'... that's why... *this* is why."

Turning the monitor toward Simon, he humbly presents us with a top-secret document from a government database. He points directly to the documents subject that read; 'Anti-Matter Weapon: Final Stage.'

The unlikely assemblage of Simon and Obedience Member's stand eerily awe. The implications of this innovative but possibly cataclysmic discovery are pestilential at best. Amidst this silence, Matthew frantically fills the multiple monitors in front of us with a variety of governmental documents heralding the same declaration. Ardently scanning the screens, he studiously researches every facility doing that sort of research.

Suddenly, I have a revelation. Enthusiastically intent on contributing, I voice; "Years ago, I vaguely remember my father researching something allegedly related to The Spear. Specifically, I remember him saying that he was overwhelmed by the gross amount of outrageous rumors and narratives that accompanied it."

"I can't be sure, but I think my father believed a little-known rumor that a nail used in the crucifixion was actually rooted inside of the authentic Spear of Longinus. Hitler, being obsessed with the occult, after he acquired it, had a both a small fragment of the Spear's tip and a tiny portion of the nail removed and secretly implanted into a necklace. Specifically hanging near his heart, he wanted to forevermore have a part of the power-wielding object with him at all times. They say he never took the chain off. He truly believed this would grant him the mystical omnipotent power he so desperately craved. Even if the Spear was taken from him, he would always retain a small portion."

Member John carelessly interjects; "What happened to the necklace? Did your father have it? Did he know where it is?"

"After Hitler's death, the seemingly innocuous necklace was thought to have disappeared. About fifteen years ago, my father was absolutely convinced he had found it. Somehow the necklace had found its way into the hands of an eccentric millionaire that later passed away. Utterly oblivious to its bawdy history, the bank sold it at an auction. My father bought it for next to nothing and immediately joined it with the rest of his personal collection of rare and questionable finds."

Perpetually anxious John blurts; "What *did* he do with them?"

Continuing in negligible annoyance I proceeded; "Whenever he had obtained a sensitive piece such as this, he discreetly tucked them away; temporarily hidden until other evidence could be collected. Unequivocally dedicated to the sanctity of the church, my father always kept any controversial artifacts a total secret. These delicate matters could unjustly and unnecessarily alter history and the reputation of the holy church.

His controversial collectables were always securely hidden away. No one, including myself, ever knew where he stowed these disputable items."

Briefly, I hesitate, promptly reflecting on my own words. I am suddenly stricken with a shocking realization: my mother's locket!

Reaching into my shirt, I retrieve my mother's pendant. I gingerly swing the aged hinges open and delicately begin to peel back the tiny picture of me; revealing an auspiciously diminutive metallic fleck. Stricken with intimidating disbelief I bafflingly utter; "*This* is where he hid it; my mother's locket."

We are all momentarily stupefied in far-fetched astonishment.

Shattering the tension filled moment of wonderment, Simon emphatically ascertains; "If that truly contains either a piece of the Spear or nail, or even the tiniest drop of Jesus' blood; we may be able to use it to carve a new curse that could reverse his pledge of flesh."

Suspended in his provocative postulation, Simon optimistically adds; "Ela, that little artifact could very well be the key to destroying Judas."

Likewise, Matthew and John now anxiously aroused with ardent enthusiasm, present the group with their possible leads to finding Judas.

Young Matthew proudly displays his newest results, declaring;

"Geneva... Batrava...Berkley."

Matthew rapidly dispatches across the conglomeration of screens the three possible locations. Immediately, we all review the data, eager to uncover a hint to Judas' whereabouts. In seconds, Matthew has another possible lead.

An impassioned Matthew recites aloud, the conceivably promising report. "From the CIA's database; here is a story of a team at Berkley, who currently has the definitive and groundbreaking research on anti-matter."

Upon the hectic retrieval of this most recent revelation, Matthew brusquely carries on. "It seems their research has yielded the most significant advances in anti-matter; but has remained highly classified because of its possible weapons applications."

Echoing with dejection, John queries; "You think he is actually planning on obliterating the Spear?"

Simon severely responds, "The Spear, along with any other questionable artifact. Judas intends to eventually erase anything capable of challenging his immortality. If they are indeed this close to manufacturing anti-matter; God help us."

Faithfully optimistic Matthew uneasily scratches his forehead and heartily injects, "I think I know where it is!"

We all keenly turn our attention to the enthusiastic Matthew.

"Even though none of these documents mention a location; they all have this same grouping of numbers somewhere on the page. These numbers looked very familiar to me. The Obedience used this same code a long time ago, to transmit a location. The numbers are basically coordinates; Dirac Field in the Sierra Mountains!"

"Then we can't waste any time, he is going to use it soon." Simon retorts with hell-bent conviction.

"We need to get to California discreetly and as quickly as possible."

With staunch devotion, Simon readily insists; "I think I know just the person to get us there."

Simon takes my hand and initiates our hasty retreat from The Sanctum. As we impetuously sprint away from the Matthew and John, Simon yells back in obstinate potency, "I *will* stop him, by any means necessary. You do what you must; but he must not succeed."

This forcefully dynamic exclamation echoes throughout the hallowed corridors of The Sanctum as we rapidly ascend back atop the congested and unsuspecting streets of Rome.

21

"There are moments when even to the sober eye of
reason, the world of our sad humanity may
assume the semblance Hell."
-Edgar Allan Poe

SONORA, CALIFORNIA
PRESENT

Following the remarkably constructive consultation with
The Obedience that led to an unlikely fellowship between
an immortal and the band of immortal hunters, Simon
immediately phoned his contact in the aeronautics industry. From
what I can gather, this veiled acquaintance seems to be military mogul
with a significant position inside of a government aerospace company.
Through use of the infamous and somehow confidentially unretired
Concorde; at supersonic speed, we are deposited only minutes from
our destination in California.

In addition to the use of the high-speed passenger transport,
we were advantageously supplied with our ground transportation
in the form of a high-performance motorcycle. Upon landing we
hurriedly race to our awaiting carriage. The onyx Ducati motorcycle
serves as our succeeding carrier to our ensuing objective in Sonora.
While handing me a helmet, Simon assures me; "Just hold on tight."

He has been my intrepid guardian so far; hesitation never

even crossed my mind. Slipping the helmet on, I tightly constricted my arms around Simon as he revved the bike's robust engine. In a flash we are propelled toward our destination.

Directly east of Berkley, California just outside the city of Sonora, is a vast expanse of mountainous desert known as Dirac Field. Set on the edge of the Sierra National Forrest, Dirac Field is owned and operated by the University of California, Berkley. It has been used as a scholastic playground for the University's unconventional science department. Immersed below Dirac Field is situated the Dirac Anti-Matter Device. The particle accelerator turned anti-particle creator is the revolutionary result of a top-secret collaboration between the University and the U.S. military. According to those classified reports, the device can make actually make anti-matter. Once produced; this anti-matter should be able to entirely eliminate normal matter therefore truly obliterating the object and wiping it from existence.

Because of this colossal advancement in what used to be only theoretical technology, Simon's sincerest belief is that with the help of the Dirac Device, Judas now has the ability to permanently protect his unholy pledge. If the device works, Judas will undoubtedly use it to nullify any religious relic that threatens his immortal existence. Simon is thoroughly convinced that Judas not only has the authentic Spear of Destiny but that he has also somehow reassembled his precious pieces of silver. By destroying his collection of ceremonial artifacts using their exact opposites and subsequently canceling each other out; he makes any attempt to reverse his vile vow altogether non-existent.

At an outrageous speed, we arrive at the official outer and ostensibly commonplace gates of Dirac Field.

Abandoning the bike, we approach the edge of the perimeter. Peering through the openings of the excessively tall fence, Simon focuses his scouting gaze on the field's surprisingly nominal security. The perimeter guards, though more than adequately armed, appear to be simple humans. Once again, I recognize Simon ascertaining the scent of both Bleeders and Feeders. Accompanying the immortals' foul pheromones however, is the distant but distinct trail of Judas himself.

Simon guardedly advances us closer to the gate. Taking a robust pull from his flask, he advises me to remain where we stand. As I attentively stand stationary, Simon swiftly swings into action. Leaping forward, he turbulently smashes into six of the guards; fluently overpowers the six with ease. With one forward gusting movement of his sufficient batons, he renders the men entirely incapacitated.

Rapidly rolling onward and rising back to his feet, looking back with a firm brow and a slight nod, Simon signals me to follow. I confidently stride to his side. Swiveling his neck from side to side; intensively scanning the grounds, he takes another swallow of blood. His eyes are lock and focus on a single steel doorway in front of us. That is the gateway to the Dirac Device stationed deep below us.

Dexterously unfastening the sealed entryway, Simon instantly gains us access into the surprisingly stunted lobby of the machine's elevator shaft. Immediately the warm California air turns stagnantly cool as we cross the threshold into the corridor. The simple square space is uniquely void of décor. Rudimentary bare, this silvery brushed steel box simply housed the lift that led to the deep caverns below the Sierra Mountains.

Taking his customary lead, Simon punches the solitary button. As the steel doors slide open, we boldly step into the cold restricted lift. Without hesitation Simon pushes the "down" button, propelling us downward at a rapid but stable rate. During our descent my considerable concern swells as the chill in the air increases. Under the pressure of our sudden declination, my ears grow increasingly disagreeable. As we plunge downward, I widen my mouth and repeatedly wiggle my jaw from side to side in hopes of relieving the accumulating pressure.

Along with my ears, I also take notice of the peculiar decline of anxiety. My uneasiness of our impending engagement with

Judas is considerably less substantial than expected. Though we are hastily advancing toward an ominous encounter with the infamously iniquitous Judas, at this moment in time Simon is absolutely the only person in the world that I trust.

With a minor bump, we gradually slow down to a subtle stop. Upon our cessation, the satiny doors slide back open. Just as our new surroundings are revealed, Simon defensively steps directly in front of me. Looking over his shoulder, he looks me steadfastly in the eyes and then progresses us into the surprisingly unsophisticated passageway. We are obviously not just heading for the device, but we are headed straight toward an abhorrently large assemblage of immortals.

The slender hallway stretches roughly thirty meters out and the flat grey walls slightly bow to the left; signaling we are in a tiny segment of a gigantic circle. Just above our heads is a network of metal tubes and wiry pipelines that stretch the entirety of the prolonged hallway. Continuing to the end of the arched corridor, another singular doorway begins to come into view. Still too far away to distinguish what it is; there appears to be a something on the floor just in front of the impending entryway. As we cautiously walk closer, the bodies of two guards sharply come into focus. It seems Simon's intuition is proving to be rather spot on. Remaining steadfastly in front of me, Simon continues us toward the blue painted door. Just beyond the two bodies and past the lead door is the Dirac Device's primary chamber.

Pushing past the guards, as approach the entryway, the door is suddenly swung wide open. Out of the entrance emerges a riotous faction of Bleeders and Feeders. Rushing toward the two of us, the obnoxious band of brutes roars and shrieks with the rawness of feral beasts.

Procuring his swords out from his lengthy coat, Simon brashly bolts directly into the aggressive mass. Voraciously commanding his blades, he nimbly begins disposing of them. Slashing through flailing figures and hacking off fluttering limbs, Simon solidly slaughtered the seven beasts in mere seconds. Customarily authoritative, he waves the sign of the cross above as the bodies reduce to piles of debris.

As the grisly ash recedes, I return to my post at Simon's back. With a fluid twirl, he tucks one of his blades back inside of his flowing jacket, while clenching the other cutlass with intense acuity.

Briefly paused in observant contemplation Simon reveals, "It is safe to say that Judas is well aware of our presence."

Accompanying his innate discernment of distinctive aromatic essences he adds; "There are at least twenty or maybe even thirty more."

With a stunted sniff he adds, "*He* is on the other side."

Upon taking a generous swig of blood, Simon securely clutches my hand and crosses past the threshold and into the tremendously vast chamber that is the control room of the Dirac Device.

Well over eight stories tall, the immense expanse is lined from floor to ceiling with an intricate web of soaring scaffolding and spiring staircases. We seem to be in the middle of the fifth floor, overlooking the center of the colossally broadly expansive room. Weaving wires and bundles of blinking lights are littered across the voluminous area. Straight ahead of us looks to be the huge octagonal nucleus of the high-tech facility. I am entirely awestruck from the magnitude of this oversized machine. Bulging bulky ducts protrude from the eight corners of the titanic opening. The massive ductwork bends back into the center of the contraption. The stunningly prodigious centerpiece is made up of shimmery silver and burnished copper colored components.

Oddly indifferent with our arrival, Judas' henchmen drone around the mechanical apparatus before us; suspiciously they ignore our very presence. Interspersed about the various levels and assorted avenues of the chamber, the Bleeders and Feeders seem unconcerned with our appearance. The lecherous group simply carries on; bustling about the lofty platforms with intensive ambition.

Their inexplicably inattentive reactions make me nauseous. Like a weighty stone, my heart sinks deep into pit of my stomach. This all feels wrong.

Thankfully, as usual Simon endured in rock solid certainty.

Suddenly, a boisterous voice from somewhere below us bellows; "My prodigal brother has returned. I was beginning to think the two of you would never arrive."

At that very moment, a high-reaching red crane steadily hoists up an encased platform. Confidently standing atop the uplifting stage is a slender, bearded man with an intensely deranged look on his face. From the telling proclamation, I can only assume this swaggering braggart is Judas.

The up-surging crane comes to a slow and steady halt, placing Judas directly in front of the two of us. Suspended over five stories, he now stands face to face with his sworn archenemy. One meter is all that divides the two legendary rivals. The two heated adversaries maintain a stalwart stare-down, fiercely fixated on each other's unflinching gaze. The level of intensity was already palpable, but this aggressively tense encounter was a frighteningly still but oddly dynamic silent impasse.

Confident in my capable benefactor, Simon; I stand completely puzzled as to why Judas and his loathsome lackeys aren't rapidly charging us? The utter lack of an assault is truly troublesome. The stiff and stress filled seconds feel like an eternity. Is it possible Judas has the upper hand?

Breaking the stubborn impasse, Judas blares out; "Welcome. Welcome to the realized consummation of my perfect eternity."

Turning his profoundly maniacal glance toward me; "Why Angel, you are even more ravishing in person." He divulges with a perverted wink of his eye.

"You are just in time to witness the concluding procedures

that will unconditionally guarantee my irreversible perpetuity."

As Judas smugly utters the conceited remarks, multiple monsters suddenly seeped down from the landing above. We are similarly flanked by another cluster of henchmen. Both Bleeders and Feeders alike, the crowd of immortals stood at least thirty of forty strong; all of them characteristically tinted the transparent tinge of alabaster and donning some shade of black. Dangling precariously above our heads, a particularly obnoxious and upside down Bleeder audaciously slithers closer and coarsely hisses in Simon's seething face.

"I have already obliterated my silver along with the extensive collection of spears; liberating, to say the least. All that remains is the eradication of true Spear of Longinus. Before I destroy you, both of you will be witness to the unmitigated assurance of my life everlasting."

Judas mockingly mutters while grimly grimacing emphatically into Simon's ready stance; "Like my faithful little pet, you Simon, have unknowingly retrieved for me the imperative article to achieving this illustrious reinstitution."

"Pet? You're the miserable dog, remember." Simon responds with downright disdain.

Marginally irritated, Judas responds in a frisky tone; "Hyena, actually... but thank you all the same for that sentiment, brother."

Judas abruptly stretches out his arm and reaches out to me.

Immediately, Simon initiates a spirited motion of protective retaliation, but Judas has already fiercely taken hold of my throat. Securely seizing my esophagus in his sturdy grip; his threatening action is enough to impede Simon's impending response. Frightened more than ever before, I struggle to take a breath. Simon stands utterly still; calmly incensed and fuming with animosity. During his reluctant halt, the blanched immortals frenziedly converged upon him. Snarling and grunting, the advancing immortals suddenly extend and fix their various guns and blades toward Simon.

214

Judas' hold, though deliberately not lethal, is gradually getting tighter.

"No, no, no; not so fast!" Judas gratingly giggles, languidly waving his finger in the air. Unexpectedly, he releases his hold. With a sharp snap, the delicate chain of my locket breaks as Judas' tightly clasped fist retreats. The fragmented necklace plummets five stories down to the chamber floor as Judas holds the antique heirloom in his hand.

It was obvious Judas knew the only recently discovered contents of my mother's locket. How in God's name did he know?

Dismally perplexed, I look to Simon for his proficient reassurance. Sword securely in hand, Simon and his incessant vigilance still stand at the ready. My only recourse is my utmost dependence in my cleverly capable bodyguard to deliver us from yet another ominous set of circumstances.

Judas beams down with gross gratification at the newly obtained object in his hand. Absolutely appeased, he howls out to his subservient minion; "Monkey, my boy, regale me with your boundless brilliance; initiate the appropriate sequences."

Devotedly standing at what can only be the primary control panel of the anti-matter mechanism five stories below us is Monkey. With a jittery nod and stumbling finger gestures, Monkey tawdrily replies to his commanding supervisor; "Won't be a minute, sir."

Perseveringly rooted in his defensive stance and surrounded by degenerates, Simon remains deathly still. His eyes meticulously survey the entirety of the situation while Judas is gradually carried away and lowered by the retracting crane. While that rotten ringmaster recedes down towards his devoted Monkey, he wails out to the serpentine soldiers that surround us; "Snuff out the whore and bring Lazarus to me!"

Judas looks up into Simon's eyes and ferociously articulates; "I am going to rip out that damn bleeding heart of yours for good!"

In the blink of an eye, as the cretins close in to finish us off, I notice an acute change in Simon's manner. Suddenly, he was emitting pure indignation like I had never seen before.

Impossibly accelerated, Simon snatches the suspended assailant from above while simultaneously slicing through the other encroaching beasts. His swift movements are virtually imperceptible as he hurls the dangling Bleeder downward while unrestrainedly whirling his swords. In an indistinct blur, Simon scourges every one of the immortals in our immediate vicinity. In an instant, the substantial swarm of brutes is diminished to a fraction of its original breadth. His dazzling display of indescribable dexterity is far beyond any previous exhibition of his incredible capabilities.

Guilelessly, I maintain my still position, utterly unqualified to respond. There had always been an air of calm and rigor to Simon's technique, but his current conduct is dramatically more primeval and quite vicious. At the conclusion of his ritualistic diminishing of the immortals bested remains, Simon swiftly hooks his arm around my hips; attentively tucking me close to his frame. Spontaneously, he vaults from the platform; springing us away from the lofty terrace we quickly cascade down toward the chamber floor away from the remaining mass of onrushing combatants.

Under Simon's complete control, we prudently land on the inflexible cement, entirely unscathed. Visibly vexed, my provoked protector expeditiously flings a set of throwing knives upward. The hurling projectiles thwack deeply into a set of narrow pipes suspended above the remaining horde of Bleeders and Feeders. His missile-like knives penetrate the pipes, spewing out a puff of grayish gas that engulfs the mob in a cloud of vapor. One of the Feeders foolishly fires off a round amidst the fog; instantly igniting the swamping gas. The explosion discharges the remaining troops off of the lofty level. The blast propels them out into the capacious center of the room.

As their seared bodies are shot across the room, Simon

vigorously leaps toward the flailing figures. In fascinating disbelief I watch him soar through the air and steeply slice the toppling bodies. In a dazzling display of aerial acrobatics and fastidious maneuvers, Simon rapidly beheads the charred figures as they rain down from above. Thud after thud, burnt bodies and sizzling heads crash all around. Simon swoops back down; already chanting his recitation. As he forcefully lands on the floor, the butchered carcasses abruptly dissolve in swirling puffs of odious debris. Simon cautiously lands only a short distance from me, bearing a curious cast of contemplative concern.

All at once, I feel a dank and balmy breath huffing against the back of my neck. It doesn't take me long to realize what has Simon so tensely preoccupied. The muggy respiration sourly saturates the nape of my neck just as a hand grabs hold of my waist. Spellbound at the vociferous proceedings, I failed to realize that Judas had managed to once again get his paws on me.

As troubling as Simon's hauntingly hesitant gaze is it is not nearly as distressing as Judas' rotten embrace. His uncomfortably oppressive arm gathers me further into his enveloping embrace, while his other hand slowly undulates over my throat. Like a vicious vice, he progressively compresses my windpipe into his taut grip.

With crumbling corpses dissolving all around us, Simon glares at Judas with exasperating enmity.

Visually struck with exceptionally umbrage, Simon stands with both blades; anxiously anticipating Judas' next move.

As I ineffectively writhe and struggle, Judas takes notice of a minor laceration on my cheek from the explosion. He tightens his dastardly grasp of my trachea as I desperately gasp for air. Heaving me even closer to his body, he shamelessly uses me as a human shield. My hysterical breaths seem increasingly futile. Judas yanks my head backward; stiffly peer up at him, his sodden breath oozes across my face. I wheeze as his impure exhalation slowly seeps above my skin.

217

Vulgarly sticking out his tongue, he grotesquely slides it against my cheek. With swelling discomfort and fright, I stand powerless as he nauseatingly skims his tongue against the bleeding wound and drags it across my cheek. With an uncharacteristic unsettling look of defeat, Simon looks on in woeful vulnerability. Still firmly grasping my neck, Judas releases the hold on my waist and slowly raises his hand to my weeping face. Dipping his fingers into the now oozing laceration, he makes another streak; macabrely smearing a perversely primitive inverted cross across my terrified cheek.

Utterly petrified; I can't help but anticipate the worst; Judas is going to kill me!

Although he had just relinquished dozens of immortals with relative ease, it was painfully obvious Judas' deft abilities where of tremendous concern to Simon. Though undeniably strengthening his overall resolve, his previous encounters with Judas had clearly left him slightly and uncharacteristically insecure. His tentatively calculating watch could only be a result of an intimate knowledge of Judas. Unrelenting and without principle, Judas' deathly apt capabilities made him Simon's ultimately formidable opponent.

After completing the sick crimson cross on my face, Judas satirically shrieks out; "What was it that *He* so eloquently said; 'It is finished?'"

Unexpectedly, Judas lets loose of his lethally compact grasp of my neck and releases me. Taking an immensely imperative breath in; tears stream down my battered face as air rushes into my grateful lungs.

Simon instantly responds; promptly sprinting to my position. Without hesitation, Judas reinstates his hold; sturdily snagging me by the back of my hair. Simon instantly comes to a halt as Judas forcibly bends my neck backwards. With an unscrupulously tone of excessive self-gratification, Judas coerces me to look up at his crass expression and daintily whispers in my ear; "Goodnight, my sweet, sweet Angel."

Entirely debilitated, I feebly shudder with scathing disgust and promptly spit in his fetid face.

Unfazed, he retorts; "Shall I seal it with a kiss?"

I am slightly lifted off the floor as he violently snaps my head back even further. Upon that last wrenching jerk, I cry out "Simon!"

Thereafter hearing my desperately despondent plea, Judas pounds his open mouth into the outstretched side of my exposed neck. I can distinctly discern the excruciating sensations of his gnashing teeth inside of me. Grisly gnawing his fangs deeper into my shredded neck, he torturously takes an agonizingly plentiful bite. With a smugly satiated smirk, he spits out the hefty chunk of flesh as I slump to the ground. Judas neglectfully kicks me to the side as I sluggishly sag to the floor. My blood spills out like a pool all around me. Saturated by warmth; motionless against the cold chamber floor, I feel both my consciousness slipping away.

"You and your women!" Judas says with a smirk.

Venomously snarling out to a progressively infuriated Simon, he adds; "Weep for your ravishing graceful gash, brother...weep!"

Vehemently appalled by Judas' grotesquely baleful actions, Simon unleashes a growl that rattles throughout the vast compartment. No longer bound by Judas' hold on me, he savagely dashes directly toward his murderous adversary. Judas nimbly avoids a collision by spryly sliding to the side; successfully avoiding his aggressor.

Progressively weakened by a severe loss of blood, I endure in scarce consciousness. In a haze, I lay witness to the unimaginable interactions of the inhumanly potent enemies.

Cowardly springing away from Simon, Judas scampers toward the opposite corner of the vast chamber. Simon gives chase. In his brisk pursuit of Judas, Simon scoops up an abandoned machine gun and promptly emits a barrage of bullets toward Monkey sending showers of sparks bursting from the operational panel. The controls are destroyed, but Monkey disappears under the cover of the flaring explosions.

Momentarily distracted by the percussive eruptions, Simon is unexpectedly struck by a substantial kick to his back. Inexplicably taking Simon by surprise, Judas began to deliver a multitude of ruthless punches; momentarily causing him to actually struggle. With another stout kick to the side, Judas brings Simon all the way down to the ground. Joyously dominant, Judas stands triumphantly above him. Simon begins to torturously crawl across the floor, but the assuredly victorious Judas kicks him repeatedly; keeping him on his knees. With coarse confidence, Judas exclaims; "My dear Lazarus, you haven't the vaguest concept of the amusing festivities I actually have in store, do you?"

Woefully gory, Simon strains to stand up as Judas delivers another mighty blow directly to his temple. This stiff fisted punch sends Simon right back to the ground. Supremely confident in his capabilities, Judas yells out; "And if you don't know what I have arranged, brother... then how the hell would you even attempt to stop me?"

I watch in agonizing defeat as a wobbly and bloodied Simon receives another sequence of debilitating punches. Judas blaringly decries; "I wasn't *going* to kill you, Lazarus. What kind of fun would it be without you? But I admit, seeing you, my lingering rival, reduced to this pathetic pulp... it will be worth it! Unlike my glorious life eternal, this too must come to an end. *You,* my dear brother, have come to an end."

Commandingly poised over Simon, Judas hoists his foot above his thrashed face and looking down at his bested mark; Judas crashes down his heel upon Simon's cheek. But, just as the thick stomp is delivered, a resounding roar erupts from the nethermost depths of Simon's unremitting lungs. Incomparably provoked, a sudden surge of sheer irrepressible rage gives him the resilient ability to suddenly retaliate! Before Judas can stomp on his face, Simon swings his arm upward and sharply stabs Judas with a metal shard from the recent explosions. The slivery fragment sinks soundly into Judas, penetrating deep into the upper portion of his cavalierly exposed inner thigh. This reprisal allows Simon to escape from Judas' prevailing restraint.

Simon rises back to his feet; reclaiming his providential authority. Righteously roused, he is swiftly face to face with Judas.

Briskly responding to the unthinkable retort, Judas rapidly sprints away from his clearly rejuvenated rival. Desperate, he fastidiously flees to distance himself from his volatile foe. As Judas attempts to escape, Simon swiftly hurls a trio of golf ball sized projectiles skillfully at Judas' legs. Judas may be fast, but it would seem Simon is still faster. The string of round weighted weapons wildly winds and wraps around his retreating feet. In mid-scramble, Judas uncontrollably flops forward and crashes down to the callous concrete.

Recognizing that Judas would only be momentarily stalled from the fall, Simon immediately produces yet another precarious instrument from the inside of his jacket. Wielding a thin chain-linked line like a whip, Simon snares the barbed line around Judas' neck, spiraling around his collar like a virulent leash. With a snappy tug, Simon further tightens the barbed band.

The thorny chain is actually garnished with tiny crosses, ruins and other religious charm-like tokens. The more Judas writhes and thrashes, the further the collar contracts; cutting deeper into his shredded neck. Simon continues to produce even more similarly suppressive weaponry to completely subdue his chronic opponent.

Simon quickly peppers Judas' body with a swift succession of five slender throwing knives. The sleek, cross-handled blades powerfully pierce him: one in each hand, one in his outstretched right arm, and one through each ankle. Tearing into his flesh they drill through his body and pin him to the floor.

Judas flails and jerks in a futile attempt to free himself

as Simon expeditiously approaches his harshly bloodied captive. Outwardly satisfied that he has detained his elusive enemy, Simon ambles toward a pile of debris. Picking up a lengthy fragment of pipe left over from the blasts, Simon marches to Judas' side. Utterly unhinged, Judas looks up toward Simon with infuriated frustration. In order to guarantee his unabridged subjugation, Simon contemptuously plunges the pipe into Judas' chest; through his restrained frame and deep into the concrete below.

Distracted by Simon's miraculous revival from a seemingly inevitable defeat, I am quickly reminded of my own grim condition. Shivering uncontrollably, I realize the certainty of my dire situation. I can feel the life steadily seeping out of my body. At this, the upsetting moment of my passing, I looked up toward Simon, my fervent protector and began to breathe the last of my breaths. Simon turned around from his conquering position over Judas and my weary eyes tightly locked with his disquieted stare. He instantly recognizes my dying demeanor. Saturated in bleak severity, Simon mournfully watches as I helplessly succumb to the unsparing grip of death.

Suddenly I felt nothing and in another instant, my surroundings fade from blurry dim, to unqualified black. Upon watching the extinguishing expression flushed from my withering face, Simon is despondently furious. Strenuously clenching his fuming fists, Simon looks fiercely back to Judas and releases a deafening roar that assuredly reached both Heaven and Hell.

Entirely subdued by the firmly fixed lance through his body, a derisive Judas saucily convulses with uproarious laughter. Grinning from ear to ear, he begins to madly giggle with peculiar flippancy. Though overcome with curious amusement, he maintains an incessantly intense stare into Simon's enraged eyes.

Rigorously responding to his sniggering hostile, Simon vehemently swears; "You are a vile fiend; I *will* permanently eradicate you from this world!"

Wallowing in disturbing delight, Judas continues to gush with baffling glee.

With a spritz of blood and saliva spraying from his enraged lips, Simon continues to articulate with exceptionally censuring disdain; "Good, then you can properly occupy your vacancy in hell."

Enmeshed in thorny twine, impaled by a protruding pipe and infused with a multitude of miniature metallic cross-handled stakes, a fully detained Judas exclaims in a soft but stern tone; "Be still and know that I am *he* Lazarus. I am the boogieman, the monster and the wicked witch! I *am* the permanent reminder of your failures and your decadent past! I am eternal."

A rambunctious gasping laugh exits his simpering mouth as his maimed and hampered body becomes perfectly still. Solitarily poised in contemplative sentiment, Simon stands reticent over both of the motionless figures. Though temporarily tranquil and ritually controlled, Judas was far from vanquished.

22

"Where then is my hope—who can see any hope
for me? Will it go down to the gates of death?
Will we descend together into the dust?"
-Job 7:15

SONORA, CALIFORNIA
PRESENT

A midst the ragged rubble of what used to be the Dirac Device,
Simon despondently reflects upon the grave chain of events.
Lamenting the provisional care and supervision of his detained
adversary Judas, he stands stationary in hushed in meditation. Arms
firmly crossed, he woefully observes two members of The Obedience
as they tend to Ela's lifeless body; mournfully watching as her
previously angelic form is carried off. Now entirely in the care of the
newly collaborating members of The Obedience, her inanimate corpse
is prudently placed into a chalky black bag. With the slow slide of the
bag's zipper, Jacob and Marcus solemnly haul her corpse away.

As the two oddly kindred members carry her toward the
chambers exit, they cross paths with their Brother John. With a
reverent look of doleful regard, John looks down to her departing
corpse. Gravely approaching him, he comes to a halt just behind
Simon's steadfast and contemplative stance.

"The Vault has held our own for centuries; we are honored to have her laid to rest there."

Without a word, Simon persevered in static rumination.

With earnest solemnity, John states. "I have taken the liberty and already started adjusting her activities and whereabouts for the last couple of days. You have temporarily convinced the Brothers of your 'righteous intent.' For now, they have agreed to take full possession of Judas until a permanent solution is devised. We have an impermeable chamber at The Elysium that can temporarily contain him."

Chuckling with mild amusement, John inserts; "It was built to hold *you*."

Simon remains dolefully unresponsive.

"I still don't understand why we just can't cut off his head. You will find a way to destroy him; we *will* find a resolution."

Slightly nodding while bitterly maintaining his brooding focus, Simon lingers on in absolute silence.

Suppressed by a massive casket-shaped transparent vessel, Judas is uprightly suspended in chilling serenity. Deprived of blood, flesh and any other form of sick sustenance, the technically advanced clear crate has been uniquely constructed to suitably house the unholy. The enclosure is fashioned from an impenetrable resin set into a frame built from an advanced compound that is one of the lightest and most durable materials in existence. Molded into each side of this see-through sarcophagus are a variety of crosses, ruins, and other ancient religious symbols. Each of these signs effectively confines Judas, temporarily imprisoning him until they can devise a suitable way to altogether obliterate him.

Like a recession of pallbearers, eight members of The Obedience escort Judas' case. Transported out of the sunken chamber and brought up to the surface, he is hoisted into the back of spacious black semi trailer. Using its hydraulic ramp, the eight men elevate and then solidly secure the high-tech casket into the eighteen-wheeler.

Once it is soundly suspended and meticulously fastened inside, the men take their seated positions along each side of the case.

Upon competently purging the area of any evidence of the immortals and their epic encounter, the Obedience members begin their journey to their safest of retreats: The Elysium. Opportunely located on American soil, this secluded sanctuary is furtively situated amongst the field of factories in the industrial district of South Chicago.

Uncharted, unmarked and entirely unknown to the government or the public, The Elysium is The Obedience's state of the art detainment facility. It has confidentially and securely housed some of the most nefarious immortals of all time. Discreetly hidden in plain sight among the cities manufacturing region, the advanced shelter should sufficiently harbor Judas for a while. Using the utmost spiritually progressive and experimental technologies, Judas' new residence will be a cold and impermeable chamber located in the centermost area of the fortified facility. He will be tightly guarded and closely monitored by no less than ten Obedience members at any given time. Even though the facility is entirely comprised of the foremost innovative applied sciences and other supernatural and religious accoutrements, there is absolutely no conclusive method known that would eradicate Judas with absolute certainty. In short, everything Simon has used to combat him up to now has been merely theoretical spiritual speculation. Judas' schemes have been thwarted before, but remarkably he has never been successfully caught. Now that they actually have him; Simon and The Obedience are not leaving anything to chance.

"We could definitely use you as additional security on the way to Chicago. Once we reach The Elysium, he will be firmly positioned into the hold. There he will remain entirely incapacitated until we can produce the proper method of expulsion." John says with persuasive determination.

Simon replies with anguished conviction; "I'll escort you to The Elysium; once he is inside; I'm off. I *will* find the means. I just need some time."

"Don't blame yourself, Lazarus." John responds. "Judas and only Judas, is responsible for her death and all of this. Do not burden yourself. You already have your own cross to bear. In due time you will be held accountable, but for now, our only and mutual task is him."

Simon pressingly withdraws from the vastly marred chamber.

John adds with staunch understanding; "Do what you must, Lazarus."

As he vacates the scene, Simon sternly articulates, "I will discover a viable way to destroy him."

"Go with God, brother." John responds with a low toned whisper of rooted concern.

Nearly reaching the chamber's exit, with his back to John, Simon sensitively divulges; "Centuries of all of this; she was the only person who has genuinely made me feel human again. Her death *is* on me. God should be with innocents like her, not wasting His time on beasts me."

Simon turns to face John and soberly imparts; "I have a retreat directly north of here; deep in the woods, just across the US/Canadian border. It is completely secluded and it should be the perfect place for me to pray and meditate on how to displace him. Until then, you and your men just keep him out-of-commission. His reign of terror is over; this all ends now."

Simon walks out with inflexible conviction.

23

"Solitude sometimes is best society."
-John Milton, *Paradise Lost*

SOUTH CHICAGO, ILLINOIS
PRESENT

S truggling to control his shaking bloody fingers, John frantically fumbles his mobile, in an urgent attempt to contact Simon. It has only been a couple of days since Judas was securely confined inside of the ultra-fortified Elysium. In hopes of surmising a means to finally eradicate his infernal enemy, Simon isolated himself somewhere in the depths of the Canadian wilderness. This self-quarantine also provided him proper time to ponder Ela's tragic death. Conclusively isolated, Simon only intended to reflect, pray and meditate. Though predominantly off the grid, he still maintained a singular mode of communication. This exclusive mobile is only known to The Obedience and is designated only to be used in cases of severe emergencies regarding Judas.

Desperate, John phones the emergency line and leaves a panicked message. With his voice quivering with obvious trepidation he grimly exclaims; "Elysium has fallen! The Sanctuary is no more. The deceiver has escaped! *He* is at large."

Somehow, though proficiently restrained within the professedly impenetrable confines of The Elysium, Judas managed to escape. The fortified refuge of The Obedience has been annihilated.

The highly secretive facility had to have been infiltrated from within. Twenty-two bodies of Obedience members are buried underneath the distressing remain; Auspiciously, John was the only one who survived the incursion.

After leaving the burning dispatch for Simon, John concealed himself discreetly inside of a ramshackle building adjacent to the scattered remains of The Elysium. The familiar sonority of distant sirens drawing near gets unmistakably louder. Not entirely unscathed and snuggly folded inside of the abandoned garage, John must somehow wait for Simon to respond while conjointly avoiding the inevitable authorities. The Elysium was not only skillfully stationed far below its industrial exterior but it was also fully equipped with a self-destruct button. In reaction to the unlikely event of an unauthorized breech, a collection of multiple detonations would appropriately seal off the Elysium's secretive chambers. This emergency implosion mandate would securely blockade entomb the chambers; guaranteeing they remain undiscovered. In order to not draw widespread attention of Chicago's finest, the controlled implosions would have to extensively bury the Elysium while appearing entirely accidental and not of any immediate grave threat to the surrounding structures.

Even with the lack of any gigantic blast or blustering explosion, there was still enough of a commotion to capture the attention of some of the local law enforcement. John watched from his concealed position as the police furiously scampered about to determine the cause of the disturbance and seemingly innocuous collapse. In a matter of hours, the assemblage of emergency vehicles and first responders that had charged in were already parading back out. Given the non-lethal ruin of abandoned buildings, the fire department quickly concluded their preliminary investigation. Except for a few routine patrols for safety, everyone had essentially deserted the area.

Diligently, John watched as the dwindling responders dissipated into an insignificant collection of amateur security guards and out of shape patrolmen; essentially babysitters with guns.

John is startled by the familiar inflection of the quietly convergent Simon. "I need to evaluate the wreckage; take me to into the chamber."

Outwardly jounced, John turns and refreshingly greets his anticipated colleague.

Without delay, Simon sternly queries, "How is it you are the only one to survive?"

Still shaken, John responds with overcast reprieve; "It was an ambush. I don't know how, but I barely escaped. It was a goddamn bloodbath."

Invariably rigid but clearly concerned Simon suggests, "We'll find him."

With that, he promptly leads John to the other side of the greasy garage. Crimped in the corner of the deserted carport is a drainage grate that connects to the city's sewer system. Well below the surface, the system of tunnels could covertly deliver them into the sunken remnants of The Elysium.

Bending down, Simon lifts up the barred grate then pauses. He has detected a familiar essence. Beyond the smoldering soot and burnt devastation was the incontrovertible foul stench of none other than Legion.

Retrieving a flashlight from the inside of his flowing coat, Simon turns it on and directs the beam downward into the dim darkness. Without delay, he proceeds to remove the beefy drain covering. After discarding the grate, he jumps into the drain; dropping directly into the dingy cavern. Staunchly following his confederate, John leaps into the aperture. Lacking the benefit of a proper flashlight, John fetches an old metallic cigarette lighter from his trouser pocket for a bit more luminance. Bustling through the recessed brick channels that connected to the entombed Elysium, the two quickly arrive at the structures only contingency entrance. Both men progress through the dismantled interior of The Elysium. Simon's excessively sharpened faculties hone in on Legion's distinguishable aroma and he persists into the innermost cavity of what used to be the unassailable containment facility.

Traipsing through the scattered remnants of the former stronghold, Simon muddles around with profound concentration in devout eagerness to uncover where the collection of demons is hiding.

Accelerating through the devastation and dredging through the voluminous rubble, Simon instantly comes to a stop. Looking down to the littered floor, he realizes he has reached his target. Rearing both his head and his flashlight upward, Simon evaluates the condition of his attained objective, Legion.

Lagging only a few steps behind, John quickly reconvenes with Simon. Standing directly behind Simon, John stretches out his curious neck in the hopes of catching a glimpse of what has Simon so captivated. John abruptly covers his nose and mouth with his hand as the rank smell of wasting flowers and fetid feces smacks into his senses. As Simon's bright beam of light surveys the scene. John is taken aback by the unexpected spectacle before them.

Hanging in the murky corner of the subterranean system, is Legion, remarkably restrained inside of his newest bulky figure. Secured to the upper corner of the disheveled room, once again, he is occupying the body of a young, muscular and heavily inked black man. Recognizably weakened, Legion has been somehow actually been rendered entirely powerless. Not only has he been thoroughly wrapped in cumbrous chains, but also there are two "x's" charred over his eye sockets. Taking a closer look, his eyes have been completely seared shut; branded in the shape of an inverted crosses. His enervated arms have been twisted and fastened around a horizontally suspended rusted iron pipe. He has been manacled and bound with lumbering chains and thoroughly tethered to the corner of the slimy sewer ceiling. With his strapping arms outstretched in the recognizable pose of the crucifixion, Legion is suspended directly above them in the corner of the room. Additionally subdued by a variety of crosses and crucifixes, he is also secured by a multitude of razor sharp wire firmly wrapped about his struggling human form. The squalid band of demons is decidedly at bay and what can only be described as a spiritual straightjacket.

Simon glares contemptuously at the repressed faction of hellions as Legion insufficiently struggles in vain. Slashed and crippled by the ritualistic restraints, his lacerated body drips with rich red blood and mud colored sweat. Glossy from slime and smothered in grit, Legion lets out a blustery gnarl, savagely growling at Simon. With a disdain-filled snarl, he haughtily spits in their direction. Visibly anemic and entirely abated, Legion still tussles in a futile attempt to free himself. Every losing outburst movements only further the depth and perforation of his array of spiritual restraints. The filthy blood and greasy secretions continue to trickle from his impaired body.

With irrefutable contempt and a sort of binding revelry, Simon looks back to John and commands; "Go. Contact the remaining brothers and report everything that has happened. Don't worry about him; he's not going anywhere."

With a fidgety nod of affirmation, John turns around. With the flittering faint glow of his lighter he carefully retraces his steps backwards; rapidly withdrawing from the polluted passageways. As the flickering of his flame diminishes, Simon turns his attention back to the subjugated collection of spirits.

"Oh, Lazarus; 're-born again brother of the dark' Lazarus; you're not still trying to worm your way back into *His* good graces, are you?"

"You're a pathetic wretch. You have to admit; this isn't exactly your style. Tell me Legion, what did he promise you?"

Legion pallidly grins and stridently utters, "Your prized turncoat, Lazarus...where, did he go? He is a fraud; he is just as tainted and impure as the rest of us. All of your beloved sheep and treasured little maggots, they are all susceptible."

With an exuberant chuckle he continues; "Even *you* can be deceived."

"Are you suggesting that John's extraction was staged?" Simon responds with burning inquiry.

"Did we not tell you that you had no idea of what was really going on? You gullible ninny twit; we agreed to free that immortal degenerate Judas. The entire incursion was an elaborate scheme!"

In an excessively sarcastic tone, Legion continues, "You don't actually believe that John 'barely managed to get free; narrowly escaping the massacre.' It was your very own Benedict Arnold who let us in. Now he has betrayed you too, Lazarus."

Legions gleeful cast soon turned profoundly bitter. "However, once we freed him, Judas immediately double-crossed us. First he infected this body with his deadly concoction; then he imprisoned us inside of this reprehensible flesh suit using some sort of reverse-exorcism."

Legion continues, "We all hold you in unqualified eternal contempt, but, Judas is on the threshold of realizing his consummate dominion. Billions of mortals will be destroyed and he will become an everlasting omnipotent demigod."

Legion's compulsion for revenge against Judas ultimately moves him to fully divulge his comprehensive covert plan to Simon.

Legion elaborates; "Your bastard brother has been a busy little bee. He has been cultivating his magisterial ruse of a planetary epidemic. Judas is behind the development of the Human Vaccination. The poison that courses through these veins is the very same solution that will soon be injected into most of the world's population!"

Only recently developed, the universally celebrated Human Vaccination HV is the celebrated serum believed to be the first ever-universal vaccine. The incredible immunizer was expected to drastically improve the state of the world's prevalent infectious position. HV is said to have been conclusively proven to eradicate a number of deadly diseases and fatal viruses. Miraculously able to kill off most strains of both HIV and Ebola; it has also been shown to assist in the weakening of certain cancer cells in only a matter of 2-5 years after initial injection. Due to a recent increase in fatal outbreaks around the world, most everyone has been anxiously anticipating the revolutionary preventative pharmaceutical. Already hailed as a success, it has become the highest priority of countless world leaders.

Discovered entirely by accident while attempting to develop a highly resistant antibody for grains, HV originally derived from the DNA of jellyfish. Only when it was advantageously combined with another component originally developed to combat Alzheimer's, did it prove to be such a remarkably effective vaccination. Developing it into a complex treatment, similar to an influenza vaccine, it delivers a formulation of four strains of viruses into the subject. Acting like a Trojan horse, the virus carries the HV directly to the infected cells. This incredible remedy was now the predominant focus of the United Nations. Along with the U.N., various other humanitarian organizations spanning the globe have collaboratively concentrated all of their efforts to this one laudable advancement in human health. This quickly developed but amazingly efficient vaccination may in fact be capable of halting the world's current deadly outbreaks. In tandem with a worldwide census, the Human Vaccine will soon be available and willingly welcomed by nearly 75% of the world's population.

Still ineptly squirming about, Legion sorely snarls with wronged disdain; "Judas injected me with that disgusting slop."

Simon sarcastically adds with a bitter beam; "Oh, come now Legion. Certainly you cannot be spooked by something as minor as a simple serum?"

"You still don't get it, do you? You really don't have a clue, do you? HV isn't a 'Human Vaccine.' Quite the opposite, HV actually stands for the 'Herod Vaccination. ' Judas is finally going to bring about his own 'flood-like' annihilation; his sadistic solution. In their feeble attempts to stay alive, millions upon millions of your pathetic puppets will perish."

"That is impossible, even for Judas. There would be hundreds of hurdles during the testing phases alone. That alone is enough to question its fulfillment." Simon states with challenging disbelief.

"You overestimate your humans, Lazarus. In retrospect, Germany was far too complicated. Why work harder, when you can work smarter."

Seething inside of his ensnaring restraints, Legion gasps and petulantly continues; "The test subjects chosen for the later stages of the human trials were simply secretly turned *after* they were injected. Once they were injected with immortal blood, the subjects were cured of any and all mortal diseases; so simple, yet so perfect. And you'll love this; over the last couple of years, his lap dog Monkey even embedded sequences of imperceptible subliminal messages into digital downloads in order to guarantee the worlds unconditional compliance. Your dumb little susceptible mammals were so easily encouraged to not only approve the drug, but willingly accept and receive the inoculation. Your cattle unknowingly welcomed their own extermination with open arms."

Riled and squirming inside his unremitting restraints, Legion tirelessly continues; "After this exquisite apocalyptic masterpiece, Judas plans to hand-pick certain individuals he deems necessary to his new world of magnificent carnage and unadulterated anarchy. Some mortals for battle and some mortals for cattle; those are the few little piggies that he has apportioned to survive."

"You are telling me all of this because you are upset with Judas because you made a deal with him and now he has forsaken you."

Simon snickers with sarcastic amusement.

"No honor amongst thieves. You understand the irony, don't

you? You are genuinely surprised that *Judas* betrayed you."

Spitting and squirming Legion yells; "Damn the backstabbing rat and curse his impish minions! To Hell with you and your deplorable quest for absolution; may flames engulf the kingdom of God and obscure the light of His mercy and grace to all of its inhabitants."

With viscous drool dangling from his bottom lip, Legion boorishly belts out; "I am my own god! Damnation and chaos upon you and your little pigs; your beloved cattle. But all of this fulfilled in the exalted name of Legion, Lucifer, Beelzebub and eternal sin-soaked darkness; not in the traitorous name of Judas!"

As Lazarus composedly observes the miserable moans of a lamenting Legion, he gently places his flashlight down on the cold moist ground; leaning it against the slimy brick wall. The propped up light dramatically illuminates the scene with an upward glowing beam. Slowly stepping closer to the sequestered faction of fiendish spirits, Simon stares directly into Legions emerald bloodshot eyes and rigidly utters; "And so you shall reap what you have sown. All of you will be punished as much as your deeds deserve."

Glancing over his shoulder, Simon swivels his head from side to side, looking around he jestingly says; "Well, there doesn't seem to be a herd of pigs around; that only leaves one other place."

Simon continues with derisive contempt; "I command you, unclean spirits; obey my words. I, an unworthy minister of God cast you out, In the name of God who flung you headlong from the heights of heaven and into the depths of hell. No longer shall you be emboldened to harm the human bodies you inhabit. Be gone, you hostile scamps of Satan, be gone!"

As Legion tosses in agonizing desperation, Simon gradually elevates his hand up to the twisting demon's face. Outstretching two of his fingers, Simon gestures the sign of the cross. Legion frailly laughs with dwindling gusto. Drawing his hand back to his face, Simon places his two fingers against his own mouth and firmly presses them against his lips. Then, he forcefully depresses his fingertips deep into Legion's twitching forehead. Turbulently jerking, the tormented form before him squeals in unsubtle anguish. Upon this moistened touch, Legion's skin instantly sizzles. The rebellious demons shriek with excruciating vexation as the body smolders uncontrollably.

Precisely dragging his fingers against Legions forehead, he meticulously gestures the holy sign of the cross once again. As the suffering band of demons wail in toilsome discomfort, a stream of stringy smoke fizzes from his searing cross-shaped head wound. With impassioned conviction, Simon calmly closes his eyes; he earnestly whispers; "In nomine Patris, et filii, et spiritus sancti."

Upon these words, Legion's captive form vehemently tenses every one of his considerable muscles and strains into a tightly stiff state. The gushing smoke emanating from his now bubbling forehead is now dispersed around the entirety of his figure. The crazed collection of frenzied demonic wraiths, cry out in earsplitting agony. A multitude of deafening shrieks echo throughout the subterranean shaft as the body is entirely engulfed in lucid phosphorescent bursts of sparking green flames. In a flash of light and puffs of murky smoke, Legion has been properly cast into the igneous abyss of Hell.

Simon stands entirely alone inside of the clammy recessed chamber that resides amid the ruins of what once was The Elysium.

24

*"Or if I send a pestilence into that land,
and pour out my fury upon it in blood,
to cut off from it man and beast:"*
-Ezekiel 14:19

STEIN, SWITZERLAND
PRESENT

A blinding sun set into a cloudless sky of brilliant blue is not exactly what I would consider the perfect conditions for a stealthy attack; but, with less than ten hours to work with, there is no time waste. I am paused at the base of a soaring security fence capped with spiraling barbed wire and an elaborate compilation of heat sensors and multiple motion detectors. The state of the art fortification safeguards a network of buildings run by Pharchemtech, the primary producer of the 'Human' Vaccine. This is not only their main production lab but their warehouse also currently contains their largest supply of HV. I am taking a brief moment to clear my mind before I begin my 'not so discreet' incursion. Over the last couple of days, I have gone around destroying every auxiliary HV supply station. This, the main production facility, should be all that remains. I need all of my concentration because in a moment; all hell is going to break loose.

Once Legion divulged Judas' cataclysmic intentions and the

truth behind HV, I finally had the pleasure of relocating him back to the fiery depths of hell. Though I should have relished the long overdue act of his expulsion, the impending weight of Judas and his madly monolithic scheme overshadowed the entire occasion.

Only a few decades ago, Judas had come closer to accomplishing his quest for worldwide extermination than ever before. Undoubtedly, if afforded the occasion, that miscreant will most certainly try again and the mankind would never survive another one of his attempts.

Following Legions abolition, I immediately contacted every last resource at my disposal that could aid in locating every last supply of HV. As I waited in tense anticipation; I finally caught a break. I received a report from a former pharmaceutical engineer turned chemical weapons advisor. The anonymous company that won the bid to produce, facilitate and distribute the Human Vaccine, was the actually the company UniCorp. Auspiciously, the Swiss based company has only one primary production facility. To maintain anonymity, UniCorp's secretive HV headquarters and chief production laboratory were cloaked under the fake name, "Pharchemtech." Pharchemtech was outwardly just an innocuous manufacturer of an anti-anxiety medication.

Fortunately, HV has only just recently been approved and is still only in its earliest stages of production. The main facility would not be distributing an actual shipment until at least seventy-two hours from now. But unfortunately, some small batches of HV have already been distributed. In response to the latest outbreaks, the worldwide test phases were interrupted and a meager amount of the virus was doled out to a small amount of clinics across the globe. The locations were so desperate for any hope of containment, that the U.N. unanimously approved the temporary use of the drug but only specifically in those extremely dire locations. The intense security of the facilities was due in part from the increasing demand of the life-saving treatment, but also in direct response to threats from both terrorist organizations and anti-drug groups that had been exceedingly vocal against the distribution of a Human Vaccination.

With the ultrasonic aircraft once again at my disposal, I was able to make the nearly impossible jaunts necessary to destroy the auxiliary locales, in an incredibly small window of time. I swiftly traveled from the outskirts of London to the edges of Africa. By the grace of God I was able to successfully annihilate every outlying location. There was no time or need for stealth and subtlety. Heaping allocations of petrol and flame were basically all that was necessary. Since these lesser centers were considerably smaller and therefore had limited security in place, I effectively destroyed them with relative ease. Within hours of each other, all of the lesser HV holding sites were completely leveled. By the time news of the first explosion could be reported and subsequently associated to the others, I had already arrived here, my final target.

Luckily, the advanced detection systems guarding Pharchemtech's perimeter are easily bypassed from my lack of a normal human temperature. Though the building itself is quite immense, it should promptly surrender to the rather liberal amount of explosives at my side. Not just any explosives; my own particular mixture of plastic explosives were certain to bring the tyrannical drug giant down. Every terrible ounce of the Herod Virus must be devoured by flame.

As of now, the sentinel headcount concernedly stands at only twelve men strong; all of which are human. Curiously, there are no Bleeders or Feeders to speak of. That is rather odd considering the significance of this facility.

My wait for the proper moment had arrived; I quickly hurdle the fence. In moments, the guards unknowingly position themselves in perfect position for my assault. Springing forward, the twelve unsuspecting sentinels yielded promptly to my less than lethal batons. Now, the only remaining resistance was just beyond the main entrance. Ripping through the glistening glass doors I am utterly bewildered at the sight before me. The spacious lobby of the multi-billion dollar drug company is unexpectedly deserted. There isn't a single individual in sight.

A weighty sense of uncertainty washes over me from the sight of the perplexingly vacant surroundings. Suspicious, I proceed with caution. Why was the exterior sufficiently guarded if the inner workings of the HV headquarters were entirely barren?

Pressing past the airy and pretentiously ornamental lobby I progress onto the service lift that delivers me down to the lowest level. The integral infrastructure was the optimum region to plant my explosives. The doors slide open and I distribute my munitions in unsettling isolation. There still remains the suspicious lack of any other individuals. Sweeping across the sizable substructure, from pylon to pylon, I rapidly apportion out the charges. In a matter of minutes, the last of the Herod Virus will be totally incinerated.

Just at the location of my final rigging sat a shocking discovery. Fastened to the concrete pillar was a tablet; above it was a note that read "Play me!"

Deliberately placed in the logical methodical appointment of my crowning explosive, the taunting tablet lay paused. I am promptly flooded with inundated with furious mortification. Pressing down on the screen; the broadcast reveals Judas self-assuredly sitting comfortably behind a lavish desk. He begins to confidently explain his truly damnable cataclysmic intentions.

"My dear brother Lazarus, welcome to the era of my enmity. I applaud your valiant efforts brother, but truth be told you are conclusively out of your element; you never stood a chance of preventing my beautiful virus from being delivered. This was all part of my plan. I know you even better than you know yourself. I anticipated your every move and response to what you thought was my plan. Those trivial locations you crushed were all decoys. The actual production labs have been masterfully hidden; I assure you, they are perfectly intact and ready to distribute my virus!"

Judas haughtily chuckles with devilish glee.

"I am the nameless faceless network of unprecedented degradation and carnage. Destroying this tiny structure is entirely inconsequential and insignificant, just like you.

"The world and all of God's creatures will involuntarily submit to me. Some with their very lives and some with their will, but all will surrender their virtue to me. The world as you know it, has expired and gasped its last pitiful breath. As the cities decay and the highways and towers melt from neglect... my new empire will blossom. I, along with those who I have deemed worthy, will survive. Not only survive, but thrive and flourish.

"I will turn his perfect little planet into a deplorable den of unfathomable despair. The previous boundaries of depravity will be immeasurably shattered. Tormenting the pure, ravaging the righteous and blissfully smiting the innocent will be the worlds' new anthem. The soft skulls of innocent children will be smashed against stones while their mothers are violated to unspeakable measures. As every one of his chosen ones burn, I will look on with not just glorious indifference, but sheer satisfaction. I think Picasso said it best; 'Every act of creation is first an act of destruction.' Or maybe Alice Cooper said it best; 'Welcome to my nightmare.'"

Abundantly confident I am unquestionably incapable of thwarting his ambitious plot, he insolently delivers an invitation; disclosing the location of his enigmatic lair.

"My dear blood-brother, I know that you will predictably feel your obligatory need to try and stop me. Like continuing to claw at a mosquito bite until it's rendered painfully raw and sloppy with blood or like a child habitually wiggling at a loosened tooth I find myself utterly unable to resist our immortal union. That piercing, pleasing sensation that oozes over you: that is what forever bonds us together.

I will make it easy on you. Here I am. I will be waiting for you."

Just as Judas articulates his final contention, the camera slowly pans to the right. It briefly scans across what looks to be a sparsely lit cityscape under the cover of night. As the lens struggles to regain focus, the hazy camera zooms closer to a confined faint figure. The dim lights of the background are just not enough to distinguish who the figure is. Just as the blurry camera seems to resume focus, it jarringly swings to the right; tightly zooming in on what looks to be a giant skull. Once focused, the camera retracts from the massive skull and reveals the location in its entirety. Like the simulated rock habitats inside of zoos, the massive skull is part of the castle-like edifice of a pirate themed building. Behind the decorative façade, is a soaring iron tower that resembles a lesser version of the Eiffel Tower. Once again, the camera concentrates on the indistinguishable figure being held captive in front of these decorative buildings. Sharply, the blurred individual is deliberately brought into focus; to my consummate trepidation, it is Ela.

Now knowing her fate had been worse than death; I was utterly devastated.

Just like a disgusting dog to purposely turn one of his virtuous victims into a Feeder simply to spit in my face. I can only assume that sometime during our encounter at the Dirac enclosure, he waited for me to be distracted and turned her sometime before he seemingly killed her. He must have suspended her conversion because I had watched over her lifeless body until The Obedience took it away. When he escaped, he had to have taken her with him.

He *is* a shameless bastard. As the exclusive exporter of immortals, he set this all up so that I would be the one that would have to kill her. He obviously reveled in the hopes of watching me contend with the loss of yet another cherished woman in my lingeringly penitent life.

As the message abruptly concluded with the paused image of

Ela's new immortal face, I ruminated in introspective quietude. Void of any emotion; she displayed the familiar signs of a weakened Feeder; one weak from not yet feeding on human flesh.

Impossibly infuriated by this additional display of sadistic maliciousness, I was left with no other choice other than to accept his invitation. I know it's a trap, but no matter what sort of sick subterfuge he has prepared, from the location on the video, I know exactly where to find him. I took a vow to rid the world of every single immortal; I meant to keep my pledge.

25

*"What the caterpillar calls the end of the world
the master calls a butterfly."*
-Richard Bach

BLACKPOOL, ENGLAND
PRESENT

After viewing Judas' derisive message, I apprehensively accepted his invitation and proceeded to the imparted venue. The excessively theatrical backdrop made it unmistakably clear of where he was. The seaside town of Blackpool is England's own version of Las Vegas. Flashy and flamboyant, its one giant extravagant tourist attraction; Blackpool is perfectly appropriate for someone as melodramatic as Judas. Though overtly suspicious by design, I remained unconditionally compelled to acquiesce to Judas' brash supplication. For centuries now, that mongrel has always persisted one step ahead of me. By my hand and my deed, Judas and his deplorable ascendancy to world subjugation have come to an end. The stage was set and the conclusion of our epic struggle was at hand. It was time to deliver that duplicitous dog into the hands of the devil himself; only then will his rotten reign of terror be over.

As I approach the kitschy scene, I am astonished by the utter lack of any activity. The customary raucously bustling and ornamentally illuminated town is bizarrely silent and remarkably dark. The usual lively hurried herds of scampering people, even at this time of the evening have given way to a haunting hush. Only the occasional faint police siren or auto horn breaches the mostly monotonous dull hum. Roving closer to the carnival town, I notice it has been extensively barricaded and plastered with signs that all read: "Temporarily closed for renovations." Immediately upon reading the notice, the radiant lights of the town's colossal Ferris wheel at the end of the long-reaching pier suddenly come ablaze. Standing over 30 meters tall, The Big Wheel's dazzling display of twinkling lights is quickly joined by the instant illumination of a multitude of the town's other attractions. From a whirling carousel to the town's decoratively dangling street lamps, a string of attractions are sequentially switched on. The presentation was purposely directing me toward Judas' location; so without delay, I follow the illuminated route.

At the end of the vivid lit pathway was the now fully illuminated, Blackpool Tower; the sick emphasis of Judas' invitational video. The high-reaching tower is situated above a complex that houses a variety of different attractions. One of the set of buildings is the opulent, Tower Ballroom.

Just as I near the Ballroom's exterior, the Ballroom's sign promptly flickers on. What a surprise, the dramatic dog himself has dramatically stationed himself inside of a picturesque ballroom. No doubt he has is behind the temporary closure. With most of the attractions cordoned off; he would have relative carte blanche of the grounds.

Before me are the reddish-brown brick and lavish arched windows of the Ballroom's exterior. Just beyond the exterior lies the ageless elegance of a surpassingly striking dancehall. It seems that this impressive display of majestic, turn of the century architectural is now the most recent retreat for Judas and his entire noxious band of Bleeders and Feeders.

As the Tower's complex is summarily illuminated, I take notice of the handful of henchmen positioned just outside of the Ballroom's main entrance. From my advancing position roughly 50 meters away, I survey the immortal threats currently surrounding the building. Judging by my hurried count and their usual pungency, there seem to be only ten of them. I was expecting more of a welcoming party than this; I wonder what Judas has up his sleeve. He is taunting me simply to quench his own malicious appetite; I am in no mood to toy around with his raffish goons. For now, I will comply with his proposed terms. The sooner I barge through the Ballroom's doors, the faster we are face to face.

With no more time to waste, I expend the bungling brutes. Seething with righteous fury, I bombard the bastards; bashing, slashing and piercing them as firmly fast as inhumanly feasible.

Once I retired those reprobates, there was unexpectedly no retort from any other Bleeders of Feeders. Still, their scent was acutely abundant. Whatever lay beyond this old-fashioned exterior, I was whole-heartedly prepared to face the unexpected.

Alone on the street just outside of the Ballroom, I pause; lingering in a sedate moment of silence. With a trivial last pull from my flask, I purposely release my grasp; crashing to the ground, it splinters into tiny pieces.

I am guaranteed nothing less than bleak uncertainty. I do not know what foul ruse Judas has in store; undoubtedly he has some screwball scheme arranged. No longer disquieted with self-preservation, I am more than willing to surrender myself in order to put the animal down.

Without warning, the bitter bone-chilling English air brusquely turned acutely dank as the already darkened sky became soggy with a heavy stream of driving rain. Drenched by the sudden downpour, I along with my surroundings seemed to be appropriately purified by the torrent showers. The ashen piles of the recently rescinded washed away in the abrupt deluge. How fitting to be bathed in the untainted waters from heaven just before I tear into Hell.

Soaked to the bone, I initiate my voluntary admission into the building; ready to encounter the unimaginable. Walking through the front doors, I step into the expansive and unoccupied vestibule. Regardless of the eerie reserve that pervades the airy chamber; the proverbial trail of both Bleeders and Feeders intensifies. Proceeding with caution through the lobby, their patented stink guides me to the back of the corridor. As I advance toward the main entrance to the grand ballroom, the middle doors swing open; presenting me with a glimpse of the darkened hall. While the doors fully open, the lights of the ballroom are swiftly switched on, completely illuminating the refined space. Brightened by the multitude of hanging chandeliers, I take notice of both the room's richly intricate architecture and the gigantic horde of Bleeders and Feeders occupying the otherwise elegant expanse.

Momentarily paused in the doorway, I survey the expectant group of hundreds of immortals. The uncharacteristically static crowd calmly stands almost uniformly at attention; gathered in a dense clump in the middle of the rooms dance floor. Obviously anticipating my arrival, the band of mostly Feeders, gawks at me with blatant, emphatic contempt. Undoubtedly they have been anxiously awaiting my arrival: just like good little dogs. Passing through the gate and into the generous area I wittingly cross the threshold into the Tower Ballroom and toward the gathered group of oddities.

Pacing closer to the swarm of pests, I look up at the room's lavish ceiling. The painted scene above has a quality similar to that of the Sistine Chapel. Just as I passingly admire the room's grandeur while advancing toward the vast parquet ballroom floor, the voluble tones of the facilities trademark organ suddenly resonate throughout the majestic expanse. I march to the edge of the impressively patterned complex arrangement of rich woods of the regal dance floor. Sardonically playing the melodic "Always," the massive Wurlitzer organ thunderously provides a theatrical soundtrack to the relentlessly tense atmosphere.

At the back of the elaborate dance floor, is an immensely striking stage framed by a velvet richly red curtain. Above the inset stage, embellished with intricate gold molding, there is an inscription: "Bid me discourse, I will enchant thine ear." Shakespeare; oh how fittingly overly dramatic this entire scene is. This exaggerated space was less of a villain's fortified command center and more of an exaggerated Atlantic City style lair of luxury. How entirely appropriate this to be an actual stage of our final tryst. At the foot of the stage, just beyond the shoulder-to-shoulder faction of savages; was a golden grand staircase. A velvety dark violet curtain obscures the rest of the stage; without a doubt, this is the opulently plush platform Judas has arranged for our encounter.

I sluggishly continue striding through the room as small pack of the miscreants dash to callously greet me. I slowly extend my arms outward in serene surrender, just before I calmly bring myself to a halt. These four Feeders immediately paw and scrape at my exterior. The first three are scruffy men tritely decked in macabre black get-ups, customarily characteristic of conventional creeps. The gristly long black hair coupled with the silly inescapable leathery and senselessly slippery regalia. However, the third is a shockingly dissimilar strain of degenerate.

Abnormally outfitted in the contrastingly uncommon-place burning bright red jumpsuit, the feral redheaded Feeder was a unique and unhinged cross between a pin-up girl and a demented mechanic. With her razor straight bangs and wavy hairstyle she clearly had a thing for Bettie Page. In addition to her notable vogue inclinations, I notice a peculiar device attached to her waist. A compact wand dangled from her black oversized belt. Looking closer, it wasn't just a wand; it was a tiny metal detector. She must be the one tasked with clearing me of any weapons of mass immortal expulsion.

Quietly standing in complacent composure I remain entirely

passive as their steamy breaths splash against my face. The boorish boys diligently shuffle through my person as the fashion conscious hell-harlot positions herself directly in front of me. A monotonously humming buzz softly sounds from her detector as she sweeps and waves it over and around my entire form. Gliding up toward my chest, the evocative empress is further agitated as her instrument wildly bleeps. Repetitiously undulating the wand atop my chest, the detector noisily alerts her of something metallic. Without delay the brutes riotously remove my overcoat. The curvy Feeder looks on in loathing gratification.

Aggressively confiscating my jacket, the two mongrels riffle through my trench coat; searching it thoroughly for any concealed munitions. Extricating an item from the depths of my coat pocket, one of the Feeders flashes a suspicious expression as he proudly presenting it to the awaiting minions. Dangling down from his hand hangs the silver crucifix that had belonged to Ela's father. The cursed crowd of reprobates cackles in derisive bliss. Solidly self-elated with his exploratory skills, he retains the confiscated trinket in his grasp. Upon concluding their inspection, they carelessly discard my coat.

While I maintain my docile demeanor, the she-feeder routinely reestablishes the wand atop my chest and scrolls it back and forth, again and again. As the detector noisily bleeps once again, she grits her toothy grin in grave gratification. As the fanfare of chirps and beeps clearly signals to the area around my chest, a lively voice emanates from the stage. Crying out from behind the stages lofty curtain; is the familiar resonant tenor of Judas.

"Can you still feel me inside of you, brother?" Judas roguishly referring to the sharp-edged fragment discarded inside of me, his immortal counterpart, ages before.

"I will always be a part of you Lazarus." In an instant, the curtains are swept open, melodramatically revealing my contemptuous adversary. Emerging out from behind the veiling drapes he proudly displays the now immortal Ela, who is firmly secured in his daft grasp. Forcibly wielding her around, he struts them both into the light. Reluctantly constricted in his warped embrace, she is folded into the shoulder of his ivory three-piece suit. Donning his flamboyantly pearl white ensemble, he shamelessly seizes her by the neck and saunters them both toward the edge of the stage.

While Judas maneuvers across the stage, a throng of Bleeders and Feeders slowly start to shuffle. The abundant mass parted their sea of sinful subjects directly down the middle, clearing a singular designated pathway between myself and a staircase at the foot of the stage. Durably devoted, the sycophantic shape-shifters and mongrel bloodsuckers are overtly delighted to see me die at the hand of their murderous master. Now partitioned in half, the immortals are poised in long sections that form semi-uniformed columns to my left and to my right. There is nothing but the decorative dance floor between Judas and me. The awful sight of Ela's dire state is distressingly tragic, but fortunately she looks as if she has not yet fed for the first time.

After receiving a nod from Judas, the she-feeder, immediately begins to hack into me; frenziedly scratching away at my unshielded chest. All the while Judas proudly observes with overt reparation as the other hairy brutes hold my outstretched arms. Debilitated by her lack of flesh, an anemic Ela is involuntarily forced to lay witness as I am maliciously lacerated.

Two more brash and impish immortals dart to the scene. These new arrivals are readied with substantial wrist restraints. As the appended obnoxious oafs ascend upon me and apply the hefty chains, the eccentric female has reduced both my shirt and my chest to bloody ribbons. My flesh sagged and dangled from my body. With a self-contented scoffing hiss, the 'she-feeder' concludes her activities. Removing the remnants of my tattered shirt, she stands behind me. Still entirely nonresistant, I look to Judas with callous indifference.

"Forgive my dreadful etiquette, brother, but you should see

your fucking face." Judas brazenly blusters out as he initiates their decent down the illustrious staircase.

"I wish you could see yourself right now."

Still pressed against his side, Ela is coercively guided by Judas down the steps. Each of their imbalanced but coextending strides slowly brings them down and closer to me. The cretins continue their inflexible retentions of my figure, regardless of my already accommodating temperament. The army of Bleeders and Feeders is consummately washed over with awe-filled wonder; the multitude of bastards marvels at their vile supervisor and fawn over his every word.

Judas snootily scolds, "Poor little Lazarus, still depriving yourself of the simple pleasures."

On the other side of the long line of immortals, Judas along a weak and reluctant Ela by his side, steps onto the ballroom floor. Judas confidently takes a firm stance when another figure emerges from the crowd. Taking a position on the other side of Judas is my former mole John. Once my indispensable insider, John the traitor stands proudly adjoined with Judas; displaying his true colors as an aspiring immortal. What a disappointment. John, along with all the other Bleeders and Feeders are partially paused, pending their dark pundit's direction.

"Don't be concerned with this cattle lover, children. As you can see, he hasn't properly fed for quite some time. He is merely a shallow husk of his former, god-like self." Judas assuredly addresses his expectant minions.

Receiving another nod from Judas, the eager she-beast promptly pushes me forward. My hands tethered together, she forcefully shoves me down the clearing of hostiles and toward Judas. As I am thrust forward, a Feeder to my left socks me with a stout fist across my jaw, then from my right comes another blow, from an even bulkier Bleeder. Every step I take, another immortal joyously maims me. With every bustling belt, the swarm of bloodthirsty savages took out their resentments of purity and their aversion to virtue. Continuing down the lengthy line of enthusiastic immortals, I persevere without any attempt of retaliation. While I can feel each blow mutilating my appearance, I focus on retaining my composure. I must void of any visible emotion; they will get no such pleasure from me. I was their sacrificial stooge and I was being bitterly disciplined for the unforgivable betrayal of their kind. The line of louts, taking great pleasure in my disfigurement, propelled me into the hands of their master; my eternal arch nemesis.

After enduring the bastards' excessive abuse, I am placed in front of a bald headed bulky beast of a Feeder. More like a rhinoceros than the average feral Feeder, the well-built brute kicks in the back of my legs. Both his unusual strength and his steel-tipped boot instantly force me to my knees. The massive muscle-head childishly grins and recedes back into the crowd.

Reduced to shambles of shredded tissue, I gaze up and peer into Judas' devilishly dilated eyes. After a few seconds, I turn my agitated attention to the man to his side: my former asset, John. Confidently located beside his new master, John looks down at me with mocking melancholy. It takes him a moment to actually look me in the eye. I sharply scowl back at his treasonous face. Slowly closing my eyes, I calmly drop my head in brooding disappointment. Taking a deep breath, I break my sustained silence and address Judas; "Dearest King of dogs, can I have a brief moment with John?"

Laughing tempestuously, Judas glances indifferently over to John and then turns back to me responding; "My darling Lazarus, of course."

With blithesome accommodation, Judas gestures to John with an express nod: "Well then, get on with it."

Judas lively pushes John closer toward my position and cautions; "But keep in mind Lazarus, disorderly conduct will result in your immediate expulsion."

With little sign of trepidation, John tentatively takes another step closer and slowly leans nearer to my fractured figure. Judas states; "Go on, look the man you once called brother in the..."

Before Judas can complete his command, I slam my forehead into John's expression; shattering his nose and instantly killing him. Resuming my serene composure; I look back to Judas as John's lifeless body plops to the floor. His surrounding disciples turn silent in unpredicted surprise. Gazing back at Judas with blank tranquility; mildly stunned, Judas pauses in brief irritation. After his momentary lapse of hushed agitation, he uproariously hollers out "Yes!"

Convulsing with laughter, he haughtily snickers; "He certainly was a snotty little stain, wasn't he?"

I submissively endure in the compliantly tame position on my knees.

"Does that hurt John?" Judas mockingly roars out, still giggling with sick satisfaction. Firmly pressing his finger against his right nostril, he forcefully blows a sudden burst of mucus onto John's motionless body.

Shouting downward to the double-crosser's corpse, Judas adds; "Karma; it is a bitch: reap it, you prissy little prat!"

The malcontents boisterously erupt in deafening merriment. Each and every loathsome letch and uncivilized immortal celebrates the actions of their magnified alpha-male. Like a rapacious pack of illicit freaks, the mob of mongrels bursts with resonant howls and rowdy growls. Brazenly reveling in their racket; Judas wholeheartedly delights in their praise.

Turning his jubilant disposition back to me, his subjugated foe, Judas slams his beefy fist into my face. His trifling playfulness has evolved into exacting scorn. With every blow to my gory countenance, he zealously shouts; "All of your wretched repentance and all of your worthless reconciliation and for what?"

With every punch, both his disdain and intensity grow greater. "How far will you go for these swine?"

Blood splashes against his once spotless ivory ensemble; he doesn't seem to mind.

After six or seven intensely enthusiastic blasts to the head, he turns his attention to my threadbare gut. Continuing to smack his mitts deep into my ragged torso, he avidly blurts; "What lengths will you go to for your precious cattle?"

Purposely immersing his claws deep into my shoulder, he squawks; "Is it worth it, dear brother?"

Burying his paws even further into the back of my neck and securely plants a constraining penetrating grasp of my shoulder. Without hesitation, he veraciously punches me square in the gut. This shot forces my crippled body to uncontrollably double over. Involuntarily hunched over in devastating pain, I watch as the amassment of Bleeders and Feeders look on with abiding elation.

Relishing each moment of my suffering, Judas transparently savors every ounce of my martyrdom. Judas boastfully insists; "You are comprehensively helpless to stop me; your self-sacrifice is absolutely pointless!"

Punishing my diminishing body with a robust slug he boisterously continues; "How can you continue to love such a selfish God escapes me. We deserved better and He's never going to have you back. Have you forgotten, both of us have corrupted countless individuals and carried out dazzling genocides; just to spite the God who turned His back on us? Somehow, you managed to sprout a conscience; leaving me as the only one to oppose Him. Amsterdam, Tijuana; I have already affectionately curated sanctuaries of sin across the globe. But now, I am going to make you watch as I accomplish the World's grandest human liquidation in history!

Curled up in a tucked position from his grueling jolts, I turn my head to Judas and raspingly petition; "Is she not free to go?"

Judas responds with a faintly offended tone; "Regardless of what you truly think of me, Lazarus, I *am* a man of my word."

Judas gleefully asserts. "Always have... always will be."

I know my immortal counterpart and his warped nature all too well. There is only one likely reason behind authorizing Ela's release; she is dead no matter what. By the look of her current condition, she is already suffering the insatiable hunger for human flesh. Once she gives in; the completion of her total transformation into a Feeder only leaves a couple outcomes. In his ageless efforts to continuously spite and further torture my remorse-filled soul, she will either fully become one of his depraved immortals, or, if she somehow continues to reject the urge to feed, she will become even more fragile and undoubtedly die along with the rest of the world from the utilization of the "HV" virus.

Doubled over and on my knees, I lift up my head and utter to the regrettably altered Ela; "I have something for you..." Gesturing to the rotten rogue that confiscated my belongings, I continue; "...your father's crucifix."

Looking on with captive fascination, Judas smirks and flashes his minion a nod of approval. The impish immortal begins to place the pendant around Ela's neck. As the cross slips past her head and down to her neck, I sputter, "*Never* lose your faith, Ela."

Gently cupping it into her trembling pale palm, she dubiously inspects the necklace with despondent sentimentality. I watch with abundant gratification as I notice she has observed the discernible difference of weight between her original heirloom and the cross currently in her grasp. Though it looks identical to her father's crucifix, something has been altered. From her faint but implicit analysis, she recognizes this is a slightly modified crucifix. I am certain she sees the possible purpose of the augmentation.

The mystical fragments that were confiscated from the Spear of Destiny and then providentially left to her by her late father, was now fused into the pendant around her neck. She could destroy immortals or even Judas or she could use the fragment to kill her new corrupted self before it is too late. It was a dreadful gift; but a necessary one.

The gross gravity of the object is apparent and recognizably understood. Releasing the jewelry from her hand; the new trinket slides downward to its weighted position against her pallid bosom. Now that I had compliantly delivered myself as the crowning ransom for Judas' prized hostage, Ela, she was now altogether free to flee. Judas shoos her away with the exaggerated pouty expression and arm motions of someone releasing an addled young pup into the untamed wild.

Physically discombobulated and mentally debilitated by her newly acquired thirst for blood, she stares at me in confusion. I glance back at her with obligation. Ela directly dashes toward the ballroom exit. As she progresses to liberate herself through the main entryway, she pauses; gazing backward in concerned recognition. With a tender look of earnest gratitude, Ela extricates herself. I am certain; she absolutely knows what to do.

I resort back down to my relinquishing crouch; satisfied that she has been released.

"Was she worth it?" Judas unabashedly queries as she departs the room.

Overconfident as ever, Judas bends down and leans into my squatted post. Aligning his vindictive lips to my aggravated ear, he acrimoniously sighs; "Ooh, sampling her was a truly religious experience; you should have partaken."

He sneeringly continues with a grudging whisper, "She certainly *tasted* like she was worth it."

Elated in euphoric rapture, Judas drives his callous fist into my jowl one more time and with enthusiastic sedition, he hollers; "Your humanity has always betrayed you, brother!"

Brimming with abundant bliss, he furthermore attests; "The

sour smell of virtuous concern pathetically oozes out from your pours: the very stink of which offends me to my core."

Accompanying his additional contemptuous statements and fueled by an overabundance of acrimony, Judas rigorously kicks me again in the chest; his hearty hoof hurls me backwards. Extensively exhausted, I lay flush against the ballroom floor. Exultantly poised above me, Judas proudly punts me in my side; rolling me facedown against the intricate floor.

Teeming with exultation, Judas amusedly queries; "You actually believed that you had successfully thwarted my scintillating scheme? How rich! My sweet little Lazarus, you didn't even mildly delay my extinction of God's precious little pets."

Striding around my disassembled form, Judas condescendingly remarks; "I am genuinely disappointed in you, Lazarus. You have been pitifully ineffective. I have once again triumphantly succeeded and once more, you have dismally failed. I can't imagine how disenchanting that must feel."

With his swaggering declarations resonating in my mind, I am repulsed, but not surprised by his assertions. Struggling from my doleful position, I manage to twist onto my side. Placing my hand over my marred chest, I prop myself up by the elbow and solemnly respond; "You self-indulgent, God-forsaken Hellhound; I have something for you too."

Judas retorts with a frisky snark; "Hyena actually."

With observable offense he articulates; "Watch your tongue. I am not just a mere mutt; I am a god, you pathetic keeper of the faith!"

By now, I was certain that I had given Ela the appropriate time to escape. She should have vacated the premises and reached a safe distance. Mustering up one more furious burst of energy, I begin my plan of action.

Plunging my right hand into my chest, I burrow it into my flesh. My bizarre feat, without a doubt, is effectively amusing Judas.

Clawing past my ribcage, I dig around as my rival looks on in odd interest. Entrenched inside of my own tattered torso, I dig in even further. The novelty of my gruesomely impulsive deed has Judas utterly fascinated: I have definitely aroused his curiosity.

Solidly submerged, I retract my tightly clenched fist out from my now gushing cavity. Heaving my hand outwards, I have extracted a considerable chunk of my own flesh. I present the gory offering to Judas, the flesh guzzler.

My immortal nemesis jauntily laughs with unadulterated intoxicating carnality. Wholly immersed in hedonistic bliss and masturbatory merriment, Judas cackles and exclaims; "A pound of flesh then, is it?"

Arrogantly sniggering, he willingly accepts my bloody offering with self-certainty. His eager attention and open hand lunge toward my submission. Inspecting the warm and bloody slab, Judas peers further into the bestowed batch of matter lying in my opened palm. I watch as he takes notice of a curious object inside of the hemorrhaging chunk. The diminutive device is suppressed amongst blood and fleshy debris. The precarious mechanism is intriguingly equipped with a tiny illuminated blinking red button.

Judas inquisitively peers at the unusual flickering apparatus and then slowly looks back to me. I glare deep into his captivated gaze as the intriguing mechanism continuously flashes. I delight in watching his expression of curiosity transform into a strained stare of awkwardly suspicion.

Wasting no more time, I push the blinking button; promptly changing the blinking button to a constant glow or red. Assertively flashing a sharp sneer to Judas I proudly mutter; "Boom!"

Remaining in steadfast overconfidence, the white-suited, blood splattered Judas stands strangely still among the crowd of unabashed cronies. Extending his hand inside of his coat, he reaches into his inner pocket. Coolly retrieving his ever-present miniature tablet, Judas glances down at the device. After prudently examining it, he serenely turns back to me. The psychotic ensemble of immortal subordinates restlessly linger; waiting for their intrepid director's reaction. I too, wait intently for his elicited response.

26

"Thy lips are like a scarlet ribbon, and thy mouth
is lovely; Thy temples behind your veil are like
the halves of a pomegranate."
-Song of Solomon 3:3

BLACKPOOL, ENGLAND
PRESENT

Hastily escaping the wicked accommodations of my damnable donor of involuntary immortality, Judas I struggle to flee my fumbling body out of the grand ballroom. Once again, Simon had rescued me; selflessly sacrificing his life for mine. But he was too late. Although I was temporarily released from the physical hold of that monster, I was still permanently in the stronghold of his nasty gift of immortality. There is an excruciating hunger inside of me that has purposely been neglected. On my own; I'm terrified I may surrender to it.

Nearing the perimeter doors of the ballroom, I am startled by a flash of lightning. Fleetingly illuminating the obscure outdoors just outside of the sinful haunt, the murky streets are absolutely saturated by a torrential rain. Shortly after the streak of bright light, I am surprised by the snappy crack of booming thunder. Following the brief and frightening flash, the momentarily elucidated exterior promptly reverts back to its shadowy reality.

Clutching the newfangled crucifix in my hand, I dash out the main corridor of the complex and into the damp street. Instantly doused by the driving rain, I am further plagued by the savage appetite stringently streaming through my veins. This unquenchable and unholy hunger is growing increasingly stronger as my transforming body becomes progressively exhausted. Even though Judas had purposely turned me into one of his obnoxiously vile Feeders, he still had to keep me under his control. By deliberately depriving me of the necessary diet of flesh, my transformation proceeded at a laboriously sluggish pace. I am uncertain whether that now works to my benefit or regrettably against it.

Though Simon had allotted me with the possible means of nullifying my new nefarious immortality, I stood uncertain if I would actually have the ample occasion to exploit it. My aching body feels exceptionally closer to death due to the lack of fleshy sustenance. Staggering into the unusually abandoned street, I battle with the overwhelming immortal influence exerting its will upon me. Teetering into the street, my dulled senses faintly detect that I am not alone. Despite being terribly disoriented by this disturbing transformation, I can still distinguish a mass of assailants attempting to stealthily ascend upon me.

Inopportunely, my body is slowly beginning to shut down just as I am being surrounded by six of Judas' Feeder flunkies. Tightening my rigid clamp of my fathers modified cross, I defenselessly wait as goons close in. Wholeheartedly, I quickly accept that I am about to be killed; permanently. As my assailants advance, I use what is left of my fading consciousness to recite the Lord's Prayer; "Our Father who art in heaven, hallowed be thy name."

Sedately voicing the words of faith and forgiveness, I calmly close my eyes and stand still; peacefully primed for my inevitable demise.

"Thy kingdom come, Thy will be done, on earth as it is in

Heaven. Give us this day our daily bread, and forgive us our trespasses, as we forgive those who trespass against us..."

Just as my vanishing intellect is drifting to a gloomy halt, I am surprised by an earsplitting "BANG!"

Startled by the boisterous boom of a bullet, despite the pouring rain, I immediately feel my skin showered by a sizeable spray of warm and syrupy liquid. Upon opening my diminishing eyes, I am astonished to see one of the advancing Feeder's head has been entirely blown off. Entirely saturated by the degenerate's blood, I simply stood stunned and motionless. Cascading down my face, a stream of blood steadily gushes toward my lips; gushing into my mouth and down my throat.

As the warm blood hastily invades my expiring system, I remarkably receive an instantaneous shot of transcendent energy. Despite the collapsing failure of my familiar faculties, suddenly my unnatural cognitive capabilities begin to exponentially increase. I am flourishing from the blood and I am suddenly profoundly alert of my surroundings. The true nature of my regrettable Feeder disposition has been triggered. My dying senses have ignited into a dynamic frenzy of verve and acute sensitivity.

Instantly, I clearly perceive the exact position of the six approaching Feeders as well as the keenest particulars of the dusky surroundings. Amidst the barrage of Feeders and the deluge of rain and blood, I place the source of the gunshot. About to administer his second lethal round into my stupefied invaders, Agent Morretti confidently marches out from around the corner of the adjacent building.

With his a tense finger on the trigger of a weighty revolver, Morretti angrily ambles toward the group of attacking immortals. Striding across the sodden sidewalk with his sopping wet tan trench, he intently trudges closer to the now infuriated flock of Feeders. Uncompromisingly trekking onward toward them, Morretti fires off another round. As he delivers his second shot, I have the unnerving compulsion to consume some flesh.

Just as my senses have been extraordinarily amplified, so has my freshly acquired appetite for flesh too intensified. To my amazement, by the time the agent's timely second bullet is propelled through the clammy air toward his second target, I have already begun to feed. While the projectile soars to the second Feeder, I speedily reach out to the dropping headless body before me and quickly draw it close; instinctually pulling the falling Feeder's flesh against my ravenous lips. Firmly gripping his body, I plunge my eager teeth into his pathetic flesh.

With inhumanly incredible speed, I ruthlessly feed on the Feeder; instantly bolstering my blossoming baleful abilities. All of this before Moretti's second bullet enters his ensuing target. My newfound supernatural faculties have provided me with the necessary means to vanquish these beasts. Hyper-heightened senses instantaneously offer the compulsory knack to legitimately combat the remaining batch of Feeders.

Moretti's second shot delivers a bullet directly to the face of yet another Feeder. I swiftly shift and spin toward the remaining three. As the agent jogs closer to the gory scene, I briskly slay the lingering Feeders with my bare hands. Armed with the element of surprise extended from both agent Moretti's accuracy and my rapid transformation, we have skillfully annihilated our immortal assailants. As the last of their bodies collapses to the pavement, I recite Simon's words of expulsion. Passionately gesturing the sign of the cross over the heap of remains, my recitation reduces the pile of beasts into dwindling remnants of sooty ash. As the bested miscreants are hurled to hell, the smoldering mass diminishes in the densely flowing rain. In penetrating ferment, the two of us stand and face.

Flaunting a contented grin from the far edge of his stiffened lips, agent Moretti gasps, briefly catching his breath in a moment of calmly collecting his impulsive composure. Positioned only a few steps in front of me; Moretti noticeably recognizes the grisly signs of my full transformation. He stands poised with his gun at the ready; cautiously pointed squarely between my eyes.

He blurts out with strict curiosity; "Ela?"

Wiping some of the blood from my mouth with my sopping sleeve, I placidly respond, "Fear not, agent Moretti; I am merely a Feeder in body, *not* in mind."

Bathed in gooey blood and rain, I reach up to clean the richly red blood from my face. Only able to smudge and smear the profuse amount of grisly blood, I slowly extend to him my other arm. Revealing my father's cross, still clutched tightly in my pallid hands I assuredly petition; "I still have my soul."

Inquisitively gazing into my immortal eyes, Moretti gradually lowers his gun. Temporarily frozen in static meditation, the two of us attempt to absorb the far-fetched reality of our current situation. The enduring rain cascades over our reflective selves: washing away the lingering blood from my inert figure. The surrounding streets are remarkably void of activity as the intermittent lightening continues to flicker and the mighty clang of thunder resonates throughout the empty street.

27

"Forasmuch then as the children are partakers of flesh and blood, he also himself likewise took part of the same; that though death he might destroy him that had the power of death, that is, the devil."
-Hebrews 2:14

DOVER, ENGLAND
THREE DAYS PRIOR

Intermittently illuminated by a blue neon sign flashing "Jesus Saves," I attentively combine hefty sums of my explosive ingredients. Inside a dodgy hotel room poignantly adjacent to a dilapidated mission for vagrants, I assemble a massive assortment of homemade explosives. The critical concoction is my own unique blend of volatile materials that is remarkably lightweight and extraordinarily pliable. Similar to Semtex, my explosive substance had been useful in discreet demolitions in the past. The volatile material was so proficient; an effective amount could be fashioned into a sheet as shockingly thin as a single piece of paper. This made it easy to conceal and therefore virtually undetectable.

Constructing these necessary quantities for my upcoming offensive, I reflect on the intensely turbulent events of the last couple of days. Dramatic measures and bizarre lengths were entirely necessary to realistically contest the world's most nefarious killer. Because of this, I reached out to two unlikely collaborators to unite with me in a plan to permanently destroy Judas.

First, I had made contact with my first set of implausible partners. Earlier under the streets Rome, I had proposed the unusual alliance to the devout members of The Obedience. However, in addition to my absurd suggestion of cooperation, I offered a significant snippet of decidedly deceitful news. For quite some time now, I have been aware that John was actually a double-crossing traitor. At first I thought he was merely reporting my actions appropriately back to his betters at The Obedience. However, as the recent events unfolded, it became increasingly clear that someone other than just The Obedience employed him. The instant Judas exposed himself as the culprit behind the sordid situations I knew that he was who John was reporting to.

Appealing to their moral nobility and decency, I apprised them of John's duplicitous activities. I explicitly disclosed the details of our ongoing arrangement as well as my immediate disquieting notion of his double disloyalty. Justifiably outraged, the reverent members of The Obedience granted me temporary amnesty. This provisional pardon was only reached because of the disastrous complexity of the imminent events. The fate of both Heaven and Earth was in our hands. The lot of us were now liable for the future; and the only defense against the forthcoming cataclysmic events. For the moment, they need me just as much as I needed them.

As soon as I had encouragingly gained their temporary confidence, I immediately shared with them my plan of attack. Mindful of John's traitorous tendencies as well as having an ample understanding of Judas and his tediously theatrical but strategically adept nature, I could confidently anticipate some of his efforts. They agreed to momentarily house Judas in The Elysium. Once suppressed inside of the ultra-secure facility, I was entirely certain John would disclose the information to his immortal cohorts. That is exactly what happened. Upon Judas' insertion into the containment cell, his henchmen led a destructive incursion to retrieve him. Covertly directed by John himself, the brutish Feeders clumsily breached The Obedience's facility; tactlessly bulldozing into the heart of The Elysium. After freeing their weakened master, the mischievous mob hastily withdrew from the scene; placing explosive charges as they left. While they arranged their detonating devices, John planted himself inside of an elected station that protected him from the coming explosions. When John was safely in place, the others exited The Elysium. Triggering the explosives, they left a trail of vast devastation and ruin. They assumed they had properly disposed of any Obedience members on the premises. After the blasts, John miraculously emerged; making it look as though he scarcely escaped the devastating carnage.

Unbeknownst to those sloppy rogues, the members of The Obedience present at The Elysium were all privy to their intrusion. Knowing the Feeder's point of entry as well as their explosive exit strategy, the residing Obedience members perfectly played the role of being surprised and ill-prepared; totally shocked by the abrupt infiltration. Protected by body armor, the members standing guard played dead as other members covertly congregated in the depths of The Elysium. From their station, they monitored John's every movement. Once he deposited himself into his protected station, the Obedience members secretly lodged themselves into the secure confines of an impermeable bunker. This highly secretive hatch hidden among the internal structure of The Elysium had remained unidentified for years. Intended as an emergency shelter to safely house the head of The Obedience in the unlikely case of a natural or man-made disaster, this safe-room was built to withstand almost anything.

The Obedience had taken heed of my warnings and our temporary partnership had proved to be vital to the prevention of Judas' plot. The villains' treacherous scheme had been initiated, but so had my campaign to combat him.

With The Obedience momentarily on my side, I moved on to

my secondary aide. The other fundamental piece of my pivotal puzzle was Interpol Agent, Sandro Moretti.

His virile impulsiveness and veritable integrity, teamed with his invaluable links to international law enforcement, made him an indispensable confederate. Unfortunately, I lacked the appropriate time and customary means to properly explain my outrageous origins. So, without my conventional tactics of disclosure, I set forth to undertake the most forward path possible.

With regrettable but essential abruptness, I let myself into his French flat. In the middle of the night, I quietly crept to the foot of his worn out leather couch in the middle of the room. Still fully clothed and sprawled out on the uncomfortably short love seat, somehow the agent was fast asleep. I calmly took sat in an adjacent wooden chair. Rudely interrupting his slouchy slumber, I secured his attention by brashly exclaiming; "Forgive my intrusion, Agent Moretti."

My sudden interjection curtly jolted the sleeping agent wide-awake. Instinctively, Moretti draws his sidearm. Predictably disturbed and ever impressively vigilant, Moretti promptly points the firearm in my face. I tranquilly implore; "Ela Vlcek needs our help. I am desperately in need of your assistance."

With steadfast keenness, he squints; skeptically prolonging his attentive attitude. With his alert posture and point blank range, he holds his revolver bluntly between my eyes; probingly blurting out, "Who the hell are you?"

I began to tell the condensed version of my far-fetched tale. Given the preposterous nature of my narrative, I think he handled it quite well. In an attempt to pass over any of the conventional doubt and logical trepidation, I further augmented the aspects of my true origins with the particulars of Judas' latest conspiracy. I had assembled a comprehensive report of the current events. All the latest evidence and theories were printed inside.

Amidst the tense silence, I somberly asked for permission to retrieve something from my pocket. Prompted by the consenting nod of his head, I gently flop the packet onto the concave couch cushion beside him. Cautiously reaching out his hand, he timidly touches the file. Snatching up the collection of evidence, he places it on his lap. Riffling through the documents, he quickly glances over the lengthy information that supported my ludicrous claims. The two of us remained in the rigid standstill as he continued to skim through my bizarre, but hopefully, persuasive brief. Though short on time, I allotted him with the necessary moments to even begin to remotely grasp the astounding circumstances.

Relying on his honorable nature as well as his requisite for justice, I straightforwardly pose to him; "Whether or not you chose to believe my ridiculous story is entirely up to you. However, these facts are irrefutable. All I ask of you is to continue the duties of which you have already been persistently performing; please carry on in protecting Ela."

Even if it was just his burgeoning curiosity or just simply humoring me, I managed to persuade my honorable convert to dig even deeper into the grave intelligence. Hopefully, after looking at the details he would feel compelled to aid in retrieving Ela.

"Agent Moretti, I believe you to be an honorable man. If you are in any way convinced by these documents, meet me at platform No.3 at the train station at 7a.m."

Amongst the bustling businessmen and scampering crowds, I tuck myself into the corner of a gigantic steel beam and the cold concrete wall of the train station. Punctually, at 7 o'clock sharp, I encouragingly looked on as a determined Agent Moretti darted through the rushing masses. Through the multitude of hectic humans, he spots my location. I march across the crowds to meet him. Impatiently eager, he says, "I must be crazy. Your story is completely ridiculous, but I must admit, your intel is undeniable. If even part of your conspiracy is true, you'll need all the help you can get."

Responding in gracious validation, I admit to Moretti; "As time ticks on and technology erupts, his evil capabilities grow impossibly worse. As his degenerate disposition grows predominantly greater, I am unsure how long I can combat his plans on my own."

Once I had beneficially enlisted my newest capable recruit, I afforded him the necessary invaluable instructions of engaging immortals. Brief though it may be, he proved to be a bright and talented student of my crash course of Bleeders and Feeders. I also equipped him with munitions from my revolutionary arsenal of anti-immortal weapons. The prized innovation was my freshly fabricated bullets of banishment. Meticulously engraved by a laser with the Latin words of expulsion, these progressive projectiles would optimistically add the much-needed efficiency to our upcoming confrontations. Judas had been busy with his schemes; but so had I. I can't let him be the only one using cutting edge technologies to his advantage.

During our immortal instruction, I proposed my strategy to locate the secret facilities that held the HV. Just before I sent Legion back to Hell, he had disclosed that Judas runs the entirety of his global operations through one singular device; a tiny custom made digital tablet. Hand-crafted by his dutiful underling Monkey, this personal device never leaves his possession. It efficiently organizes and precisely coordinates every detail of the HV and its dispersion.

Legion woefully howled; "Judas never trusted anyone, not even Monkey. He only gives out scraps of information. No one but Judas knows every detail of his plan, but it is all inside of that tablet. Find the device: discover the plan."

Because of this, I ask Moretti to access to Interpol's massive global data network. Between The Obedience's and Interpol's resources, we could likely locate most, if not all, of the purposely-obscured HV locales. However, upon my urgent supplication of his assistance, Agent Moretti turned me down.

Instead of just accessing a database, he proposed an even

more constructive alternative. With our time running out by the hour, Moretti brilliantly suggests an even more direct solution; "Why not just hack the thing: fight fire with fire."

28

"The sorrows of oblivion surrounded me;
the snares of death confronted me."
-2 Samuel 22:6

LUXEMBOURG CITY, LUXEMBOURG
THREE DAYS PRIOR

P roperly contending with the likes of Monkey would be a near impossible task. Agent Moretti, a man of well-intentioned moral grit, has offered an irrefutably more effective revision to my strategy. Incidentally, he may currently be able to access an invaluable instrument able to possibly contest Judas' hacker mastermind. As proficient as any of Interpol's and The Obedience's vast resources may be, nothing could supersede this providential possibility that could be afforded by the use of another computer virtuoso.

Opportunely detained inside of a government facility in Luxembourg, presently resided one of the world's most wanted computer criminals. Cyber-felon, Ophelia also known as "The Shadow Queen" could be the key to fittingly preventing Judas' catastrophe. At the age of 23, Ophelia is one of the world's most dangerous computer anarchists of all time. Widely considered to be just as precariously proficient as Monkey, she may be the only person with the technological prowess to challenge his superlative computer capability.

She was only recently seized by Interpol agents while secretly settled in the Netherlands. Her equipment was inadvertently stumbled upon during a utilities company's general maintenance of the gas lines of her apartment building in Amsterdam. While using special equipment to detect any seepages or weak spots in the pipelines knit within the shabby walls, her unusually large accumulation of digital hardware gave off an irregular heat signature; instantly serving as red-flag to the encroaching crew. With unrestricted access to the entire building, the maintenance crew entered her apartment unannounced; discovering the conspicuous computer hardware inside of her modest, one-bedroom flat. Understandably suspicious, the workers instantly phoned the local authorities. Explicitly cautious and protectively paranoid concerning even the slightest hint of cyber-terrorism, the local authorities immediately contacted Interpol.

Hours later, after returning from an ordinary trip to the grocer, Ophelia discovered the multitude of law enforcement officers encompassing her building. Taken by surprise, she stood utterly stunned as she watched the waves of police move about her building. Keeping her distance, she paused in brief contemplation when suddenly; she was taken by surprise by two officers who had identified her from a description from one of her neighbors. Handcuffed and promptly placed into police custody, she was transported to a local Interpol facility.

Initially, they presumed she was just a small time cyber terrorist; they had absolutely no idea who they really had in their custody. Once she was deposited into one of their interrogation rooms, they let her silently stew in her own uncertainty. After all, it was only by sheer dumb luck that they actually managed to capture the dangerous international cyber-criminal. Allowing her own imagination to get the best of her, the Interpol agents endeavored to let her simply self-implode. As they waited for further intelligence they also waited to see if she would break her silence. For hours on end, they failed to recognize that they had actually apprehended the criminal computer mastermind known as "The Shadow Queen."

Though she managed to maintain total silence while in custody, one of the investigators' searching her seized hardware, uncovered a conspicuous indications of a seasoned hacker. This led to a full-on investigation of all of the confiscated belongings. Within a couple of hours the agency's data detectives were hunting through all of her equipment and hard drives. Upon their deeper exploration; they acquired some rather incriminating indicators of massive amounts of fraudulent activities. Moreover, they found a couple of communications that contained her actual identity.

Once totally exposed, she was promptly transported to a separate and much smaller Interpol detainment facility in Luxembourg. This particular reformatory explicitly housed some of the most exceptionally non-violent but highly dangerous felons. Stubbornly preserving her perpetual reticence, Ophelia's relocation to this considerably more intimate detention center was their best chance of extracting any additional information from her. Typically occupied by a dozen or so of the world's top "cyber-villains" the secure unit was an infamous penitentiary amongst the technological underworld. Tall tales and cryptic accounts of the facilities' goings on have circulated throughout the garrulous hacker community for years.

Notoriously reputed for their "not so legal" techniques of intelligence gathering, what the detention center lacked in stature, its representatives made up for in aggressively determined but sometimes questionable methods. Not only were the felonious hackers intentionally incarcerated for prolonged periods of time to intimidate and antagonize them; but more importantly it was to buy more time for the investigators to uncover additional evidence against them. Understood to be "legal" under the ambiguous duplicities of international cyberspace laws, the constables of Interpol's digital crimes division, though alleged to be brazenly brutal in their procedures, still essentially operated within the confines of their conveniently confusing set of laws.

Following her weeks of being confined inside of the facility, Interpol's sordid tactics eventually wore her down. Because of the widespread whispers of their unconventional means of procuring intelligence, Ophelia suspended her silence for one brief instant. Momentarily deviating from her strategy of muteness, she teasingly admitted to having "dabbled in some computer stuff."

She endured weeks of solitary confinement and lengthy sessions of extensive and repetitive interrogation, but eventually, Ophelia was forced to abandon her campaign of silence. During the purposely-delayed interlude, they had acquired the necessary evidence to convict her; they blissfully approached her with their findings. Charge after charge came in. The more they had dug into her hardware, the more illegal activities they found; vastly beyond what they had initially supposed. Over fifty felony counts of knowingly transmitting an illegal program, thirty separate charges of constructing illegal codes and commands resulting in the irreparable damage to corporate mainframes and computer networks, and the kicker; 11,728 individual accounts of unauthorized use of an illegally attained credit card which was used to acquire over $80,000,000. Though the evidence established she was more of a thief than a cyber-terrorist, they were able to manipulate enough of what they had to insinuate her all but assured conviction as one.

In return for her unrestricted cooperation, Interpol agreed not to try her as an international terrorist; an intolerable offense that could feasibly be punishable by life in prison or even death. Bullied by the doctored evidence and stricken with panic, with no other feasible options in sight, Ophelia reluctantly agreed to plead guilty to a number of her computer crimes. In doing so, she was guaranteed to avoid the probability of permanent imprisonment or even possible execution.

In a statement she later made to Interpol investigators, Ophelia accepted their charges of hacking into over 10,000 computers. However, upon her admission she quickly amended that in actuality, it was more like over 10 million corporate security systems. Shortly thereafter, when questioned why she engaged in these fraudulent activities, she offered only one curt explanation behind her illegal escapades, simply stating; "Because I can."

Agent Moretti filled me in with some of the more notable particulars of her illicit background; "During the exploratory investigation into just one of the first allegations, federal agents discovered she had gained unauthorized access to the computer systems of nearly every major prestigious university in the world: Harvard, Oxford, and even MIT. She had intercepted usernames, codes and passwords from multiple Embassies, NASA, and even The United States Secret Service." Her adept computer capabilities and cyber-skill set were so proficient; in all likelihood she can access almost any informational system in the world! Once she is in; there is no limit to what she can do."

Knowing she could basically modify, temporarily disconnect or entirely shutdown any computer system in existence, Moretti believed Ophelia to be our best chance of competing with Monkey and thwarting Judas' apocalyptic plot.

"To have any chance of finding those locations, we need Ophelia; we need The Shadow Queen." Morretti stated to me in wholesome certainty.

"She is a super-genius cyber-hack and I believe she is our only hope of uncovering their data and finding Monkey. Once we find Monkey, with any luck, we should also find Judas."

Remarkably persuaded, I enthusiastically agreed. With very little time at our disposal, we advanced to the facility where she was being held.

Though he had agreed to help me and even suggested that we exploit a convicted felon, Moretti still considered himself to be bound, to some extent, by the limits of the law. Honorably retaining this obligation to operate predominantly within the parameters of the law, he was not prepared to let her go; but only to offer her a restricted deal for her assistance.

In his gruff tenor, he sternly specified; "In exchange for her cooperation and our successful acquisition of the HV locations, I will do all that is within my power to have some of her charges dismissed or at the very least, to reduce her overall sentence."

Upon our arrival in Luxembourg as we approached the detention facility, Moretti placed his handcuffs around my wrists. With me in "custody" we marched toward the unmarked center's adequately guarded entrance. He had full confidence this rudimentary rouse, though crude, would be the most effective tactic to unsuspectingly deliver us both inside. Flaunting his appropriate governmental credentials, we briskly progressed past the entrance and down a long hallway. Down another corridor, we reach the door of her room.

Exhibiting an intense scowl and dense inhalation, Agent Moretti flashes me an imitation smile and then determinedly strides into her barren cell. Slipped into the far right corner of the snowy-white cell, stood Ophelia; the rather petite and strikingly attractive young criminal. The five foot two inch asset looks no older than nineteen and has the most flawless, dark complexion that is only contrasted by the light silvery make-up outlining her salient eyes. The youthful eastern beauty's lengthy black hair was mostly dreadlocked; interlaced with twisted bursts of radiant red and pink streaks. The bright colors splayed atop her center-issued white jumpsuit; the sleeves of which have been hacked off and are frayed at the shoulders while the legs have been tightly rolled up almost to her knees. Her eyes were duteously embellished with skillfully applied liners and shadows and her nose was ornamented with a tiny diamond stud. There she coolly stood, enveloped into the corner of her colorless cell; as if she was anticipating our arrival.

Only a few years earlier, she had been brashly banished by her very prosperous but rather traditional family in India. Born Sadhika Malhotra, the daughter of an affluent businessman from Mumbai, was disowned for her habitual disregard for her father's conventional guidelines. Like Monkey, she possessed an incredibly brilliant mind capable of retaining astounding amounts of information. Her amazing abilities flourished and she rapidly developed an uncanny knack with computers. Interesting enough; even though her father owned one of the larges IT companies in Mumbai, he immovably maintained that the women in his family should not be tainted by modern technology. Regularly reprimanded for her relentless kinship with technology, her father constantly attempted to deprive her of what he called, "detrimental diversions."

Ignoring her father's wishes, she secretly continued to cultivate her profound connection with computers. From the simplest vintage arcade game to elaborate computer role-playing games, Ophelia became engrossed with and extraordinarily proficient at nearly program she touched. After teaching herself how to write code, she began to craft complicated computer viruses entirely for her own amusement. At the time, she never implemented any of her innovations; she simply created them and then subsequently constructed another virus that would then destroy the original.

One day, after finding a thirteen-year-old Ophelia incessantly occupied by a laptop she had smuggled into the house, her father issued a rigid warning. He commanded her never to bring any of these distractions into his home ever again.

Outwardly, she returned to her everyday acceptable routines, but almost every moment away from her family, she continued to secretly exercise her digital appetites. She remained entirely unnoticed for quite some time. For years, she carefully concealed every one of her technological tendencies; that is until the one day her father delivered a shocking bit of news. Brusquely, her father candidly revealed to her the irrevocable details of her forthcoming arranged marriage.

His out-of-date mandate was the apex to her domestic frustration. Fuming with explosive resentment and rage, she managed to preserve her composure. Without a single word, she snatched up a small backpack and promptly filled it with a minute assemblage of some of her personal belongings. Persisting in her acidic silence, she stoically approached her exacting father and kissed him tenderly on the cheek. With that kiss, she immediately left her home; never to see her father or any of her family ever again.

Disenchanted by her father's cold decisiveness, she fled for Europe; excited at the prospect of experiencing life outside of clutches of her restrictive patriarch. Expending all of the money she currently had on her, she selected to head for Amsterdam. Out of money; she summarily exploited her burgeoning aptitudes to attain some quick cash. From that first illegal activity, she was penetratingly addicted. Her knack for hacking quickly became an out-of-control obsession. She became frenziedly fixated with pushing her cyber capabilities to their limits. Poaching individual bank accounts for pocket cash soon became large-scale larceny with enormous withdraws from hundreds of accounts from multiple banks. These currency antics soon became oversized embezzlement extravaganzas.

Evidently, after improving her hardware and equipment, she would distribute most of her confiscated capital to various charities and humanitarian organizations. Movingly, this criminal mastermind undoubtedly still had a soul. Clearly she was never in it for the money; she was simply hooked on the thrill of the hack.

Agent Moretti and I progressed into her cell and Moretti asks her to take a seat.

She takes a few moments and ponders his cordial but authoritative proposition. Poised with assured self-reliance, in her own time, she sits down at the heavily built white table. As she leisurely takes a seat, both Moretti and I sociably convene at the table as well. The three of us continue together in taut silence.

Overwrought with passionate intensity, Moretti disrupts the awkward verbal stalemate. "I will cut right to the chase, Ophelia. I am Agent Sandro Moretti and this is my colleague, Simon. We need your help."

Tapping her black chipped fingernails against the white ceramic-coated steel table, she snaps her chewing gum between her teeth with a noisy "crack!" Preserved in customary quiet, she seems utterly bored with our presence.

Moretti optimistically continues; "In return for your aid with this difficult matter, I am prepared to offer you a dramatically reduced sentence. Help us; you can get some of your life back."

The busy pitter-patter of her rhythmic tips comes to an abrupt stop. Slowly closing her gilded eyes, she calmly responds; "Unless you dismiss *all* of the charges completely, you can't give me my life back."

Reluctant to grant her out-and-out amnesty, Moretti counters with; "I think you overestimate how much we need you; you completely underestimate how much trouble you are already in."

"No Agent Moretti, it is you who underestimate my ability to recognize a desperate man when I see one. The situation must be truly dire to drive an Interpol agent to strike a deal with me, an alleged cyber-terrorist."

Relentlessly tapping her fingertips to the table once more, she sits and patiently waits for Moretti's, certain to be fiery, response.

"Agreed, there is a certain level of complexity, but there must be at least a dozen or more cyber-junkies out there that can help us. Hell, I bet there are at least five hackers in here right now that would jump at the chance to help us find Monkey." Moretti expresses with a minor grin.

"Akira?" Ophelia derisively blurts out in direct response to Moretti's appended disclosure.

Immediately I recognize the particular angle to his carefully chosen words. Obviously playing to her technical vanity, his timely utterance of her archrival's name is a spark big enough to ignite the venerable rivalry between the two best hacks in the world. Giving her a moment to let the newest divulgence steep, he waits for her restructured response.

After a few seconds of contemplation, she chirpily blurts out; "First, I want to be permanently removed from the 'No Tech'" list. Second and most importantly, I want the credit. I want to be recognized as the one who took Monkey down."

Acknowledging her zealous response to our imperative proposition; with an approving nod of his head Moretti commences Ophelia's indispensable efforts. Without delay, the "Shadow Queen" swiftly springs into action; eyeing us up and down, she demands: "Gimme me your phones."

Ever mindful of our decreasing timeframe and the increasing severity of the impending circumstances, the both of us automatically surrender our mobiles. Without further ado, Ophelia astutely grabs the phones and immediately begins to disassemble them. With the twist of a wire and the skillful push of a button, in no time flat she has them reassembled and begins vigorously typing away at the screens. With elegant ease, she presents us with a screen that looks like she has accessed a back door into one of Monkey's databases. If this was an audition, she certainly nailed it. Moretti and I looked at each other with bewildered consent. The promptly executed demonstration of her invaluable merit, proved her to be an unquestionably invaluable ally.

Without delay, we promptly hauled her off to the facilities control room. Abundantly furnished with more than just our mobiles, it hopefully contained sufficient instruments for her to appropriately pursue Monkey. At once, Ophelia rigorously sprang into action. She hustles to a seat at some computers while Moretti assures his puzzled associates this was legitimately authorized. We watched in awe as she keenly cracked codes and gained access to secured sites in mere moments. Energetically entering data into multiple computers at the same time; furiously striking her fingers against three separate keyboards, she was impressively efficient to say the least.

As she persisted, I offer some additional pertinent information; "Currently, Monkey and his financier Mr. Shepherd are secretly commanding the manufacturing and distribution of the Human Vaccine. Unfortunately, HV is a Trojan horse; it's actually a deadly virus. We need to find the locations of every facility."

The Shadow Queen endures in focused investigative inquiry.

I insert with further disquiet; "Apparently, Mr. Shepherd monitors all activity from one single tablet."

Diligently tending to her virtual excavation of Monkey's nefarious affairs, Ophelia soundlessly continues on with her intense probe. Though vigilant at the workstation, she maintains an air of juvenile playfulness. Given this light and casual attitude, maybe she does not entirely grasp the genuine magnitude of the situation.

We look on as the screens are suddenly inundated with vast collections of a variety of data. As Ophelia hurriedly delves deeper into Monkey's activities, it becomes patently obvious she is beginning to realize the actuality behind the true nature of HV. Moretti and I watch and in pure astonishment as she is able to unravel the restricted relevant details of Judas' plot. With every reaped detail, the sheer scope of his plan is all the more apparent to each one of us.

Despite the fact I had previously revealed most of the particulars of Judas' scheme to Moretti; to his credit, he was still genuinely overwrought with righteous indignation. While Ophelia exposed the finer facets of the global plague, he agitatedly stated; "I still don't understand how he could have had this poison approved and distributed. There would be far too many hoops to jump through; even someone with his vast resources...how did he get away with this?"

Craftily retrieving Monkey's most confidential records, Ophelia offers an explanation; "Unfortunately the simplest solution is usually the best. Right here..." Displaying a set of documents onto one of the monitors, she points at a particular segment of letters and numbers.

"This is an encrypted list that is connected to the data base of the FDA and other international agencies. It looks like the test subjects were chosen at random by the government and kept entirely anonymous; little Monkey simply accessed that list. It looks as if they located all of the test subjects."

Baffled by the blatant austerity of Judas' conspiracy, I authenticate her simplistically crude but compelling claim: "So he could turn them." I add with accepting comprehension.

Ophelia and Moretti take note in burdensome interest as I state aloud my newly exposed supposition. "That is exactly how he did it. He located the test subjects *after* they were selected and then secretly turned them into Feeders. Once turned, they could easily survive the deadly injection of HV. Unknowingly immortal, the naïve subjects would also be cured of any sickness or disease; wickedly brilliant."

Abruptly and understandably taken aback; Ophelia queries; "Immortals?"

I confirm her inquiry and nod with solemn sincerity.

Eyes brightened with exciting intrigue, she simply responds; "Wild."

Following her odd moment of unusually calm acceptance, Ophelia punctually reports; "Here...I think these are the actual locations of the HV."

Gesturing to an extensive list of locales currently presented on the largest monitor in front of us, she constructively offers up the highly sought after sites. It seems that the additional support of The Shadow Queen has proved to be indispensable.

According to the timeline, we still had a few days until the release of the HV reserves. Moretti was right: Fight fire with fire; one Trojan horse for another. While Ophelia continued to located and verify the real HV facilities, I could prepare a large enough portion of my explosives to be unknowingly inserted into the facilities. With the aid of Agent Moretti, and the recently accrued members of The Obedience, once Ophelia had pinpointed the actual production facilities, we could feasibly distribute explosives to every one of the newly exposed HV locations. If we tactfully hijacked some shipments on their way to different facilities and then quietly positioned explosives inside of the containers; within the a few days, tainted containers would be distributed to every distribution centers. Only one uncertainty remained; how to successfully simultaneously detonate them all at once?

Once more, while we formulated our strategy, Ophelia liberated our overloaded intellects with a bit of genius. She offers the imaginative suggestion to concurrently detonate the scattered interred explosives. "I can create a transmitter that broadcasts an indiscernible digital frequency."

Moretti unconvincingly queries, "But we can't possibly..."

Ophelia adds with profound simplicity; "That tablet, Mr. Shepherd's tablet; I could use it to distribute the frequency to every one of his various HV locations."

Excitedly summarizing her clever solution, I solicit; "If I could guarantee that he establishes contact with all of the HV sites..."

"Making him the bloody trigger; setting off the total destruction of his own diabolic design." Ophelia enthusiastically blurts out in spirited stimulation.

Overt confidence and methodical curiosity have always been a potential chink in Judas' proverbial armor. If I could plant even the slightest bit of suspicion inside of that narcissistic intellect of his, I could persuade him to reach out to every one of his HV locations; the crucial centerpieces of his conspiracy. Judas literally held the key to his own defeat in the palm of his hand.

To ensure that our calculated plan is executed with

incomparable precision, Moretti hastily enlisted the help of some of his trustworthy associates at Interpol. While he solicited additional agents, I phoned the members of The Obedience and fully apprised them of our developing plan of action. After distributing the lists of HV locations to both Moretti and The Obedience, Ophelia ardently began construction of her frequency device.

As she diligently assembled the frequency device, I asked her to make a slight modification. I needed a miniature vile attached to the exterior of the device. Once completed, I planned to insert and carefully lodge the apparatus into my chest. The petite container held a precise mixture of blood and just the right amount of my homemade explosive. Judas will no doubt be suspicious of my surrender, which means he will predictably have his goons thoroughly search me. I placed the device into the exact site of the knife-tip he placed inside of me centuries ago. Even if they detect it, Judas will simply think it is that very same splintered souvenir. These tiny modifications will give me a gigantic advantage going into our final engagement.

That only left me with one more task. Before I could follow through with my voluntary submission to Judas, I had to carefully deprive myself of blood in order to appear incredibly debilitated. If I seemed even the slightest bit weakened, I could give him some rather compelling but false reassurance. For good measure, I also downed a considerable quantity of petrol. Upon the timely retrieval of the implanted device, I could rupture the vile; promptly giving me the necessary burst of strength to instantly take him and anyone else down with me.

So, here I sit; assembling my explosives in the middle of the night as the intermittent indigo neon flickers its offering of redemption. There are only two possible outcomes: Either I finally deliver Judas to Hell or he ruthlessly rains down Hell on earth. The obnoxious dog needed to be put down, for good.

29

"When God desires to destroy a thing, he entrusts its destruction to the thing itself. Every bad institution of this world ends by suicide."
-Victor Hugo

BLACKPOOL, ENGLAND
PRESENT

Though abundantly confident, Judas maintains a taut grip on his tablet while tapping away at the screen. Mockingly maimed and brought to my knees, I retain my firm grip on the activated mechanism in my gory palm. In reaction to the haunting shred of slight uncertainty tirelessly swirling inside of his evil intellect, Judas taps away at his device. Though tremendously painful, our final encounter has providentially gone unerringly according to plan. At the very moment I uttered the word "Boom!" I peered deep into the depths of Judas' soulless eyes. Just what I had hoped for; flickering inside of those cantankerous eyes, I saw a faint trace of doubt.

Just as projected, believing he has called my seemingly implausible bluff; Judas immediately dispatched an urgent transmission from his exclusive device. Simultaneously distributing communiqués to both his chief production facilities as well as all of the superfluous storehouses, he demands confirmation from every HV location that they are intact. Upon sending off his critical request, the arrogant brute smugly looks down at me with a derisive smirk.

In his hasty attempt to disprove or authenticate my alleged and quite improbable claim, Judas unknowingly triggers his own annihilation. My frequency device instantly transmits the digital detonator to all of his HV facilities. Once the concealed explosives are triggered by the frequency delivered through his transmission, it is only a matter of minutes until every one of his facilities is leveled to the ground. In order to properly contest his grand go at global destruction, one only needed to understand the basic nature of the beast.

Fervently awaiting replies from his numerous subordinates around the globe, Judas looks down at me with palpable contempt. Seemingly depleted to a gravely feeble position, I look down in feigning disillusionment. I remain face down as Judas stridently proclaims with victorious zeal; "You can't get rid of me that easy, brother. You of all His creatures know that best: for better or for worse darling, we are linked for all eternity."

Conceitedly Judas continues his immodest diatribe; "I am the repugnant churning in the innermost expanse of your gooey guts! I am the shameless, irritating melody, forever stuck inside your head! I am the disturbingly vicious brutality eternally featured in your recurring nightmares! I am the abhorrent taste of bitter bile; seeping and burning the rear of your throat that will drip for all eternity!"

Smugly brandishing his signature toothy smirk, he elatedly articulates; "All that you hate, dear brother Lazarus; I am."

Judas continues to roar with self-consummation: "We deserved so much better from Him, you and I. So, I have nobly delivered unto this world the religion it deserves. Unlike your merciless master, I do not condemn: No, I simply convert, with only the purest offering of 'anything goes!' Entitlement, divisiveness and voyeurism; these are my sacred vocations. Social media is my narcissistic house of worship. There, you can profess and you can also confess all that you have done. I am the vicar of vanity; the counselor of corruption. I have instilled my own resplendent sacraments: litigation is reconciliation and abortion is a sacred rite of confirmation! Marriage has been replaced with excessive promiscuity and all one must contribute to charity is unadulterated apathy and ill-bred indifference. I have successfully anointed the world in iniquity, brother and they have been baptized in perfect ignorance!"

Lingering over me; intoxicated by sureness, Judas reaches out and impatiently seizes the blood-slathered device out of my hand and hurls it to floor. The fellowship of anxious Bleeders and Feeders look on in blithe interest as the gadget is smashed into tiny pieces.

"Your impassioned pursuit to rescind me and this incessant ridiculous yearning for redemption has once more proved to be entirely meaningless." Judas expounds in elated self-satisfaction.

As I look around at the culmination of sordid psychopaths and unnatural creatures that Judas and I are responsible for, I receive the sudden rush of vigor provided by the surge of blood now coursing through my veins.

Bristling with a potent swell of energy, I respond to my overconfident captor; "I look forward to seeing you in Hell, Judas!"

Gazing around at his huddled assembly of reprehensible cohorts and rejects, Judas proudly retorts: "Good! You can wait for me there, dear brother. It might feel like an eternity, but you can wait! It seems your precious question of redemption... you have answered yourself. Once again you have dismally failed Him and once again He has selfishly abandoned you."

His ingratiating followers cackle with zesty enthusiasm. As the manic mob rejoices, I satisfy the final portion of my plot. Taking advantage of the fleeting eruption of strength, as the ignorant immortals revel in their assumed superiority, I immediately grab Judas firmly by his puffed-up shoulders and forcefully thrust him to the ground. Face to face with my eternal adversary, I glare into his eyes with incited placation. In eager defense of their malevolent mentor, the mass of Bleeders and Feeders impulsively pounce upon me. Expeditiously descending upon their demented demagogue, and myself the single-minded goons act in absolute accordance with my strategy.

Looking him squarely in the eyes for the very last time, I offer a direct response to his counterfeit concern for my aspirations of redemption. I simply and solemnly say; "My dear brother, it's not up to me."

Just at that, the most momentous occasion of our transecting existences, the frequency fulfills its providential vocation. Activated by Ophelia's digital spark, the assorted warehouses and facilities of apocalyptic HV are almost simultaneously incinerated. Obliterated by the miniature but aptly proficient explosive materials meticulously circulated to the undisclosed locales; the massive blasts destroy every hope of Judas' dastardly attempt at global decimation.

Barely seconds after the first facility is rescinded, I continued to gaze into Judas' roguish eyes. Uncontaminated by decorum, we shared an absolutely impeccable moment. At that exact instant, the slight amount of ingested gasoline and the explosives stitched into the lining of my discarded jacket, ignite with the rest of the other explosives.

In one instantaneously coordinated effort, all of us wretched immortals are engulfed in flashes of flame. My abysmal antagonist and all of his foul followers rapidly burst into righteous flames. In this massive combusting inferno of fiery flame, all of us are entirely obliterated. We are all reduced to seething smoke and sooty ash. It has been accomplished.

30

"You will not abandon me to the realm of the dead,
nor will you let your faithful one see decay."
-Psalm 16:10

BANGKOK, THAILAND
PRESENT

*My name is Ela Vlcek, and I am dead. This is the story of my death
and of my rebirth as an immortal.*

The elaborate network of explosives concurrently detonated just as Simon designed; thoroughly destroying every awful ounce of the Herod Virus. The explosion that exhaustively incinerated Judas; additionally devoured the hundreds of Bleeders and Feeders that surrounded them. But Simon still had one more trick up his ever-sly sleeve. Taking a cue from Judas' exploitation of subliminal messaging, Simon had Ophelia layer an imperceptible message underneath the triggering frequency. The message was simple; it just repeated the Latin words of expulsion. Regrettably, the devastating set of successful measures not only put an end to Judas and his attending reprobates, but Simon had to selflessly sacrifice himself in order to conclusively defeat his ceaseless rival. But I am committed to making sure his death was not in vain.

Thousands if not tens of thousands of immortals are still

among us. Brackish breeds of Bleeders and Feeders and other types of monsters still endure; just as hungry for mass devastation and corruption.

Feeding on the flesh of fiends, I am now the new ageless ambassador of the afterlife. I have assumed Simon's righteous charge of eradicating the immortal infestation currently plaguing the earth. Lazarus, Simon, the immortal riddled with regret, never sought his own redemption, but only desired the appropriate retribution for the twisted creatures that he had created. He did manage to provide me with the proper means to kill myself and end my newfound bloodthirsty nature. That day is inevitable, but before it arrives, I will take all of these beasts down with me.

In truth, there already exists a type of Hell on earth. The world is tormented by an aberrant evil that threatens every single human being. With the continued truce between The Obedience and myself I have also joined forces with the infinitely adept Agent Morretti. We travel the globe; intent on eradicating every immortal from this earthly realm. Immortals have christened me 'The Angel of Death.' Today and tomorrow there waits a reckoning for all of the infected and the corrupt. All Bleeders, Feeders and all other forms of freaks and monsters take heed; I will find you. And when I do, I will swiftly deliver you into the fiery pits of Hell of which you belong.

CPSIA information can be obtained
at www.ICGtesting.com
Printed in the USA
FSHW020445191219
65260FS